# CLASSICS OF AMERICAN SHORT FICTION
## (VOLUME II)

# 美国短篇小说经典
## （下卷）

徐华东　朱　源 / 主编

图书在版编目(CIP)数据

美国短篇小说经典.下卷/徐华东,朱源主编.—北京:北京大学出版社,2019.10
ISBN 978-7-301-30887-5

Ⅰ.①美… Ⅱ.①徐… ②朱… Ⅲ.①短篇小说–小说集–美国 Ⅳ.①I712.4

中国版本图书馆CIP数据核字(2019)第226895号

| | |
|---|---|
| 书　　　名 | 美国短篇小说经典（下卷）<br>MEIGUO DUANPIAN XIAOSHUO JINGDIAN（XIAJUAN） |
| 著作责任者 | 徐华东　朱源　主编 |
| 责任编辑 | 刘爽 |
| 标准书号 | ISBN 978-7-301-30887-5 |
| 出版发行 | 北京大学出版社 |
| 地　　　址 | 北京市海淀区成府路205号　100871 |
| 网　　　址 | http://www.pup.cn　新浪微博:@北京大学出版社 |
| 电子信箱 | nkliushuang@hotmail.com |
| 电　　　话 | 邮购部010-62752015　发行部010-62750672　编辑部010-62759634 |
| 印刷者 | 河北滦县鑫华书刊印刷厂 |
| 经销者 | 新华书店 |
| | 720毫米×1020毫米　16开本　17.25印张　430千字<br>2019年10月第1版　2019年10月第1次印刷 |
| 定　　　价 | 58.00元 |

未经许可,不得以任何方式复制或抄袭本书之部分或全部内容。
**版权所有,侵权必究**
举报电话: 010-62752024 电子信箱: fd@pup.pku.edu.cn
图书如有印装质量问题,请与出版部联系,电话: 010-62756370

## 《美国短篇小说经典》（下卷）

**主　编**　徐华东　朱　源
**副主编**　常少华　刘　生
**译　者**　徐华东　朱　源　尹铁超　霍跃红　井卫华
　　　　　　丁海彬　裴瑞成　鹿清霞　周玉芳　王玉华
　　　　　　杜　松　杜洪峰　葛　颂　徐永志　罗俏娟

# 代序

## 好的短篇小说集就是一座精品博物馆

——呼唤英汉对照版英美短篇小说经典问世

  2016年7月，华东师大校园美丽的丽娃湖畔风景宜人，高朋满座，迎来了来自世界近20个国家两百多位知名作家和学者参加的盛会。这是第十四届世界短篇小说大会，也是首次在亚洲召开的、以"短篇小说中的影响与汇合：西方与东方"为主题的大会。这次大会是由世界英语短篇小说研究会组织的，每两年召开一次。中国作家、学者、翻译家更是积极贡献，打破语言障碍，中外交流，其乐融融；华东师大是东道主，上海文化界、文学界做了全面的部署和多方面的配合，会议开得十分成功，也产生了持久的影响。

  及至今日，这使我们应然有了一个直接的积极的理由，来谈论一下英美短篇小说在中国的译介。其中由北京大学出版社即将推出的《英国短篇小说经典》（上、下卷）和《美国短篇小说经典》（上、下卷），恰好给了我们一个实体文本，让我们有所依凭地讨论一下这个话题。当然啦，这也给了我一点勇气，让我能够借题发挥，不拘一格，坦露一下自己的观点，开启这两套书的序言——犹如拉开一道无形中被遮掩了的序幕。

## 一

  提起短篇小说（short story/fiction, novelette），许多读者可能不以为然，何必小题大做？时下人们都在务长篇，谁还看短篇，写短篇？更何况是外国短篇小说。花花草草、莺莺燕燕，美则美矣，要不是余闲多多，谁还顾得上？其实，短篇小说不像人们所想象的那样"小"，更不是小事一桩，不值一提，要是推介一本短篇小说集，也不至于需要特殊的理由吧？

  只要说起短篇小说，人们就会以短小精悍作为其审美特征。可篇幅短小也不是短篇小说存在的充足理由，虽然可以说是必要条件。就文学作品的篇幅而言，可以说，长有长的好处，短有短的理由。在中国长篇小说大行其道的今天，许多人只知道长，不知道短，还要说长道短，就不能不令人担忧了。可我既不是击长护短，也不是主张不长不短，而是主张大家了解短，知道长。这就不得不从长说起，从长计议。

其实，长篇小说（novel），在国外往往等同于通俗小说（popular fiction）或消遣小说（light fiction）。走进一家书店或图书馆，最高的一层就是长篇小说的专库，堆满了顶到天花板的书架，排满了大部头的长篇小说。貌似庞然大物，其实光顾者寥寥无几。而靠近底层的短篇小说集、诗集和散文集，当然也有立于经典而不倒的长篇巨著，倒是读者络绎不绝、流连忘返之地。在大饱眼福之后，出来时也要买上一本，免得空手而归。国内的书店正相反，大部分把长篇小说摆在一层显赫的位置，甚至等同于世界名著。其实许多人看也不看，就直接上楼了，寻找他想要的"其他"书籍去了。这难道不发人深思？

这是什么原因呢？

这是因为，在国外许多有识之士看来，短篇小说才是精品，是艺术品，值得仔细挑选和阅读领会。而在国内，则把长篇小说当作文学经典和代表作，作为某一作家成功的象征和试金石，有的甚至作为获奖的必要条件。不错，据说鲁迅先生当年与诺贝尔文学奖失之交臂，就是因为没有长篇。而沈从文因《边城》获得提名，假若他再多活半年，诺贝尔文学奖的桂冠也许就会降临在他的头上。而《边城》，最多是个中篇。其实，许多中篇小说（novelette）和短篇小说可以等同视之，只是容量稍大，情节也不太复杂，写作上并没有太大的差异。英文本身以novelette兼指短篇和中篇，就是这个道理。而fiction，则是所有小说的统称（所谓"虚构性叙事作品"，无论是韵体还是散体），或者狭义地指长篇小说。路遥的代表作诚然是长篇《平凡的世界》，但他的中篇《人生》却是成名作和代表作，较早地拍成电影，在作者生前就获得了承认。至今重读，发现其结构之严谨，人物之生动，主题之深刻，并不逊色于《平凡的世界》。人们也许会说，前者是单一线索，后者则是复线发展，不错，但这不是长篇与中短篇小说区分的关键。

也许按照中国的惯例，对于一个作家而言，短篇只是装饰和点缀——有了长篇而出了名，何愁不能出个人短篇小说集？但这是夹带策略，算不得正途。许多人连短篇也没写好，就写长篇，缺乏训练基础，反倒弄巧成拙。而中篇是成名的敲门砖，进了此门，真正瞄准的目标是长篇。可惜，中篇在中国也不发达，也许在国外也是个另类。几乎很少会有人光顾这个不短不长、"飞短流长"的折中领域。要不就是短篇写长了，长篇写短了。幸而这一"惯例"，并非放之四海而皆准，也非举世所公认。

退一步而言，路遥当年病入膏肓，来日无多，却拒绝治疗，而拼命要一口气写完《平凡的世界》，其理由无非是认为，长篇作品在于贯气，若写作中止，则文气中断，再接续实为不可能。看来，路遥的选择是正确的，他的生命没有白费。相反，被路遥视为导师的柳青，作为关中作家的先辈，却因为"文化大革命"，被迫中断了《创业史》的写作。第一部的完成也略显仓促，待到他缓过劲来，重操旧业，全力投入第二部写作，已经晚矣，终于没有完成，留下了千古遗憾。再由此想到，柳青还计划写完互助组写合作社，写完初级社写高级社，再写人民公社，胃口很大，倘若不是好大喜功，也是为长篇所累，终于功败垂成。归根结底，以有限之人生，写无限之长篇，甚至"悠悠万事，唯此为大"，悖论一也。

可是话又说回来，古今中外，写长篇小说出名者多，反而是短篇小说，貌似容易，却难出精品，成功者寡。就世界范围而言，从古希腊的奴隶伊索口述的寓言算起，古阿拉伯的《一千零一夜》、意大利的《十日谈》，到了近代，以语言论，唯有英语中的欧·亨利，法语中的莫泊桑，德语中的茨威格，俄语中的契诃夫，独能以短篇名世。此外，斗转星移，虽然名家辈出，集子不断，但若考究起来，在短篇小说领域，至今称为圣手巧匠者，仍然百不一遇，除了天才与时代因素而外，文体、文类自身的因素，民族语言敏感之程度，难道不也应当考虑在内？

本来，语言问题就够复杂的。文体、文类，难道也成为问题？是的。就写作的难度而言，短篇小说不仅不比中长篇小说容易，甚至更难。且听知者言之：

> 短篇小说是一种极具挑战性的文体，不仅需要娴熟高超的叙事技巧、精巧严密的布局，还需要博大的心志和深邃的思想。真正优秀的短篇小说既不允许有叙述上的败笔，更不允许有思想上的平庸，它是技巧与思想完美结合的产物。（《世界上最精彩的小说》，华文出版社，2010年）

诚哉斯言！

这使我想起美国诗人、小说家爱伦·坡的诗论。爱伦·坡认为长诗之不可能，因为诗歌须让人一口气读完，反复回味，才是正品。诗歌之外，散文和短篇，也符合此原理。书画亦然。

我个人觉得，短篇小说犹如美术博物馆里的古典精品，凡·高绘画、罗丹雕塑、青藤花鸟、白石草虫，皆是小幅作品，方寸之间，显示乾坤气象，而一笔之弱败，导致整幅作品成为废品。哪个不是集终生之学养，得一时之观察，苦心经营，心有所悟，形诸笔墨，才能成功？篆刻较之绘画更甚！

长篇之奥妙，或者说其难处，看来首要的在于结构，因为语言与经验的缘故。短篇亦然。短篇之结构，旨在精巧，卒章显志，出人意料，但不宜过于复杂曲折。而长篇之结构，却是要大气浑成，不炫技巧，从头至尾，一气呵成，容不得拖沓、无聊。如此看来，长篇完全符合此原理者，实乃凤毛麟角。就连有些世界名著，例如《战争与和平》，也不是没有缺点，唯其皇皇巨著，山丘起伏，林壑茂盛，能遮丑而已。更有《红楼梦》，总体设计匠心独运，中间难免冗长拖沓，反复修改，年谱错落，细节照应不周，而续书的缘故，更难免有狗尾续貂之嫌。石涛的《搜尽奇峰打草稿》，顾名思义，更是草创之作，观其结构，虽然巨笔浓墨，气势有之，但缺乏小心收拾，不能说是上品。其原因就是，他是从局部起笔绘制全景，这样的画法并不适合长篇，只能用于小品。小说亦然。

观古人之长篇巨著，如《千里江山图》《富春山居图》《清明上河图》，乃是稀世珍品，而有作者如此心胸和丘壑者，如此精道之笔墨者，历代实为罕见。而如今的艺术馆，尤其是现代书画馆，动辄参天巨幅，除了吸引眼球之外，许多技巧未熟，笔墨未精，丘壑未成，却自命出手不凡，巍然高悬厅堂，夺人眼目，让人瞠目，旋即欲逃走。纽约现代艺术馆里，整座墙壁一幅巨画，或整个展示铺地而来，堆满了瓶瓶罐罐，也令人想起我们的长篇小说，一年据说出两千部，有的人几个月就写一部，可观者毕竟少数，多数艺术残缺，思想平庸，如时下的电视剧，摇头摆尾，重复拉长，捉襟见肘，不堪卒读者，不在少数。这不徒是创作态度轻率所致，与作者的艺术观、文学观，想必也有关系。

作为一种体裁，短篇小说古已有之，以中国文学史为例，最早的先秦寓言，可作为它的前身和雏形，只是因主题而设故事，目的在于道德教训或击败论敌，非纯文学之属；而明代冯梦龙书中的短篇，已具有规模和高度，与世俗生活市井文学相表里，有自然主义之风；到了蒲松龄，人鬼莫辨，狐媚成精，精于构思，文笔摇曳，文言短篇遂攀上了高峰。至于民国以降，乃至新文学运动中的白话短篇，也有不少成就，名家虽不为多，也绝非罕有。倒是后来逐渐衰落了，长篇急剧增长了。这二者之间虽无必然联系，但也不是一点关系没有。世风和心态，体制和褒奖，理论和评论，都有关系。

## 二

回到英美短篇小说的主题上，始觉得也有一些话要说。

英语世界，原是以叙事见长的，别的不论，就连英语诗歌，也是叙事成分较多，精品接连不断。现代长篇小说自笛福始，名家辈出。近世报业发达，狄更斯得以长篇连载；萨克雷之锋利，哈代之老辣，毛姆之博闻，康拉德之深刻，加上爱尔兰、威尔士，便有乔伊斯之意识流，再加上诗人写小说者，便有王尔德、迪伦·托马斯等。长篇小说叙事传统优厚，短篇与散文，也不例外。美国更是后来居上，华盛顿·欧文、霍桑开其端，海明威、莫里森断其后，作家是黑白并举，作品是长短并收，而欧·亨利，乃跻身世界级短篇小说大师之列，与法国之莫泊桑、奥地利之茨威格、俄国之契诃夫，并驾齐驱。不过，相比于英美的经验论和实用主义，法国审美之感观，德国哲思之神秘，在文史方面，尤见其长。近世以来，法国的小说理论，特别是叙事学和符号学，后来居上，独占鳌头，英语小说似乎有点难以招架，至少在理论上给人这种印象。好在西方世界的现代文学理论，从现代主义到后现代主义，乃是一整体现象，作为文学创作和理论批评，甚至艺术观点和潮流，则是交互的整体的影响。

这使得英语小说的选编和出版，独成别致的景观。

既然是英美短篇小说，自然是英美的资料要充足得多，因为那里是原产地。同样，出版的个人选集和综合选集也要多。个人的集子姑且不论，综合性的集子，以《诺顿短篇小说集》为最全，除了《诺顿文学选读》，还有《小说一百篇》，也是重要的选集。还有一些大学文学课教材，也有按国别分类的，基本上是英国短篇小说选，或美国短篇小说选，而一般通识性文学教材，则是按小说、诗歌、散文、戏剧分类，当然也包括短篇小说。其中大部分集子，既有总序也有作者介绍，还有必要的注释，可以说是应有尽有。这为我们国内的选编提供了原材料。另有一部分，是专门供英美学生作教材用的，包括原作欣赏和写作手册，欣赏部分按主题、情节、人物、语言等方面分类，写作部分则有积累资料、选题写作、修改润色等分类，甚至发表推介都有，十分方便。

就我所见，国内的短篇小说选编，大多数直接取材于上述不同的集子，但也有不同的选编目的和方法。一类是原作鉴赏型的，其中多数不分国别，有原文和注释，有的还有思考题。作者介绍，有用英语写的，也有用汉语写的。这类教材，也有按国别分类的，或按写作技巧分类的，例如情节结构、人物性格、象征隐喻、语言风格等。重庆大学出版社出版的《英语短篇小说赏析》，就是这种类型的，全英文的不分国别。南京大学出版社出版的《英美短篇小说》，除了作品本身、阅读资料和思考题是英文的，其他部分都是中文的，这样便于中国学生接受和讨论，除按主题、情节、人物、视角、象征分类之外，还有实验小说，单列一章，附录则有批评术语解释；每一部分，不仅有作者及其创作概况，还有作品赏析与相关评论，是直接针对这篇作品的，甚至还有问题与思考，更有阅读链接，可以说是体制最完备的了。这套书是《英美小说》的修订版，实际上，原先所选内容也全是名副其实的短篇小说，这也可以看出选编者的学术底线。

外研社出版的《英美小说选读》，却是前英后美，长短不分，即有的是短篇小说，有的则是长篇小说的节录，这样混杂的编排，至少在概念上混淆了短篇小说和中长篇小说，应该说是不够严谨的。不过，这个集子除了与选文密切相关的其他内容之外，还有文学术语或文学知识（理论与批评），其中有的是西方文学理论流派观点介绍，有的是对具体作品的分析。可见这个本子的编选的实用目的和学术倾向。

还有一类是英汉双语编撰的英美短篇小说集，例如华文出版社出版的《世界上最精彩的小说》，甚至封面上有"影响一生，感动一生，珍藏一生"的宣传推介语，号称"最美的英文经典"。乍看起来是有点商业化倾向，但实际上却是严格的短篇小说选集，不仅收录的全是小说名家，而且其译文也流畅可读。

本书以中英文对照形式编排，译者均为文学界的知名翻译家和研究专家，不仅原汁原味地呈现了作品的风采，醇美的译文更能帮助我们深刻体会小说的荒诞、诙谐、幽默与真情，感受大师们的艺术功底和写作才华，是广大文学爱好者和英语学习爱好者的必备读物。（《世界上最精彩的小说》，华文出版社，2010年）

阅读这本书的译文，也有这样的感觉，此番说法感觉并不过分。不过，名家并非全是以短篇小说而著名，有的作品长达二三十页，是否仍然算作短篇小说，也值得思考。这好像又回到了何谓短篇小说，它的文体特征和审美特点是什么这样一些根本的问题上来了。

## 三

该回到我们手头的这两套书上了。

放在读者诸君手头的这两套书，一套是《英国短篇小说经典》，一套是《美国短篇小说经典》，都是英汉对照，而且分为上下卷，可见出编选者的雄心勃勃和内容的丰富全面。两位主编一位是从事英语语言文学的教授，一位是立足出版界但从未丢弃学问的实业家。他们除了完成自己的本职工作以外，始终在学术研究和出版上谋求发展，而且取得了可喜的成绩。这四卷部头不小的书，就是他们多年心血和努力的见证。大约十二年前，他们就启动了这项浩大的工程，从三千多篇原文中选出一百篇左右，其中大部分是没有翻译的，大约用了三年时间，完成了翻译工作，又继续精选，淘汰掉不满意的，再加上反复的修改，觉得可以出版了，才准备付梓。结果就是现在的七八十篇了。但和同类书籍相比，已经是鸿篇巨制了。

他们的初衷，是按照《英语专业本科教学质量国家标准》，为大学生和青年人阅读英美文学经典提供食粮，所以这两套书，只是按照时间顺序选编最好的英语短篇小说，并且提供上佳的译文，并没有其他的条件限制。原文之前有用英文写出的作者介绍和作品提示。原文之后，用英文提供了供讨论和思考的问题，以便于课堂讨论。最后还提供了参考译文。之所以是参考译文，因为短篇小说作家百人百姓，作品面貌各异，语言风格悬殊，是不可能统一的。且不说英国英语和美国英语差异明显，汉语译文也不可能一样。至于如何体现英美语言的差异，并且反映在汉译中，迄今还是一个没有得到充分讨论的问题，也有待于在实践中努力解决。而我在阅读的过程中，看到个别地方还有改动余地的，便不揣冒昧，顺手改了几处，希望能有助于译文质量的提高。

所选的短篇小说，我还是根据个人兴趣抽取看了几篇。英国的短篇小说，看了哈代写英法战争的《1804年的传说》，使我想起哈代的诗剧《列王》，属于重大题材；王尔德写的《没有秘密的斯芬克斯》（讽刺性很强），以及迪伦·托马斯的《真实的故事》（是写一个少女杀人案的，风格凄美）。因为他们三位同时都是诗人，而且代表了英格兰、爱尔兰和威尔士三个区域文化的创作风格和文化底蕴，可以说是有目的地选取。美国的短篇小说，我看了三个不太熟悉的作家，分别是安布罗斯·比尔斯的《枭河桥纪事》（印象深刻，堪称绝唱），斯蒂芬·文森特·波奈特的《巴比伦河畔》（被题材所吸引，但观感比较模糊），还有著名作家梅尔维尔的《小提琴手》，是天才无名声而快乐的主题（结构精巧，寓意深刻）。这几位作家固然是我所感兴趣的，有的是因为熟悉，有的则是因为陌生而感兴趣，多数作品也都是有兴味的，那些随手翻翻而没有阅读或者看了几行就进不去的作品，没有记录下来，也没有留下太深的印象。

我的一个总体印象是，惯于写长篇小说的，要么把短篇作为长篇来写，要么把不能写长篇的资料用来写短篇，而在写法上基本没有什么不同。而不太写长篇的，或者诗人等其他艺术家，他们写的短篇要好看得多，往往有一个特殊的题材和视觉，特别适合写短篇，或者给人以深刻而新颖的印象，令人过目难忘。而专门写短篇的作家，则有自己写短篇的经验和资料，写起来得心应手，令人叫绝，但他们的短篇小说集，也不是篇篇都是精品，写得多了，重复是难免的，所以，真正传世的，值得一看或反复阅读的，还是那几个短篇作品。这便引出了一个话题，也许最好看的短篇小说集子，是集最佳短篇作家的最佳作品的集子。

以下仅举这个集子中的一例，来验证一下自己的感觉。

在《美国短篇小说经典》（上卷）中有介绍安布罗斯·比尔斯的一篇《枭河桥纪事》，我以为可作为代表。安布罗斯·比尔斯（1842—1914）是美国记者、专栏作家、小说家，一生充满传奇色彩。他以苦涩辛辣的风格赢得了"辛辣比尔斯"的绰号。他的代表作是《魔鬼词典》，而战争中的骇人事件则是他写作短篇的焦点。南北战争中他参加了北方部队，战后，在旧金山做报刊编辑。1913年，他只身前往革命中的墨西哥，在那里失踪，死因不明。可以说，他的一生就是一段传奇，而他的《枭河桥纪事》，是其代表作。

《枭河桥纪事》被称为安布罗斯·比尔斯短篇小说中的佳作。故事的主人公佩顿·法科尔是一个南方种植园主，他因企图破坏北方部队在枭河桥上修建铁路而被处以绞刑。犯人临死前的心理活动描写堪称大家手笔，逼真细腻的描写背后又流露出事件的过程和起因，对人性的深刻洞察和战争的残酷的描写互为表里。一开头被吊在桥上的汉子，以及整个桥面的军方布置，被写得惊心动魄又真实可感，着实发人深思：

> 一个汉子站在北亚拉巴马一座铁路桥上，俯视着桥下20英尺处湍急的河水。他双手反扣，手腕上缚着绳子。另一根绳子紧紧地套在他的脖子上，系在他头顶上方一个结实的木头十字架上，绳头下垂及膝。几块松动的木板铺在支撑铁轨的枕木上，成为汉子和行刑人的落脚之处。行刑人是两个北方军列兵，由一位中士指挥。这位中士如果在地方上，很可能会成为一名负责治安的官员。不远处，在临时搭建的平台上，站着一位身着军阶制服、全副武装的军官。他是个上尉。桥两端各有一位哨兵，站立成"放哨"的姿势，也就是步枪位于左肩前方，枪机抵住横过胸前的前臂——这样的姿势迫使人身体笔直挺立，动作规范却很别扭。看来他们两个无须知道在桥中央发生的事情，只要封锁好横贯桥面直抵两端的木板通道就可以了。

这一段精彩的描写使人想起南斯拉夫电影《桥》的一个镜头，但比那个要震撼人心，因为有一个人即将被处死在桥上。这里的文字略有调整，因为翻译还是要语句松弛，描写从容些，才能阅读顺畅，有思考的余地。

结局可想而知，但仍然给人以思考：

> 佩顿·法科尔死了。他的尸身（脖子已经断掉），吊在枭河桥的横木下方，缓缓地荡来荡去。

最后，就自己的观察，谈几点短篇小说的写作特点或技术要求，以求教于方家：

1. 短篇的容量有限，要尽快进入主题，引起读者的兴趣。即使描述也要引人入胜,平淡中也要有趣味,有悬念,否则读者会丢弃不读。

2. 结尾要出人意料,或者在逼近必然的结局时,要么不可逆转,要么能做出新的或令人信服的解释,否则读者会有上当的感觉,甚至不再读这个作家的作品了。

3. 虽然短篇的结构也可以多姿多彩,但最好的结构,是简单而又引人入胜的,内涵无限丰富和寓意深刻的。不要把长篇的宏大题材用来写短篇。

4. 因为展开和铺垫的时间和篇幅有限,要流露足够的信息作为暗示和启示的线索,揭示和解释进程与结局的合理性和必然性,所以要惜墨如金。

5. 过分精巧的布置和细密的文笔,虽然称为"匠心独运",但终会有不自然的感觉。这在长篇中是忌讳,在短篇中尚可容忍,但最好不要重复地犯这种错误。

6. 过于晦涩或深奥的短篇,如同绘画缺少鲜明的调子,灰掉了。这在长篇中可以说是隐藏很深的技巧,在短篇中却是缺乏鲜明的色彩和感觉,使人莫名其妙,失之朦胧。

7. 生活经验的局限,或者艺术观念的单一,表现手法的雷同,都可能限制一个人的短篇小说创作水平和成就。没有就不要写,不要变着法儿写,否则也会让人看出来。

8. 太像小说的短篇,终究不是上品。上品应是富于诗意或像散文的短篇小说,太像小说会流于精巧或耽于说教,虽然诗歌和散文也难免,但毕竟要好一些。戏剧性强也是太像小说的一类,有看点就行。

9. 无论何种艺术作品,大凡是过目难忘的,或有价值的,需有趣、细腻、深刻、博大、奇妙,但不必平分秋色,切忌过犹不及;一滑入精巧、烦琐、古奥、混沌、怪诞,就走入魔道了。短篇小说亦然。

无论如何,读短篇小说要有心情,今日之时代迸发,时间紧迫,长篇固然要潜下心来读,才有收获,即便要读短篇小说,也要平心静气,不可过于草率。心不定,则思不宁,难于入定,何谈收获与感受?

至于短篇小说的翻译,只能有一个大概的认识。首先是废除翻译腔和狭义的忠实观,使其在语言和语气上达到翻译文学的程度。其次,深谙作者的意图和文笔,竭力向译文靠近。再下来,就是一口气译完,不要半途而废。实在不行的,也要反复修改,使其气韵贯通,文采内敛,切忌浮躁和花哨。毕肖人物语言和精于描述,长于叙事,乃是常识性的说法了。

坦率地说,本来是短篇序言,却写得很长,实不足观。好在这两部英国和美国的短篇小说经典,都没有各自的绪论,以序言充绪论,固然难当重任,而序言本身杂糅中外,兼谈艺术,近乎东拉西扯,也非正途。倘若有可观处,倒是编译者和广大读者抬爱了。

  但愿大家能够喜欢汉英对照版的英美短篇小说经典,也不枉费了我在这里苦口婆心地发了一番议论。

王宏印(朱墨)

2018年12月22日星期六

于古城长安西外专家楼

# 前　言

　　现代意义上的英语短篇小说形成于19世纪。美国作家埃德加·爱伦·坡既是该文学体裁的早期实践者也是理论家。他在1842年为霍桑的第一部短篇小说集《重述的故事》所写的书评中表明了对短篇小说的看法。他将短篇小说界定为"需要在半小时至一二个小时内读完的短篇散文体叙事作品",这样才能保证读者在阅读过程中不受任何干扰,以获得总体效果。短篇小说家还必须有意识地安排每一个细节,以取得某种预设的独一无二的突出效果。其实短篇小说发展的实际情况要复杂得多。其篇幅从500个英语单词到20000个英语单词不等;其形式变化多样,可以聚焦于某个场景、一段经历、一次行动、对某个或几个人物内心的揭示,甚至还可以是离奇的幻想。但相对于长篇小说来讲,短篇小说无论在形式和内容上都保持了其简洁、经济、紧凑、完整的鲜明特征,基本上遵循了"一人一事""一线到底"的情节发展模式,因而才能产生爱伦·坡所谓的强烈的"单一效果"。一篇短篇小说是一件精心构思、精细雕琢的精美艺术品。19世纪前期的英语短篇小说大多还遗留着西方古代传奇故事的痕迹,同时也受当时西方浪漫主义文学思潮的影响,其中的人物、情节类似于中国古代传奇笔记小说中的"志怪""志人",往往是现实生活与鬼怪等超自然力夹杂在一起,强调故事的趣味性与新奇性。19世纪后期至20世纪初的英美文学是以现实主义、自然主义为主流的时代,短篇小说也不例外,注重对人生、社会现实的细致描述与深刻揭露。20世纪以降的英美短篇小说侧重于用心理手法描写人物的内心世界,发掘故事内所暗含的对人性、社会以及自然的批判与思考。

　　早在18世纪,英国作家笛福、爱迪生、斯梯尔、哥尔德斯密斯就已经开始写短篇故事,刊登在当时开始盛行的期刊上,着重描绘环境气氛与刻画人物。1827年发表的《两个牲畜贩子》一般被英美评论界认为是现代英语短篇小说之祖,作者是苏格兰小说家、诗人瓦尔特·司各特。虽然这一时期的英国短篇小说还多与神秘和超自然元素纠葛在一起,但已经开始注意人物性格刻画和对人性与社会的揭示。狄更斯和哈代皆属于维多利亚时代老派的讲故事高手,前者诙谐幽默,后者阴郁悲怆。自史蒂文森开始,英国短篇小说的风格焕然一新,化陈腐平常为神奇新鲜,充分体现了奇妙构思与文字表述的功效。继而有吉卜林将传统叙事技巧推向了一个新的高度,显示出其故事的复杂性与多样性。威尔斯的短篇小说同他的长篇小说一样,同样显示出他的科幻色彩和对社会问题的忧虑。萨基的短篇小说擅长以别出心裁的情节和气氛讽刺社会的虚伪、冷酷和愚蠢。毛姆的短篇以简洁而富有悬念著称，描述了欧洲人在异域的冲突，也体现了他对人性的洞察。德·拉·梅尔的短篇充满了唯美、理想化的诗意幻象，其复杂程度与阅读难度极具挑战性。康拉德、乔伊斯、伍尔夫、劳伦斯皆为现代主义小说大师。康拉德突显了异域的叙事文体风格，从语言表述到叙事结构都有创新，同时反应了在英国殖民统治背景下人性、种族的冲突。伍尔夫的短篇小说创作于长篇小说写作的间歇，她探寻的是意识的心理本质，认为在生活表象之下才是超越时间的现实，描写当下的精神活动比描写外在行为更加重要。劳伦斯以精炼的措辞、微妙的节奏感，表现了对现代复杂人际关系的困惑。乔伊斯在短篇小说领域同样开一代新风，在独创的印象与象征的框架下，突出了"顿悟"这一现代小说的关键要素。凯瑟琳·曼斯菲尔德专注于短篇，她以敏锐的观察力和对人物心理冲突的描写见长，在内容和形式上对短篇小说作为独立的文学叙事体裁的发展做出了突出贡献。

现代短篇小说在美国的发展尤为迅猛，成绩斐然。其中早期华盛顿·欧文和霍桑的作品充满浪漫、神秘色彩。爱伦·坡只写短篇，其作品结构严谨、恐怖怪异。梅尔维尔的作品已经初显现代人的精神困惑。马克·吐温和布雷特·哈特展现出西部的幽默与写实风格。安布罗斯·比尔斯在其短篇中尝试了现实与梦幻的结合以及意识流叙事手法的运用。亨利·詹姆斯突出心理现实主义，其晦涩、繁复的文体同样体现在其短篇之中。欧·亨利也只写短篇小说，特点是通俗化、程式化、大众化。史蒂芬·克莱恩、西奥多·德莱赛、杰克·伦敦呈现出对现实更逼真、更无奈、不加道德评价的新闻报道式的自然主义风格。薇拉·凯瑟返回到更朴实、传统的叙事风格。司各特·菲茨杰拉德以浪漫理想化的视角观察浮夸、颓废的现实生活。舍伍德·安德森虽然非一流作家，但他对极端闭关狭隘的地方人物的描写影响了福克纳对于美国南方乡土生活的详尽描述，其简明的语言叙事风格也影响了海明威的写作风格。福克纳以揭示美国南方传统的解体与人类命运的主题而闻名，他常以创作短篇开始，继而将其拓展为长篇小说。他认为短篇小说集中的内在形式同长篇小说中的一样，都必须具有内容与结构上的统一性。海明威的经历极富传奇性，他以短篇与长篇小说创作并重，以描写"硬汉"形象与运用简洁、凝练的"冰山"写作原则而著名。以上三位作家虽然风格迥异，对英语现代叙述艺术形式多有创新，但在描述与揭示现代人面对快速发展的现代工业、商品社会所遭遇的困惑与异化感方面多有契合之处。凯瑟琳·波特的南方题材与福克纳相近，但在叙事风格上却保持了经典的传统英语小说形式。另一个美国南方女作家弗兰纳里·奥康纳既凸显了哥特式、怪异的描述风格又揭示出现代人道德沦丧、精神异化的主题。

# 前言

短篇小说作为现代叙事艺术形式具有很强的国际性,欧美的长篇小说家几乎都涉足此领域,除了英美之外,成就最突出的还包括俄国的果戈理、屠格涅夫、契诃夫、托尔斯泰,法国的梅里美、福楼拜、都德、莫泊桑,德国的霍夫曼,奥地利的卡夫卡等。

本套美国经典短篇小说选编和翻译共分上下两卷,精选了从19世纪至20世纪中叶美国主要短篇小说家的重要作品。体例上包括四个部分:作家作品简介及所选作品简评、正文、思考问题、对正文及简介简评的全译。我们选编和翻译本套书的主要目的有四。其一,为美国短篇小说课以及美国文学课提供一种适宜的教材。短篇小说的完整性和凝练性有利于学生在有限的时间内有效掌握文学的基本特征,也便于教师的授课安排与要求。其二,本套书是严格意义上的全译,这有助于学生透彻理解原文,借鉴译文,进行文学翻译本身的练习。其三,通过阅读完整的原文,使学生亲历英语语言的历时与共时特点,不同的文体特征,丰富独特的表现力,帮助学生提高自己的英语表达能力。其四,帮助学生深层次地了解英美人士的生活习惯、思维方式、情感表现,以及民族心理特征。本套书适用于高年级英语专业本科生与研究生以及较高级阶段的英语学习者。

编选名家作品常留有遗憾。由于版权或是篇幅限制,我们只能割舍少数名家或名作。同时我们也尽量避免重复翻译,努力保证选材的代表性和译文的文学性。文学翻译往往是"费力不讨好"之事,但有志于文学翻译的人却乐在其中。我们虽然在选编与翻译过程中尽心尽力,但其中仍会存在各种问题,希望有关专家与读者批评指正,不吝赐教。

我们要衷心地感谢南开大学外语学院英语系博士生导师、中国文化典籍翻译研究会会长王宏印教授。先生学贯中西、博古通今、治学严谨、著作等身。能够在繁忙的教学和学术研究中,抽出时间为小书作序,令学生后辈感激之至。他的序言引文如小溪流水、娓娓道来、内涵丰富、沁人心脾……同时要特别感谢北京大学出版社的领导和外语编辑部的编辑对本书出版所给予的大力支持和帮助。

主编

2019年2月

# 目 录

Stephen Crane (1871—1900) ································································ 1
An Episode of War ·································································· 1
斯蒂芬·克莱恩（1871—1900）················································· 6
硝烟背后 ·················································································· 6
The Bride Comes to Yellow Sky ············································· 10
新娘来到黄天镇 ······································································· 21

Theodore Dreiser (1871—1945) ············································· 30
The Lost Phoebe ····································································· 30
西奥多·德莱塞（1871—1945）··············································· 45
失去的菲比 ············································································· 45

Willa Cather (1873—1947) ····················································· 57
The Sculptor's Funeral ···························································· 57
薇拉·凯瑟（1873—1947）····················································· 71
雕塑家的葬礼 ········································································· 71

Clarence Day (1874—1935) ··················································· 82
Father Wakes Up the Village ·················································· 82
克劳伦斯·戴伊（1874—1935）··············································· 89
雄鸡一唱 ················································································· 89

Jack London (1876—1916) ····················································· 94
The Law of Life ······································································ 94
杰克·伦敦（1876—1916）····················································· 101
生命的法则 ············································································· 101
To Build a Fire ······································································· 106
生火 ······················································································· 121

| | |
|---|---|
| Sherwood Anderson (1876—1941) | 132 |
| Hands | 132 |
| 舍伍德·安德森（1876—1941） | 138 |
| 手 | 138 |
| Paper Pills | 143 |
| 纸团 | 146 |
| | |
| H. L. Mencken (1880—1956) | 149 |
| A Girl from Red Lion, P.A. | 149 |
| H. L. 门肯（1880—1956） | 156 |
| 来自宾州红狮村的姑娘 | 156 |
| | |
| Ring W. Lardner (1885—1933) | 161 |
| Old Folk's Christmas | 161 |
| 林·威·拉德纳（1885—1933） | 172 |
| 一对双亲的圣诞节 | 172 |
| | |
| John McNulty (1895—1956) | 181 |
| Cluney McFarrar's Hardtack | 181 |
| 约翰·麦克纳尔蒂（1895—1956） | 186 |
| 柯拉内·麦克法若的硬饼干 | 186 |
| | |
| William Faulkner (1897—1962) | 190 |
| Dry September | 190 |
| 威廉·福克纳（1897—1962） | 202 |
| 干旱的九月 | 202 |
| | |
| Stephen Vincent Benét (1898—1943) | 212 |
| By the Waters of Babylon | 212 |
| 斯蒂芬·文森特·波奈特（1898—1943） | 224 |
| 巴比伦河畔 | 224 |
| | |
| Ernest Hemingway (1899—1961) | 234 |

| | |
|---|---|
| A Clean, Well-Lighted Place | 234 |
| 欧内斯特·海明威（1899—1961） | 240 |
| 一个干净、明亮的地方 | 240 |
| | |
| Thomas Wolfe (1900—1938) | 245 |
| Circus at Dawn | 245 |
| 托马斯·沃尔夫（1900—1938） | 251 |
| 黎明时的马戏团 | 251 |

# Stephen Crane
## (1871—1900)

Stephen Crane was born in a Methodist minister's family in New Jersey. After attending public school, Crane enrolled himself into the College of Liberal Arts at Syracuse University, but did not graduate. A penniless artist, he led a down-and-out life before becoming famous as a poet, journalist, social critic and realist. His contemporaries noted him as being an "original" in his field of work.

After school, Crane began writing short stories for newspapers. Started as a serial, Crane's *The Red Badge of Courage* was a booming success and gained him almost instant fame and the esteem of a bachelor. Crane's ensuing travels inspired further works including *The Black Riders and Other Lines* (1895), *The Little Regiment* (1896), *The Blue Hotel* (1898), *War Is Kind* (1899), *Active Service* (1899), and his finest yet last short work, *The Open Boat* (1898), an account of his own experience in a boat after the ship he was aboard sank. The poems Crane produced were published in *War Is Kind & Other Lines* (1899) and some were posthumously included in *The Black Riders & Other Lines* (1905).

## An Episode of War

*In the following short story, the author presents a lieutenant who is wounded in the right arm while resting with his troops between combats. The main part of the story is comprised of the lieutenant's perceptions of the war going on around him as he retreats to a field hospital. At the hospital, the wounded man has a brief yet unpleasant encounter with a surgeon, who is rude and has him amputated. The theme of the story, that is, the lack of medical humanities in wars, is highlighted in the author's ability to draw the reader into the lieutenant's reactions to his wound and the dramatic illustration of the surgeon's absence of empathy.*

The lieutenant's rubber blanket lay on the ground, and upon it he had poured the company's supply of coffee. Corporals and other representatives of the grimy and hotthroated men who lined the breastwork had come for each squad's portion.

The lieutenant was frowning and serious at this task of division. His lips pursed as he drew with his sword various crevices in the heap until brown squares of coffee, astoundingly equal in size, appeared on the blanket. He was on the verge of a great triumph in mathematics, and the corporals were thronging forward, each to reap a little square, when suddenly the lieutenant cried out and looked quickly at a man near him as if he suspected it was a case of personal assault. The others cried out also when they saw blood upon the lieutenant's sleeve.

He had winced like a man stung, swayed dangerously, and then straightened. The sound of his hoarse breathing was plainly audible. He looked sadly, mystically, over the breastwork at the green face of a wood where now were many puffs of white smoke. During this moment, the men about him gazed statue-like and silent, astonished and awed by this catastrophe which had happened when catastrophes were not expected—when they had leisure to observe it.

As the lieutenant stared at the wood, they too swung their heads so that for another moment all hands, still silent, contemplated the distant forest as if their minds were fixed upon the mystery of a bullet's journey.

The officer had, of course, been compelled to take his sword at once into his left hand. He did not hold it by the hilt. He gripped it at the middle of the blade, awkwardly. Turning his eyes from the hostile wood, he looked at the sword as he held it there, and seemed puzzled as to what to do with it, where to put it. In short this weapon had of a sudden become a strange thing to him. He looked at it in a kind of stupefaction, as if he had been miraculously endowed with a trident, a sceptre, or a spade.

Finally he tried to sheath it. To sheath a sword held by the left hand, at the middle of the blade, in a scabbard hung at the left hip, is a feat worthy of a sawdust ring. This wounded officer engaged in a desperate struggle with the sword and the wobbling scabbard, and during the time of it he breathed like a wrestler.

But at this instant the men, spectators, awoke from their stone-like poses and crowded forward sympathetically. The orderly-sergeant took the sword and tenderly placed it in the scabbard. At the time, he leaned nervously backward, and did not allow even his finger to brush the body of the lieutenant. A wound gives strange dignity to him who bears it. Well men shy from this new and terrible majesty. It is as if the wounded man's hand is upon the curtain which hangs before the revelations of all existence, the meaning of ants, potentates, wars, cities, sunshine, snow, a feather dropped from a bird's wing, and the power of it sheds radiance upon a bloody form, and makes the other men understand sometimes that they are little. His comrades look at him with large eyes thoughtfully. Moreover, they fear vaguely that the weight of a finger upon him might send him headlong, precipitate the tragedy, hurl him at once into the dim, gray unknown. And so the orderly-sergeant, while sheathing the sword, leaned nervously backward.

There were others who proffered assistance. One timidly presented his shoulder and asked the lieutenant if he cared to lean upon it, but the latter waved them away mournfully. He wore the look of one who knows he is the victim of a terrible disease and understands his helplessness. He again stared over the breastwork at the forest, and then turning went slowly rearward. He held his right wrist tenderly in his left hand, as if the wounded arm was made of very brittle glass.

And the men in silence stared at the woods, then at the departing lieutenant, then at the wood, then at the lieutenant.

As the wounded officer passed from the line of battle, he was enabled to see many things which as a participant in the fight were unknown to him. He saw a general on a black horse gazing over the lines of blue infantry at the green woods which veiled his problems. An aide galloped furiously, dragged his horse suddenly to a halt, saluted, and presented a paper. It was, for a wonder, precisely like an historical painting.

To the rear of the general and his staff, a group, composed of a bugler, two or three orderlies, and the bearer of the corps standard, all upon maniacal horses, were working like slaves to hold their ground, preserve their respectful interval, while the shells bloomed in the air about them, and caused their chargers to make furious quivering leaps.

A battery, a tumultuous and shining mass, was swirling toward the right. The wild thud of hoofs, the cries of the riders shouting blame and praise, menace and encouragement, and, last, the roar of the wheels, the slant of the glistening guns, brought the lieutenant to an intent pause. The battery swept in curves that stirred the heart; it made halts as dramatic as the crash of a wave on the rocks, and when it fled onward, this aggregation of wheels, levers, motors, had a beautiful unity, as if it were a missile. The sound of it was a war-chorus that reached into the depths of man's emotion.

The lieutenant, still holding his arm as if it were of glass, stood watching this battery until all detail of it were lost, save the figures of the riders, which rose and fell and waved lashes over the black mass.

Later, he turned his eyes toward the battle where the shooting sometimes crackled like bush-fires, sometimes sputtered with exasperating irregularity, and sometimes reverberated like the thunder. He saw the smoke rolling upward and saw crowds of men who ran and cheered, or stood and blazed away at the inscrutable distance.

He came upon some stragglers, and they told him how to find the field hospital. They described its exact location. In fact these men, no longer having part in the battle, knew more of it than others. They told the performance of every corps, every division, the opinion of every general. The lieutenant, carrying his wounded arm rearward, looked upon them with wonder.

At the roadside a brigade was making coffee and buzzing with talk like a girl's boarding-school. Several officers came out to him and inquired concerning things of which he knew nothing. One, seeing his arm, began to scold. "Why, man, that's no way to do. You want to fix that thing." He appropriated the lieutenant and the lieutenant's wound. He cut the sleeve and laid bare the arm, every nerve of which softly fluttered under his touch. He bound his handkerchief over the wound, scolding away in the meantime. His tone allowed one to think that he was in the habit of being wounded every day. The lieutenant hung his head, feeling, in this presence, that he did not know how to be correctly wounded.

The low white tents of the hospital were grouped around an old schoolhouse. There was here a singular commotion. In the foreground two ambulances interlocked wheels in the deep mud. The drivers were tossing the blame of it back and forth, gesticulating and berating, while from the ambulances, both crammed with wounded, there came an occasional groan. An interminable crowd of bandaged men were coming and going. Great numbers sat under the trees nursing heads or arms or legs. There was a dispute of some kind raging on the steps of the schoolhouse. Sitting with his back against a tree a man with a face as gray as a new army blanket was serenely smoking a corn-cob pipe. The lieutenant wished to rush forward and inform him that he was dying.

A busy surgeon was passing near the lieutenant. "Good morning," he said, with a friendly smile. Then he caught sight of the lieutenant's arm, and his face at once changed. "Well, let's have a look at it." He seemed possessed suddenly of a great contempt for the lieutenant. This wound evidently placed the latter on a very low social plane. The doctor cried out impatiently: "What mutton-head had tied it up that way anyhow?" The lieutenant answered, "Oh, a man."

When the wound was disclosed the doctor fingered it disdainfully. "Humph," he said. "You come along with me and I'll tend to you." His voice contained the same scorn as if he were saying: "You will have to go to jail."

The lieutenant had been very meek, but now his face flushed, and he looked into the doctor's eyes. "I guess I won't have it amputated," he said.

"Nonsense, man! Nonsense! Nonsense!" cried the doctor. "Come along, now. I won't amputate it. Come along. Don't be a baby."

"Let go of me," said the lieutenant, holding back wrathfully, his glance fixed upon the door of the old school-house, as sinister to him as the portals of death.

And this is the story of how the lieutenant lost his arm. When he reached home, his sisters, his mother, his wife, sobbed for a long time at the sight of the flat sleeve. "Oh, well," he said, standing shamefaced amid these tears, "I don't suppose it matters so much as all that."

## Questions

1. Crane is known as a realistic novelist. Can you find some examples of realism in this story?
2. At the beginning of the story, the lieutenant is shot while rationing coffee. How does this incident add to the realistic flavor of this story?
3. Why does the author choose "An Episode of War" as the title while the main part of the story has little to do with battles or heroic combats?
4. How does the surgeon's reaction to the lieutenant's wound help to highlight the theme of the short story?
5. Since the captain lost his arm in such an unheroic way, do you think he is still a hero? Why?

# 斯蒂芬·克莱恩
## （1871—1900）

斯蒂芬·克莱恩出生于新泽西的一个牧师家庭，父亲是基督教卫理公会会长。克莱恩读完公立中小学后，入锡拉丘兹大学人文学院就读。肄业后从事自由写作工作，一度身无分文，贫苦交加。后来他声名渐起，成为著名的诗人、新闻记者、社会评论家及现实主义作家，在当时被认为在他所从事的领域"有独特建树"。

克莱恩的写作生涯始于为报纸撰稿。《红色英勇勋章》最初在报纸连载，使他一举成名，并成为当时最受追捧的单身汉。随后克莱恩曾出国游历，足迹遍布中美洲、欧洲各国，并创作了《黑骑者》（1895）、《小军团》（1896）、《蓝色旅馆》（1898）、《战争是仁慈的》（1899）、《服现役》（1899）等脍炙人口的小说。《海上扁舟》（1898）取材于他本人一次真实的海上沉船经历。克莱恩的多数诗作收录于他的诗集《战争是仁慈的》，也有部分诗篇在他逝世后，被收录于诗集《黑骑者》。

## 硝烟背后

《硝烟背后》这部短篇小说一开始描写了美国内战中一位中尉军官正在给部下分配给养时被流弹击伤手臂的情形。随后作者浓墨重彩地描写中尉返回后方医院时一路上亲眼所见的战争情景。故事结尾中尉在医院与一位外科医生有一次短暂且不愉快的交谈，正是这位缺乏同情心的医生给中尉做了截肢手术。这段描写虽笔墨不多，却升华了故事的主题，谴责了战争的残酷。作者巧妙地驾驭语言，在刻画众人对中尉伤势的反映及医生对中尉伤势的漠视方面使读者有身临其境之感。

中尉就地而铺的胶皮垫子上摆着连里配给的咖啡，各部派来领给养的士兵在齐胸高的防御掩体里排成一排站在一旁，一个个灰头土脸，口干舌燥。

中尉眉头紧锁，分配给养之事他丝毫不敢疏忽。他嘴角微翘，抽出佩剑，将垫子上成堆的咖啡切成一个个棕色的小块，每份大小都出奇的均匀。就在分配工作即将大功告成，士兵们蜂拥上前来领取本单位的那一份之际，中尉猛然大叫一声，迅速将目光移向他身旁的那个士兵，好像是怀疑遭其暗算。其他士兵一看到中尉衣袖上渗出的鲜血，也不禁大声呼喊。

中尉就像被蜂蜇了一样表情痛苦，身体摇晃得厉害，挨了一阵子才站直。他粗重的呼吸声清晰可闻，神情怆然，疑惑的目光越过掩体墙，投向远方一片葱茏的密林，股股白烟正从林中升腾而起。此刻，他身旁的士兵都一动不动静静地看着他，表情愕然。战士们好像被眼前这突如其来的意外吓到了——谁能料到会出这事儿啊！

中尉依旧目视着远方的密林，士兵们也转头向那边望去，全体都警惕着可能再次发生意外的瞬间，却毫无异样，于是大家陷入了沉思之中，好像在思考着这里到丛林的距离是否在子弹的射程之内。

中尉右臂受了伤，只好左手持剑。但他没握剑柄，而是用手握住剑身的中央，虽然这么持剑相当不便。他的目光缓缓从远方收回，落到了手中的剑上，表情中掺杂着迷茫，似乎不知道用手中这把利剑能做些什么。一时间，手中的武器似乎变得陌生了，持剑的人神情茫然，似乎手中握的不是军人所熟悉的利剑，不知是那海神的三叉戟，还是君王的权杖，抑或是农民的铁锹。

中尉试图归剑入鞘，可是他左手持剑，且握的是剑身中央，要将剑收回到挂在左腰上的剑鞘内，简直是难于登天。他竭力尝试，可右臂受伤无法借力，剑鞘又摇晃不定，挣扎努力中他气喘吁吁，像个摔跤手。

此时的一幕，才让所有站在一旁呆呆观望的士兵们回过神儿来，大伙关切地拥上前来查看中尉的伤势。勤务兵从中尉手中接过剑，轻轻地把它插入鞘中。与此同时，他上身微微后仰，很是谨慎，手上的动作丝毫没有碰到中尉。伤者往往会让他人感到一种莫名的敬畏，神情庄重肃穆，令人不敢靠近。此时，受伤的中尉好像正伸手触碰着一层帘幕，撩开帘幕就会昭示世间万象——穴中蝼蚁，廷上君王有何意？战事纷争，城池陷落有何意？阳光普照，白雪消融，飞鸟振翅，轻羽飘落又有何意？这世间所衍射出的那股力量，让一人身形血染，他人自感形秽。士兵们眼睛都睁得大大的，若有所思地看着中尉，心头笼罩着一种难以名状的恐惧感，好像只要有人手指尖轻轻一碰，他就会一头栽进一个灰洞洞的、阴森森的无底深渊，酿成可怕的悲剧。所以勤务兵动作轻柔，不敢靠他太近。

其他人也上前帮忙。一个士兵怯生生地走上前来，表示想让中尉靠在自己肩上，但中尉冲他摆了摆手示意不必。中尉神色有些悲伤，不禁令人想起身患重症、求治无门的病人。此时，他的眼光又一次越过防御工事，投向远处的树林，没过多久，他便转过身来缓缓离去。他左手轻轻托在受伤的右手手腕下面，仿佛动作稍重，右臂就会像玻璃杯一样破碎。

士兵们默默地注视着远处的树林，然后又看看中尉远去的背影，转头再望望树林，之后再看看渐行渐远的中尉。

他一路沿战线走去，此刻作为一个战争参与者所无法洞察的情景纷纷映入眼帘。他看到一位将军骑着一匹黑色战马，注视着步兵队列，葱茏的密林成了掩护这些身着蓝色制服步兵的天然屏障。将军的副官策马急驰而来，行至将军面前猛地勒马收缰，行过军礼后，交给了将军一份文件。说来也怪，这一幕在中尉眼中就是一幅活生生的记载历史的画卷。

将军及其随从人员的后面还跟着一群人，有一个司号员，一个司旗手，两三个勤务兵，他们都立身烈马，彼此间保持着一定的距离。此时，弹片就在他们四周横飞，他们却毅然履行着军人的职责，而战马却在纷然四起的爆炸声中躁动不安。

炮群正在向阵地的右翼转移，炮身闪亮，马蹄嘈杂，骑手嬉笑怒骂，炮车轰隆作响，士兵步枪上肩，刺刀闪亮。目睹斯情斯景，中尉不由得定住了脚步，眉宇间流露出热切的神情。远远望去，移动中的车马人流构成了一条条曲线，有时突然停止前进，就如同巨浪拍石般震撼人心；继续前进时车马人流泾渭分明整齐划一，给人以视觉上美的感受。所有的声响交织在一起，如战鼓齐鸣般振聋发聩。

中尉左手托着受伤的右臂，一动不动地站在那里，目不转睛地看着眼前的这一幕。随着炮群的远去，最后他只能看见在黑压压的一片中，骑手的身影在马背上上下起伏，挥舞着马鞭。

中尉又把目光转向了战场，那里时而枪炮齐鸣，如山火，如怒雷；时而又枪声零落，扰思绪，乱心神。远处浓烟滚滚升起，人群时而涌动，时而欢呼，时而原地不动，向不可知处枪炮齐发。

中尉碰到了几个掉队的士兵，从他们口中得知战地医院的确切位置。事实上因为没上战场，这些事他们知道的反而最清楚。他们还告诉中尉哪个部队英勇善战，哪个将军指挥若定。中尉手托在受伤的胳膊下面，带着奇怪的神情打量着这几个士兵。

路边一支部队正在休整，士兵们边煮咖啡边闲聊着，开心得就像寄宿女子学校的姑娘们。几个军官向中尉走来，问了一些他既不知道也无从回答的问题，其中一个军官发现了他右臂的伤势，以一种责备的口吻说："怎么搞的，你那样托着没用，得包扎一下。"他走上前来撕掉中尉右臂的衣袖让伤口露出来，伤口在他的触碰下一阵阵疼痛。他用手帕包住伤口，边包扎边责备，那语气就好像他天天受伤，这对他来说是家常便饭。中尉低头听着，感到莫名其妙，难道战场负伤还有对错之分？

一所废弃学校的四周支了许多低矮的白色小帐篷，那就是战地医院。医院前有两辆救护车交错着陷在泥里，进退不得，两个司机互相埋怨，边比画边吵吵，场面混乱不堪。两辆车里都塞满了伤员，时不时地发出呻吟声。医院里进进出出的人川流不息，多数是缠着绷带的轻伤员，更有大批大批的伤员坐在树荫下，多数是头部和四肢受伤，护士们正在给他们包扎。学校门口的台阶上有些人不知在争论什么事。不远处有个人背靠着树干坐着，面色如新式灰色军毯一般灰暗，一声不响地抽着烟，手里握着的烟斗居然是用掏空了的玉米棒子做成的。这会儿中尉真想冲上前去告诉他，如果再没人给他治伤他就离死不远了。

一个外科医生正进进出出忙得不可开交，走到中尉身前时，他微笑道："早上好。"他脸上的神情很友好，随即注意到了中尉右臂的伤势，脸上的神情立刻为之一变。"让我看看伤口，"可一看之后，脸上立刻显现出极度轻视的神色。伤口处置成这样，这人肯定不是什么大人物。"究竟是哪个笨蛋这样给人包扎伤口的？"医生很不耐烦地问道。中尉回答道："不过就是个普通人。"

医生解开绷带，用手碰了碰伤口，一脸轻蔑之情。"嗯，你跟我过来吧，我来给你处理一下。"说这话时他的声音冷冷的，就如同在对犯人说："你进监狱去吧。"

从受伤到现在，中尉一直话不多，别人说什么就是什么，可这会儿他突然显得很激动，脸都有点儿红了，他盯着医生说："我想用不着截肢吧？"

"你胡说什么呀，截什么肢啊，快跟我来，别跟小孩似的。"医生不耐烦地说。

"放开我。"中尉愤然向后退去，此时，学校的大门在中尉眼里变得如同地狱之门般狰狞可怖。

这是一个关于中尉如何失去手臂的故事。他回到家后，他的姐姐、妈妈和妻子看到他袖子里空荡荡的，一个个不由得悲从中来，哭个不停。他感到一阵愧疚，安慰她们道："别哭了，这没什么大不了的。"

# The Bride Comes to Yellow Sky

*"The Bride Comes to Yellow Sky" was published in* **The Open Boat & Other Tales of Adventure.** *Set at the end of the 19th century in a town called Yellow Sky, the story concerns the marshal, Jack Potter, and his unnamed bride and the effect their marriage has on the town. The drunken, belligerent Scratchy Wilson, a cowboy who represents the Old West tries to effect a showdown with Jack, his nemesis. When Jack refuses to fight, responding to the cowpoke's taunts with "I'm married," Scratchy leaves without fighting, bewildered that the old rules have changed.*

## I

The great pullman was whirling onward with such dignity of motion that a glance from the window seemed simply to prove that the plains of Texas were pouring eastward. Vast flats of green grass, dull-hued spaces of mesquite and cactus, little groups of frame houses, woods of light and tender trees, all were sweeping into the east, sweeping over the horizon, a precipice.

A newly married pair had boarded this coach at San Antonio. The man's face was reddened from many days in the wind and sun, and a direct result of his new black clothes was that his brick-colored hands were constantly performing in a most conscious fashion. From time to time he looked down respectfully at his attire. He sat with a hand on each knee, like a man waiting in a barber's shop. The glances he devoted to other passengers were furtive and shy.

The bride was not pretty, nor was she very young. She wore a dress of blue cashmere, with small reservations of velvet here and there and with steel buttons abounding. She continually twisted her head to regard her puff sleeves, very stiff, straight, and high. They embarrassed her. It was quite apparent that she had cooked, and that she expected to cook, dutifully. The blushes caused by the careless scrutiny of some passengers as she had entered the car were strange to see upon this plain, under-class countenance, which was drawn in placid, almost emotionless lines.

They were evidently very happy. "Ever been in a parlor-car before?" he asked, smiling with delight.

"No," she answered, "I never was. It's fine, ain't it?"

"Great! And then after a while we'll go forward to the diner and get a big layout. Finest meal in the world. Charge a dollar."

"Oh, do they?" cried the bride. "Charge a dollar? Why, that's too much—for us—ain't it, Jack?"

"Not this trip, anyhow," he answered bravely. "We're going to go the whole thing."

Later, he explained to her about the train. "You see, it's a thousand miles from one end of Texas to the other, and this train runs right across it and never stops but four times." He had the pride of an owner. He pointed out to her the dazzling fittings of the coach, and in truth her eyes opened wider as she contemplated the sea-green figured velvet, the shining brass, silver, and glass, the wood that gleamed as darkly brilliant as the surface of a pool of oil. At one end a bronze figure sturdily held a support for a separated chamber, and at convenient places on the ceiling were frescoes in olive and silver.

To the minds of the pair, their surroundings reflected the glory of their marriage that morning in San Antonio. This was the environment of their new estate, and the man's face in particular beamed with an elation that made him appear ridiculous to the negro porter. This individual at times surveyed them from afar with an amused and superior grin. On other occasions he bullied them with skill in ways that did not make it exactly plain to them that they were being bullied. He subtly used all the manners of the most unconquerable kind of snobbery. He oppressed them, but of this oppression they had small knowledge, and they speedily forgot that infrequently a number of travelers covered them with stares of derisive enjoyment. Historically there was supposed to be something infinitely humorous in their situation.

"We are due in Yellow Sky at 3:42," he said, looking tenderly into her eyes.

"Oh, are we?" she said, as if she had not been aware of it. To evince surprise at her husband's statement was part of her wifely amiability. She took from a pocket a little silver watch, and as she held it before her and stared at it with a frown of attention, the new husband's face shone.

"I bought it in San Anton' from a friend of mine," he told her gleefully.

"It's seventeen minutes past twelve," she said, looking up at him with a kind of shy and clumsy coquetry. A passenger, noting this play, grew excessively sardonic, and winked at himself in one of the numerous mirrors.

At last they went to the dining-car. Two rows of negro waiters in glowing white suits surveyed their entrance with the interest and also the equanimity of men who had been forewarned. The pair fell to the lot of a waiter who happened to feel pleasure in steering them through their meal. He viewed them with the manner of a fatherly pilot, his countenance radiant with benevolence. The patronage, entwined with the ordinary deference, was not plain to them. And yet as they returned to their coach they showed in their faces a sense of escape.

To the left, miles down a long purple slope, was a little ribbon of mist where moved the keening Rio Grande. The train was approaching it at an angle, and the apex was Yellow Sky. Presently it was apparent that as the distance from Yellow Sky grew shorter, the husband became commensurately restless. His brick-red hands were more insistent in their prominence. Occasionally he was even rather absent-minded and far-away when the bride leaned forward and addressed him.

As a matter of truth, Jack Potter was beginning to find the shadow of a deed weigh upon him like a leaden slab. He, the town marshal of Yellow Sky, a man known, liked, and feared in his corner, a prominent person, had gone to San Antonio to meet a girl he believed he loved, and there, after the usual prayers, had actually induced her to marry him, without consulting Yellow Sky for any part of the transaction. He was now bringing his bride before an innocent and unsuspecting community.

Of course, people in Yellow Sky married as it pleased them in accordance with a general custom; but such was Potter's thought of his duty to his friends, or of their idea of his duty, or of an unspoken form which does not control men in these matters, that he felt he was heinous. He had committed an extraordinary crime. Face to face with this girl in San Antonio, and spurred by his sharp impulse, he had gone headlong over all the social hedges. At San Antonio he was like a man hidden in the dark. A knife to sever any friendly duty, any form, was easy to his hand in that remote city. But the hour of Yellow Sky, the hour of daylight, was approaching.

He knew full well that his marriage was an important thing to his town. It could only be exceeded by the burning of the new hotel. His friends could not forgive him. Frequently he had reflected on the advisability of telling them by telegraph, but a new cowardice had been upon him. He feared to do it. And now the train was hurrying him toward a scene of amazement, glee, and reproach. He glanced out of the window at the line of haze swinging slowly in towards the train.

Yellow Sky had a kind of brass band, which played painfully to the delight of the populace. He laughed without heart as he thought of it. If the citizens could dream of his prospective arrival with his bride, they would parade the band at the station and escort them, amid cheers and laughing congratulations, to his adobe home.

He resolved that he would use all the devices of speed and plains-craft in making the journey from the station to his house. Once within that safe citadel, he could issue some sort of a vocal bulletin, and then not go among the citizens until they had time to wear off a little of their enthusiasm.

The bride looked anxiously at him. "What's worrying you, Jack?"

He laughed again. "I'm not worrying, girl. I'm only thinking of Yellow Sky."

She flushed in comprehension.

A sense of mutual guilt invaded their minds and developed a finer tenderness. They looked at each other with eyes softly aglow. But Potter often laughed the same nervous laugh. The flush upon the bride's face seemed quite permanent.

The traitor to the feelings of Yellow Sky narrowly watched the speeding landscape. "We're nearly there," he said.

Presently the porter came and announced the proximity of Potter's home. He held a brush in his hand and, with all his airy superiority gone, he brushed Potter's new clothes as the latter slowly turned this way and that way. Potter fumbled out a coin and gave it to the porter as he had seen others do. It was a heavy and muscle-bound business, as that of a man shoeing his first horse.

The porter took their bag, and as the train began to slow they moved forward to the hooded platform of the car. Presently the two engines and their long string of coaches rushed into the station of Yellow Sky.

"They have to take water here," said Potter, from a constricted throat and in mournful cadence as one announcing death. Before the train stopped, his eye had swept the length of the platform, and he was glad and astonished to see there was none upon it but the station-agent, who, with a slightly hurried and anxious air, was walking toward the water-tanks. When the train had halted, the porter alighted first and placed in position a little temporary step.

"Come on, girl," said Potter hoarsely. As he helped her down they each laughed on a false note. He took the bag from the negro, and bade his wife cling to his arm. As they slunk rapidly away, his hang-dog glance perceived that they were unloading the two trunks, and also that the station-agent far ahead near the baggage-car had turned and was running toward him, making gestures. He laughed, and groaned as he laughed, when he noted the first effect of his marital bliss upon Yellow Sky. He gripped his wife's arm firmly to his side, and they fled. Behind them the porter stood chuckling fatuously.

## II

The California Express on the Southern Railway was due at Yellow Sky in twenty-one minutes. There were six men at the bar of the "Weary Gentleman" saloon. One was a drummer who talked a great deal and rapidly; three were Texans who did not care to talk at that time; and two were Mexican sheep-herders who did not talk as a general practice in the "Weary Gentleman" saloon. The barkeeper's dog lay on the board walk that crossed in front of the door. His head was on his paws, and he glanced drowsily here and there with the constant vigilance of a dog that is kicked on occasion. Across the sandy street were some vivid green grass plots, so wonderful in appearance amid the sands that burned near them in a blazing sun that they caused a doubt in the mind. They exactly resembled the grass mats used to represent lawns on the stage. At the cooler end of the railway station a man without a coat sat in a tilted chair and smoked his pipe. The fresh-cut bank of the Rio Grande circled near the town, and there could be seen beyond it a great, plum-colored plain of mesquite.

Save for the busy drummer and his companions in the saloon, Yellow Sky was dozing. The new-comer leaned gracefully upon the bar, and recited many tales with the confidence of a bard who has come upon a new field.

"—and at the moment that the old man fell down stairs with the bureau in his arms, the old woman was coming up with two scuttles of coal, and, of course—"

The drummer's tale was interrupted by a young man who suddenly appeared in the open door. He cried: "Scratchy Wilson's drunk, and has turned loose with both hands." The two Mexicans at once set down their glasses and faded out of the rear entrance of the saloon.

The drummer, innocent and jocular, answered: "All right, old man. S'pose he has. Come in and have a drink, anyhow."

But the information had made such an obvious cleft in every skull in the room that the drummer was obliged to see its importance. All had become instantly solemn. "Say," said he, mystified, "what is this?" His three companions made the introductory gesture of eloquent speech, but the young man at the door forestalled them.

"It means, my friend," he answered, as he came into the saloon, "that for the next two hours this town won't be a health resort."

The barkeeper went to the door and locked and barred it. Reaching out of the window, he pulled in heavy wooden shutters and barred them. Immediately a solemn, chapel-like gloom was upon the place. The drummer was looking from one to another.

"But, say," he cried, "what is this, anyhow? You don't mean there is going to be a gun-fight?"

"Don't know whether there'll be a fight or not," answered one man grimly. "But there'll be some shootin' — some good shootin'."

The young man who had warned them waved his hand. "Oh, there'll be a fight fast enough, if anyone wants it. Anybody can get a fight out there in the street. There's a fight just waiting."

The drummer seemed to be swayed between the interest of a foreigner and a perception of personal danger.

"What did you say his name was?" he asked.

"Scratchy Wilson," they answered in chorus.

"And will he kill anybody? What are you going to do? Does this happen often? Does he rampage around like this once a week or so? Can he break in that door?"

"No, he can't break down that door," replied the barkeeper. "He's tried it three times. But when he comes you'd better lay down on the floor, stranger. He's dead sure to shoot at it, and a bullet may come through."

Thereafter the drummer kept a strict eye upon the door. The time had not yet been called for him to hug the floor, but, as a minor precaution, he sidled near to the wall. "Will he kill anybody?" he said again.

The men laughed low and scornfully at the question.

"He's out to shoot, and he's out for trouble. Don't see any good in experimentin' with him."

"But what do you do in a case like this? What do you do?"

A man responded: "Why, he and Jack Potter—"

"But," in chorus, the other men interrupted, "Jack Potter's in San Anton'."

"Well, who is he? What's he got to do with it?"

"Oh, he's the town marshal. He goes out and fights Scratchy when he gets on one of these tears."

"Wow," said the drummer, mopping his brow. "Nice job he's got."

The voices had toned away to mere whisperings. The drummer wished to ask further questions which were born of an increasing anxiety and bewilderment; but when he attempted them, the men merely looked at him in irritation and motioned him to remain silent. A tense waiting hush was upon them. In the deep shadows of the room their eyes shone as they listened for sounds from the street. One man made three gestures at the barkeeper, and the latter, moving like a ghost, handed him a glass and a bottle. The man poured a full glass of whisky, and set down the bottle noiselessly. He gulped the whisky in a swallow, and turned again toward the door in immovable silence. The drummer saw that the barkeeper, without a sound, had taken a Winchester from beneath the bar. Later he saw this individual beckoning to him, so he tiptoed across the room.

"You better come with me back of the bar."

"No, thanks," said the drummer, perspiring. "I'd rather be where I can make a break for the back door."

Whereupon the man of bottles made a kindly but peremptory gesture. The drummer obeyed it, and finding himself seated on a box with his head below the level of the bar, balm was laid upon his soul at sight of various zinc and copper fittings that bore a resemblance to armor-plate. The barkeeper took a seat comfortably upon an adjacent box.

"You see," he whispered, "this here Scratchy Wilson is a wonder with a gun—a perfect wonder—and when he goes on the war trail, we hunt our holes—naturally. He's about the last one of the old gang that used to hang out along the river here. He's a terror when he's drunk. When he's sober he's all right—kind of simple—wouldn't hurt a fly— nicest fellow in town. But when he's drunk—whoo!" There were periods of stillness. "I wish Jack Potter was back from San Anton'," said the barkeeper. "He shot Wilson up once—in the leg—and he would sail in and pull out the kinks in this thing."

Presently they heard from a distance the sound of a shot, followed by three wild yowls. It instantly removed a bond from the men in the darkened saloon. There was a shuffling of feet. They looked at each other. "Here he comes," they said.

## III

A man in a maroon-colored flannel shirt, which had been purchased for purposes of decoration and made, principally, by some Jewish women on the east side of New York, rounded a corner and walked into the middle of the main street of Yellow Sky.

In either hand the man held a long, heavy, blue-black revolver. Often he yelled, and these cries rang through a semblance of a deserted village, shrilly flying over the roofs in a volume that seemed to have no relation to the ordinary vocal strength of a man. It was as if the surrounding stillness formed the arch of a tomb over him. These cries of ferocious challenge rang against walls of silence. And his boots had red tops with gilded imprints, of the kind beloved in winter by little sledding boys on the hillsides of New England.

The man's face flamed in a rage begot of whisky. His eyes, rolling and yet keen for ambush, hunted the still doorways and windows. He walked with the creeping movement of the midnight cat. As it occurred to him, he roared menacing information. The long revolvers in his hands were as easy as straws; they were moved with an electric swiftness. The little fingers of each hand played sometimes in a musician's way. Plain from the low collar of the shirt, the cords of his neck straightened and sank, straightened and sank, as passion moved him. The only sounds were his terrible invitations. The calm adobes preserved their demeanor at the passing of this small thing in the middle of the street.

There was no offer of fight—no offer of fight. The man called to the sky. There were no attractions. He bellowed and fumed and swayed his revolvers here and everywhere.

The dog of the barkeeper of the "Weary Gentleman" saloon had not appreciated the advance of events. He yet lay dozing in front of his master's door. At sight of the dog, the man paused and raised his revolver humorously. At sight of the man, the dog sprang up and walked diagonally away, with a sullen head, and growling. The man yelled, and the dog broke into a gallop. As it was about to enter an alley, there was a loud noise, a whistling, and something spat the ground directly before it. The dog screamed, and, wheeling in terror, galloped headlong in a new direction. Again there was a noise, a whistling, and sand was kicked viciously before it. Fear-stricken, the dog turned and flurried like an animal in a pen. The man stood laughing, his weapons at his hips.

Ultimately the man was attracted by the closed door of the "Weary Gentleman" saloon. He went to it, and hammering with a revolver, demanded drink.

The door remaining imperturbable, he picked a bit of paper from the walk and nailed it to the framework with a knife. He then turned his back contemptuously upon this popular resort, and walking to the opposite side of the street, and spinning there on his heel quickly and lithely, fired at the bit of paper. He missed it by a half inch. He swore at himself, and went away. Later, he comfortably fusilladed the windows of his most intimate friend. The man was playing with this town. It was a toy for him.

But still there was no offer of fight. The name of Jack Potter, his ancient antagonist, entered his mind, and he concluded that it would be a glad thing if he should go to Potter's house and by bombardment induce him to come out and fight. He moved in the direction of his desire, chanting Apache scalp-music.

When he arrived at it, Potter's house presented the same still front as had the other adobes. Taking up a strategic position, the man howled a challenge. But this house regarded him as might a great stone god. It gave no sign. After a decent wait, the man howled further challenges, mingling with them wonderful epithets.

Presently there came the spectacle of a man churning himself into deepest rage over the immobility of a house. He fumed at it as the winter wind attacks a prairie cabin in the North. To the distance there should have gone the sound of a tumult like the fighting of 200 Mexicans. As necessity bade him, he paused for breath or to reload his revolvers.

## IV

Potter and his bride walked sheepishly and with speed. Sometimes they laughed together shamefacedly and low.

"Next corner, dear," he said finally.

They put forth the efforts of a pair walking bowed against a strong wind. Potter was about to raise a finger to point the first appearance of the new home when, as they circled the corner, they came face to face with a man in a maroon-colored shirt who was feverishly pushing cartridges into a large revolver. Upon the instant the man dropped his revolver to the ground, and, like lightning, whipped another from its holster. The second weapon was aimed at the bridegroom's chest.

There was silence. Potter's mouth seemed to be merely a grave for his tongue. He exhibited an instinct to at once loosen his arm from the woman's grip, and he dropped the bag to the sand. As for the bride, her face had gone as yellow as old cloth. She was a slave to hideous rites gazing at the apparitional snake.

The two men faced each other at a distance of three paces. He of the revolver smiled with a new and quiet ferocity. "Tried to sneak up on me," he said. "Tried to sneak up on me!" His eyes grew more baleful. As Potter made a slight movement, the man thrust his revolver venomously forward. "No, don't you do it, Jack Potter. Don't you move a finger toward a gun just yet. Don't you move an eyelash. The time has come for me to settle with you, and I'm goin' to do it my own way and loaf along with no interferin'. So if you don't want a gun bent on you, just mind what I tell you."

Potter looked at his enemy. "I ain't got a gun on me, Scratchy," he said. "Honest, I ain't." He was stiffening and steadying, but yet somewhere at the back of his mind a vision of the Pullman floated, the sea-green figured velvet, the shining brass, silver, and glass, the wood that gleamed as darkly brilliant as the surface of a pool of oil—all the glory of the marriage, the environment of the new estate. "You know I fight when it comes to fighting, Scratchy Wilson, but I ain't got a gun on me. You'll have to do all the shootin' yourself."

His enemy's face went livid. He stepped forward and lashed his weapon to and fro before Potter's chest. "Don't you tell me you ain't got no gun on you, you whelp. Don't tell me no lie like that. There ain't a man in Texas ever seen you without no gun. Don't take me for no kid." His eyes blazed with light, and his throat worked like a pump.

"I ain't takin' you for no kid," answered Potter. His heels had not moved an inch backward. "I'm takin' you for a—fool. I tell you I ain't got a gun, and I ain't. If you're goin' to shoot me up, you better begin now. You'll never get a chance like this again."

So much enforced reasoning had told on Wilson's rage. He was calmer. "If you ain't got a gun, why ain't you got a gun?" he sneered. "Been to Sunday-school?"

"I ain't got a gun because I've just come from San Anton' with my wife. I'm married," said Potter. "And if I'd thought there was going to be any galoots like you prowling around when I brought my wife home, I'd had a gun, and don't you forget it."

"Married!" said Scratchy, not at all comprehending.

"Yes, married. I'm married," said Potter distinctly.

"Married?" said Scratchy. Seemingly for the first time he saw the drooping, drowning woman at the other man's side. "No!" he said. He was like a creature allowed a glimpse of another world. He moved a pace backward, and his arm with the revolver dropped to his side. "Is this the lady?" he asked.

"Yes, this is the lady," answered Potter.

There was another period of silence.

"Well," said Wilson at last, slowly, "I s'pose it's all off now."

"It's all off if you say so, Scratchy. You know I didn't make the trouble." Potter lifted his valise.

"Well, I 'low it's off, Jack," said Wilson. He was looking at the ground. "Married!" He was not a student of chivalry; it was merely that in the presence of this foreign condition he was a simple child of the earlier plains. He picked up his starboard revolver, and placing both weapons in their holsters, he went away. His feet made funnel-shaped tracks in the heavy sand.

**Questions**

1. Why is Jack Potter so ambivalent about his marriage?
2. What is the point of view, and how is it critical to the reader's understanding of the story?
3. The name of the saloon has symbolic significance. What does the name suggest? Can you find other symbolic names or images in the story? What's the meaning of each symbol?
4. How are the four sections of Crane's story thematically related to one another?
5. How does Crane manage to avoid sentimentality?

## 新娘来到黄天镇

《新娘来到黄天镇》收录在小说集《海上扁舟及其他历险故事》里。该小说以19世纪末一座名为"黄天镇"的小镇为背景,以警察局局长杰克·波特和他的新娘以及他们的婚姻带给这座小镇的影响为主线。而醉醺醺、好斗的斯克赖奇·威尔逊则是旧时代西部的代表,他准备与教训过他的人杰克一决高下。当杰克拒绝同他决斗并对这位牛仔的嘲骂做出"我结婚了"的回应时,斯克赖奇放弃了挑衅,对旧时代规则的改变迷惑不解。

一

巨人的豪华列车正飒爽英姿地向前驰骋着,从窗外放眼望去,仿佛觉得得克萨斯的大片草原在向东奔去。一片片辽阔的绿草地,一片片暗色调的牧豆树和仙人掌,一排排低矮整齐的木屋,一丛丛轻盈婆娑的树木,仿佛都直奔悬崖般的地平线,一直向东蔓延开去。

一对新婚夫妇在圣安东尼奥登上了这列客车。新郎的脸色由于多日的风吹日晒而泛红,而这身黑色的新装带来了一个结果:他那双砖红色的手,总是不自在地动来动去,还不时地低头恭敬地看看自己的打扮。他双手扶膝坐在那里,就好像在理发店里等待理发一样。他的目光总是隐秘而羞涩地投向其他乘客。

新娘既不算漂亮,也不十分年轻。她穿着一条蓝色的开司米长裙,上面零零星星镶嵌着天鹅绒,裙子上点缀了无数的钢扣。她不断地扭头去打量她那又硬又挺而且高高鼓起的泡泡袖。这身装扮使她觉得尴尬。显而易见她是下过厨的,甚至还尽职地热衷于此。上车时,一些乘客不经意的打量使她脸上泛起了害羞的红晕,衬在她那张貌不惊人的下层人面孔上显得有些不可思议。她脸上神情安静,几乎没有任何表情。

他们显然很幸福。"以前坐过豪华列车吗?"男子兴高采烈面带微笑地问她。

"没有,"她回答道,"从来没有。感觉真棒,是吧?"

"太棒了!等会儿咱们就去餐车实现咱们的宏伟计划,去享受世界一流的美食,要一美金呢。"

"噢!是吗?"新娘很惊讶,"要一美金吗?对我们来说会不会太贵了,杰克?"

"无论如何,这次旅行例外,"他毅然地说,"我们要彻底享受一回。"

然后,他向妻子介绍了列车的情况。"你看,得克萨斯从西到东有一千英里远,这趟列车穿过整个州只停四次。"他带着骄傲的口吻,好像就是列车的主人。他将车厢里眼花缭乱的装饰一一指给她看,而她也瞪大了眼睛,凝视着带有海蓝色图案的天鹅绒,闪闪发亮的铜器、银器和玻璃制品,还有如同油池表面一样发出暗色光芒的木制品。在车厢一端,一尊铜像牢牢地支撑出一个独立隔间,在天棚触手可及的地方总能看见些橄榄色和银色的壁画。

在这对夫妻心里,他们所在的环境体现了当天早上他们在圣安东尼奥喜结良缘的荣耀。这正是他们人生新阶段应有的境界,男子脸上散发出得意扬扬的神采。一名黑人服务员觉得他有点儿可笑。此人不时地从远处审视着他们,开心的笑容里透出些傲慢。他偶尔也会去欺负他们一下,不过巧妙得让他们察觉不到受到了欺负。他狡猾地使出了一切不可抵挡的势利手段。他压制他们,但他俩对此却浑然不觉,他们很快便忘记有一些旅客偶尔用嘲讽而寻开心的眼光打量他们。自古以来,他们这样的情景自然而然会蒙上一层滑稽的色彩。

"我们三点四十二分就要到黄天镇了,"新郎含情脉脉地看着新娘的双眼。

"噢,是吗?"新娘说,好像她之前没有意识到一样。对丈夫所说的话表示惊讶,这在她看来是表达妻子温柔的一种方式。她从口袋里掏出一只小巧的银表,放在眼前,微微蹙眉仔细端详了一番,此时新郎不禁喜形于色。

"这是我在圣安东尼奥时从一个朋友那里买的,"他美滋滋地告诉新娘。

"十二点十七分了,"新娘仰头望着新郎说道,娇媚中带着些许羞涩和笨拙。一位乘客察觉到这一幕,不无嘲讽地对着无数镜子中的一面,向自己眨巴眼睛。

最后他们来到餐车。两排身着雪白制服的黑人侍者列队而立,带着训练有素的镇定表情,饶有兴趣地注视着他们的到来。小两口开始用餐时,碰巧遇上一个侍者愿意在旁引导他们用餐。他以一副慈父般的表情看着他们,脸上洋溢着慈爱。这样的服务司空见惯,但对他们来说却不同寻常。最后,当他们回到自己的车厢时,都感到如释重负。

往左,沿着一道紫色的斜坡往前几英里,里奥格兰德河如同一道迷雾在欢快地流淌着。列车呈斜角向河流靠近,而角度的顶点便是黄天镇所在地。随着离黄天镇的距离越来越短,新郎显然也越来越坐立不安,他砖红色双手的动作越发引人注目。有几次新娘靠过来呼唤他时,他甚至心不在焉,神情恍惚。

事实上,杰克·波特渐渐开始感觉有件事情在他心里像压了块铅板一样。他是黄天镇的警察局局长,一个在当地受人爱戴,让人敬畏的赫赫有名的人物。他到圣安东尼奥去见一位他自以为喜爱的姑娘,经过一番平常的恳求之后,竟然诱使姑娘嫁给了他。他没有就此事的任何环节征求过黄天镇人的意见,如今他把新娘带回来了，天真的镇民们却还都蒙在鼓里。

当然，按照常规惯例，黄天镇人的婚姻是自主的，要让自己称心如意。可是波特想起他对朋友的责任和义务，想起一种未及言明的习俗，并不能在这种事情中对人们加以控制，于是对自己深恶痛绝。他自己犯下了滔天大罪。在圣安东尼奥和这个女子相见后，因为一时的冲动，便贸然跨越了一切社会障碍。在圣安东尼奥，他就像是一个藏在暗处的人，在那座遥远的城市里，他可以轻易地用刀切断对朋友的情谊和责任，忘记一切规定。然而，到达黄天镇的时刻，真相大白的时刻就要来临了。

他心里清楚，对镇民们来说，除了放火烧掉新旅馆这样的事情以外，似乎没有什么比他的婚姻更重要的了。他的朋友不会宽恕他的所作所为。他也曾无数次想过最明智的办法是打电报告诉他们这一切，然而另一种胆怯却涌上心头。他不敢那么做。列车正在急速往前行驶，迎接他的将是令人惊诧而兴奋，或是备受责骂的一幕。他向窗外看去，一缕薄雾正缓缓地朝着列车飘过来。

黄天镇有一支铜管乐队，为了讨百姓欢心他们演奏时很卖力。他一想到这儿，便漫不经心地笑了。如果镇民们能料到他将携妻子如期而至，说不定会带着乐队游行至车站，在一片欢呼道喜声中护送他们回新郎的土砖房。

波特决定以最快的速度和最巧妙的办法，尽快从车站回到家里。只要进入他的保险之地，他就可以发表一项口头声明，一段时间不出现，直到镇民们的热情减退下来。

新娘急切地看着他，问道："你有什么心事吗，杰克？"

杰克又笑了。"没有，亲爱的。只不过想起了黄天镇。"

新娘会意，脸颊绯红。

两人忽然间对彼此产生了一种内疚感，这却使他们更加缠绵悱恻。他们用满含柔情的炽热目光注视着对方。不过波特的笑声中总是带着些不安和紧张，而新娘的脸上似乎总是飞着红霞。

波特这个背弃了黄天镇人感情的人，专注地看着飞驰而过的风景。"我们快到了，"他说。

过了一会儿，列车员过来通知波特快要到站了。列车员手里拿着一把刷子。这次他全然没有了之前的傲慢，为波特刷起了新衣，任由他慢慢地转过来转过去。波特摸出一枚硬币递给他，他以前见过别人这样做。这是个粗活，让人肌肉紧张，就像一个人给他第一匹马钉铁掌那样。

列车员拎起他们的提包，随着列车慢慢减速，他们朝着车厢带篷的平台走去。不久，两个火车头和一长串车厢终于驶进了黄天镇车站。

"他们得在这里加水，"波特说，其喉咙哽咽，语调忧伤，就好像谁在宣布噩耗一样。没等火车停稳,他的目光已经把整个站台扫视了个遍,他惊喜地发现,那里除了站台管理员之外没有其他人。车站管理员有些行色匆匆地向水槽急步走去。火车停了,列车员先下了车,安放了一个临时踏板。

"下来吧,亲爱的,"波特用沙哑的声音说道。他把新娘搀下车时,两人一起笑了起来,但笑得很假。波特从黑人手里接过提包,嘱咐妻子紧搀他的胳膊。两人正在急忙往外溜时,波特鬼鬼祟祟的目光察觉到有两个人正在往下卸行李箱,在前方远处的行李车旁,站台管理员转身向他跑过来,一面打着手势。波特注意到,这就是警察局局长新婚之后回到黄天镇所引起的第一个反应,于是他忍不住笑了,还边笑边发出呻吟。他紧紧抓住妻子的胳膊,一溜烟儿地逃了。列车员站在他们身后,咯咯地傻笑起来。

## 二

南方铁路段的加利福尼亚快车再有21分钟就要到达黄天镇了。"疲乏先生"酒吧间里有六个男子。一个是旅行推销员,一直滔滔不绝,语速极快;三个是得克萨斯人,他们这个时候不喜欢说话;另外两个是墨西哥牧羊人,按"疲乏先生"酒吧的惯例,他们一言不发。酒吧老板的狗躺在门口的木板人行道上,脑袋枕着双爪,睡眼惺忪地四处张望,好像被人偶尔踢怕了似的总是提防别人。在沙地街道的对面,是几片绿油油的草地,顶着炎炎的烈日,旁边的沙子被晒得滚烫,草地郁郁葱葱叫人心生疑问。草地看起来就像舞台上代表草坪的草垫子一样。车站里比较凉爽的一端,一个没穿外套的男子坐在斜椅上,吸着烟斗。里奥格兰德河新建的河岸环绕过小镇,穿过河堤可以看见一片梅红色的牧豆树。

除了那个喋喋不休的旅行推销员及其同伴之外,整个黄天镇都在昏昏欲睡之中。这位初来乍到的人士颇有风度地倚在柜台前,满怀自信地朗诵了许多故事,犹如一位吟游诗人刚踏上一片新土地。

"——正当老人抱着五斗柜从楼梯上摔下来的时候,老太太提着两桶煤上来了,当然——"

这时一位年轻人突然来到门口,打断了旅行推销员的故事。他大声嚷道:"斯克赖奇·威尔逊喝醉了,又大打出手了。"一听这话,两个墨西哥人连忙放下酒杯,从酒吧间的后门溜走了。

旅行推销员性格率真,善于逗趣,于是回答道:"行了,老兄。就算如此,那又怎样?不管怎样,还是进来喝一杯再说。"

然而这消息显然让在座的所有人的脑子炸裂,旅行推销员不由地意识到此事非同小可。众人立刻都板起了面孔。"说啊!"他疑惑不解地问,"这是怎回事？"他的三个同伴刚要滔滔不绝地说明原委，不想却被站在门口的年轻人阻止了。

"我的朋友，这意味着，"他一面走进酒吧间一面回答，"接下来的两个小时里，小镇将不会是安生之地。"

酒吧间老板走到门口，将门锁住并闩好。然后伸手到窗外把厚厚的窗板拉进来，也给闩上了。霎时间，酒吧里就像小教堂一样，笼罩着一种阴暗沉寂的气氛。旅行推销员看看这个，再望望那个。

"说啊！"他嚷道，"这究竟是怎么回事？你们的意思不会是要有一场枪战吧？"

"不知道能不能打起来，"有个人冷冷地答道。"不过肯定有人会开枪——会很激烈。"

来报信的年轻人挥挥手。"谁要是想动武，肯定马上就能打起来。谁上街去都会打起来，有人正等着打呢。"

旅行推销员心神不定，时而对陌生人好奇，时而又感到自己受到威胁。

"你刚才说他叫什么来着？"他问道。

"斯克赖奇·威尔逊。"大家异口同声地回答。

"他会杀人吗？你们打算怎么办？经常发生这种事吗？他如此横冲直撞，是不是几乎每周一次？他能冲破那道门吗？"

"不，他冲不破那道门，"酒吧间老板答道。"他试过三次了。不过，一旦他来了，这位外乡人，你最好趴在地上。他肯定会对着门开枪，子弹会穿进来。"

因此，旅行推销员目不转睛地盯着门。还没到他趴在地上的时候，他还是采取了一个小小的防范措施，侧身移到了墙角。"他谁都杀吗？"他又问。

众人听到这个问题，都轻蔑地低声笑了起来。

"他出来是要开枪惹事的。如果谁招惹他，我看没什么好果子吃。"

"可是遇到这样的事，你们怎么办？你们怎么办啊？"

有个人做出了回答："噢，他和杰克·波特——"

"可是，"其他人异口同声地打断了他，"杰克·波特还在圣安东尼奥呢。"

"啊，他是谁？他和此事有什么关系？"

"噢，他是本镇的警察局局长。每次闹事，他都挺身而出和斯克赖奇一决高下。"

"哇！"旅行推销员蹙了蹙眉头，说道。"这差事不错啊。"

只听说话的声音越来越低，后来几乎成了耳语。旅行推销员变得越来越焦急,越来越疑惑,便想再问些问题。但是,当他准备发问时,众人只是愤怒地看着他,示意他不要出声。大家都在安静而紧张地等待着。在屋内幽暗的阴影中,人们个个目光炯炯,倾听街上有什么动静。有人向老板打了三个手势,老板的动作像幽灵,他递给那人一个杯子和一瓶酒。那人斟满一杯威士忌,悄悄地放下酒瓶。那人把威士忌一饮而尽,又悄无声息地转向门口。旅行推销员看见老板一声不响地从柜台底下拿出一支温切斯特连发步枪。随后,他又见老板向他招手,于是他蹑手蹑脚地穿过屋子。

"你最好跟我到柜台后面来。"

"不用了,谢谢,"旅行推销员浑身冒汗地说。"我还是待在一个好往后门冲的地方吧。"

酒吧间老板听了这话,做了个友好而命令式的手势。旅行推销员不得不从。他坐在一只箱子上,将头低于柜台台面,看见那些近似装甲板的锌铜装饰时,心里多少得到些安慰。老板自己舒坦地坐在旁边的一只箱子上面。

"知道吗,"老板低声地说道,"这位斯克赖奇·威尔逊是个神枪手——枪法百发百中,堪称一绝。他一猖狂起来,我们自然就会四处躲避。以前有一群匪徒在这条河沿岸活动,他大概是他们中的最后一个匪徒。他一喝醉可真让人害怕,不过清醒的时候倒挺好的——挺直率的——连只蚂蚁也不踩的——镇上的小伙子数他不错了。可是一醉起来就——噢!"

又是一阵沉寂。"要是杰克·波特从圣安东尼奥回来就好了,"老板说道。"有一回他朝威尔逊开了一枪——打在了腿上——在这种情况下他总是挺身而出,化险为夷。"

此时,他们听到远处传来一声枪响,接着是三声狂吼。顿时,酒吧间黑暗中的人们开始乱了套,只听见嚓嚓的脚步声。他们个个面面相觑。"他来了,"众人说道。

## 三

一个身穿栗色法兰绒衬衫的汉子拐过街角,走到黄天镇主街的中央。他这件衬衫是特意为了装扮自己而买的,是由纽约市东区一些犹太妇女制作的。男子握着又长又重的深黑色左轮手枪,一手一支。他不时大喊大叫,这喊叫声好像回荡在荒废的村落之间,厉地冲破一层层屋顶。音量之巨大与普通人发声力度大相径庭。周围的沉寂好像一座圆拱坟墓将他罩住。他那挑衅的狂妄叫嚣冲破了沉寂的壁垒。他穿着一双带有镀金图案的红面靴子,这是新英格兰山坡上乘雪橇的男孩们最钟爱的一种靴子。

在酒的作用下他开始发怒，脸涨得通红。两只眼睛滴溜溜地转着，机敏地警惕着周围的埋伏，目光搜索着沉静的门道和窗口。他的行走姿势仿佛野猫蹑手蹑脚地在穿行。他突然间爆发出恐吓性的吼叫。他轻松地握着两支长长的左轮手枪，就像抓着两根稻草，闪电般地挥舞着。双手的小指头不时动弹着，像是音乐家在演奏。衬衫的领子很低，很容易看到，他情绪上来时，脖筋在一鼓一瘪，一鼓一瘪。唯一能听见的是他挑衅的嚎叫。当这个小东西打街中央经过时，平静的土砖屋依旧如故。

没人应战——没有人应战。那人仰天长啸一声，可惜没有反应。他大吼大叫，怒不可遏，端着枪到处挥舞。

"疲乏先生"酒吧间老板的那条狗对事态的发展毫无察觉，还躺在主人门前打盹儿。那人一瞅见这狗，便停下脚步，滑稽地举起了枪。狗一看见那人，蹦起来斜着身子溜走了，耷拉个脑袋狂吠不止。那人一声怒吼，狗听见撒腿就跑。它刚想往巷子里钻，只听一声喧嚣，一声口哨，什么东西砰的一声正好砸在狗的前方。狗嗷叫了一声，恐惧地回转身，飞快地往另外一个方向逃奔。又是一声喧嚣，一声口哨，狗前面的沙子被射得四下飞溅。狗被吓得魂飞魄散地转过身去，就像栏里的牲畜一样，惊恐万状。那人站在那里哈哈大笑，两支枪贴在臀部。

最后，这家伙被"疲乏先生"酒吧间紧闭着的门吸引住了。他来到门口，用枪砸着门，嚷着要进去喝酒。

门却纹丝不动，于是他从人行道上捡起一张纸片，用刀钉到门框上。随即他蔑视地背对着这个好去处，转身走到街对面，脚跟轻快敏捷地旋转了一圈，回身向纸片开枪射击。没料到差了半英寸，没有击中。他骂了自己一声，然后走开了。后来，他又惬意地朝他最亲密的朋友的窗口猛烈射击。这家伙跟黄天镇玩起了游戏，黄天镇俨然成了他的玩具。

然而，还是无人应战。他脑海里闪现出他的老对手杰克·波特的名字，于是决定最好是去波特家，用怒斥的方法诱他出来交手。他朝要去的目的地走去，嘴里还哼着阿帕切奏捷曲。

他来到波特屋前，发现这里和其他土屋一样平静。这家伙选了一个战略位置，叫嚣着要一决高下。然而，房子犹如石头神像一般地注视着他，里面没有任何回应。那人悠闲地等了一会儿，接着号叫着要决斗，叫声中混杂着奇妙的字眼。

随后，看见房子没有任何动静，那人越发起劲地勃然大怒起来。他对着房子大发雷霆，犹如凛冽的寒风袭击着北方平原上的小屋。这动静就像远处有二百名墨西哥人在搏斗。到了必要之时，他就停下来缓口气，或是装子弹。

## 四

波特和新娘怯生生地快步走着。有时,他们会同时发出低沉而羞怯的笑声。

"下一个拐角,亲爱的,"波特终于说道。

他们双双弯腰向前走,像是顶着烈风前行似的。波特刚想抬手去指他那初现的新居,不料才拐过街角,便面对面地撞上一名身穿栗红色衬衫的男子。他正急忙地往一支左轮手枪里上子弹。突然间,枪掉在了地上,那人闪电般地从枪套里又拔出了一支。第二支枪直直地瞄准了新郎的胸口。

一阵沉默。波特的嘴巴此时就像是舌头的坟墓。出于本能,他立即挣脱了妻子紧握着的手臂,手提包落到了沙地上。再看新娘,她的脸色变得蜡黄。她成了烦琐的祭拜仪式前的奴仆,盯着眼前鬼怪般的毒蛇。

两位男子隔着三步远,面面相觑。拿枪的汉子再次露出一副凶相,静静地狞笑着。"你想偷袭我,"他说。"你想偷袭我!"他的眼光变得更加凶狠。波特稍微动了一下,那人就恶狠狠地把枪往前一戳。"别动,你不许动,杰克·波特。别向枪挪动一个指头。连根睫毛也别想动。该到和你算账的时候了,我要按照自己的方式做,自行其是,谁也别想干涉。所以,你要是不想让枪对着你,最好乖乖地听我的话。"

波特看着自己的对手。"我没带枪,斯克赖奇,"他说。"实话告诉你,我没带枪。"他直起身子想镇定一些,但是在他心灵深处掠过了豪华列车的幻影:带有海蓝色图案的天鹅绒,闪闪发亮的铜器、银器和玻璃制品,还有如同油池表面一样发出暗色光芒的木制品——一切都是新婚之喜的荣耀,一切都是新生活的开始。"斯克赖奇·威尔逊,你是知道的,我该出手时就出手,不过我没带枪。你自己开枪就得了。"

对手脸色发青。他往前迈了一步,拿枪在波特的胸前晃来晃去。"别跟我说你没带枪,你个兔崽子。少跟我说这种骗人的鬼话。在得克萨斯,谁见你没带过枪。别把我当孩子耍。"他两眼发亮,喉咙咕咚作响,像个水泵。

"我可没把你当小孩,"波特答道。他的脚跟没有后退一步。"我是把你当成蠢货。我告诉你我没带枪,没带就是没带。你要是想开枪毙了我,最好马上动手。机不可失,时不再来啊。"

这番突如其来的理论让那人火气渐消,镇定了下来。"要是没带枪的话,干嘛不带一支呢?"他讥讽道。"去主日学校啦?"

"没带枪是因为我刚跟妻子从圣安东尼奥回来。我结婚了,"波特说道。"我要是知道带妻子回家时会遇到你这样的蠢货四处游荡,我肯定会带枪的,你可别忘了。"

"结婚了！"斯克赖奇大惑不解地说。

"没错，结婚了。我结婚了。"波特明明白白地说。

"结婚了？"斯克赖奇说。他仿佛这才注意到对手旁边那个颓丧惶恐的女人。"不可能！"他说。他就好像某个家伙被允许瞧了一眼另一个世界。他后退了一步，举枪的手放了下来。"这就是新娘吗？"他问道。

"是的，这就是新娘。"波特答道。

又是一阵沉默。

"好了，"威尔逊最后慢悠悠地说，"我看一切就此了结了。"

"你这么说的话，那咱们就算了，斯克赖奇。要知道，我可没招惹你。"波特拿起了手提包。

"行了，我承认作罢了，杰克，"威尔逊说。他望着地面。"结婚了！"他并不是一个侠义之徒，只不过在此陌生情景之下，他仍不失早期大草原之子的秉性。他拾起右侧的手枪，把两支枪都装进枪套，走开了。他的双脚在厚厚的沙地里留下了漏斗形的足迹。

# Theodore Dreiser
# (1871—1945)

Theodore Dreiser was one of America's greatest representatives of Naturalism. Born to a German immigrant in Terra Haute, Indiana, Dreiser experienced in his formative years what poverty would face him with. Under the monetary help of a former teacher, Dreiser studied at the University of Indiana in 1889, but left for Chicago one year later. After attempts on various jobs, he began his literary career in 1892, as a reporter for the *Chicago Globe* and the following eighteen years saw his gradual success in journalistic career in St. Louis, Pittsburgh and New York. In 1927 he traveled to the Soviet Union, which contributed to his left views about socialism and capitalism. He died of heart attack in Hollywood, California, with two novels unfinished.

His first novel, *Sister Carrie* (1900), depicts the life of a country girl, transgressing the moral code, in her pursuit of American dream in Chicago, but finally prospering. Its theme — life is purposeless — is the same with that of his next novel, *Jennie Gerhardt* (1911). His "The Trilogy of Desire," including *The Financier* (1912), *The Titan* (1914) and *The Stoic* (1947), tells of a powerful businessman in modern society. Dreiser's social consciousness is perfectly manifested through an "anti-hero," in his masterpiece, *The American Tragedy* (1925).

## The Lost Phoebe

*The following story from* **Free and Other Stories** *(1918) is among Dreiser's most widely anthologized short stories. It relates the story of an old Hoosier farmer, who loses his sanity after his beloved wife's death, searches for her at doors of the neighborhood, running after her specter in his hallucination, and finally falls to his death at the foot of a cliff. Though, in this shorter narrative, his writing style may seem circuitous, Dreiser paints a pathetic picture of the old couple's decline and reveals the isolation and confinement of life.*

They lived together in a part of the country which was not so prosperous as it had once been, about three miles from one of those small towns that, instead of increasing in population, is steadily decreasing. The territory was not very thickly settled; perhaps a house every other mile or so, with large areas of corn- and wheat-land and fallow fields that at odd seasons had been sown to timothy and clover. Their particular house was part log and part frame, the log portion being the old original home of Henry's grandfather. The new portion, of now rain-beaten, time-worn slabs, through which the wind squeaked in the chinks at times, and which several overshadowing elms and a butternut-tree made picturesque and reminiscently pathetic, but a little damp, was erected by Henry when he was twenty-one and just married.

That was forty-eighty years before. The furniture inside, like the house outside, was old and mildewy and reminiscent of an earlier day. You have seen the what-not of cherry wood, perhaps, with spiral legs and fluted top. It was there. The old-fashioned four poster bed, with its ball-like protuberances and deep curving incisions, was there also, a sadly alienated descendant of an early Jacobean ancestor. The bureau of cherry was also high and wide and solidly built, but faded-looking, and with a musty odor. The rag carpet that underlay all these sturdy examples of enduring furniture was a weak, faded, lead-and-pink-colored affair woven by Phoebe Ann's own hands, when she was fifteen years younger than she was when she died. The creaky wooden loom on which it had been done now stood like a dusty, bony skeleton, along with a broken rocking-chair, a worm-eaten clothes-press—Heaven know how old—a lime-stained bench that had once been used to keep flowers on outside the door, and other decrepit factors of household utility, in an east room that was a lean-to against this so-called main portion. All sorts of other broken-down furniture were about this place; an antiquated clothes-horse, cracked in two of its ribs; a broken mirror in an old cherry frame, which had fallen from a nail and cracked itself three days before their youngest son, Jerry, died; an extension hat-rack, which once had had porcelain knobs on the ends of its pegs; and a sewing-machine, long since outdone in its clumsy mechanism by rivals of a newer generation.

The orchard to the east of the house was full of gnarled old apple-trees, worm-eaten as to trunks and branches, and fully ornamented with green and white lichens, so that it had a sad, greenish-white, silvery effect in moonlight. The low outhouses, which had once housed chickens, a horse or two, a cow, and several pigs, were covered with patches of moss as to their roof, and the sides had been free of paint for so long that they were blackish gray as to color, and a little spongy. The picket-fence in front, with its gate squeaky and askew, and the side fences of the stake-and-rider type were in an equally run-down condition. As a matter of fact, they had aged synchronously with the persons who lived here, old Henry Reifsneider and his wife Pheobe Ann.

They had lived here, these two, ever since their marriage, forty-eight years before, and Henry had lived here before that from his childhood up. His father and mother, well along in years when he was a boy, had invited him to bring his wife here when he had first fallen in love and decided to marry, and he had done so. His father and mother were the companions of himself and his wife for ten years after they were married, when both died; and then Henry and Phoebe were left with their five children growing lustily apace. But all sorts of things had happened since then. Of the seven children, all told, that had been born to them, three had died; one girl had gone to Kansas; one boy had gone to Sioux Falls, never even to be heard of after; another boy had gone to Washington; and the last girl lived five counties away in the same State, but was so burdened with cares of her own that she rarely gave them a thought. Time and a commonplace home life that had never been attractive had weaned them thoroughly, so that, wherever they were, they gave little thought as to how it might be with their father and mother.

Old Henry Reifsneider and his wife Phoebe were a loving couple. You perhaps know how it is with simple natures that fasten themselves like lichens on the stones of circumstance and weather their days to a crumbling conclusion. The great world sounds widely, but it has no call for them. They have no soaring intellect. The orchard, the meadow, the corn-field, the pig-pen, and the chicken-lot measure the range of their human activities. When the wheat is headed it is reaped and threshed; when the corn is browned and frosted it is cut and shocked; when the timothy is in full head it is cut, and the hay-cock erected. After that comes winter, with the hauling of grain to market, the sawing and splitting of wood, the simple chores of fire-building, meal-getting, occasional repairing, and visiting. Beyond these and the changes of weather—the snows, the rains, and the fair days—there are no immediate, significant things. All the rest of life is a far-off, clamorous phantasmagoria, flickering like Northern lights in the night, and sounding as faintly as cow-bells tinkling in the distance.

Old Henry and his wife Phoebe were as fond of each other as it is possible for two old people to be who have nothing else in this life to be fond of. He was a thin old man, seventy when she died, a queer, crotchety person with coarse gray-black hair and beard, quite straggly and unkempt. He looked at you out of dull, fishy, watery eyes that had deep-brown crow's-feet at the sides. His clothes, like the clothes of many farmers, were aged and angular and baggy, standing out at the pockets, not fitting about the neck, protuberant and worn at elbow and knee. Phoebe Ann was thin and shapeless, a very umbrella of a woman, clad in shabby black, and with a black bonnet for her best wear. As time had passed, and they had only themselves to look after, their movements had become slower and slower, their activities fewer and fewer. The annual keep of pigs had been reduced from five to one grunting porker, and the single horse which Henry now retained was a sleepy animal, not over-nourished and not very clean. The chickens, of which formerly there was a large flock, had almost disappeared, owing to ferrets, foxes, and the lack of proper care, which produces disease. The former healthy garden was now a straggling memory of itself, and the vines and flower-beds that formerly ornamented the windows and dooryard had now become choking thickets. A will had been made which divided the small tax-eaten property equally among the remaining four, so that it was really of no interest to any of them. Yet these two lived together in peace and sympathy, only that now and then old Henry would become unduly cranky, complaining almost invariably that something had been neglected or mislaid which was of no importance at all.

"Phoebe, where's my corn-knife? You ain't never minded to let my things alone no more."

"No you hush, Henry," his wife would caution him in a cracked and squeaky voice. "If you don't, I'll leave yuh. I'll git up and walk out of here some day, and then where would y' be? Y' ain't got anybody but me to look after yuh, so yuh just behave yourself. Your corn-knife's on the mantel where it's allus been unless you've gone an' put it somewhere else."

Old Henry, who knew his wife would never leave him in any circumstances, used to speculate at times as to what he would do if she were to die. That was the one leaving that he really feared. As he climbed on the chair at night to wind the old, long-pendulumed, double-weighted clock, or went finally to the front and the back door to see that they were safely shut in, it was a comfort to know that Phoebe was there, properly ensconced on her side of the bed, and that if he stirred restlessly in the night, she would be there to ask what he wanted.

"Now, Henry, do lie still! You're as restless as a chicken."

"Well, I can't sleep, Phoebe."

"Well, yuh needn't roll so, anyhow. Yuh kin let me sleep."

This is usually reduced him to a state of somnolent ease. If she wanted a pail of water, it was a grumbling pleasure for him to get it; and if she did rise first to build the fires, he saw that the wood was cut and placed within easy reach. They divided this simple world nicely between them.

As the years had gone on, however, fewer and fewer people had called. They were well-known for a distance of as much as ten square miles as old Mr. and Mrs. Reifsneider, honest, moderately Christian, but too old to be really interesting any longer. The writing of letters had become an almost impossible burden too difficult to continue or even negotiate via others, although an occasional letter still did arrive from the daughter in Pemberton County. Now and then some old friend stopped with a pie or cake or a roasted chicken or duck, or merely to see that they were well; but even these kindly minded visits were no longer frequent.

One day in the early spring of her sixty-fourth year Mrs. Reifsneider took sick, and from a low fever passed into some indefinable ailment which, because of her age, was no longer curable. Old Henry drove to Swinnerton, the neighboring town, and procured a doctor. Some friends called, and the immediate care of her was taken off his hands. Then one chill spring night she died, and old Henry, in a fog of sorrow and uncertainty, followed her body to the nearest graveyard, an unattractive space with a few pines growing in it. Although he might have gone to the daughter in Pemberton or sent for her, it was really too much trouble and he was too weary and fixed. It was suggested to him at once by one friend and another that he come to stay with them awhile, but he did not see fit. He was so old and so fixed in his notions and so accustomed to the exact surroundings he had known all his days, that he could not think of leaving. He wanted to remain near where they had put his Phoebe; and the fact that he would have to live alone did not trouble him in the least. The living children were notified and the care of him offered if he would leave, but he would not.

"I kin make a shift for myself," he continually announced to old Dr. Morrow, who had attended his wife in this case. "I kin cook a little, and, besides, it don't take much more'n coffee an' bread in the mornin's to satisfy me. I'll get along now well enough. Yuh just let me be." And after many pleadings and proffers of advice, with supplies of coffee and bacon and baked bread duly offered and accepted, he was left to himself. For a while he sat idly outside his door brooding in the spring sun. He tried to revive his interest in farming, and to keep himself busy and free from thought by looking after the fields, which of late had been much neglected. It was a gloomy thing to come in of an evening, however, or in the afternoon and find no shadow of Phoebe where everything suggested her. By degrees he put a few of her things away. At night he sat beside his lamp and read in the papers that were left him occasionally or in a *Bible* that he had neglected for years, but he could get little solace from these things. Mostly he held his hand over his mouth and looked at the floor as he sat and thought of what had become of her, and how soon he himself would die. He made a great business of making his coffee in the morning and frying himself a little bacon at night; but his appetite was gone. The shell in which he had been housed so long seemed vacant, and its shadows were suggestive of immediate griefs. So he lived quite dolefully for five long months, and then a change began.

It was one night, after he had looked after the front and the back door, wound the clock, blown out the light, and gone through all the selfsame motions that he had indulged in for years, that he went to bed not so much to sleep as to think. It was a moonlight night. The green-lichen-covered orchard just outside and to be seen from his bed where he now lay was a silvery affair, sweetly spectral. The moon shone through the east windows, throwing the pattern of the panes on the wooden floor, and making the old furniture, to which he was accustomed, stand out dimly in the room. As usual he had been thinking of Phoebe and the years when they had been young together, and of the children who had gone, and the poor shift he was making of his present days. The house was coming to be in a very bad state indeed. The bed-clothes were in disorder and not clean, for he made a wretched shift of washing. It was a terror to him. The roof leaked, causing things, some of them, to remain damp for weeks at a time, but he was getting into that brooding state where he would accept anything rather than exert himself. He preferred to pace slowly to and fro or to sit and think.

By twelve o'clock of this particular night he was asleep, however, and by two had waked again. The moon by this time had shifted to a position on the western side of the house, and it now shone in through the windows of the living-room and those of the kitchen beyond. A certain combination of furniture—a chair near a table, with his coat on it, the half-open kitchen door casting a shadow, and the position of a lamp near a paper—gave him an exact representation of Phoebe leaning over the table as he had often seen her do in life. It gave him a great start. Could it be she—or her ghost? He had scarcely ever believed in spirits; and still— He looked at her fixedly in the feeble half-light, his old hair tingling oddly at the roots, and then sat up. The figure did not move. He put his thin legs out of the bed and sat looking at her, wondering if this could really be Phoebe. They had talked of ghosts often in their lifetime, of apparitions and omens; but they had never agreed that such things could be. It had never been a part of his wife's creed that she could have a spirit that could return to walk the earth. Her after-world was quite a different affair, a vague heaven, no less, from which the righteous did not trouble to return. Yet here she was now, bending over the table in her black skirt and gray shawl, her pale profile outlined against the moonlight.

"Phoebe," he called, thrilling from head to toe and putting out one bony hand, "have yuh come back?"

The figure did not stir, and he arose and walked uncertainly to the door, looking at it fixedly the while. As he drew near, however, the apparition resolved itself into its primal content—his old coat over the high-backed chair, the lamp by the paper, the half-open door.

"Well," he said to himself, his mouth open, "I thought shore I saw her." And he ran his hand strangely and vaguely through his hair, the while his nervous tension relaxed. Vanished as it had, it gave him the idea that she might return.

Another night, because of this first illusion, and because his mind was now constantly on her and he was old, he looked out of the window that was nearest his bed and commanded a hen-coop and pig-pen and a part of the wagon-shed, and there, a faint mist exuding from the damp of the ground, he thought he saw her again. It was one of those little wisps of mist, one of those faint exhalations of the earth that rise in a cool night after a warm day, and flicker like small white cypresses of fog before they disappear. In life it had been a custom of hers to cross this lot from her kitchen door to the pig-pen to throw in any scrap that was left from her cooking, and here she was again. He sat up and watched it strangely, doubtfully, because of his previous experience, but inclined, because of the nervous titillation that passed over his body, to believe that spirits really were, and that Phoebe, who would be concerned because of his lonely state, must be thinking about him, and hence returning. What other way would she have? How otherwise could she express herself? It would be within the province of her charity so to do, and like her loving interest in him. He quivered and watched it eagerly; but, a faint breath of air stirring, it wound away toward the fence and disappeared.

A third night, as he was actually dreaming, some ten days later, she came to his bedside and put her hand on his head.

"Poor Henry!" she said. "It's too bad."

He roused out of his sleep, actually to see her, he thought, moving from his bedroom into the one living-room, her figure a shadowy mass of black. The weak straining of his eyes caused little points of light to flicker about the outlines of her form. He arose, greatly astonished, walked the floor in the cool room, convinced that Phoebe was coming back to him. If he only thought sufficiently, if he made it perfectly clear by his feeling that he needed her greatly, she would come back, this kindly wife, and tell him what to do. She would perhaps be with him much of the time, in the night, anyhow; and that would make him less lonely, this state more endurable.

In age and with the feeble it is not such a far cry from the subtleties of illusion to actual hallucination, and in due time this transition was made for Henry. Night after night he waited, expecting her return. Once in his weird mood he thought he saw a pale light moving about the room, and another time he thought he saw her walking in the orchard after dark. It was one morning when the details of his lonely state were virtually unendurable that he woke with the thought that she was not dead. How he had arrived at this conclusion it is hard to say. His mind had gone. In its place was a fixed illusion. He and Phoebe had had a senseless quarrel. He had reproached her for not leaving his pipe where he was accustomed to find it, and she had left. It was an aberrated fulfillment of her old jesting threat that if he did not behave himself she would leave him.

"I guess I could find yuh ag'in," he had always said. But her cackling threat had always been:

"Yuh'll not find me if I ever leave yuh. I guess I kin get some place where yuh can't find me."

This morning when he arose he did not think to build the fire in the customary way or to grind his coffee and cut his bread, as was his wont, but solely to meditate as to where he should search for her and how he should induce her to come back. Recently the one horse had been dispensed with because he found it cumbersome and beyond his needs. He took down his soft crush hat after he had dressed himself, a new glint of interest and determination in his eye, and taking his black crook cane from behind the door, where he had always placed it, started out briskly to look for her among the nearest neighbors. His old shoes clumped soundly in the dust as he walked, and his gray-black locks, now grown rather long, straggled out in a dramatic fringe or halo from under his hat. His short coat stirred busily as he walked, and his hands and face were peaked and pale.

"Why, hello, Henry! Where're yuh goin' this mornin'?" inquired Farmer Dodge, who, hauling a load of wheat to market, encountered him on the public road. He had not seen the aged farmer in months, not since his wife's death, and he wondered now, seeing him looking so spry.

"Yuh ain't seen Phoebe, have yuh?" inquired the old man, looking up quizzically.

"Phoebe who?" inquired Farmer Dodge, not for the moment connecting the name with Henry's dead wife.

"Why, my wife Phoebe, o' course. Who do yuh s'pose I mean?" He stared up with a pathetic sharpness of glance from under his shaggy, gray eyebrows.

"Well, I'll swan, Henry, yuh ain't jokin', are yuh?" said the solid Dodge, a pursy man, with a smooth, hard, red face. "It can't be your wife yuh're talkin' about. She's dead."

"Dead! Shucks!" retorted the demented Reifsneider. "She left me early this mornin', while I was sleepin'. She allus got up to build the fire, but she's gone now. We had a little spat last night, an' I guess that's the reason. But I guess I kin find her. She's gone over to Matilda Race's; that's where she's gone."

He started briskly up the road, leaving the amazed Dodge to stare in wonder after him.

"Well, I'll be switched!" he said aloud to himself. "He's clean out'n his head. That poor old feller's been livin' down there till he's gone outen his mind. I'll have to notify the authorities." And he flicked his whip with great enthusiasm. "Geddap!" he said, and was off.

Reifsneider met no one else in this poorly populated region until he reached the whitewashed fence of Matilda Race and her husband three miles away. He had passed several other houses en route, but these not being within the range of his illusion were not considered. His wife, who had known Matilda well, must be here. He opened the picket-gate which guarded the walk, and stamped briskly up to the door.

"Why, Mr. Reifsneider," exclaimed old Matilda herself, a stout woman, looking out of the door in answer to his knock, "what brings yuh here this mornin'?"

"Is Phoebe here?" he demanded eagerly.

"Phoebe who? What Phoebe?" replied Mrs. Race, curious as to this sudden development of energy on his part.

"Why, my Phoebe, o' course. My wife Phoebe. Who do yuh s'pose? Ain't she here now?"

"Lawsy me!" exclaimed Mrs. Race, opening her mouth. "Yuh poor man! So you're clean out'n your mind now. Yuh come right in and sit down. I'll git yuh a cup o' coffee. O' course your wife ain't here; but yuh come in an' sit down. I'll find her for yuh after a while. I know where she is."

The old farmer's eyes softened, and he entered. He was so thin and pale a specimen, pantalooned and patriarchal, that he aroused Mrs. Race's extremest sympathy as he took off his hat and laid it on his knees, quite softly and mildly.

"We had a quarrel last night, an' she left me," he volunteered.

"Laws! Laws!" sighed Mrs. Race, there being no one present with whom to share her astonishment as she went to her kitchen. "The poor man! Now somebody's just got to look after him. He can't be allowed to run around the country this way lookin' for his dead wife. It's terrible."

She boiled him a pot of coffee and brought in some of her new-baked bread and fresh butter. She set out some of her best jam and put a couple of eggs to boil, lying whole-heartedly the while.

"Now yuh stay right there, Uncle Henry, till Jake comes in, an' I'll send him to look for Phoebe. I think it's more'n likely she's over to Swinnerton with some o' her friends. Anyhow, we'll find her. Now yuh just drink this coffee an' eat this bread. Yuh must be tired. Yuh've had a long walk this mornin'." Her idea was to take counsel with Jake, " her man," and perhaps have him notify the authorities.

She bustled about, meditating on the uncertainties of life, while old Reifsneider thrummed on the rim of his hat with his pale fingers and later ate abstractedly of what she offered. His mind was on his wife, however, and since she was not here, or did not appear, it wandered vaguely away to a family by the name of Murray, miles away in another direction. He decided after a time that he would not wait for Jack Race to hunt his wife but would seek her for himself. He must be on, and urge her to come back.

"Well, I'll be goin'," he said, getting up and looking strangely about him. "I guess she didn't come here after all. She went over to the Murrays', I guess. I'll not wait any longer, Mis' Race. There's a lot to do over to the house today." And out he marched in the face of her protests taking to the dusty road again in the warm spring sun, his cane striking the earth as he went.

It was two hours later that this pale figure of a man appeared in the Murrays' doorway, dusty, perspiring, eager. He had tramped all of five miles, and it was noon. An amazed husband and wife of sixty heard his strange query, and realized also that he was mad. They begged him to stay to dinner, intending to notify the authorities later and see what could be done; but though he stayed to partake of a little something, he did not stay long, and was off again to another distant farmhouse, his idea of many things to do and his need of Phoebe impelling him. So it went for that day and the next and the next, the circle of his inquiry ever widening.

The process by which a character assumes the significance of being peculiar, his antics weird, yet harmless, in such a community is often involute and pathetic. This day, as has been said, saw Reifsneider at other doors, eagerly asking his unnatural question, and leaving a trail of amazement, sympathy, and pity in his wake. Although the authorities were informed—the county sheriff, no less—it was not deemed advisable to take him into custody; for when those who knew old Henry, and had for so long, reflected on the condition of the county insane asylum, a place which, because of the poverty of the district, was of staggering aberration and sickening environment, it was decided to let him remain at large; for, strange to relate, it was found on investigation that at night he returned peaceably enough to his lonesome domicile there to discover whether his wife had returned, and to brood in loneliness until the morning. Who would lock up a thin, eager, seeking old man with iron-gray hair and an attitude of kindly, innocent inquiry, particularly when he was well known for a past of only kindly servitude and reliability? Those who had known him best rather agreed that he should be allowed to roam at large. He could do no harm. There were many who were willing to help him as to food, old clothes, the odds and ends of his daily life—at least at first. His figure after a time became not so much a common-place as an accepted curiosity, and the replies, "Why, no, Henry; I ain't see her," or "No, Henry; she ain't seen here to-day," more customary.

For several years thereafter then he was an odd figure in the sun and rain, on dusty roads and muddy ones, encountered occasionally in strange and unexpected places, pursuing his endless search. Undernourishment, after a time, although the neighbors and those who knew his history gladly contributed from their store, affected his body; for he walked much and ate little. The longer he roamed the public highway in this manner, the deeper became his strange hallucination; and finding it harder and harder to return from his more and more distant pilgrimages, he finally began taking a few utensils with him from his home, making a small package of them, in order that he might not be compelled to return. In an old tin coffee-pot of large size he placed a small tin cup, a knife, fork, and spoon, some salt and pepper, and to the outside of it, by a string forced through a pierced hole, he fastened a plate, which could be released, and which was his woodland table. It was no trouble for him to secure the little food that he needed, and with a strange, almost religious dignity, he had no hesitation in asking for that much. By degrees his hair became longer and longer, his once black hat became an earthen brown, and his clothes threadbare and dusty.

For all of three years he walked, and none knew how wide were his perambulations, nor how he survived the storms and cold. They could not see him, with homely rural understanding and forethought, sheltering himself in hay-cocks, or by the sides of cattle, whose warm bodies protected him from the cold, and whose dull understandings were not opposed to his harmless presence. Overhanging rocks and trees kept him at times from the rain, and a friendly hay-loft or corn-crib was not above his humble consideration.

The involute progression of hallucination is strange. From asking at doors and being constantly rebuffed or denied, he finally came to the conclusion that although his Phoebe might not be in any of the houses at the doors of which he inquired, she might nevertheless be within the sound of his voice. And so, from patient inquiry, he began to call sad, occasional cries, that ever and anon walked the quiet landscapes and ragged hill regions, and set to echoing his thin "O-o-o Phoebe! O-o-o Phoebe!" It had a pathetic, albeit insane, ring, and many a farmer or plowboy came to know it even from afar and say, "There goes old Reifsneider."

Another thing that puzzled him greatly after a time and after many hundreds of inquiries was, when he no longer had any particular door-yard in view and so special inquiry to make, which way to go. These cross-roads, which occasionally led in four or even six directions, came after a time to puzzle him. But to solve this knotty problem, which became more and more of a puzzle, there came to his aid another hallucination. Phoebe's spirit or some power of the air or wind or nature would tell him. If he stood at the center of the parting of the ways, closed his eyes, turned thrice about, and called "O-o-o Phoebe!" twice, and then threw his cane straight before him, that would surely indicate which way to go for Phoebe, or one of these mystic powers would surely govern its direction and fall! In whichever direction it went, even though, as was not infrequently the case, it took him back along the path he had already come, or across fields, he was not so far gone in his mind but that he gave himself ample time to search before he called again. Also the hallucination seemed to persist that at some time he would surely find her. There were hours when his feet were sore, and his limbs weary, when he would stop in the heat to wipe his seamed brow, or in the cold to beat his arms. Sometimes, after throwing away his cane, and finding it indicating the direction from which he had just come, he would shake his head wearily and philosophically, as if contemplating the unbelievable or an untoward fate, and then start briskly off. His strange figure came finally to be known in the farthest reaches of three or four counties. Old Reifsneider was a pathetic character. His fame was wide.

Near a little town called Watersville, in Green County, perhaps four miles from that minor center of human activity, there was a place or precipice locally known as the Red Cliff, a sheer wall of red sandstone, perhaps a hundred feet high, which raised its sharp face for half a mile or more above the fruitful corn-fields and orchards that lay beneath, and which was surmounted by a thick grove of trees. The slope that slowly led up to it from the opposite side was covered by a rank growth of beech, hickory, and ash, through which threaded a number of wagon-tracks crossing at various angles. In fair weather it had become old Reifsneider's habit, so inured was he by now to the open, to make his bed in some such patch of trees as this to fry his bacon or boil his eggs at the foot of some tree before laying himself down for the night. Occasionally, so light and inconsequential was his sleep, he would walk at night. More often, the moonlight or some sudden wind stirring in the trees or a reconnoitering animal arousing him, he would sit up and think, or pursue his quest in the moonlight or the dark, a strange, unnatural, half wild, half savage-looking but utterly harmless creature, calling at lonely road crossings, staring at dark and shuttered houses, and wondering where, where Phoebe could really be.

That particular lull that comes in the systole-diastole of this earthly ball at two o'clock in the morning invariably aroused him, and though he might not go any farther he would sit up and contemplate the darkness or the stars, wondering. Sometimes in the strange processes of his mind he would fancy that he saw moving among the trees the figure of his lost wife, and then he would get up to follow, taking his utensils, always on a string, and his cane. If she seemed to evade him too easily he would run, or plead, or, suddenly losing track of the fancied figure, stand awed or disappointed, grieving for the moment over the almost insurmountable difficulties of his search.

It was in the seventh year of these hopeless peregrinations, in the dawn of a similar springtime to that in which his wife had died, that he came at last one night to the vicinity of this self-same patch that crowned the rise to the Red Cliff. His far-flung cane, used as a divining-rod at the last cross-roads, had brought him hither. He had walked many, many miles. It was after ten o'clock at night, and he was very weary.

Long wandering and little eating had left him but a shadow of his former self. It was a question now not so much of physical strength but of spiritual endurance which kept him up. He had scarcely eaten this day, and now exhausted he set himself down in the dark to rest and possibly to sleep.

Curiously on this occasion a strange suggestion of the presence of his wife surrounded him. It would not be long now, he counseled with himself, although the long months had brought him nothing, until he should see her, talk to her. He fell asleep after a time, his head on his knees. At midnight the moon began to rise, and at two in the morning, his wakeful hour, was a large silver disk shining through the trees to the east. He opened his eyes when the radiance became strong, making a silver pattern at his feet and lighting the woods with strange lusters and silvery, shadowy forms. As usual, his old notion that his wife must be near occurred to him on this occasion, and he looked about him with a speculative, anticipatory eye. What was it that moved in the distant shadows along the path by which he had entered—a pale, flickering will-o'-the-wisp that bobbed gracefully among the trees and riveted his expectant gaze? Moonlight and shadows combined to give it a strange form and a stranger reality, this fluttering of bog-fire or dancing of wandering fire-flies. Was it truly his lost Phoebe? By a circuitous route it passed about him, and in his fevered state he fancied that he could see the very eyes of her, not as she was when he last saw her in the black dress and shawl but now a strangely younger Phoebe, gayer, sweeter, the one whom he had known years before as a girl. Old Reifsneider got up. He had been expecting and dreaming of this hour all these years, and now as he saw the feeble light dancing lightly before him he peered at it questioningly, one thin hand in his gray hair.

Of a sudden there came to him now for the first time in many years the full charm of her girlish figure as he had known it in boyhood, the pleasing, sympathetic smile, the brown hair, the blue sash she had once worn about her waist at a picnic, her gay, graceful movements. He walked around the base of the tree, straining with his eyes, forgetting for once his cane and utensils, and following eagerly after. On she moved before him, a will-o'-the-wisp of the spring, a little flame above her head, and it seemed as though among the small saplings of ash and beech and the thick trunks of hickory and elm that she signaled with a young, a lightsome hand.

"O Phoebe! Phoebe!" he called. "Have yuh really come? Have yuh really answered me?" And hurrying faster, he fell once, scrambling lamely to his feet, only to see the light in the distance dancing illusively on. On and on he hurried until he was fairly running, brushing his ragged arms against the trees, striking his hands and face against impeding twigs. His hat was gone, his lungs were breathless, his reason quite astray, when coming to the edge of the cliff he saw her below among a silvery bed of apple-trees now blooming in the spring.

"O Phoebe!" he called. "O Phoebe! Oh, no, don't leave me!" And feeling the lure of a world where love was young and Phoebe as this vision presented her, a delightful epitome of their quondam youth, he gave a gay cry of "Oh, wait, Phoebe!" and leaped.

Some farmer-boys, reconnoitering this region of bounty and prospect some few days afterward, found first the tin utensils tied together under the tree where he had left them, and then later at the foot of the cliff, pale, broken, but elate, a molded smile of peace and delight upon his lips, his body. His old hat was discovered lying under some low-growing saplings the twigs of which held it back. No one of all the simple population knew how eagerly and joyously he had found his lost mate.

**Questions**

1. When does the couple's decline really begin?
2. How are the opening paragraphs painted as a bleak picture?
3. How many times does "lichen" appear in the story? Do you think it is given a symbolic meaning? If yes, what does it symbolize? Are there any other symbols in the story?
4. Do you conceive of this story as a typical piece of naturalistic writing? Give your reasons.

# 西奥多·德莱塞
（1871—1945）

　　西奥多·德莱塞是美国自然主义杰出代表作家之一。他出生于印第安纳州的特雷霍特镇，父亲是来自德国的移民。德莱塞在其性格形成期，经历了贫穷带来的种种困苦。在一位昔日教师的资助下，他1889年就读印第安纳大学，但一年后便去了芝加哥。他尝试过多种工作，并于1892年成为《芝加哥环球报》的记者，由此开始了自己的写作生涯。在随后的18年间，德莱塞在圣路易斯、匹兹堡和纽约逐步发展他的新闻事业，并在这一领域获得了成功。他对于社会主义和资本主义的左翼观点得益于1927年的苏联之行。因突发心脏病，德莱塞于加利福尼亚州的好莱坞逝世，留给世人两部尚未完成的遗作。

　　德莱塞的第一部小说《嘉莉妹妹》（1900）描绘了一个乡村女孩的人生，她在芝加哥追寻自己的美国梦，虽然违背了道德的准则，最终却飞黄腾达。这部作品的主题——生活是漫无目的而又毫无意义的——与其下一部小说《珍妮姑娘》（1911）的主题异曲同工。他的《金融家》（1912）、《巨人》（1914）和《斯多葛》（1947）被称为"欲望三部曲"，所讲述的故事都围绕着一个现代社会有权有势的商人而展开。在他的杰作《美国的悲剧》（1925）中，德莱塞通过"反英雄"式的主人公完美地表达了自己的社会意识。

## 失去的菲比

　　下面的故事选自短篇小说集《自由故事集》（1918），是德莱塞短篇小说中广为收录的一篇。故事讲述了一个印第安纳州的老农在妻子死后精神失常，挨家挨户地寻找妻子，并在幻觉中追逐妻子的亡灵，最终跌下山崖死去。虽然德莱塞的文风在这篇短小的故事中似乎有些迂回曲折，但他为读者描绘出一对夫妇衰朽残年的哀婉画卷，并由此揭示出生活中的疏离与禁锢。

　　他们住在乡间，那时的乡村已不复往日的繁华，距离他们住所大概三英里外的那个小镇，如今人口不但没有增加，反而越来越少。他们这一带人烟稀少，大概每隔一英里左右才会见到一幢房子，房子的周围是种植玉米和小麦的大片土地以及在个别时节用来播种猫尾草和三叶草的休耕地。他们那幢房子一部分是原木结构，一部分是框架结构。原木结构的部分是亨利的祖父原先居住的老屋。较新的那部分是亨利21岁刚刚结婚时用木板搭建的，经过风吹雨打，木板如今已经年久失修，风时常在木板的缝隙间呼啸，几棵荫翳的榆树和一棵灰胡桃令木板既如画一般美丽，又如追忆往事般令人感伤，但也使得木板些许潮湿。

48年过去了。房子里的家具与房子的外表一样，陈旧并且已经发霉，看起来不免令人缅怀往事。你可能见过樱桃木的古董架，螺旋形的支柱，顶部刻有凹槽。这里就有个这样的古董架。这儿还有老式的、带有四根帷柱的床，上面还有球形的突起和深深的弧形切口，风格上沿袭了詹姆士一世早期的家具，孤零零的样子略显忧伤。樱桃木的书桌又高又宽，做工结实，但颜色已经褪去，还散发着一股子霉味儿。所有这些都可谓持久耐用的家具中的典范，而它们下面铺着的是一块质地并不密实、褪了色的、深灰与粉色相间的碎呢地毯。这是由菲比·安亲手编织的，当时她比故去时年轻15岁。地毯是在那架吱吱作响的木质织机上完成的，如今它就好似一副落满灰尘的骷髅，与一把坏掉的摇椅，一个破旧不堪的衣橱——天知道用了多久，一把从前被用来搁在户外摆放花朵还带着几个石灰点儿的长凳，以及其他一些陈旧的家庭用品，一同放在一个单坡屋顶的东向房间。它就紧挨着这个所谓的主体部分。各种其他破旧的家具都随意地摆放在这里；一个古色古香的衣架，它的两个肋条已经裂开；一面破碎的镜子，陈旧的镜框是樱桃木的，他们最小的儿子杰瑞死去的三天前，镜子从钉子上滑落下来，结果把镜框也摔裂了；一个镶在墙上的衣帽架，帽挂的末端原本是有瓷钮的；还有一台缝纫机，粗陋的机械结构早已被新型号比了下去。

房子东面的果园里满是疙疙瘩瘩的老苹果树，树干和枝杈都被虫蛀过，而且长满了绿色和白色的苔藓，月光之下，看上去白中透着青，还泛着银光，添一抹忧伤。低矮的外屋曾经养过鸡、一两匹马、一头牛和几头猪，屋顶上布满一块块的青苔，墙面由于久未粉刷，颜色已经变成灰黑色，而且有点儿松软。屋前是一排尖桩篱栅，门吱吱嘎嘎、歪歪斜斜的，侧面是用树的丫杈和倾斜的木桩支起的围栏，也是一样的破败。它们其实同住在这里的老亨利·瑞夫施奈德以及他的妻子菲比·安一道在一天天变老。

打从48年前结婚时起，夫妇俩便住在这里，亨利还在这儿度过了从童年到结婚前的时光。在他小时候，父母的日子过得和和睦睦。他初次恋爱并决定结婚时，父母让他和妻子与他们在这儿共同生活，他也就照做了。他们婚后的十年间，父母陪伴着他和妻子，直到两位老人双双故去。此后，亨利和菲比的身边就只剩下五个孩子，他们飞快而又茁壮地成长。不过从那时起，事情接踵而至。据说，他们生的七个孩子中有三个夭折了；一个女儿去了堪萨斯州；一个儿子去了苏福尔斯市，走后便没了音信；另一个儿子去了华盛顿；最小的女儿与他们住在同一个州，相隔五个县，不过她自己家里的负担太重，她很少把心思放在他们身上。时间与平淡普通的家庭生活让这些孩子彻底断了对父母的依恋，结果无论身在何处，他们都很少考虑父母的生活会是个什么样子。

老亨利·瑞夫施奈德和他的妻子菲比是一对恩爱的夫妇。你也许知道纯朴的本性是如何令他们好似石头上的苔藓般在适宜的条件下紧密相连一直到天荒地老、海枯石烂的。非凡的世界听起来广袤无垠，可他们却毫不在意。他们没有超群的才智。果园、草地、玉米地、猪圈和鸡舍便是他们一切活动的天地。麦子成熟了，就会被收割、脱粒；玉米变成棕色并经过了霜冻，就会被割下来，堆成堆；猫尾草的穗饱满了，就会被割下来，堆成干草垛。此后便是冬天的到来。他们会把粮食拉到市场去卖，锯些木头劈成柴火，干些生火做饭这样简单的家务杂事，偶尔做点儿修补的工作，还会去访亲探友。除了这些以及阴晴雨雪的天气变化，没有什么要紧的大事。生活中其他的一切都是遥远、吵闹而又千变万化的风景，如同夜空中的北极光忽隐忽现，如同远处奶牛身上叮当作响的铃铛声微弱难辨。

老亨利和他的妻子菲比都把对方视作一生挚爱。亨利是个瘦老头儿，妻子去世时他70岁，有些疯癫，脾气又坏，粗糙的花白头发和胡须乱蓬蓬的，从不梳理。他用那双失去光泽、目光呆滞、颜色暗淡的眼睛望着你，眼睛周围满是深褐色的皱纹。和许多农夫一样，他的衣服旧旧的，有棱有角，像袋子一样松松垮垮的，口袋突出着，脖领处的剪裁不太合身，肘部和膝盖处都鼓了起来并且磨出了洞。菲比·安是个清瘦的女人，身材扁平，活像一把雨伞，穿着破旧的黑色衣服，头戴一顶黑色软帽，这便是她最好的装扮。光阴荏苒，他们只需要照顾自己了。他们的行动日渐迟缓，活动也越来越少。每年饲养的猪从五头减少为一头咕咕噜噜的小肥猪，亨利现在留下的那匹马是个无精打采的家伙，吃得不是很多，也不是很干净。从前的那一大群鸡已经差不多死光了，一方面因为白鼬和狐狸，另一方面因为缺乏适当的照看而生了病。曾经绿意盎然的花园如今已成凌乱的回忆，从前用来装饰窗台和天井的藤蔓植物和花圃现在已经变成碍事的树丛。在立下的遗嘱中，这一小处需要纳税的房产被平均分给剩下的四个孩子，结果孩子们都对这里没有兴趣。不过老两口的日子还是安宁和睦的，只不过老亨利会时而乱发脾气，不是抱怨有什么事情疏忽了，就是抱怨有什么东西放错了地方，都是些鸡毛蒜皮的小事。

"菲比，我那把割玉米的刀在哪儿？你总是乱动我的东西。"

"好了，你安静点儿吧，亨利，"他的妻子会用嘶哑而尖细的嗓音警告他。"不然，我就离开你。总有一天我会打扮一番，然后离开这儿，看你到时候去哪儿？除了我没人会照看你，所以你就老实点儿吧。那把刀在壁炉架上，一直都放在那儿，除非你把它放在别的地儿了。"

老亨利知道妻子无论如何都不会离开自己，不过，有时他也会猜想如果她死了自己会怎么办。以死亡的方式离开是真正令他感到恐惧的。晚上，当他爬到椅子上去给那座陈旧的、带有长长的钟摆和两个钟锤的时钟上弦时，或是最后去前门和后门确保房门已经安全地锁上时，知道菲比就安坐在床上她睡的那一侧，知道如果他在夜里不安地翻身，她便会在旁边问他需要什么，这都是种安慰。

"好了，亨利，躺着别动！别像只小鸡一样动来动去。"

"嗯，我睡不着啊，菲比。"

"可怎么着你也不用这样翻来覆去的。你就让我睡一觉吧。"

通常这会使他处于一种昏昏欲睡的安逸之中。如果她要一桶水，他会去取来，可嘴里总要嘟囔上几句；如果她先起来生火，他会确保柴火已经劈好并且伸手便能拿到。他们甜蜜地分享着这一方简简单单的小天地。

不过随着时间一年一年地流逝，登门的人越来越少。大家都知道他们是老瑞夫施奈德先生和太太，住处足足有十英里远，为人诚实，是温和的基督徒，但是年纪太大了，实在让人感到无趣。写信几乎成了无法承受的负担，实在没法继续下去，甚至没法请人代写。不过住在彭伯顿县的女儿偶尔还是会寄来一封信。一些老朋友时而会带着一个派或蛋糕，或者一只烤鸡或烤鸭来访，或是仅仅来确定一下他们过得还好；但即便是这样善意的拜访也不再那么频繁了。

瑞夫施奈德太太在她64岁那年的早春生了病，从发低烧演变成某种不明原因的小病。因为上了年纪，这点儿小恙却成了不治之症。老亨利乘车去邻近的小镇斯温纳顿找来医生。一些朋友过来看她，从他手中接替了眼下对她的看护。然后在一个春寒料峭的夜晚她死了，老亨利在哀伤而无常的薄雾中，跟随她的遗体来到最近的墓地。这里长着几棵松树，并不引人注目。尽管他本可以到彭伯顿县的女儿那儿或是让人把她找来，可这实在太麻烦，而他又太过疲惫、太过固执。一两个朋友立刻建议他去和他们住一阵子，可他却觉得不合适。他的年纪太大了，太固执于自己的观念，又太习惯于这辈子他所熟悉的环境，他是不会考虑离去的。他想留在靠近安葬他的菲比的地方。必须独自生活这一点丝毫不会令他烦恼。那几个还在世的孩子得到消息后都表示如果他想离开的话，他们会照顾他，可他不想离开。

"我能自己想法儿应付，"他不断郑重其事地向这次来照看他妻子的老莫罗医生说。"我能自己做点儿饭，而且，再者了，早上我吃不了多少，只要喝点儿咖啡、吃点面包也就饱了。现在我能过得不错。你就别管了。"人们多次恳求他，给他这样那样的建议，还会按时给他送些咖啡、培根和烤面包，东西他也都收下了。在此之后，便没人再管他了。有一阵子，他会在春日的阳光下懒散地坐在门外沉思。他试着重拾对农活的兴致，让自己忙碌些，侍弄侍弄早已被扔在脑后的田地，免得自己想东想西。然而，晚间或是下午进屋时，他就会感到沮丧，屋子里处处都让他想起菲比，可她的身影却无处找寻。逐渐地，他一点点地把她的东西收拾起来。晚上他会坐在灯前，读着人们偶尔留给他的报纸或是已经遗忘了多年的《圣经》，可这些给不了他多少慰藉。他通常会挂着下巴，盯着地面，坐着思量她的亡灵何在，自己的生命要过多久才会终结。早上他正经八百地煮点咖啡，晚上又像模像样地给自己煎点儿培根；可他并没什么胃口。这个居住了多年的房子看起来空荡荡的，看到一处处阴暗的角落都立刻叫他心中一痛。他愁苦万分地挨过了漫长的五个月，然后日子开始有了变化。

　　一天夜里，他检查了前门和后门，给时钟上了弦，熄了灯，把多年来每天都会重复的事做了个遍，然后他上了床。可是，与其说他是为了睡觉，还不如说是为了思考。那一晚月光皎皎。窗外的果园被绿色的苔藓覆盖着，他躺在床上，望出去就能看到果园闪着银色的光泽，好似幽灵般美妙。月亮照着东面的窗户，在木头地板上洒下窗格子的图案，他所熟悉的老家具在房间里显得朦朦胧胧的。和往常一样，他一直在想菲比，想他们年轻时共度的时光，想着那些离开的孩子，想着近来他为了应付生活做出的那点儿可怜的转变。房子的状况实在变得十分糟糕。床上的用品乱糟糟、脏兮兮的，因为在洗衣服这件事上他有些应付不来，对于他来说，洗衣服是件恐怖的事情。房顶漏了，有些东西一下子就好几个星期都潮乎乎的，可他开始处于一种沉思的状态，只要不用他费劲儿，他就能接受任何事情。他更喜欢慢悠悠地来回踱着步子，或是坐着思考。

　　不过，这天晚上，他12点便睡着了，到两点钟又醒了过来。此时，月亮已经移到房子的西侧，现在正透过起居室和前面厨房的窗户照进来。桌旁的一把椅子，上面挂着他的外套；半遮半掩的厨房门，在月光下投下一片阴影；还有一盏放在报纸附近的灯——这些家具把菲比完完全全地展现在他面前，她正俯身靠在桌子上，她生前他常常看到她会这样做。他心头一惊。那是她吗——或是她的鬼魂？他不怎么相信灵魂，而且依然如此——他在微弱的光线中目不转睛地看着她，头皮发麻。然后，他坐起身来。那个人影没有动弹。他把自己那瘦弱的双腿从床上挪了下来，坐在那儿看着她，心想这是否真的是菲比。在她生前，他们经常谈论鬼魂、幽灵和预兆；但是对于这些东西是否存在他们却看法不一。他妻子从不相信自己是有灵魂的，并且死后灵魂能够重返人间。她往生的世界那可是另外一回事，那是个影影绰绰的天堂，一点儿不假，那儿的好人可不会费神返回到人间。可如今，她就在这儿，穿着她的黑裙子，披着灰色的围巾，俯身靠在桌子上，月光衬托出她那朦胧的轮廓。

　　"菲比，"他从头到脚都在颤抖，伸出一只瘦骨嶙峋的手喊道，"是你回来了吗？"

那个人影没动，于是他起身怯怯地朝门口走去，其间一直目不转睛地望着她。可是等他走近，那幻影化作了最初的几样东西——挂在高靠背椅子上的外套、报纸旁边的灯、半遮半掩的门。

"好吧，"他张着嘴，自言自语道，"我想我确实看到她了。"然后他以一种奇特而又含糊的方式用手梳了梳头发，这一刻他紧张的神经松弛了下来。尽管那幻影消失了，他却觉得她或许还会回来。

另一晚，因为有了第一次的幻觉，加之他现在始终惦念着她，而且又上了年纪，他认为自己又看到了她。当时，他朝着离床最近的窗外望去，从这扇窗子可以清楚地看到一个鸡笼、猪圈和四轮车棚的一角，就在这里，地面的潮气令一层淡淡的薄雾弥漫开来。那是一小缕雾霭，是经过了一天的温暖、在凉爽的夜晚从地面散发出来的薄雾中的一缕。在消散之前，那缕缕薄雾犹如小束的白色柏树枝一般摇曳。她生前常常从厨房门口穿过这一小块地方，到猪圈去把做饭时剩下的零零碎碎扔掉。现在她又出现在这里。他坐了起来，因为上一次的事奇怪地看着它，有些怀疑，但又因为身体中那股躁动的兴奋感而倾向于相信真的有灵魂存在。他相信菲比一定在惦念着他，因为他的孤独难耐而担心着他，因此就回来了。她还能有什么别的办法呢？如果不这样她还能以什么方式表达自己的情感呢？以她的恻隐之心，她应该会这样做，而且凭她对他的爱恋，她也应该会这样做。他颤抖着，热切地望着它；但是，空气的流动即便如呼吸一般微弱，还是令它朝着围栏迂回而去，然后便消失不见了。

还有一晚，大概是十天之后，他正在睡梦之中，她来到他的身旁，把手放在他头上。

"可怜的亨利！"她说，"这太糟了。"

他从睡梦中惊醒，真切地看到了她，他是这样认为的。她正从他的卧室朝起居室移动，身形犹如一团黑漆漆的阴影。他竭尽全力地睁大眼睛，可视力却不济，没看到几缕闪烁在她轮廓周围的微光。他站起身来，惊愕不已，在凉爽的房间里踱来踱去，对于菲比就要回到他的身边来深信不疑。只要他足够地想念她，只要他在情感上充分地表明他非常需要她，他体贴的妻子，就会回来，告诉他该怎么做。也许，无论如何她都会在夜里的大部分时间和他在一起；如此一来，他也就不再那么孤单，一切也就更容易忍受了。

人上了年纪，脑筋又不灵光，从似幻似真的微妙想象到真正的幻觉之间，并未隔着多远的距离。对于亨利来说，这种转换便适时地出现了。他夜夜等待着，期盼着她的归来。有一次，他认为自己看到了一束微光在房间里四处移动。还有一次，他认为自己看到她走在黄昏过后的果园里。这都是他的心绪在作怪。一天早上，他孤单生活的点点滴滴再也令他无法忍受了，一觉醒来后，他便认为她并没有死。很难说他是如何得出这个结论的。他已丧失了理智。取而代之的是固执的幻觉。他和菲比发生了无谓的争吵。他责怪她没把他的烟斗放在老地方，于是她就离开了。她这个反常的举动倒应了她总挂在嘴边的玩笑话，威胁说如果他不老实点儿，她就离开他。

"我想我会再次找到你的，"他总说。可她却会噼里啪啦地威胁道：

"我要是离开你，你才不会找到我呢。我想我会找个地方让你找不到。"

这天早上，他在起床时并没有考虑去按照惯例生火，或是，按照他的习惯，磨咖啡、切面包，而仅仅是冥思苦想在哪儿能找到她以及如何才能劝她回来。近来，亨利已经把那匹马解决掉了，因为觉得它麻烦，而且他也用不着它。他穿好衣服，取下那顶柔软但已变了形的帽子，眼中闪过一丝兴致与果断。他从门后拿出那根黑色弯柄手杖，他总是把它放在那儿，然后他便干脆利落地出了门，去最近的邻居那儿找她。他走路时，那双破旧的鞋子在尘土中咚咚作响，如今已经长长的花白头发从帽子下面散落出来，形成有趣的一圈儿，还有点儿像光环。他的短身外套在他走路时不停地呼扇，而他那瘦削的双手和尖尖的脸庞都毫无血色。

"哎呀，你好，亨利！这一早上去哪儿啊？"农夫道奇问道。在大路上遇到亨利时，道奇正拉着一车小麦到市场去。看到亨利这么充满生气，他心想，他已经好几个月没见到这个老农夫了，自从他妻子去世就没见过。

"你没看到菲比，是吧？"老头儿问道，疑惑地抬起头。

"谁家的菲比啊？"农夫道奇问道，一时没能把菲比和亨利的亡妻联系在一起。

"嗨，当然是我的妻子菲比啦。你以为我说的是谁？"他抬起头瞪眼看着他，浓密的花白眉毛下闪过一丝锐利的目光，看起来怪可怜的。

"啊，我发誓，亨利，你不是在开玩笑，是吧？"壮实的道奇说道。他是个胖子，面色红润，皮肤光滑，一脸严肃。"你说的不可能是你妻子。她死了。"

"死了！呸！"疯狂的瑞夫施奈德反驳道。"她今天一大早离开我的，我当时在睡觉。她总是起床去生火，可现在她走了。我们昨晚吵了一架，我猜她是因为这个才走的。可我想我能找到她。她去了马蒂尔德·莱斯家；她就是去那儿了。"

他干脆利落地上了路，身后是惊讶的道奇，纳闷地瞪着他。

"好吧，你要能找到，我把脑袋砍下来给你。"道奇大声地自言自语道。"他真是疯了。那个可怜的老家伙一直一个人住，结果现在发疯了。我得通知县里一声。"于是他起劲儿地轻挥鞭子。"快跑！"他说道，然后便出发了。

这一带人烟稀少，瑞夫施耐德一直走到三英里外马蒂尔德·莱斯和她丈夫用白石灰粉刷的栅栏前，才遇到别人。他在路上经过了其他几栋房子，不过这些房子都与他的幻觉不相关，也就没被他考虑在内。他的妻子和马蒂尔德相熟，她一定在这儿。他打开了人行道上的篱笆门，干脆利落地朝房门口走去。

"哎呀，瑞夫施奈德先生，"应声来开门的马蒂尔德也上了年纪，身材臃肿，朝门外看了看便喊道，"今早是什么风把你吹到这儿来啦？"

"菲比在吗？"他急切地问道。

"谁家的菲比？哪个菲比？"莱斯夫人答道，对他突如其来的旺盛精力觉得挺好奇。

"嗨，当然是我家的菲比啦。我妻子菲比啊。你以为是谁？她现在不在这儿吗？"

"天哪！"莱斯太太张着嘴巴惊呼一声。"可怜的家伙！这么说你现在什么都不记得了。你先进来坐下。我给你弄杯咖啡。你妻子当然不在这儿；但你先进来坐下。我过会儿去替你找她。我知道她在哪儿。"

老农夫的眼神柔和下来，进了屋。穿着马裤、一副元老派头的他瘦骨嶙峋，脸色苍白，看他取下帽子，把它轻柔地放在膝盖上，莱斯太太不禁充满对他的无限同情。

"我们昨晚吵架了，她就离开了我，"他主动说道。

"哎呀！哎呀！"莱斯太太叹着气，一个人去了厨房，心中的震惊也没处说与人听。"真可怜！现在得有个人照顾他才行。不能让他这样跑来跑去地找他死去的妻子啊。真是太糟了。"

她给他煮了一壶咖啡，还给他拿来一些新烤的面包和新鲜的黄油。她把最好的果酱也摆上了桌，还拿出几个鸡蛋来煮，同时还编着善意的谎话。

"你现在就待在这儿，亨利大叔，等杰克进来，我让他去找菲比。我想她很可能和几个朋友去了斯温纳顿。无论如何，我们会找到她的。现在你就喝点儿咖啡，再把面包吃了。你一定累了。你今天一早可走了不少的路。"她想着和"她男人"杰克商量一下，然后或许他能通知县里。

她一边忙碌着，一边思索着生命的无常。此时，老瑞夫施奈德用苍白的手指不断轻轻敲打着帽檐儿，然后心不在焉地吃着她拿来的食物。可他的心思却在他妻子身上。既然她不在这儿，或者没出现在这儿，他的思绪便模模糊糊地游荡到叫莫瑞的人家上，他们住在另一个方向几英里远的地方。不久，他便决定不等杰克·莱斯去寻找他妻子了，他要自己去找她。他必须上路了，然后催她回来。

"好了，我要走了，"他说，站起身来古怪地打量着四周。"我想她根本就没来这儿。我想，她去莫瑞家了。我不再等了，莱斯小姐。家里今天还有好多事要做呢。"然后他走出房门，没有理会她的反对，在温暖的春光中，再次踏上了满是尘土的大路，一边走路一边用他的拐杖戳着地面。

两小时后这个苍白的身影出现在莫瑞家的门口,一身的尘土,汗流浃背,一脸的急切。他迈着沉重的步伐赶了五英里的路,现在已是正午时分。年届六旬的夫妇二人一脸惊愕地听着他那奇怪的问题,然后也意识到他疯了。他们请他留下共进晚餐,想着随后通知县里看看该做些什么;可是尽管他留下来吃了点儿东西,却没待多久便再次出发要去另一处人家,距离这里并不近。他自认为有许多事要做,而且他需要菲比,这都催促着他赶紧动身。那天的状况就这样继续着,接下来的一天天也是如此,他询问的圈子也在不断扩大。

他的行为怪异却无害,一个人的性子变得古怪,这一过程常常是复杂而又令人感伤的。如前所述,这一天见证了瑞夫施奈德在其他人家的门口急切地提出他那反常的问题,然后在他身后留下一连串的惊异、同情和惋惜。尽管有人通知了县里——县治安官,一点儿不假——可拘捕他并不是明智之举;考虑到县精神病院的状况,那些认识老亨利并且已经认识他很久的人便决定让他仍旧随心所欲,毕竟精神病院里的病人精神错乱的程度令人愕然,而且环境令人作呕,这都是由于本地区的贫困造成的。说来也怪,人们在打听一番后发现,晚上他会平静地回到他那孤单的住所,看看妻子是否已经回来,然后孤独地陷入沉思,一坐就是一整夜。有谁会把一个头发灰白,温和而又天真地询问他人的老头儿关起来呢?尤其是瘦弱、急切地想找寻妻子的他,过去出了名的任劳任怨、老实可靠。那些最了解他的人非常赞同让他随心所欲地游荡下去。他不会伤害谁。有许多人愿意帮他,给他拿些食物、旧衣服以及他日常生活中的零星杂物——至少起初如此。过了一段时间,人们对他的身影都习以为常,不再感到奇怪了,对他的回答则变成了"哎呀,没有,亨利;我没看到她。"或是"不,亨利;她今天不在这儿。"这是人们更经常给他的回答。

那以后的几年里,他成了个怪人,阳光下、雨水中、尘土飞扬和泥泞不堪的道路上都能看到他的身影,偶尔人们会在奇怪而又出乎意料的地方遇见他,看到他仍在不懈地继续找寻妻子。又过了一阵子,尽管邻居们和那些了解他过去的人乐于给他拿这拿那,可他的身体还是因为营养不良每况愈下;因为他走路走得太多,却吃得太少。这样在公路上游荡得越久,他那奇异的幻觉就越严重;当他发现从旅途越来越长的远游归来变得越发困难时,他便开始从家里拿些器皿,打个小包,带在身上,这样就不用非得回家不可。他把一个洋铁质地的小茶杯、一副刀叉和勺子以及一些盐和胡椒都放在一个大号的破洋铁咖啡壶里。他把壶钻出个小孔,穿了根线绳,把一个盘子绑在壶上。盘子可以被解下来,在林地里,它便成了他的餐桌。对他来说,弄到他所需要的那点儿食物不是什么麻烦事,出于一种奇特的、近乎宗教般神圣的尊严,他会只要求那么点儿,毫不犹豫。逐渐地,他的头发越来越长,曾经的黑色帽子变成了土黄色,衣服也磨破了,上面满是尘土。

没人知道在他不断行走的整整三年中他所徘徊的地域有多大,在暴风雨和寒冷中他是如何捱过来的。以人们对乡村居家生活的理解和考虑,他们不会想到他把自己藏在干草垛里,或是挤到牛群里,用牛的温暖身躯为自己抵御严寒,而愚笨的牛也不会反对他的存在,反正这不会给它们带来任何伤害。突出的岩石和树木有时会为他挡雨,他也会考虑住进干草棚或是玉米穗仓库,这些都是不错的地方。

幻觉那错综复杂的进程是奇特的。总是站在门口询问却不被理会或是得到否定的答复,他从中得出了这样的结论:尽管在他挨家询问的房子中没有菲比的身影,她却可能存在于他自己的嗓音之中。于是,从耐心的询问,他开始偶尔发出悲伤的叫喊。喊声时时唤醒寂静的田野和凹凸不平的丘陵。于是它们便开始随声附和他那飘忽的"哦——菲比!哦——菲比!"这尽管听起来疯狂,却令人悲伤。许多农夫和耕童,甚至是那些相距遥远的农人,都开始熟悉这喊声,并会说:"那是老瑞夫施奈德。"

一段时间之后,在数百次的询问之后,另一个使他极其迷惑的问题出现了:当他再也想不出可以去哪家的门口询问时,他该走哪条路。这些有时会指向四个或六个方向的交叉路口过一阵子便会使他迷惑不解。但要解决这个越发令人迷惑的难题,却让另一个能帮助他的幻觉出现了。菲比的灵魂或是某种蕴藏在空气、风或自然中的力量会告诉他去往何方。如果他站在道路分界处的中心,闭上眼睛,转上三圈,喊上两声"哦——菲比!"然后把手杖径直扔到面前,手杖便自然会指引寻找菲比的方向,或者其中一种神秘力量会自然掌控手杖的方向,并让它落下!不论手杖指向何方,即便它多次将他带回到来时的路上,或是来时穿越的田野中,他也不会完全丧失理智,而是在又一次疯狂叫喊之前,给自己充裕的时间来寻找妻子。而且,那令他认为也许哪天他一定会找到她的幻觉似乎仍旧顽固。有时他的双脚会酸痛,他的四肢会疲倦。有时他会在酷热中停下来擦拭皱巴巴的额头,或在严寒中拍打自己的双臂。有时,在将手杖扔出之后,他会发现手杖指引的方向是他刚才来时的方向。这时他会疲惫而冷静地摇摇头,似乎思量着这难以置信的情形或是不幸的命运,然后便干脆利落地出发。他奇怪的身影最终连最远三四个县的人都知道。老瑞夫施奈德是令人感伤的家伙。他声名远播。

在格林县有一个名叫沃特斯韦尔的小镇,那里人口不多,附近有个地方或者说悬崖,人称红崖,距离小镇大概四英里。陡峭的岩壁大概半英里高,下面是果实累累的玉米田和果园,上面则被茂密的小树林所覆盖。岩壁背面的缓坡上生长着山毛榉、山胡桃和白杨,其间贯穿着众多纵横交织的小道可以供四轮马车通行。天气晴好时,老瑞夫施奈德习惯在某个像这样的小片树林中安身。如今他已经十分习惯待在户外,在躺下睡觉前,他会在某棵树底下煎培根或煮鸡蛋。偶尔,他会因为睡不踏实而在夜间赶路。当他因为月光、林中突然吹起的风或是出来巡查一番的动物而醒来时,他通常会坐起身来思考,或者在月光或黑暗中继续找寻。他的样子奇怪反常,一半疯癫一半野人似的,不过绝不会伤害谁。他会在孤寂的十字路口叫喊,朝黑洞洞的、关着百叶窗的房子里凝望,想知道菲比到底在哪儿,在哪儿。

深夜两点钟,心脏伸缩与舒展的间歇总会令他醒来。他尽管不会继续前行,可还是会坐起来凝视着黑暗与星辰,暗自纳闷。有时,在他思维的奇特进程中,他会想象自己在林中看到了失去的妻子。然后他便会起身,拿起总是系在一根线绳上的器皿,还有他的手杖,追随她的身影。如果她极其容易地躲开他,他便会奔跑,或乞求,或是因为突然失去了想象中那身影的踪迹而站住,一脸的惊叹或失望,为他在找寻的过程中那几乎不可逾越的艰难,进行短暂的哀悼。

当他无望地游历到第七个年头时,在一个春日的拂晓,他来到一片树林附近,这是他在这里度过的最后一晚。那天与他妻子去世的日子有些相似,而那片树林则有一条通往红崖顶的山路。那根能被扔得远远的、在最后那个十字路口被用作探寻方向的手杖把他带到了此处。他已经走了好几英里的路。那时已过了晚上十点钟,他非常疲倦。由于长时间的徘徊却吃得很少,他只剩下往日的依稀身影。如今是精神上的耐力而并非体力在支撑着他。这一天他吃得很少,现在筋疲力尽的他在黑暗中躺下来歇一歇而且很可能会睡着。

奇怪的是,这次他被某种奇特的迹象所围绕。这一迹象似乎表明妻子的存在。尽管数月来一无所获,他却劝导自己如今距离见到她并能和她说话的时候不远了。不一会儿,他便头枕着膝盖进入了梦乡。午夜时分,月亮开始升起。到了两点钟,他通常醒来的时刻,月亮仿若一个大大的银盘透过东面的树林闪着光芒。他睁开双眼。此时,月亮的光线变强,在他的脚下形成一个银色的图案,并以奇特的光泽和银色的朦胧光线将树林照亮。和往常一样,他心头又升起了妻子一定在附近的老念头。于是他环顾四周,眼神中尽是猜测与企盼。远处阴影中是什么在沿着进入树林的小径移动着?——那不过是一股微弱而又闪烁不定的鬼火在林中优雅地上下跳动,因而吸引了他期盼的目光。月光和阴影的融合令这股鬼火具有了一种奇异的形状和一种更为神奇的真实感。它可能是一团飘动着的磷火,也可能是一群在游荡中飞舞的萤火虫。那真的是他已失去的菲比吗?它迂回地绕过他,而陷入狂热之中的他却认为他刚好看到了她的双眸。令人奇怪的是,不同于他最后一次见到她的样子,身着黑色衣裙和围巾,现在的菲比更加年轻、更加愉快、更加楚楚动人,是他多年前所认识的少女时代的菲比。老瑞夫施奈德站起身来。这些年来，他一直期待并梦想着这个时刻。如今，当看到那微弱的光线在他面前轻快地舞动时，他凝视着它，满腹疑虑，一只瘦削的手插在灰白的头发里。

突然他想起了她少女时代魅力无限的身影，自己还是小伙子时便已熟识的身影，她那可爱的、富于同情心的微笑，那棕色的秀发，在一次野餐时她那曾系在腰间的蓝色饰带，还有那快乐而优雅的一举一动。他绕着树的根基穿梭于林间，竭力地睁大双眼，热切地紧随其后。这次，他忘记了手杖和那些器皿。她继续在他的前面移动着，那团春天里的鬼火，她头顶的那一小簇火焰，看起来又好像是她那年轻而轻快的手，在白杨和山毛榉的小树苗以及山胡桃和榆树的粗壮树干之间挥动着。

"哦，菲比！菲比！"他呼喊着。"你真的来了吗？你真的在回应我吗？"然后由于加紧了脚步，他跌了一跤。他一瘸一拐地站起来，只看到了远处的光线如同幻影般向前舞动。他不断地向前追赶，直到完全跑了起来。衣衫褴褛的臂膀擦过树干，双手和脸庞撞到了挡住去路的嫩枝。他的帽子不见了，肺部喘不过气来，理智则彻底步入了歧途。当他来到悬崖的边缘，他看到她在下面那片银色的苹果树中，树上的花朵正在春季里盛开。

"哦，菲比！"他呼喊着。"哦，菲比！哦，不，不要离开我！"他呼喊着。感受着那虚幻世界的诱惑——那里有年少时的爱情，还有这幻影所呈现的菲比，他们昔日青春的可爱化身——他快乐地高喊一声"哦，等等，菲比！"便一跃而起。

数日后，几个农家男孩在勘查这片丰饶而开阔的地区时，首先发现了他遗忘在树下的那些系在一起的洋铁器皿，然后在悬崖下发现了他的尸体。他已面无血色，骨头也摔断了，可却是一副兴高采烈的样子，凝固在嘴角的笑容带着一丝安心和喜悦。人们在一些低矮的小树下发现了他那顶破旧的帽子，它当时被小树的嫩枝刮落在地。在所有那些纯朴的居民中，没人知道他是多么急切而又快活地找到了他所失去的伴侣。

# Willa Cather
# (1873—1947)

Willa Cather was an American novelist and short story writer noted for her novels about immigrants struggling to make a living in the Midwest during the late 1800s. She has been placed by various critics among feminist writers, antifeminist writers, and even lesbian writers. Born in 1873 in western Virginia, she moved to a farm near Red Cloud, Nebraska with her family when she was nine. There she grew up among the immigrants from Europe, most of them coming from Scandinavia, who were establishing homesteads on the Great Plains. The people of Red Cloud played an important part in the life and work of Willa Cather. Cather was 22 when she left home to go east and begin her professional career as a writer. In 1922 Cather won the Pulitzer Prize for her novel *One of Ours*, which depicted a boy from the Western plains, who leaves home to fight in World War I and is killed in France. Ernest Hemingway expressed disdain at Cather's having received the prize.

Cather wrote 12 novels and some remarkable long and short stories. The most popular of her novels include *O Pioneers!* (1913), *The Song of the Lark* (1915), *My Antonia* (1918), and *Death Comes for the Archbishop* (1927). In her works Cather created strong female characters, who had the courage and vision to face all obstacles in their difficult lives. Her first novel, *Alexander's Bridge* was published in 1912, and from that point on Cather became a great American novelist. In the years following WW I Cather became gravely distressed by the loss of spiritual values that accompanied the growth of materialism and technology in the 20th-century. Her judgment of contemporary society was seen in works including *A Lost Lady* (1923), and *The Professor's House* (1925).

## The Sculptor's Funeral

*The following story from* **The Troll Garden** *(1905) addressed Cather's ambivalent feelings about the Midwest. "The Sculptor's Funeral" took an unromanticized look at Sand City, Kansas, a small town which reabsorbed one of its exiles, Harvey Merrick, a sculptor who escaped the town's provincialism, corruption,* *prejudices, and violence only to return in the event of his death. Cather used his funeral to examine the values of small, Midwestern towns.*

A group of the townspeople stood on the station siding of a little Kansas town, awaiting the coming of the night train, which was already twenty minutes overdue. The snow had fallen thick over everything; in the pale starlight the line of bluffs across the wide, white meadows south of the town made soft, smoke-colored curves against the clear sky. The men on the siding stood first on one foot and then on the other, their hands thrust deep into their trousers pockets, their overcoats open, their shoulders screwed up with the cold; and they glanced from time to time toward the southeast, where the railroad track wound along the river shore. They conversed in low tones and moved about restlessly, seeming uncertain as to what was expected of them. There was but one of the company who looked as though he knew exactly why he was there; and he kept conspicuously apart; walking to the far end of the platform, returning to the station door, then pacing up the track again, his chin sunk in the high collar of his overcoat, his burly shoulders drooping forward, his gait heavy and dogged. Presently he was approached by a tall, spare, grizzled man clad in a faded Grand Army suit, who shuffled out from the group and advanced with a certain deference, craning his neck forward until his back made the angle of a jack-knife three-quarters open.

"I reckon she's agoin' to be pretty late ag'in tonight, Jim," he remarked in a squeaky falsetto. "S'pose it's the snow?"

"I don't know," responded the other man with a shade of annoyance, speaking from out an astonishing cataract of red beard that grew fiercely and thickly in all directions.

The spare man shifted the quill toothpick he was chewing to the other side of his mouth. "It ain't likely that anybody from the East will come with the corpse, I s'pose," he went on reflectively.

"I don't know," responded the other, more curtly than before.

"It's too bad he didn't belong to some lodge or other. I like an order funeral myself. They seem more appropriate for people of some reputation," the spare man continued, with an ingratiating concession in his shrill voice, as he carefully placed his toothpick in his vest pocket. He always carried the flag at the G. A. R. funerals in the town.

The heavy man turned on his heel, without replying, and walked up the siding.

The spare man shuffled back to the uneasy group. "Jim's ez full ez a tick, ez ushel," he commented commiseratingly.

Just then a distant whistle sounded, and there was a shuffling of feet on the platform. A number of lanky boys, of all ages, appeared as suddenly and slimily as eels wakened by the crack of thunder; some came from the waiting room, where they had been warming themselves by the red stove, or half-asleep on the slat benches; others uncoiled themselves from baggage trucks or slid out of express wagons. Two clambered down from the driver's seat of a hearse that stood backed up against the siding. They straightened their stooping shoulders and lifted their heads, and a flash of momentary animation kindled their dull eyes at that cold, vibrant scream, the world-wide call for men. It stirred them like the note of a trumpet; just as it had often stirred the man who was coming home tonight, in his boyhood.

The night express shot, red as a rocket, from out the eastward marsh lands and wound along the river shore under the long lines of shivering poplars that sentinelled the meadows, the escaping steam hanging in gray masses against the pale sky and blotting out the Milky Way. In a moment the red glare from the headlight streamed up the snow-covered track before the siding and glittered on the wet, black rails. The burly man with the disheveled red beard walked swiftly up the platform toward the approaching train, uncovering his head as he went. The group of men behind him hesitated, glanced questioningly at one another, and awkwardly followed his example. The train stopped, and the crowd shuffled up to the express car just as the door was thrown open, the spare man in the G. A. B. suit thrusting his head forward with curiosity. The express messenger appeared in the doorway, accompanied by a young man in a long ulster and traveling cap.

"Are Mr. Merrick's friends here?" inquired the young man.

The group on the platform swayed and shuffled uneasily. Philip Phelps, the banker, responded with dignity: "We have come to take charge of the body. Mr. Merrick's father is very feeble and can't be about."

"Send the agent out here," growled the express messenger, "and tell the operator to lend a hand."

The coffin was got out of its rough-box and down on the snowy platform. The townspeople drew back enough to make room for it and then formed a close semicircle about it, looking curiously at the palm leaf which lay across the black cover. No one said anything. The baggage man stood by his truck, waiting to get at the trunks. The engine panted heavily, and the fireman dodged in and out among the wheels with his yellow torch and long oil-can, snapping the spindle boxes. The young Bostonian, one of the dead sculptor's pupils who had come with the body, looked about him helplessly. He turned to the banker, the only one of that black, uneasy, stoop-shouldered group who seemed enough of an individual to be addressed.

"None of Mr. Merrick's brothers are here?" he asked uncertainly.

The man with the red heard for the first time stepped up and joined the group. "No, they have not come yet; the family is scattered. The body will be taken directly to the house." He stooped and took hold of one of the handles of the coffin.

"Take the long hill road up, Thompson, it will be easier on the horses," called the liveryman as the undertaker snapped the door of the hearse and prepared to mount to the driver's seat.

Laird, the red-bearded lawyer, turned again to the stranger: "We didn't know whether there would be anyone with him or not," he explained. "It's a long walk, so you'd better go up in the hack." He pointed to a single, battered conveyance, but the young man replied stiffly: "Thank you, but I think I will go up with the hearse. If you don't object," turning to the undertaker, "I'll ride with you."

They clambered up over the wheels and drove off in the starlight tip the long, white hill toward the town. The lamps in the still village were shining from under the low, snow-burdened roofs; and beyond, on every side, the plains reached out into emptiness, peaceful and wide as the soft sky itself, and wrapped in a tangible, white silence.

When the hearse backed up to a wooden sidewalk before a naked, weatherbeaten frame house, the same composite, ill-defined group that had stood upon the station siding was huddled about the gate. The front yard was an icy swamp, and a couple of warped planks, extending from the sidewalk to the door, made a sort of rickety footbridge. The gate hung on one hinge, and was opened wide with difficulty. Steavens, the young stranger, noticed that something black was tied to the knob of the front door.

The grating sound made by the casket, as it was drawn from the hearse, was answered by a scream from the house; the front door was wrenched open, and a tall, corpulent woman rushed out bareheaded into the snow and flung herself upon the coffin, shrieking: "My boy, my boy! And this is how you've come home to me!"

As Steavens turned away and closed his eyes with a shudder of unutterable repulsion, another woman, also tall, but flat and angular, dressed entirely in black, darted out of the house and caught Mrs. Merrick by the shoulders, crying sharply: "Come, come, Mother; you mustn't go on like this!" Her tone changed to one of obsequious solemnity as she turned to the banker: "The parlor is ready, Mr. Phelps."

The bearers carried the coffin along the narrow boards, while the undertaker ran ahead with the coffin-rests. They bore it into a large, unheated room that smelled of dampness and disuse and furniture polish, and set it down under a hanging lamp ornamented with jingling glass prisms and before a "Rogers group" of John Alden and Priscilla, wreathed with smilax. Henry Steavens stared about him with the sickening conviction that there had been a mistake, and that he had somehow arrived at the wrong destination. He looked at the clover-green Brussels, the fat plush upholstery, among the hand-painted china plaques and panels, and vases, for some mark of identification, — for something that might once conceivably have belonged to Harvey Merrick. It was not until he recognized his friend in the crayon portrait of a little boy in kilts and curls, hanging above the piano, that he felt willing to let any of these people approach the coffin.

"Take the lid off, Mr. Thompson; let me see my boy's face," wailed the elder woman between her sobs. This time Steavens looked fearfully, almost beseechingly into her face, red and swollen under its masses of strong, black, shiny hair. He flushed, dropped his eyes, and then, almost incredulously, looked again. There was a kind of power about her face—a kind of brutal handsomeness, even; but it was scarred and furrowed by violence, and so colored and coarsened by fiercer passions that grief seemed never to have laid a gentle finger there. The long nose was distended and knobbed at the end, and there were deep lines on either side of it; her heavy, black brows almost met across her forehead, her teeth were large and square and set far apart—teeth that could tear. She filled the room; the men were obliterated, seemed tossed about like twigs in an angry water, and even Steavens felt himself being drawn into the whirlpool.

The daughter—the tall, raw-boned woman in crêpe, with a mourning comb in her hair which curiously lengthened her long face sat stiffly upon the sofa, her hands, conspicuous for their large knuckles, folded in her lap, her mouth and eyes drawn down, solemnly awaiting the opening of the coffin. Near the door stood a mulatto woman, evidently a servant in the house, with a timid bearing and an emaciated face pitifully sad and gentle. She was weeping silently, the corner of her calico apron lifted to her eyes, occasionally suppressing a long, quivering sob. Steavens walked over and stood beside her.

Feeble steps were heard on the stairs, and an old man, tall and frail, odorous of pipe smoke, with shaggy, unkept gray hair and a dingy beard, tobacco stained about the mouth, entered uncertainly. He went slowly up to the coffin and stood, rolling a blue cotton handkerchief between his hands, seeming so pained and embarrassed by his wife's orgy of grief that he had no consciousness of anything else.

"There, there, Annie, dear, don't take on so," he quavered timidly, putting out a shaking hand and awkwardly patting her elbow. She turned with a cry and sank upon his shoulder with such violence that he tottered a little. He did not even glance toward the coffin, but continued to look at her with a dull, frightened, appealing expression, as a spaniel looks at the whip. His sunken cheeks slowly reddened and burned with miserable shame. When his wife rushed from the room her daughter strode after her with set lips. The servant stole up to the coffin, bent over it for a moment, and then slipped away to the kitchen, leaving Steavens, the lawyer, and the father to themselves. The old man stood trembling and looking down at his dead son's face. The sculptor's splendid head seemed even more noble in its rigid stillness than in life. The dark hair had crept down upon the wide forehead; the face seemed strangely long, but in it there was not that beautiful and chaste repose which we expect to find in the faces of the dead. The brows were so drawn that there were two deep lines above the beaked nose, and the chin was thrust forward defiantly. It was as though the strain of life had been so sharp and bitter that death could not at once wholly relax the tension and smooth the countenance into perfect peace— as though he were still guarding something precious and holy, which might even yet be wrested from him.

The old man's lips were working under his stained beard. He turned to the lawyer with timid deference: "Phelps and the rest are comin' back to set up with Harve, ain't they?" he asked. "Thank 'ee, Jim, thank 'ee." He brushed the hair back gently from his son's forehead. "He was a good boy, Jim; always a good boy. He was ez gentle ez a child and the kindest of 'em all—only we didn't none of us ever understand him." The tears trickled slowly down his beard and dropped upon the sculptor's coat.

"Martin, Martin. Oh, Martin! come here," his wife wailed from the top of the stairs. The old man started timorously: "Yes, Annie, I'm coming." He turned away, hesitated stood for a moment in miserable indecision; then he reached back and patted the dead man's hair softly, and stumbled from the room.

"Poor old man, I didn't think he had any tears left. Seems as if his eyes would have gone dry long ago. At his age nothing cuts very deep," remarked the lawyer.

Something in his tone made Steavens glance up. While the mother had been in the room the young man had scarcely seen anyone else; but now, from the moment he first glanced into Jim Laird's florid face and bloodshot eyes, he knew that he had found what he had been heartsick at not finding before—the feeling, the understanding, that must exist in someone, even here.

The man was red as his beard, with features swollen and blurred by dissipation, and a hot, blazing blue eye. His face was strained—that of a man who is controlling himself with difficulty—and he kept plucking at his beard with a sort of fierce resentment. Steavens, sitting by the window, watched him turn down the glaring lamp, still its jangling pendants with an angry gesture, and then stand with his hands locked behind him, staring down into the master's face. He could not help wondering what link there could have been between the porcelain vessel and so sooty a lump of potter's clay.

From the kitchen an uproar was sounding; when the dining-room door opened, the import of it was clear. The mother was abusing the maid for having forgotten to make the dressing for the chicken salad which had been prepared for the watchers. Steavens had never heard anything in the least like it; it was injured, emotional, dramatic abuse, unique and masterly in its excruciating cruelty, as violent and unrestrained as had been her grief of twenty minutes before. With a shudder of disgust the lawyer went into the dining room and closed the door into the kitchen.

"Poor Roxy's getting it now," he remarked when he came back. "The Merricks took her out of the poorhouse years ago; and if her loyalty would let her, I guess the poor old thing could tell tales that would curdle your blood. She's the mulatto woman who was standing in here a while ago, with her apron to her eyes. The old woman is a fury; there never was anybody like her. She made Harvey's life a hell for him when he lived at home; he was so sick ashamed of it. I never could see how he kept himself so sweet."

"He was wonderful," said Steavens slowly, "wonderful; but until tonight I have never known how wonderful."

"That is the true and eternal wonder of it, anyway; that it can come even from such a dung heap as this," the lawyer cried, with a sweeping gesture which seemed to indicate much more than the four walls within which they stood.

"I think I'll see whether I can get a little air. The room is so close I am beginning to feel rather faint," murmured Steavens, struggling with one of the windows. The sash was stuck, however, and would not yield, so he sat down dejectedly and began pulling at his collar. The lawyer came over, loosened the sash with one blow of his red fist, and sent the window up a few inches. Steavens thanked him, but the nausea which had been gradually climbing into his throat for the last half-hour left him with but one desire—a desperate feeling that he must get away from this place with what was left of Harvey Merrick. Oh, he comprehended well enough now the quiet bitterness of the smile that he had seen so often on his master's lips!

Once when Merrick returned from a visit home, he brought with him a singularly feeling and suggestive bas-relief of a thin, faded old woman, sitting and sewing something pinned to her knee; while a full-lipped, full-blooded little urchin, his trousers held up by a single gallows, stood beside her, impatiently twitching her gown to call her attention to a butterfly he had caught. Steavens, impressed by the tender and delicate modeling of the thin, tired face, had asked him if it were his mother. He remembered the dull flush that had burned up in the sculptor's face.

The lawyer was sitting in a rocking chair beside the coffin, his head thrown back and his eyes closed. Steavens looked at him earnestly, puzzled at the line of the chin, and wondering why a man should conceal a feature of such distinction under that disfiguring shock of beard. Suddenly, as though he felt the young sculptor's keen glance, he opened his eyes.

"Was he always a good deal of an oyster?" he asked abruptly. "He was terribly shy as a boy."

"Yes, he was an oyster, since you put it so," rejoined Steavens. "Although he could be very fond of people, he always gave one the impression of being detached. He disliked violent emotion; he was reflective, and rather distrustful of himself—except, of course, as regarded his work. He was sure enough there. He distrusted men pretty thoroughly and women even more, yet somehow without believing ill of them. He was determined, indeed, to believe the best, but he seemed afraid to investigate."

"A burnt dog dreads the fire," said the lawyer grimly, and closed his eyes.

Steavens went on and on, reconstructing that whole miserable boyhood. All this raw, biting ugliness had been the portion of the man whose mind was an exhaustless gallery of beautiful impressions—so sensitive that the mere shadow of a poplar leaf flickering against a sunny wall would be etched and held there forever. Surely, if ever a man had the magic word in his fingertips, it was Merrick. Whatever he touched, he revealed its holiest secret; liberated it from enchantment and restored it to its pristine loveliness, like the Arabian prince who fought the enchantress spell for spell. Upon whatever he had come in contact with, he had left a beautiful record of the experience—a sort of ethereal signature; a scent, a sound, a color that was his own.

Steavens understood now the real tragedy of his master's life; neither love nor wine, as many had conjectured, but a blow which had fallen earlier and cut deeper than these could have done—a shame not his, and yet so unescapably his, to hide in his heart from his very boyhood. And without—the frontier warfare; the yearning of a boy, cast ashore upon a desert of newness and ugliness and sordidness, for all that is chastened and old, and noble with traditions.

At eleven o'clock the tall, flat woman in black announced that the watchers were arriving, and asked them "to step into the dining room." As Steavens rose the lawyer said dryly: "You go on—it'll be a good experience for you, doubtless; as for me, I'm not equal to that crowd tonight; I've had twenty years of them."

As Steavens closed the door after him he glanced back at the lawyer, sitting by the coffin in the dim light, with his chin resting on his hand.

The same misty group that had stood before the door of the express car shuffled into the dining-room. In the light of the kerosene lamp they separated and became individuals. The minister, a pale, feeble-looking man with white hair and blond chin-whiskers, took his seat beside a small side table and placed his Bible upon it. The Grand Army man sat down behind the stove and tilted his chair back comfortably against the wall, fishing his quill toothpick from his waistcoat pocket. The two bankers, Phelps and Elder, sat off in a corner behind the dinner table, where they could finish their discussion of the new usury law and its effect on chattel security loans. The real estate agent, an old man with a smiling, hypocritical face, soon joined them. The coal and lumber dealer and the cattle shipper sat on opposite sides of the hard coal-burner, their feet on the nickel-work. Steavens took a book from his pocket and began to read. The talk around him ranged through various topics of local interest while the house was quieting down. When it was clear that the members of the family were in bed, the Grand Army man hitched his shoulders and, untangling his long legs, caught his heels on the rounds of his chair.

"S'pose there'll be a will, Phelps?" he queried in his weak falsetto.

The banker laughed disagreeably and began trimming his nails with a pearl-handled pocket-knife.

"There'll scarcely be any need for one, will there?" he queried in his turn.

The restless Grand Army man shifted his position again, getting his knees still nearer his chin. "Why, the ole man says Harve's done right well lately," he chirped.

The other banker spoke up. "I reckon he means by that Harve ain't asked him to mortgage any more farms lately, so as he could go on with his education."

"Seems like my mind don't reach back to a time when Harve wasn't bein' educated," tittered the Grand Army man.

There was a general chuckle. The minister took out his handkerchief and blew his nose sonorously. Banker Phelps closed his knife with a snap. "It's too bad the old man's sons didn't turn out better," he remarked with reflective authority. "They never hung together. He spent money enough on Harve to stock a dozen cattle-farms and he might as well have poured it into Sand Creek. If Harve had stayed at home and helped nurse what little they had, and gone into stock on the old man's bottom farm, they might all have been well fixed. But the old man had to trust everything to tenants and was cheated right and left."

"Harve never could have handled stock none," interposed the cattleman. "He hadn't it in him to be sharp. Do you remember when he bought Sander's mules for eight-year-olds, when everybody in town knew that Sander's father-in-law give 'em to his wife for a wedding present eighteen years before, an' they was full-grown mules then."

The company laughed discreetly, and the Grand Army man rubbed his knees with a spasm of childish delight.

"Harve never was much account for anything practical, and he shore was never fond of work," began the coal-and-lumber dealer. "I mind the last time he was home; the day he left, when the old man was out to the barn helpin' his hand hitch up to take Harve to the train, and Cal Moots was patchin' up the fence; Harve, he come out on the step and sings out, in his ladylike voice: 'Cal Moots, Cal Moots! please come cord my trunk.'"

"That's Harve for you," approved the Grand Army man gleefully. "I kin hear him howlin' yet when he was a big feller in long pants and his mother used to whale him with a rawhide in the barn for lettin' the cows git foundered in the cornfield when he was drivin' 'em home from pasture. He killed a cow of mine that-a-way onc't—a pure Jersey and the best milker I had, an' the ole man had to put up for her. Harve, he was watchin' the sun set acros't the marshes when the anamile got away."

"Where the old man made his mistake was in sending the boy East to school," said Phelps, stroking his goatee and speaking in a deliberate, judicial tone. "There was where he got his head full of nonesense. What Harve needed, of all people, was a course in some first-class Kansas City business college."

The letters were swimming before Steavens's eyes. Was it possible that these men did not understand, that the palm on the coffin meant nothing to them? The very name of their town would have remained forever buried in the postal guide had it not been now and again mentioned in the world in connection with Harvey Merrick's. He remembered what his master had said to him on the day of his death, after the congestion of both lungs had shut off any probability of recovery, and the sculptor had asked his pupil to send his body home. "It's not a pleasant place to be lying while the world is moving and doing and bettering," he had said with a feeble smile, "but it rather seems as though we ought to go back to the place we came from, in the end. The townspeople will come in for a look at me; and after they have had their say I shan't have much to fear from the judgment of God!"

The cattleman took up the comment. "Forty's young for a Merrick to cash in; they usually hang on pretty well. Probably he helped it along with whisky."

"His mother's people were not long-lived, and Harvey never had a robust constitution," said the minister mildly. He would have liked to say more. He had been the boy's Sunday-school teacher, and had been fond of him; but he felt that he was not in a position to speak. His own sons had turned out badly, and it was not a year since one of them had made his last trip home in the express car, shot in a gambling house in the Black Hills.

"Nevertheless, there is no disputin' that Harve frequently looked upon the wine when it was red, also variegated, and it shore made an uncommon fool of him," moralized the cattleman.

Just then the door leading into the parlor rattled loudly, and everyone started involuntarily, looking relieved when only Jim Laird came out. The Grand Army man ducked his head when he saw the spark in his blue, bloodshot eye. They were all afraid of Jim; he was a drunkard, but he could twist the law to suit his client's needs as no other man in all western Kansas could do, and there were many who tried. The lawyer closed the door behind him, leaned back against it and folded his arms, cocking his head a little to one side. When he assumed this attitude in the courtroom, ears were always pricked up, as it usually foretold a flood of withering sarcasm.

"I've been with you gentlemen before," he began in a dry, even tone, "when you've sat by the coffins of boys born and raised in this town; and, if I remember rightly, you were never any too well satisfied when you checked them up. What's the matter, anyhow? Why is it that reputable young men are as scarce as millionaires in Sand City? It might almost seem to a stranger that there was some way something the matter with your progressive town. Why did Ruben Sayer, the brightest young lawyer you ever turned out, after he had come home from the university as straight as a die, take to drinking and forge a check and shoot himself? Why did Bill Merrit's son die of the shakes in a saloon in Omaha? Why was Mr. Thomas's son, here, shot in a gambling house? Why did young Adams burn his mill to beat the insurance companies and go to the pen?"

The lawyer paused and unfolded his arms, laying one clenched fist quietly on the table. "I'll tell you why. Because you drummed nothing but money and knavery into their ears from the time they wore knickerbockers; because you carped away at them as you've been carping here tonight, holding our friends Phelps and Elder up to them for their models, as our grandfathers held up George Washington and John Adams. But the boys were young and raw at the business you put them to, and how could they match coppers with such artists as Phelps and Elder? You wanted them to be successful rascals; they were only unsuccessful ones—that's all the difference. There was only one boy ever raised in this borderland between ruffianism and civilization who didn't come to grief, and you hated Harvey Merrick more for winning out than you hated all the other boys who got under the wheels. Lord, Lord, how you did hate him! Phelps, here, is fond of saying that he could buy and sell us all out any time he's a mind to; but he knew Harve wouldn't have given a tinker's damn for his bank and all his cattle farms put together; and a lack of appreciation, that way, goes hard with Phelps.

"Old Nimrod, here, thinks Harve drank too much; and this from such as Nimrod and me!"

"Brother Elder says Harve was too free with the old man's money—fell short in filial consideration, maybe. Well, we can all remember the very tone in which brother Elder swore his own father was a liar, in the county court; and we all know that the old man came out of that partnership with his son as bare as a sheared lamb. But maybe I'm getting personal, and I'd better be driving ahead at what I want to say."

The lawyer paused a moment, squared his heavy shoulders, and went on: "Harvey Merrick and I went to school together, back East. We were dead in earnest, and we wanted you all to be proud of us some day. We meant to be great men. Even I, and I haven't lost my sense of humor, gentlemen, I meant to be a great man. I came back here to practice, and I found you didn't in the least want me to be a great man. You wanted me to be a shrewd lawyer— oh, yes! Our veteran here wanted me to get him an increase of pension, because he had dyspepsia; Phelps wanted a new county survey that would put the widow Wilson's little bottom farm inside his south line; Elder wanted to lend money at 5 per cent a month, and get it collected; old Stark here wanted to wheedle old women up in Vermont into investing their annuities in real estate mortgages that are not worth the paper they are written on. Oh, you needed me hard enough, and you'll go on needing me!

"Well, I came back here and became the damned shyster you wanted me to be. You pretend to have some sort of respect for me; and yet you'll stand up and throw mud at Harvey Merrick, whose soul you couldn't dirty and whose hands you couldn't tie. Oh, you're a discriminating lot of Christians! There have been times when the sight of Harvey's name in some Eastern paper has made me hang my head like a whipped dog; and, again, times when I liked to think of him off there in the world, away from all this hog wallow, doing his great work and climbing the big, clean upgrade he'd set for himself.

"And we? Now that we've fought and lied and sweated and stolen, and hated as only the disappointed strugglers in a bitter, dead little Western town know how to do, what have we got to show for it? Harvey Merrick wouldn't have given one sunset over your marshes for all you've got put together, and you know it. It's not for me to say why, in the inscrutable wisdom of God, a genius should ever have been called from this place of hatred and bitter waters; but I want this Boston man to know that the drivel he's been hearing here tonight is the only tribute any truly great man could ever have from such a lot of sick, side-tracked, burnt-dog, land-poor sharks as the here-present financiers of Sand City—upon which town may God have mercy!"

The lawyer thrust out his hand to Steavens as he passed him, caught up his overcoat in the hall, and had left the house before the Grand Army man had had time to lift his ducked head and crane his long neck about at his fellows.

Next day Jim Laird was drunk and unable to attend the funeral services. Steavens called twice at his office, but was compelled to start East without seeing him. He had a presentiment that he would hear from him again, and left his address on the lawyer's table; but if Laird found it, he never acknowledged it. The thing in him that Harvey

Merrick had loved must have gone underground with Harvey Merrick's coffin; for it never spoke again, and Jim got the cold he died of driving across the Colorado mountains to defend one of Phelps's sons, who had got into trouble out there by cutting government timber.

**Questions**

1. What hints does Cather give you early in the story about Jim Laird's relationship with the townspeople?
2. Describe the reactions of Steavens, Merrick's pupil from Boston, during his visit to Sand City. What did Steavens learn about his teacher by accompanying his corpse home? How did this affect his appreciation of Merrick?
3. How did the men of the town assess Harvey Merrick? What was Jim Laird condemning in his attack on Sand City?
4. In what ways is Jim Laird's life used as a contrast to Harvey Merrick's?
5. What function does the final paragraph serve in the story? Do you think this improves or weakens the story?

# 薇拉·凯瑟
# （1873—1947）

美国女作家薇拉·凯瑟，长、短篇小说都有佳作，尤其以描写19世纪末期美国中西部欧洲移民生活的长篇小说著称。评论家对她的作品没有争议，但对她本人的评价意见不统一：有的认为她是女权主义作家，有的认为她是反女权主义的，还有人认为她是同性恋作家。她于1873年出生于弗吉尼亚西部，9岁的时候随家人搬到内布拉斯加州红云镇的一个农场。在那里她接触到大量来自欧洲的移民，他们在大草原地区安家立业。红云镇的人们对她的人生和创作都有深远的影响。22岁的时候，她离家前往东部开始职业创作生涯。1922年她的小说《我们中的一个》获得普利策奖，小说是关于一名来自大草原地区的青年参加第一次世界大战并战死在法国的故事。欧内斯特·海明威对她的获奖颇不以为然。

凯瑟一生创作了12部优秀的长篇小说和一些短篇小说。她最受欢迎的小说有《啊，拓荒者！》（1913）、《云雀之歌》（1915）、《我的安东尼娅》（1918）、《大主教之死》（1927）等。她在作品中塑造了非常坚强的女性形象，她们凭勇气和远见度过生活中的难关。1912年她发表的第一部小说《亚力山大的桥》使她成为美国著名作家。第一次世界大战后，凯瑟对20世纪初物质文明和科学技术飞速发展所带来的精神价值的迷失感到非常沮丧，这时期她的作品主要有《一个迷失的女人》（1923）和《教授的住宅》（1925）。

## 雕塑家的葬礼

短篇小说《雕塑家的葬礼》选自《精灵花园》（1905），体现了作者对于美国中西部小镇复杂的情感。小说以堪萨斯州小镇沙溪为背景，尖锐地刻画了小镇的狭隘、腐败、偏见甚至是暴力。故事中哈维·莫里克为了逃脱这一切去东部追求艺术，成名后魂归故里却遭到人们不公正的评价和耻笑。小说通过他的葬礼审视了美国中西部小镇的价值观。

一群人在堪萨斯州的一个小镇站台上等待已经晚了20分钟的夜班车。地上覆盖着厚厚的积雪，银色的星光下，从镇南那大片白茫茫的牧场延伸出来的峭壁在晴朗的夜空下形成了柔和、褐色的弧线。站台上的男人们来回换着脚，手深插在裤兜里，大衣的扣子都没系，在冷风中缩着肩膀。他们不时地向东南方顺着河岸铺陈过来的铁路张望。他们低声地交谈着，不停地来回走动，好像不太清楚到底到这里来干什么。人群中只有一个人看样子非常清楚他来这儿的使命。他与人群保持着明显的距离，一会儿踱到站台的尽头，一会儿又折回来到车站门口，然后又沿着铁轨走来走去。他的下巴缩在大衣的领子里面，宽厚的肩膀向前倾着，步伐厚重有力。不一会儿，有个头发花白、穿着有些褪色的军大衣的瘦高个儿男人从人群中朝他走来。他毕恭毕敬，脖子向前探着，后背快成了弓形。

"吉姆，我估计这车又得晚很久，"他用尖细的嗓音说道，"也许是因为路上有雪的缘故？"

"我可不清楚，"对方有点儿不高兴，声音从一大堆乱蓬蓬又浓又密的红胡子间发了出来。

瘦高个儿男子把嘴里叼着的羽毛茎做的牙签移到嘴角的另一端，考虑了一下说道："我觉得东部不会有人随车送尸体回来。"

"不知道，"语气比刚才更生硬了。

"糟糕的是他不属于任何地方社团，我有那么一天就举行个社团葬礼，这才符合有点儿身份的人。"瘦高个儿一边说着，一边小心翼翼地把牙签放到背心口袋里。他尖细的嗓音中有讨好的成分。他是镇上北军士兵会举行葬礼时扛旗的人。

对方根本没接他的茬儿就抬脚朝铁轨方向走去。那个瘦高个儿又慢慢地蹭回到有点儿心神不宁的人群中，以同情的口吻说道："还是老样子，吉姆又醉了。"

这时远处的汽笛响了，站台上的人们一阵骚动。好几个瘦高的小子，多大的都有，就像是被雷声惊醒的泥鳅一样，一下子钻了出来。他们有的是从候车室出来的，刚才还在那儿围着红通通的火炉烤火，或者是在细木条候车椅上打盹来着。还有的伸着懒腰从行李车上钻了出来，有的从邮车里溜了下来。两个小子从靠着铁轨边停放的灵车车夫的位置上爬了出来。他们都挺直了肩膀，抬起了头，呆滞的目光里刹那间闪过一丝活力。他们都听到了那一声清冷的、震撼的火车声，众所周知这是对男人的呼唤。它就像号角一样一下子把他们震醒了，这声音也曾无数次地对这个即将魂归故里的人产生过同样的作用，那时他还是个孩子。

火车像红色的火箭一样冲出了东边的沼泽地，沿着曲折的河岸，呼啸而来，震得河两岸守卫着牧场的白杨都在抖动。火车冒出的大团大团的蒸汽升腾在灰暗的天空中，挡住了银河闪烁的星光。不一会儿，车头大灯发出的刺眼的红光就倾泻在了站台前积雪覆盖的铁轨上，在湿漉漉的黑色铁轨上闪着亮光。那个长着乱蓬蓬红胡子的大块头朝着进站的火车快步走了过去，边走边把帽子摘了下来。他身后的人们有点儿迟疑，用目光互相探询着，有点儿窘迫地跟着他朝火车走去。

火车停了下来,车厢的门一开,人群就涌了过去。那个穿着旧军装的人好奇地向前探着头。列车上的邮差出现在门口,身边站着一个穿着长大衣、戴着旅行帽的年轻人。

"莫里克先生的朋友们到了吗?"年轻人问道。

站台上的人群不自然地挪动着。银行家菲利普·菲尔普斯很庄重地回答道:"我们就是来接遗体的,莫里克先生的父亲身体不好,来不了。"

邮差大声喊道:"派个列车员过来,再让报务员来搭把手。"

棺材从一个大破箱子里抬了出来,放到了落满雪的站台上。人群向后闪开,腾出地方来,然后又呈半圆形围了过来,好奇地看着蒙棺材的黑布上斜放的那片棕榈叶。没人吱声,行李员站在行李车前,等着人们拿箱子。火车头呼呼地喷着汽,司炉工在车轮间进进出出,手里拿着黄色火把式的灯和长长的油壶,弄得主轴箱发出很大的响声。随遗体前来的波士顿的年轻人,是这个刚刚逝去的雕塑家的学生。他无助地向人群看了看,然后转向那个银行家,他像是这个黑压压的人群中唯一一个看起来有所不同、可以说话的人,其他的人都勾着个身子,显得很局促。

年轻人以拿不准的口吻问道:"莫里克先生的兄弟一个都没来吗?"

那个长着红胡子的人第一次走到人群中间,搭话道:"他们还没来,他们家人住得很分散。遗体直接运到他家就行了。"他猫下腰,抓住了棺材的一个把手。

殡仪工把灵车的门咣当一声关上,正要坐到车夫的位置上,就听马车行的人对他喊道:"汤姆逊,走那条远的山路吧,这样马能省点劲儿。"

红胡子叫莱尔德,是个律师,转过身来对那个外人说:"我们原先不知道有人送遗体过来。这条道可不短,你最好坐到那个车上去。"他指着一辆单座的旧马车说。但那个年轻人挺生硬地回答道:"谢谢,我宁愿跟着灵车。"年轻人对赶灵车的殡仪工说:"你要是没意见的话,我跟你一道吧。"

他们爬上车,在星光下顺着绵延的白色山路向小镇驶去。静寂的山村里,摇曳的灯光从低矮、覆盖着积雪的屋顶下透出来。远处是一望无际的原野,空灵、宁静,就像头顶的天空一样无垠,到处是一种触手可及的白色的静谧。

在一个光秃秃、破旧不堪的木房子前,灵车倒着停在一个木头的过道上。先前在站台上出现的数不出个数、说不清是谁的人们又都聚在大门口了。房子前院的水洼结了冰,从过道到屋门口铺了几块变了形的木头板子,凑合着给人们当桥踏脚。大门只有一个合叶把着,人们费了好大劲才把它敲开。

棺材从灵车上拖下来时发出了刺耳的声音,紧跟着房子里传出哭喊声。房子的前门被猛地拽开,一个没戴帽子的、又粗又壮的妇人冲到了雪地里。她扑在棺材上，哭喊着："孩子，我的孩子。你怎么这样回到妈妈身边了！"

史蒂文斯突然感到很不舒服,说不出来的感受,他转过身去，闭上眼睛。可就在这时，从房子里又冲出来一个女人。她穿一身黑衣，也是高高的个子，但扁扁平平，瘦骨嶙峋。她把住莫里克夫人的肩膀，尖声叫道："好了，好了，妈妈，你别这样了！"但当她转过身来对着银行家说话时，语调却变得谦恭而庄重，"灵堂准备好了，菲尔普斯先生。"

人们通过木板铺成的小窄道把棺材往屋子里抬，那个殡仪工手里拿着放棺材的支架跑在前面。他们把棺材抬到一间很大、没有暖气的房间。房子里潮乎乎的，散发着一种久不住人和家具油漆的味道。棺材放在一个吊灯的下面，吊灯上装饰着叮当作响的玻璃柱。棺材放在"罗杰斯组雕"前，组雕表现的是美国早期拓荒者约翰·奥尔丁向普瑞希拉求爱的情形。雕像上装饰着卵叶天门冬做的花环。亨利·史蒂文斯环顾着四周，忽然有一种强烈的感受，他觉得自己一定是搞错了，一定是来错地方了。他看着翠绿色的布鲁塞尔地毯，鼓囊囊的长毛绒靠垫，在手绘的瓷器、窗格、花瓶中寻找可以辨认的标记，能让人们想起曾经是属于哈维·莫里克的标记。直到他从钢琴上方悬挂的一幅铅笔画上认出那个穿着苏格兰式短裙、头发有卷的小男孩是他的朋友时，他才能够接受这群人靠近他朋友的棺木。

老妇人边哭边说道："汤姆逊先生，把棺材盖打开，让我见他一面。"史蒂文斯这时用有点儿害怕、几乎乞求的目光看着老妇人的脸。她的脸在一大团浓密、油黑发亮的头发下显得红肿难看。他脸红了，垂下了目光，然后像是不相信似的，又盯着她的脸看。她的脸有一种震慑的力量，甚至是一种近乎残忍的俊朗，但这种俊朗却被一种强硬的表情所破坏，从而留下了深深的痕迹。比悲伤更强烈的情绪使她的脸看起来更红润、更粗糙，似乎悲伤根本就不能使它变得柔和。她的长鼻梁、大鼻头使她的鼻子看起来很大，鼻子两侧都有一条很深的纹路。她那粗黑的眉毛几乎连在了一起，她的牙齿又大又方，长得稀稀拉拉，看起来能撕善咬的。她的气势震住了整个房间，男人们都像急流中的小树丫一样变得渺小、无足轻重了。就连史蒂文斯都觉得自己被拽到旋涡中去了似的。

她那高高瘦瘦穿着绉绸裙子的女儿，头发上别着吊丧的梳子。这梳子使她本来就很长的脸显得更长了。她直挺挺地坐在沙发上，骨结粗大的两只手交叉放在大腿上。她的嘴角和目光都向下耷拉着，严肃地等着打开棺材盖。门口站着一个黑白混血的女人，很明显是这家的女佣，她怯怯地站在那儿，憔悴的脸既难过又温和。她不出声地哭着，撩起围裙角擦着眼睛，忍不住偶尔发出一声长长的、颤抖的啜泣。史蒂文斯走过去站在她的身旁。

楼梯上传来无力的脚步声，一位个子很高，但虚弱不堪的老人不知所措地走了进来。他一身烟味，一头乱蓬蓬未经梳理的白发，胡子邋遢，嘴边留有烟渍。他慢慢地走向棺材然后站住，两手不停地搓着一个蓝色的布手绢。妻子肆无忌惮的悲痛哭喊似乎使他伤心欲绝，局促不安，以至于他对周围的一切都没了感觉。

老人伸出一只颤抖的手，很笨拙地拍着妻子的胳膊肘，安慰道："好了，好了，安妮，亲爱的，别这么难过了！"他的声音怯怯的，有点儿打战。他的妻子哭着转过身来，一下子扑在他的肩膀上，使他一个趔趄。他甚至都没往棺材里扫一眼，只是继续用那种呆滞的、害怕的、哀求的目光盯着她看，就像是盯着鞭子的小狗一样。他凹陷的双颊由于痛苦和羞愧渐渐地发烧变红了。他的妻子撇下他走出房间，女儿一声不吭地跟着她快步出去了。女佣悄悄地走到棺木前，俯下身看了一会儿，然后就回到厨房去了。房间里现在只剩下史蒂文斯、律师和死者的父亲。老人浑身颤抖地低头看着儿子的遗容。雕塑家不凡的头颅停放在那儿，显得比活着时还要高贵。黑发滑落到他宽阔的前额上，使脸显得更长，但在他的脸上怎么也找不到死者应有的安详。他眉头紧锁，在鹰钩鼻了上方形成了两条深纹，下巴倔强地抬着。活着时似乎曾如此艰辛而痛苦，以至于死亡也没能使他解脱，也没能使他的脸完全安详地舒展开来，好像他仍然在守卫着宝贵、神圣的东西，以防有人在他死后还要把它们夺走。

老人的嘴唇在脏兮兮的胡子下嚅动着。他胆怯又满怀敬意地对律师说："菲尔普斯和其他人会回来帮着料理后事吧？谢谢您，吉姆，谢谢。"他把儿子前额上的头发拢回原处，说道："吉姆，这可真是个好孩子，一直是个好孩子。他就像婴儿般温和，是他们几个孩子中最好的，只是我们从来就没人理解过他。"泪珠顺着他的胡子流了下来，落在了雕塑家的大衣上。

"马丁，马丁！我说马丁，你过来！"妻子在楼梯顶上叫喊道。"来了，安妮，我来了！"他吓了一跳，转身要走，但又犹豫了一下，好像很痛苦地做着决定。然后他回过身来，伸出手轻轻地拍了拍儿子的头发，这才跌跌撞撞地离开了房间。

"可怜的老人，我还以为他没有眼泪了呢！好像好久以前他的眼泪就流干了。这把年纪，什么都不会让他太伤心了。"律师说道。

他语气中某种异样的东西使史蒂文斯抬起头来向他望去。死者的母亲在的时候，史蒂文斯几乎没法注意到别人。但现在，一看见吉姆·莱尔德红润的脸膛、充血的眼睛，他突然意识到在吉姆身上找到了他以前在这儿没有发现的东西——感情、理解。人所具有的品质，即便是在这样一个闭塞的地方，它们仍然存在着。他曾为这些品质在这儿的缺失感到多么痛苦啊！

吉姆脸色红润，就像他的胡子一样。他的脸有点儿浮肿，线条不是很明显，一看就是长期喝酒的表现。他蓝色的眼睛发出愤怒、炽热的光芒。他的脸有点儿扭曲，看得出他在竭力控制自己的情绪。他泄愤似地揪着自己的胡子。史蒂文斯坐在窗边，看着他走过去把亮得有点儿晃眼的吊灯调暗，很生气地把着那叮当的吊坠让它们别响，然后就背着手，盯着雕塑师的脸看。史蒂文斯禁不住感到困惑：雕塑师和律师之间，就像精美的瓷器和陶匠手里的黑泥巴一样，他们到底有什么联系呢？

这时厨房里传来了咆哮声。餐厅门开了，人们搞清楚了是怎么回事。死者的母亲正在破口大骂家里的女佣，因为她忘了调制给守灵的人们吃的鸡肉沙拉的调料。史蒂文斯就从来没听谁这样骂过人，就像是受了多大的委屈，她语调激动，抑扬顿挫。她的辱骂像刀子一样尖刻、残忍，这一出就和她20分钟前哭儿子时一样狂野和肆无忌惮。律师由于厌恶打了个冷战，他走过去关上了餐厅通向厨房的门。

"可怜的萝茜又在遭罪了。"他关完门往回走的时候说，"好几年前莫里克这家人把她从贫民院领出来。要不是她太过忠心耿耿，他们家的事都能把你说得浑身冰凉。萝茜就是刚才站在这儿的那个混血女人，用围裙擦眼泪的那个。这家的老妇人太歹毒，从来没见过她这样的人，表面上比谁都虔诚，骨子里比谁都残忍。哈维在家的时候，他妈妈让他过的简直不是人的日子。他总觉得那么羞愧，为这样的生活，这样的妈妈。我一直没弄明白，这样的家庭怎么会有他这样的好孩子。"

史蒂文斯慢慢说道："他可真了不起，了不起，但直到今天晚上我才真正明白他有多么了不起。"

"这才是真正的奇特之处，这么好的人竟出自这样的粪堆里！"律师嚷嚷着，把手一挥，似乎他所指的不仅仅是他们所待的屋子。

"我得呼吸点儿新鲜空气。这个房间太小了，我觉得有点儿透不过气来。"史蒂文斯嘟囔着去拉一扇窗户。窗框都卡着，连点儿缝都没翘。他沮丧地回去坐下，解开了领口。律师走了过来，用他那红通通的拳头朝窗框使劲一敲，窗户活动了，他把窗户开了个几英寸的缝。史蒂文斯对他表示感谢。但过去的半个小时里史蒂文斯觉得嗓子眼里越来越恶心，这使他只有一个愿望，非常迫切的愿望：带着哈维·莫里克还没被毁坏的东西赶紧逃离这个地方。哦，他现在终于能真正理解老师常挂在嘴角的那种安详而苦涩的微笑了。

有一次莫里克从家探亲回来，带来一件非常奇特、让人联想丰富的浅浮雕作品，一位瘦削、枯槁的老妇人在缝补别在膝盖上的什么东西。她的身边站着一个厚嘴唇、浑身闲不住的小淘气，他穿着单背带裤，急切地拽着她的裙子让她看刚抓到的一只蝴蝶。作品对老人瘦削、疲惫的脸进行的柔和、细腻的刻画给史蒂文斯留下了深刻的印象，他还问莫里克那上面的是不是他的母亲。他记得当时莫里克的脸变得通红通红的。

律师坐在棺材旁边的一把摇椅上，闭着眼，头向后仰着。史蒂文斯认真地打量着他，不知道他下巴的轮廓在哪。他搞不懂这个应该是棱角非常分明的人为什么非要把这一切掩藏在乱蓬蓬的胡子下。突然就像知道年轻的雕塑师在盯着他一样，他睁开了眼睛。

"他不爱吱声，是吧？"律师很突兀地问道，"小的时候他腼腆得要命。"

"他还真是少言寡语的，就是你说的不爱吱声，"史蒂文斯回答道。"即使他非常喜欢别人，也会给人一种冷冰冰的印象。他不喜欢流露强烈的感情，他总是在沉思，不太自信。当然，这不包括他的作品。对雕塑他自信、精通。他非常不信任男人，对女人就更不信任了，但他对任何人都没有恶意。他确信存在着完美，但又不敢去追求。"

"一朝被蛇咬，十年怕井绳啊，"律师冷冷地说道，说完就又闭上了眼睛。

史蒂文斯任思想驰骋，想勾画出他曾经历了怎样不幸的少年时代。所有这粗鄙、令人难忍的丑恶都曾是他人生的一部分，而他的大脑却是一个取之不尽的艺术画廊，那里装满对美丽的体验，他的体验是那么细腻、敏感，哪怕只是阳光下一片翩跹而落的白杨叶照在墙上的影子也会铭刻在他的大脑里，永远不会褪色。如果谁的手指确实具有艺术的魔力，那一定就是莫里克了。他把经手的任何作品都诠释出它最神圣的秘密；他把它从艺术的魔力中解脱出来，使它还原为最原始的美好。他就像传说中的阿拉伯王子要挣脱魔女的魔法以获得另一种魔力一样。他所接触的任何东西，都记录了他美好的体验，就像是一种超凡脱俗的签名：可能是他独有的一种味道，一个声音，一种色彩。

史蒂文斯现在终于明白老师人生真正的悲剧是什么了。不是许多人猜测的失恋或贪杯，而是比这两样都降临得早而且伤他更深的一种打击：是羞辱感，不是他的过错，但却是他无法摆脱的羞辱感。这种羞辱感从他少年时代起就在他的内心根深蒂固。他无法摆脱，边疆战争早已成过去，从戎已不可能。史蒂文斯似乎能听到那个少年想摆脱这一切的挣扎：被丢到一个陌生、丑陋、肮脏的荒漠上，却渴望所有纯洁、悠久、具有丰富传统美德的东西。

11点的时候那个瘦高个子、身穿黑衣的女人走了进来，她说守灵的人就要到了，请他们"到餐厅就座"。史蒂文斯起身要走，律师平淡地说道："你去吧，这对你无疑是一次难得的体验。今晚我是没心思搭理那些人，我跟他们打交道都20年了。"

史蒂文斯关门的时候向后瞥了一眼律师，在昏暗的灯光下，他手托着下巴坐在棺材旁边。

原先在车厢门口模糊不清的那群人都踱进了餐厅。餐厅的煤油灯下，他们四处找地方安置自己。牧师在一张小桌前就座，把《圣经》放在桌子上。他面色苍白，看起来瘦弱不堪，一头白发，却长着金黄色的络腮胡子。那个穿军装的人坐在火炉后面，把椅背舒服地靠在墙上，手在马甲兜里摸着那个羽茎做的牙签。两个银行家，菲尔普斯和艾尔德，远远地坐在餐桌后面的一个角落里，在谈论新颁布的高利贷法和它可能会对动产抵押贷款产生的影响。那个满脸堆着虚伪微笑的房地产经纪人很快就凑到他们身边去。煤炭木材经销商和牧场主面对面坐在火炉的两边，把脚都搭在炉子边上。史蒂文斯从兜里拿出一本书读了起来，周围的人谈论着各种与当地有关的话题，房间里慢慢地静了下来。当人们意识到莫里克一家都睡了的时候，穿军装的人正了正身子，伸了伸腿，把脚搭在椅子腿的横梁上。

他用尖细的嗓音小声问："菲尔普斯，他该留了遗嘱吧？"

银行家笑了起来，让人觉得非常刺耳。他用柄上镶有珍珠的小刀磨起指甲来，反问道："有这个必要吗？"

穿军装的人闲不住，调整了坐姿，使膝盖离下巴更近了。"怎么？老头儿说哈维混得可不赖，"他尖声尖气地说。

另一个银行家接茬道："我倒觉得老头儿的意思是，哈维再也没让他拿牧场抵押，供自己上学。"

穿军装的人嗤嗤地笑着说："我还真就想不起哈维什么时候不是在念书了。"

听到这儿大家都小声笑了起来。这时牧师拿出手帕，很响地擤着鼻涕。银行家菲尔普斯啪的一声把小刀合上，字斟句酌很权威地说："糟糕的是老头儿的儿子们都不争气，心也不齐。老头儿投在哈维念书上的钱都够开十多个奶牛场的了，再说了就是不开奶牛场，也可以投资到沙溪那儿去嘛。要是哈维不去念书，在家一起过日子，用下边的农场养牲畜，他们家也早就过好了。结果呢，老头儿只能一切都指望佃户打理，到头来处处挨宰。"

牧场主插话道："哈维可养不了牲畜，他天生不是那块料。你们还记得他买萨德家骡子那次不？镇上的人都知道那些骡子是18年前萨德的老丈人给他老婆的陪嫁，当时就是成年的骡子，哈维却当八岁的牲口给买了回来。"

这伙人小声笑了起来，那个穿军装的人像小孩子似的高兴得直搓膝盖。

"哈维是啥活也拿不起来啊，再说他也确实不爱干活，"那个经营煤炭木材的人接话道。"我还记得他上次回家来的时候呢。他要走的那天，老头儿去马棚里帮着伙计套车去了，好送哈维到火车站去，卡尔·穆兹正在那儿修篱笆。哈维站在台阶上，像个娘们儿似的朝着卡尔喊：'卡尔·穆兹，卡尔·穆兹，过来帮我捆下箱子。'"

穿军装的人高兴地应和道:"那是你看到的哈维,我还听过他嗷嗷哭呢。那时他都是穿长衣长裤的大小伙子了,他妈妈拿着牛皮鞭子在牲口棚里抽他。他妈揍他的原因是,放牧回来的路上他看不住,牛拐到玉米地里去啃青,都撑病了。我的一头牛就这样死在他手上,那可是纯种的泽西牛,是我最好的一头牛。后来老头儿出钱赔给我。那牛拐到地里去的时候,人家哈维正在那儿看草原落日呢。"

菲尔普斯捋着山羊胡子,慢条斯理地下结论道:"老头儿错就错在送孩子去东部念书,就是在东部他才满脑子胡思乱想。别人不说,哈维最需要的是找个一流的堪萨斯商业学校学点儿有用的东西。"

史蒂文斯觉得眼前的字都游动起来。难道这些人真的就不明白,难道他们对棺木上的棕榈叶真的无动于衷吗?他们的小镇如果不是作为哈维·莫里克的故乡常被世人提到的话,它将永远只是邮政指南上一个默默无闻的地名。史蒂文斯还记得老师临终那天对他说的话,在双肺感染失去了任何治愈的希望后,他请求史蒂文斯送他的遗体回乡。他虚弱地笑着说:"当外面的世界一直在运转、在行动、在进步,我的家乡实在不是理想的安息之所,但人总是有落叶归根的想法。到时候镇上的人们会到我家来看我一眼,等他们把所有难听的话都说完了,我就不用害怕上帝的审判了。"

牧场主继续着话题:"他才40岁就死了,对莫里克家的人来说可是不多见,他们家的人可都挺能活的。八成是威士忌要了他的命。"

"他妈妈那边的人没有长寿的,再说哈维从小就不是很壮实。"牧师很温和地替他辩解道。他本来还想对人们多说点儿什么,他是哈维主日学校的老师,他一直喜欢这个小男孩。但他又觉得自己没资格多说什么,毕竟自己的儿子们都很不争气。就在不到一年前,他的一个儿子在黑山一带的赌场被人开枪打死了,尸体也是被火车运回来的。

"不管咋说大家都知道哈维可是好酒的人,先是喝红葡萄酒,后来就啥颜色的都喝了,酒把他的脑子喝不正常了,"牧场主继续说教道。

这时通往客厅的门咯吱一声响了,屋里的人都吓了一跳。发现只是吉姆·莱尔德一个人进来的时候,他们才都长舒了一口气。当穿军装的人看见他布满血丝的蓝眼睛里喷射着怒火的时候,他赶紧把头埋了下来。人们都怕他,他是个酒鬼,但却能随意曲解法律满足客户的需要。就这一点整个堪萨斯州西部的人没人能做到,尽管许多人尝试过。律师随手把门带上,身子靠在门上,双臂交叉,头歪向一边。每次他在法庭里摆出这副架势的时候,人们都会竖起耳朵,因为他们知道紧跟着的就是一场尖酸刻薄的讽刺了。

他以一种非常平稳、不带任何感情色彩的语调说道:"我跟在座的各位经过不少这样的场合了，都是在给那些土生土长的年轻人守灵的时候。如果我记得不错的话，你们评论他们的时候，好像没有哪一次对哪一个人满意过。这到底是哪儿不对劲呢？为什么我们沙溪镇的好青年就跟百万富翁一样寥若晨星呢？对外人来说，他肯定觉得我们这个日益发展的小镇有问题。卢宾·塞叶是我们这儿培养的最聪明的律师吧？他大学毕业刚回到这里来的时候那么诚实守信，可为什么后来却开始酗酒，伪造支票，最后开枪自杀了？为什么比尔·莫里特的儿子会在奥马哈的一个酒吧里饮酒至死？为什么在场的托马斯先生，他的儿子会在一个赌场里中枪身亡？为什么年纪轻轻的亚当斯会纵火烧自己的厂子骗保，最后锒铛入狱？"

律师说到这儿停顿了一下。他把交叉的手臂放下，一只紧攥的拳头轻轻放在桌子上。"现在我来告诉你们答案。他们还是穿灯笼裤的孩子的时候你们就在他们的耳朵里灌输金钱和欺诈的概念，除了这个，再没别的；因为你们一直对他们鸡蛋里挑骨头，就像你们现在对哈维吹毛求疵一样。你们把这里的菲尔普斯和艾尔德作为他们的榜样，就像我们的父辈崇仰乔治·华盛顿和约翰·亚当斯一样。可是这些年轻人对让他们经营的行当没有任何经验，聚富敛财方面他们怎么能赶得上菲尔普斯和艾尔德这样的行家里手？你们想让他们也成为成功的无赖，可他们却成了没挣到钱的无赖。这就是两者的区别了。唯一一个在这介于荒蛮与文明之间的小镇长大的男孩没有失败，可你们却憎恨他的成功甚至超过了憎恨那些孩子们的失败。上帝，我的上帝，看你们有多恨他！在座的菲尔普斯总爱说只要他愿意他可以在任何时候把我们所有的人买卖掉。可他知道哈维对他的银行和他所有的奶牛场根本就不屑一顾，对他的财富缺少欣赏，这种蔑视，让菲尔普斯觉得很难堪。

"在座的老宁录认为哈维酗酒过度，我都不敢相信这话竟出于像宁录和我这样的酒鬼！"

"老兄艾尔德说哈维花他爸爸的钱太多，也许他觉得这是哈维不孝顺的表现。可大家都还记得在郡法庭上艾尔德诅咒他父亲是个骗子的语气吧。大家一定都还记得他爸爸跟他和伙经营的结果是两手空空，穷得比剪过毛的羊都干净。可能我这是涉及人家私事，但我还是想把心里的话说完。"

律师停顿了一下，正了正厚实的肩膀，继续说："当年我和哈维·莫里克一起去东部求学，我们都下定决心，想有一天能成为你们的骄傲。我们当时真的想做出不凡的事业，就是我，先生们，也曾想成就点儿什么来着，我现在这样说是调侃了，可当初不是。我回到家乡来做律师，可我发现你们压根就不想让我成就什么不凡的事业。你们只想让我成为一个奸诈的律师，你们只想让我这样。在座的老兵想让我为他争取更多的抚恤金，理由是他吃多了消化不良；菲尔普斯想争取让郡政府重新丈量土地，目的是把寡妇威尔逊家河下游的小农场划进他家的南地界线；艾尔德想以5%的月息放高利贷，并能按时清贷；在座的老斯达克想蒙骗佛特蒙州的老妇人们用养老金抵押贷款购买房产，而他所卖的房产连签合同的纸都不值。咳，你们总需要我做这些事，你们以后还会需要我这样做。

"我回到这儿来，变成了现在这样没有任何道德感的讼棍，这就是你们希望我成为的人物。你们都装着对我很尊敬的样子；可你们竟一起来败坏哈维·莫里克的名声，你们知道他的灵魂是你们不能亵渎的，而他也不会受你们的摆布。你们可真是一群有眼力、懂得厚此薄彼的基督徒啊！多少次看到哈维的名字出现在东部的报纸上时，我都羞愧得像个被鞭子抽打了的狗似的垂下头来，但有时一想到他能远离这个蠢猪生活的肮脏的地方而到外面去发展、去见世面、去从事自己伟大的事业，攀登为自己树立的崇高、干净的目标，我就非常高兴。"

"而我们呢？我们在这儿钩心斗角、谎话连篇、汗流浃背、狗盗鼠窃，对人们充满着憎恨，也只有生活在这种恶毒、死气沉沉的西部小镇上对生活没有了幻想的我们才会这样做。我们有什么可引以为豪展示给外人看的呢？你们知道，即使把你们所有的财富划拉到一块儿都换不来哈维·莫里克眼中湿地上的一抹夕阳，你们有什么可炫耀的？我想不明白，以上帝深奥的智慧，怎么会让这样一个天才出生在这样一个充满着仇恨、恶毒的杂乱之地；但我真心希望这个来自波士顿的人明白，他刚才在这听到的信口雌黄是任何伟大的灵魂能从你们这帮人嘴里得到的唯一的颂词。在场的沙溪镇的金融家们，你们是如此令人恶心，说话不着边际，像癞皮狗似的，你们是对土地贪得无厌的骗子，真愿上帝宽恕沙溪镇。"

律师经过史蒂文斯身边的时候，很用力地向他伸出了手，然后到道里一把拿过自己的大衣就离开了。还没等穿旧军装的人抬起他那耷拉的脑袋伸直脖子看看周围人的反应，律师已经离开了。

第二天律师喝醉了，没能出席葬礼。史蒂文斯两次去办公室找他，但都没见着，只好动身回东部了。他预感律师会跟他联系，于是在办公桌上留下了自己的地址。莱尔德是否看到这个地址无从知晓，也许在他身上哈维·莫里克所喜爱的品质都随着他入土为安而被深埋安葬了。这些品质再无人提及。后来吉姆为了赶去为菲尔普斯一个因盗伐政府木材惹上官司的儿子做辩护，在他开车行驶在科罗拉多山脉中的时候得了感冒，之后他就一病不起，死了。

# Clarence Day
# (1874—1935)

Born in New York City, Clarence Shepard Day, Jr. graduated from Yale University in 1896. The following year, he joined the New York Stock Exchange, and became a partner in his father's Wall Street brokerage firm. Day enlisted in the Navy in 1898, but developed crippling arthritis and spent the remainder of his life as a semi-invalid. Day's most famous work is the autobiographical *Life with Father* (1935), which detailed humorous episodes in his family's life, centering on his domineering father, during the 1890s in New York City. Day died in New York City shortly after finishing *Life with Father*, without ever getting to experience its success on Broadway or in Hollywood.

Scenes from *Life with Father*, along with its 1932 prequel, *God and My Father*, and its posthumous 1937 sequel, *Life with Mother*, were the basis for a 1939 play by Howard Lindsay and Russell Crouse, which became one of Broadway's longest-running, non-musical hits. A survey of Day's early short stories and magazine columns reveals that "he was fascinated by the changing roles of men and women in American society as Victorian conceptions of marriage, family, and domestic order unraveled in the first decades of the twentieth century." He was also author of *In the Green Mountain Country* (1934), *Scenes from the Mesozoic and Other Drawings* (1935), *After All* (1936), *The World of Books* (1938), and *Father and I* (1940).

## Father Wakes Up the Village

*"Father Wakes Up the Village," a short story from* **Life with Father,** *fascinates readers with diversified cultural and educational backgrounds for decades. The domineering image of a stubborn but lovable father evolves in contrast against those inefficient, slack small village tradesmen, and there cultivated in the boy's mind is an undoubted admiration for his father.*

One of the most disgraceful features of life in the country, Father often declared, was the general inefficiency and slackness of small village tradesmen. He said he had originally supposed that such men were interested in business, and that was why they had opened their shops and sunk capital in them, but no, they never used them for anything but gossip and sleep. They took no interest in civilized ways. Hadn't heard of them, probably. He said that of course if he were camping out on the veldt or the tundra he would expect few conveniences in the neighborhood and would do his best to forego them, but why should he be confronted with the wilds twenty miles from New York?

Usually, when Father talked this way, he was thinking of ice. He strongly objected to spending even one day of his life without a glass of cold water beside his plate at every meal. There was never any difficulty about this in our home in the city. A great silver ice-water pitcher stood on the sideboard all day, and when Father was home its outer surface was frosted with cold. When he had gone to the office, the ice was allowed to melt sometimes, and the water got warmish, but never in the evening, or on Sundays, when Father might want some. He said he liked water, he told us it was one of Nature's best gifts, but he said that like all her gifts it was unfit for human consumption unless served in a suitable manner. And the only right way to serve water was icy cold.

It was still more important that each kind of wine should be served at whatever the right temperature was for it. And kept at it, too. No civilized man would take dinner without wine, Father said, and no man who knew the first thing about it would keep his wine in hot cellars. Mother thought this was a mere whim of Father's. She said he was fussy. How about people who lived in apartments, she asked him, who didn't have cellars? Father replied that civilized persons didn't live in apartments.

One of the first summers that Father ever spent in the country, he rented a furnished house in Irvington on the Hudson, not far from New York. It had a garden, a stable, and one or two acres of woods, and Father arranged to camp out there with many misgivings. He took a train for New York every morning at eight-ten, after breakfast, and he got back between five and six, bringing anything special we might need along with him, such as a basket of peaches from the city, or a fresh package of his own private coffee.

Things went well until one day in August the ice-man didn't come. It was hot, he and his horses were tired, and he hated to come to us anyhow because the house we had rented was perched up on top of a hill. He said afterward that on this particular day he had not liked the idea of making his horses drag the big ice-wagon up that sharp and steep road to sell fifty cents' worth of ice. Besides, all his ice was gone anyhow—the heat had melted it on him. He had four or five other good reasons. So he didn't come.

Father was in town. The rest of us waited in astonishment, wondering what could be the matter. We were so used to the regularity and punctilio of life in the city that it seemed unbelievable to us that the ice-man would fail to appear. We discussed it at lunch. Mother said that the minute he arrived she would have to give him a talking to. After lunch had been over an hour and he still hadn't come, she got so worried about what Father would say that she decided to send to the village.

There was no telephone, of course. There were no motors. She would have liked to spare the horse if she could, for he had been worked hard that week. But as this was a crisis, she sent for Morgan, the coachman, and told him to bring up the dog-cart.

The big English dog-cart arrived. Two of us boys and the coachman drove off. The sun beat down on our heads. Where the heavy harness was rubbing on Brownie's coat, he broke out into a thick, whitish lather. Morgan was sullen. When we boys were along he couldn't take off his stiff black hat or unbutton his thick, padded coat. Worse still, from his point of view, he couldn't stop at a bar for a drink. That was why Mother had sent us along with him, of course, and he knew it.

We arrived at the little town after a while and I went into the Coal & Ice Office. A wiry-looking old clerk was dozing in a corner, his chair tilted back and his chin resting on his dingy shirt-front. I woke this clerk up. I told him about the crisis at our house.

He listened unwillingly, and when I had finished he said it was a very hot day.

I waited. He spat. He said he didn't see what he could do, because the ice-house was locked.

I explained earnestly that this was the Day family and that something must be done right away.

He hunted around his desk a few minutes, found his chewing tobacco, and said, "Well, sonny, I'll see what I can do about it."

I thanked him very much, as that seemed to me to settle the matter. I went back to the dog-cart. Brownie's check-rein had been unhooked, and he stood with his head hanging down. He looked sloppy. It wouldn't have been so bad with a buggy, but a slumpy horse in a dog-cart can look pretty awful. Also, Morgan was gone. He reappeared soon, coming out of a side door down the street, buttoning up his coat, but with his hat tilted back. He looked worse than the horse.

We checked up the weary animal's head again and drove slowly home. A hot little breeze in our rear moved our dust along with us. At the foot of the hill, we boys got out, to spare Brownie our extra weight. We unhooked his check-rein again. He dragged the heavy cart up.

Mother was sitting out on the piazza. I said the ice would come soon now. We waited.

It was a long afternoon.

At five o'clock, Brownie was hitched up again. The coachman and I drove back to the village. We had to meet Father's train. We also had to break the bad news to him that he would have no ice-water for dinner, and that there didn't seem to be any way to chill his Rhine wine.

The village was as sleepy as ever, but when Father arrived and learned what the situation was, he said it would have to wake up. He told me that he had had a long, trying day at the office, the city was hotter than the Desert of Sahara, and he was completely worn out, but that if any ice-man imagined for a moment he could behave in that manner, he, Father, would take his damned head off. He strode into the Coal & Ice Office.

When he came out, he had the clerk with him, and the clerk had put on his hat and was vainly trying to calm Father down. He was promising that he himself would come with the ice-wagon if the driver had left, and deliver all the ice we could use, and he'd be there inside an hour.

Father said, "Inside of an hour be hanged, you'll have to come quicker than that."

The clerk got rebellious. He pointed out that he'd have to go to the stables and hitch up the horses himself, and then get someone to help him hoist a block of ice out of the ice-house. He said it was 'most time for his supper and he wasn't used to such work. He was only doing it as a favor to Father. He was just being neighborly.

Father said he'd have to be neighborly in a hurry, because he wouldn't stand it, and he didn't know what the devil the ice company meant by such actions.

The clerk said it wasn't his fault, was it? It was the driver's.

This was poor tactics, of course, because it wound Father up again. He wasn't interested in whose fault it was, he said. It was everybody's. What he wanted was ice and plenty of it, and he wanted it in time for his dinner. A small crowd which had collected by this time listened admiringly as Father shook his finger at the clerk and said he dined at six-thirty.

The clerk went loping off toward the stables to hitch up the big horses. Father waited till he'd turned the corner.

Followed by the crowd, Father marched to the butcher's.

After nearly a quarter of an hour, the butcher and his assistant came out, unwillingly carrying what seemed to be a coffin, wrapped in a black mackintosh. It was a huge cake of ice.

Father got in, in front, sat on the box seat beside me, and took up the reins. We drove off. The coachman was on the rear seat, sitting back-to-back to us, keeping the ice from sliding out with the calves of his legs. Father went a few doors up the street to a little house-furnishings shop and got out again.

I went in the shop with him this time. I didn't want to miss any further scenes of this performance. Father began proceedings by demanding to see all the man's ice-boxes. There were only a few. Father selected the largest he had. Then, when the sale seemed arranged, and when the proprietor was smiling broadly with pleasure at this sudden windfall, Father said he was buying that refrigerator only on two conditions.

The first was that it had to be delivered at his home before dinner. Yes, now. Right away. The shopkeeper explained over and over that this was impossible, but that he'd have it up the next morning, sure, Father said no, he didn't want it the next morning, he had to have it at once. He added that he dined at six-thirty, and that there was no time to waste.

The shopkeeper gave in.

The second condition, which was then put to him firmly, was staggering. Father announced that that ice-box must be delivered to him full of ice.

The man said he was not in the ice business.

Father said, "Very well then. I don't want it."

The man said obstinately that it was an excellent ice-box.

Father made a short speech. It was the one we had heard so often at home about the slackness of village tradesmen, and he put such strong emotion and scorn into it that his voice rang through the shop. He closed it by saying, "An ice-box is of no use to a man without ice, and if you haven't the enterprise, the gumption, to sell your damned goods to a customer who wants them delivered in condition to use, you had better shut up your shop and be done with it. Not in the ice business, eh? You aren't in business at all!" He strode out.

The dealer came to the door just as Father was getting into the dog-cart and called out anxiously, "All right, Mr. Day, I'll get that refrigerator filled for you and send it up right away."

Father drove quickly home. A thunderstorm seemed to be brewing and this had waked Brownie up, or else Father was putting some of his own supply of energy into him. The poor old boy probably needed it as again he climbed the steep hill. I got out at the foot, and as I walked along behind I saw that Morgan was looking kind of desperate trying to sit in the correct position with his arms folded while he held in the ice with his legs. The big cake was continually slipping and sliding around under the seat and doing its best to plunge out. It had bumped against his calves all the way home. They must have got good and cold.

When the dog-cart drew up at our door, Father remained seated a moment while Morgan, the waitress, and I pulled and pushed at the ice. The mackintosh had come off it by this time. We dumped it out on the grass. A little later, after Morgan had unharnessed and hurriedly rubbed down the horse, he ran back to help us boys break the cake up, push the chunks around to the back door, and cram them into the ice-box while Father was dressing for dinner.

Mother had calmed down by this time. The Rhine wine was cooling. "Don't get it too cold," Father Called.

Then the ice-man arrived.

The old clerk was with him, like a warden in charge of a prisoner. Mother stepped out to meet them, and at once gave the ice-man the scolding that had been waiting for him all day.

The clerk asked how much ice we wanted. Mother said we didn't want any now. Mr. Day had brought home some, and we had no room for more in the ice-box. The ice-man looked at the clerk. The clerk tried to speak, but no words came.

Father put his head out of the window. "Take a hundred pounds, Vinnie," he said. "There's another box coming."

A hundred-pound block was brought into the house and heaved into the washtub. The waitress put the mackintosh over it. The ice-wagon left.

Just as we all sat down to dinner, the new ice-box arrived, full.

Mother was provoked. She said "Really, Clare!" crossly. "Now what am I to do with that piece that's waiting out in the washtub?"

Father chuckled.

She told him he didn't know the first thing about keeping house, and went out to the laundry with the waitress to tackle the problem. The thunderstorm broke and crashed. We boys ran around shutting the windows upstairs.

Father's soul was at peace. He dined well, and he had his coffee and cognac served to him on the piazza. The storm was over by then. Father snuffed a deep breath of the sweet-smelling air and smoked his evening cigar.

"Clarence," he said, "King Solomon had the right idea about these things. 'Whatsoever thy hand findeth to do,' Solomon said, 'do thy damnedest.'"

Mother called me inside. "Whose mackintosh is that?" she asked anxiously. "Katie's torn a hole in the back."

I heard Father saying contentedly on the piazza, "I like plenty of ice."

## Questions

1. Who was father and why it was he who waked up the village?
2. What is the function of ice in this story? Is it merely cold water that father most preferred?
3. What was father's attitude towards those small village tradesmen? And was that attitude justified?
4. How did the little boy view the words and deeds of his father? And what significance does this simple fact symbolize?
5. What did father really wake up the village from? And why?

# 克劳伦斯·戴伊
(1874—1935)

克劳伦斯·谢泼德·戴伊出生在纽约，1896年毕业于耶鲁大学。第二年，他进入了纽约证券交易所，成为父亲在华尔街经纪公司的合伙人。1898年，戴伊加入美国海军，却患上了严重的关节炎，拖着半残的身体度过余生。戴伊最著名的作品是自传《家有老爸》（1935），这部作品详细讲述了19世纪90年代在纽约以专横的父亲为中心发生的家庭趣事。《家有老爸》完成后不久，戴伊就在纽约去世了，来不及见证这部作品在百老汇或好莱坞取得成功。

1939年，《家有老爸》及1932年的前传《上帝与父亲》和1937年作者去世后的续篇《家有老妈》中的场景被搬上了舞台，该剧由霍华德·林赛和拉塞尔·克劳斯创作，是百老汇历史悠久的热门舞台剧。一项对戴伊早期短篇小说和杂志专栏的调查显示："在20世纪头几十年里，随着维多利亚时代关于婚姻、家庭和家庭秩序的观念逐渐瓦解，男性和女性在美国社会中的角色变化令他着迷。"戴伊还著有《青山国》（1934）、《中生代景象及图说》（1935）、《终究》（1936）、《书的世界》（1938）和《父亲与我》（1940）。

## 雄鸡一唱

《雄鸡一唱》是《家有老爸》中的短篇故事，几十年来一直吸引着不同文化和教育背景的读者。父亲固执而可爱的霸道形象与小村庄里低效率又懒散的商人形成了鲜明的对比，这些无疑让男孩在脑海中萌生出对父亲的崇拜。

父亲常说，村庄小商人的那股子懒散劲儿是农村生活最不爽的地方。父亲说，他本来还以为这些人投钱开店是想发财，而他们除了睡觉就是扯淡。他们对文明礼貌一无所知；或者他们知道，但父亲没见识过。父亲说，要是住在南非的草原或哪儿的冻土上，他自然也不再奢望什么现代生活；可要是家离纽约只有20英里，就不应该算是荒郊野外吧。

一般说来，父亲发这样一肚子牢骚的时候，都是冰闹的。如果哪顿饭没有冰水伺候着，他可坚决不干。在城里住，冰当然没问题。餐具柜上有个银色的大个儿冰水罐子，每次父亲回家的时候，罐子外面像下了一层霜。父亲上班了，罐子就不再那么凉；可晚上或星期天——父亲在家的时候——它又冷若冰霜起来。父亲说他喜欢水,说水是老天爷赐给的宝贝,又说所有的宝贝要以正确的方式提供才好;冰镇的水就是正确的方式。

更重要的是,喝酒得有合适的温度,得一直是那个温度。父亲说,文明人儿吃饭都得喝酒,稍微明白这个的人都不把酒放到热地窖里。母亲认为父亲是个鸡蛋里挑骨头的刺儿头——那些住公寓、没地窖的人,他们怎么办?父亲说,文明人儿哪有住公寓的。

在农村住的第一个夏天,父亲在哈得孙河边的欧文顿租了一座带家具的房子——这里离纽约挺近的。房子有花园、马房,还有两英亩的林子——父亲想在那里露个营啥的。每天早饭后,父亲坐八点十分的火车到纽约,下午五六点钟回来,回来时还带点儿新鲜玩意儿,一篮子桃,或者一盒他最喜欢的咖啡。

事情开始还顺利,可八月份的一天,送冰的没来。天很热,送冰的和他的马都累了,而他也不愿意来——我们的房子在山顶上。后来,他说就为了卖五毛钱的冰,他才不愿意在大热天和马拉着大冰车爬那陡峭的山路呢。再有,那么大热的天,来了冰也化了。理由一箩筐;总之,他没来。

父亲在城里,我们在家为了冰的事担心得要命。在城里过惯了按部就班的日子,我们怎么都不愿意相信,送冰的竟然没来。吃午饭的时候,母亲说,等送冰的来了,她要给他点儿脸色看看。可午饭吃完一个多钟头了,送冰的还没来。母亲担心父亲会急得蹦起来,决定干脆找人到村子里去喊送冰的。

那时候自然没电话啦,也没汽车。那几天马累得够呛,母亲心疼它,但谁让事情急得火上房呢。母亲派人叫来了马夫摩根,让他把马车拉出来。

马车来了。马夫、我和另一个男孩子出发了。太阳像烤肉机似的挂在我们头上。硬硬的马具一下下摩擦着布朗尼——我们的马,摩出了一个厚厚的、白色的大水泡。马夫拉着张驴脸:我们跟着,他不能摘下僵硬的黑帽子,不能脱下厚衣服,甚至———他知道——都不能在酒吧停下喝一杯。母亲的高明——我们跟着一起来——他是见识了。

不一会儿,我们到了小镇,我直奔煤冰办公室。一位身材瘦长的老职员正在屋角打盹儿。他头发向后散着,下巴窝在脏巴巴的衬衣上。我叫醒了他,把家里的十万火急报告给了这位老职员。

他有一搭没一搭地听着,听完后说天真热。

我等着。他吐了口唾沫。他说没办法,冰室上锁了。

我诚恳地做着解释,说我姓戴,说请他马上解决。

他在桌子上搜了半天,找到了烟卷,"好吧,小家伙儿,我研究研究。"

看起来已经大功告成,所以我对他千恩万谢。我回到马车那里。缰绳已经解开了;马儿垂头丧气地站着,又脏又累。本来拉个马车没什么大不了,但破马拉大车可就遭了大罪。马夫不见了。过了一会儿，他从街上一个侧门出来，还一边系着扣子；帽子还是向后歪着。他看起来比马还难看。

我们又检查了倦马的头，开始慢慢地往家赶，一路上燥热的微风在身后卷起的尘土如影随形。到了山脚，我们两个男孩子下了车，给可怜的布朗尼减点儿负。我们又解开了缰绳。它一路拉着沉重的车，向上，向上。

母亲正坐在阳台上。我说冰很快就到了。我们等待着。

下午过得真慢。

五点钟，又套上了马——马夫和我要回到小村子去接下火车的父亲。没办法，我们必须告诉父亲：晚饭没冰水，而他的莱茵酒也绝没办法冰镇。

村子昏睡如常，而刚下车的父亲知道了原委。他说：村子该醒了。父亲说，办公室里的一天又长又烦，城里比撒哈拉沙漠还热，他快累死了，可要是哪个送冰的天真地认为——哪怕一秒钟——他可以随便胡来，父亲准会拧下他的烂头。父亲冲进了煤冰办公室。

父亲出来时，那位老职员也出来了——他已戴上了帽子，还一直说些废话想让父亲消消气。老职员许诺说要是送冰的不在他本人会亲自送冰过去，我们要多少他送多少，一小时内绝对搞定。

父亲说："一小时个球！你得飞过去。"

老职员不干了。他说他要亲自到马棚牵马，还要找人从冰室抬冰。他说他可不怎么干这种活，都到了他吃饭的时候了。他这样干只是想帮父亲一个忙——邻居嘛，低头不见抬头见的。

父亲说是邻居就快点儿，要不他可受不了；送冰的吃错药了，竟然如此无法无天。

老职员说那不怪他，要怪就怪马夫。

这句蠢话又把父亲的火勾起来了。父亲说他对该怪谁的混账话不感冒，每个人都该怪；他只想要冰，很多冰，很多不会耽搁他吃饭的冰。这时周围已经聚集了一圈人——父亲指着那位老职员的鼻子说自己必须在六点三十分吃饭的时候，人群边听边佩服地咂嘴。

老职员大步跑到马棚去牵马，父亲一直看着他转过街角。

父亲又大踏步地走向屠户家——身后跟着那群人。

大约一刻钟的工夫，屠户和他的帮手出来了，十分不情愿地拉着一块貌似棺材但裹着黑油布的东西。好一座冰山啊。

父亲上了车，坐在马夫的位子上，一抖缰绳出发了！马夫坐在后面，和我们背对背，用腿撑着冰防滑。父亲经过几家店铺，进了一间家具店，随即又出来了。

这次我跟着父亲进去了，难得的学习机会啊。父亲发表了一番长篇大论，吆喝着要瞧瞧所有的冰箱。但冰箱没几个，父亲挑了最大的。生意似乎已经谈妥而老板憨憨笑着准备大发横财的时候，父亲说买冰箱只需要满足两个条件。

第一个是晚饭前必须运到家。必须。老板一遍遍地解释，说这完全不可能，但保证第二天一早送到。父亲严词拒绝，说第二天早上要冰箱有什么用呢，他马上就要。父亲又说，他晚饭时间是六点半，没什么时间可浪费了。

老板让步了。

而第二个条件又令他目瞪口呆。父亲宣布，冰箱送到家时，里面得有满满的冰。

老板说他卖的是冰箱，不是冰。

父亲说："很好，我不买了。"

但店老板坚持说冰箱质量不错。

父亲又发表了一个短暂的演讲，就是那个我们在家听了无数遍的关于村庄小商人的懒散劲儿的论调；但这次父亲感情丰富，讽刺犀利，他的声音嗡嗡地回荡在家具店里。父亲最后说："没有冰，要冰箱有什么用呢？做生意没有事业心？没有满足顾客一切需求的进取心？那就关门不做生意好啦！不卖冰？干脆什么都别卖好啦！"父亲大踏步地走出了门。

父亲正要上马车的时候，店老板在门口焦急地叫喊："好啦好啦，戴伊先生！我给你装满冰送到就是啦。"

父亲赶着马车，轻快地走在回家的路上。山雨欲来，惊醒的马儿跑得真快；或者父亲的力量鼓舞了它吧。这可怜的老兄又开始攀爬起陡峭的山路，它还真需要父亲的劲头儿呢。我在山脚下来走在车后，看见摩根一边用腿起劲儿地揽着冰，一边要命地弯着胳膊以防掉下来。座位下的大冰块滑滑溜溜的，一直想掉下来。一路上这个大家伙始终在亲着摩根的腿肚子，真是够凉的。

马车终于停在我们家门口。父亲在车上坐了一会儿，摩根、女仆和我开始又推又拉地搬那块大冰。我们掀下油布，铺在草地上。不一会儿，摩根卸下了马车，跑过来帮我们切这块大蛋糕。我们起劲儿地把这些庞然大物推过后门，塞到冰箱里去；而父亲已经换衣服准备吃晚饭了。

母亲终于平静下来，而莱茵酒已经冰上了。父亲喊道："别冰过头了。"

送冰的来了。

老职员也在，如同官差押解犯人一样。母亲出去接他们，并马上给了送冰的好一顿数落，说等了他一天。

老职员问我们要多少冰。母亲说："先生已经买回来了，冰箱里也没地方了，我们一点儿也不要。"送冰的看看老职员，老职员的嘴张了张，没蹦出一个字。

父亲从窗子里伸出头来："温尼，要一百磅吧。还买了一个冰箱呢。"

一百镑的大家伙搬进了屋子，放在浴盆里；女仆盖上了油布。冰车走了。

全家刚坐在饭桌旁，新冰箱到了——满的。

母亲急了。"克莱尔，你真行！"母亲吼着，"浴盆里的大家伙怎么办？！"

父亲咯咯地笑了。

母亲说父亲是个不懂持家的夯货，便匆匆和女仆去洗衣房研究去了。暴风雨来了！我们一群男孩子忙着跑去关楼上的窗户。

父亲安静了。他晚饭吃得好，还在阳台上享用了咖啡和白兰地。此时，暴风雨已经停了。父亲深深地吸了一口清新的空气，点上了雪茄。

"儿子，"父亲说，"碰上这种烂事儿，所罗门王有办法。他说，要干，就干好喽！"

母亲把我喊到里屋。"谁的油布啊？"母亲不安地问，"凯蒂挖了个洞。"

我听见父亲在阳台上高兴地叫着："我就喜欢冰。"

# Jack London
# (1876—1916)

Jack London was one of the most famous American realistic novelists and short story writers in the early 20th century, whose works not only went around widely in the native US, but also remained popular for a long time among all nations. London was born in San Francisco, California on January 12, 1876. He spent much of his poor youth in Oakland and he never got a good chance to learn formally. To support his family he had to take various jobs in his teens, even going to venture on the sea and searching for gold in Alaska. These rich life experiences left deep mark in his stories. He loved reading and turned to writing successfully through his self-education. His writing career was quite short, but he used his own efforts to earn fame and respect for himself. In 1916, he committed suicide in his beloved farm when he was only 40.

London's diligent talents made him a prolific writer compared with his literary peers. In his short life he wrote about fifty books, more than one hundred short stories and many essays and sketches. Among London's most notable works were *The Call of the Wild* (1903), dealing with the power of human will in touch with nature; *People of the Abyss* (1903), talking about the decline of the poor in England; *The Sea Wolf* (1904), based on London's experience as a sailor; *Martin Eden* (1909), an autobiographical novel, and *Lost Face* (1910), a collection of short stories.

## The Law of Life

*"The Law of Life" tells a story of an old Indian chief who was left when the tribe moved for new hunting ground. With the coming of wolves, his life ended in the lonely recalling of his past and reflection on the natural law which had to be obeyed by every living creature. The naturalistic way of story telling seems also to reveal to the readers the so called law recognized by Social Darwinism.*

Old Koskoosh listened greedily. Though his sight had long since faded, his hearing was still acute, and the slightest sound penetrated to the glimmering intelligence which yet abode behind the withered forehead, but which no longer gazed forth upon the things of the world. Ah! That was Sit-cum-to-ha, shrilly anathematizing the dogs as she cuffed and beat them into the harnesses. Sit-cum-to-ha was his daughter's daughter, but she was too busy to waste a thought upon her broken grandfather, sitting alone there in the snow, forlorn and helpless. Camp must be broken. The long trail waited while the short day refused to linger. Life called her, and the duties of life, not death. And he was very close to death now.

The thought made the old man panicky for the moment, and he stretched forth a palsied hand which wandered tremblingly over the small heap of dry wood beside him. Reassured that it was indeed there, his hand returned to the shelter of his mangy furs, and he again fell to listening. The sulky crackling of half-frozen hides told him that the chief's moose-skin lodge had been struck, and even then was being rammed and jammed into portable compass. The chief was his son, stalwart and strong, headman of the tribesmen, and a mighty hunter. As the women toiled with the camp luggage, his voice rose chiding them for their slowness. Old Koskoosh strained his ears. It was the last time he would hear that voice. There went Geehow's lodge! And Tusken's! Seven, eight, nine, only the shaman's could be still standing. There! They were at work upon it now. He could hear the shaman grunt as he piled it on the sled. A child whimpered, and a woman soothed it with soft, crooning gutturals. Little Koo-tee, the old man thought, a fretful child, and not overstrong. It would die soon, perhaps, and they would burn a hole through the frozen tundra and pile rocks above to keep the wolverines away. Well, what did it matter? A few years at best, and as many an empty belly as a full one. And in the end, Death waited, ever-hungry and hungriest of them all.

What was that? Oh, the men lashing the sleds and drawing tight the thongs. He listened, who would listen no more. The whiplashes snarled and bit among the dogs. Hear them whine! How they hated the work and the trail! They were off! Sled after sled churned slowly away into the silence. They were gone. They had passed out of his life, and he faced the last bitter hour alone. No. The snow crunched beneath a moccasin; a man stood beside him; upon his head a hand rested gently. His son was good to do this thing. He remembered other old men whose sons had not waited after the tribe. But his son had. He wandered away into the past, till the young man's voice brought him back.

"It is well with you?" he asked.

And the old man answered, "It is well."

"There be wood beside you," the younger man continued, "and the fire burns bright. The morning is gray, and the cold has broken. It will snow presently. Even now it is snowing."

"Aye, even now it is snowing."

"The tribesmen hurry. Their bales are heavy and their bellies flat with lack of feasting. The trail is long and they travel fast. I go now. It is well?"

"It is well. I am as a last year's leaf, clinging lightly to the stem. The first breath that blows, and I fall. My voice is become like an old woman's. My eyes no longer show me the way of my feet, and my feet are heavy, and I am tired. It is well."

He bowed his head in content till the last noise of the complaining snow had died away, and he knew his son was beyond recall. Then his hand crept out in haste to the wood. It alone stood between him and the eternity that yawned in upon him. At last the measure of his life was a handful of faggots. One by one they would go to feed the fire, and just so, step by step, death would creep upon him. When the last stick had surrendered up its heat, the frost would begin to gather strength. First his feet would yield, then his hands; and the numbness would travel, slowly, from the extremities to the body. His head would fall forward upon his knees, and he would rest. It was easy. All men must die.

He did not complain. It was the way of life, and it was just. He had been born close to the earth, close to the earth had he lived, and the law thereof was not new to him. It was the law of all flesh. Nature was not kindly to the flesh. She had no concern for that concrete thing called the individual. Her interest lay in the species, the race. This was the deepest abstraction old Koskoosh's barbaric mind was capable of, but he grasped it firmly. He saw it exemplified in all life. The rise of the sap, the bursting greenness of the willow bud, the fall of the yellow leaf—in this alone was told the whole history. But one task did nature set the individual. Did he not perform it, he died. Did he perform it, it was all the same, he died. Nature did not care; there were plenty who were obedient, and it was only the obedience in this matter, not the obedient, which lived and lived always. The tribe of Koskoosh was very old. The old men he had known when a boy had known old men before them. Therefore it was true that the tribe lived, that it stood for the obedience of all its members, way down into the forgotten past, whose very resting places were unremembered. They did not count; they were episodes. They had passed away like clouds from a summer sky. He also was an episode and would pass away. Nature did not care. To life she set one task, gave one law. To perpetuate was the task of life, its law was death. A maiden was a good creature to look upon, full-breasted and strong, with spring to her step and light in her eyes. But her task was yet before her.

The light in her eyes brightened, her step quickened, she was now bold with the young men, now timid, and she gave them of her own unrest. And ever she grew fairer and yet fairer to look upon, till some hunter, able no longer to withhold himself, took her to his lodge to cook and toil for him and to become the mother of his children. And with the coming of her offspring her looks left her. Her limbs dragged and shuffled, her eyes dimmed and bleared, and only the little children found joy against the withered cheek of the old squaw by the fire. Her task was done. But a little while, on the first pinch of famine or the first long trail, and she would be left, even as he had been left, in the snow, with a little pile of wood. Such was the law.

He placed a stick carefully upon the fire and resumed his meditations. It was the same everywhere, with all things. The mosquitoes vanished with the first frost. The little tree squirrel crawled away to die. When age settled upon the rabbit it became slow and heavy and could no longer outfoot its enemies. Even the big bald face grew clumsy and blind and quarrelsome, in the end to be dragged down by a handful of yelping huskies. He remembered how he had abandoned his own father on an upper reach of the Klondike one winter, the winter before the missionary came with his talk books and his box of medicines. Many a time had Koskoosh smacked his lips over the recollection of that box, though now his mouth refused to moisten. The "painkiller" had been especially good. But the missionary was a bother after all, for he brought no meat into the camp, and he ate heartily, and the hunters grumbled. But he chilled his lungs on the divide by the Mayo, and the dogs afterward nosed the stones away and fought over his bones.

Koskoosh placed another stick on the fire and harked back deeper into the past. There was the time of the great famine, when the old men crouched empty-bellied to the fire, and let fall from their lips dim traditions of the ancient day when the Yukon ran wide open for three winters, and then lay frozen for three summers. He had lost his mother in that famine. In the summer the salmon run had failed, and the tribe looked forward to the winter and the coming of the caribou. Then the winter came, but with it there were no caribou. Never had the like been known, not even in the lives of the old men. But the caribou did not come, and it was the seventh year, and the rabbits had not replenished, and the dogs were naught but bundles of bones. And through the long darkness the children wailed and died, and the women, and the old men; and not one in ten of the tribe lived to meet the sun when it came back in the spring. That was a famine!

But he had seen times of plenty, too, when the meat spoiled on their hands, and the dogs were fat and worthless with overeating—times when they let the game go unkilled, and the women were fertile, and the lodges were cluttered with sprawling men-children and women-children. Then it was the men became high-stomached, and revived ancient quarrels, and crossed the divides to the south to kill the Pellys, and to the west that they might sit by the dead fires of the Tananas. He remembered, when a boy, during a time of plenty, when he saw a moose pulled down by the wolves. Zing-ha lay with him in the snow and watched—Zing-ha, who later became the craftiest of bunters, and who, in the end, fell through an air hole on the Yukon. They found him, a month afterward, just as he had crawled halfway out and frozen stiff to the ice.

But the moose. Zing-ha and he had gone out that day to play at hunting after the manner of their fathers. On the bed of the creek they struck the fresh track of a moose, and with it the tracks of many wolves. "An old one," Zing-ha, who was quicker at reading the sign, said "an old one who cannot keep up with the herd. The wolves have cut him out from his brothers, and they will never leave him." And it was so. It was their way. By day and by night, never resting, snarling on his heels, snapping at his nose, they would stay by him to the end. How Zing-ha and he felt the blood lust quicken! The finish would be a sight to see!

Eager-footed, they took the trail, and even he, Koskoosh, slow of sight and an unversed tracker, could have followed it blind, it was so wide. Hot were they on the heels of the chase, reading the grim tragedy, fresh-written, at every step. Now they came to where the moose had made a stand. Thrice the length of a grown man's body, in every direction, had the snow been stamped about and uptossed. In the midst were the deep impressions of the splay-hoofed game, and all about, everywhere, were the lighter footmarks of the wolves. Some, while their brothers harried the kill, had lain to one side and rested. The full-stretched impress of their bodies in the snow was as perfect as though made the moment before. One wolf had been caught in a wild lunge of the maddened victim and trampled to death. A few bones, well picked, bore witness.

Again, they ceased the uplift of their snowshoes at a second stand. Here the great animal had fought desperately. Twice had he been dragged down, as the snow attested, and twice had he shaken his assailants clear and gained footing once more. He had done his task long since, but none the less was life dear to him. Zing-ha said it was a strange thing, a moose once down to get free again; but this one certainly had. The shaman would see signs and wonders in this when they told him.

And yet again, they came to where the moose had made to mount the bank and gain the timber. But his foes had laid on from behind, till he reared and fell back upon them, crushing two deep into the snow. It was plain the kill was at hand, for their brothers had left them untouched. Two more stands were hurried past, brief in time length and very close together. The trail was red now, and the clean stride of the great beast had grown short and slovenly. Then they heard the first sounds of the battle—not the full-throated chorus of the chase, but the short snappy bark which spoke of close quarters and teeth to flesh. Crawling up the wind, Zing-ha bellied it through the snow, and with him crept he, Koskoosh, who was to be chief of the tribesmen in the years to come. Together they shoved aside the under branches of a young spruce and peered forth. It was the end they saw.

The picture, like all of youth's impressions, was still strong with him, and his dim eyes watched the end played out as vividly as in that far-off time. Koskoosh marveled at this, for in the days which followed, when he was a leader of men and a head of councilors, he had done great deeds and made his name a curse in the mouths of the Pellys, to say naught of the strange white man he had killed, knife to knife, in open fight.

For long he pondered on the days of his youth, till the fire died down and the frost bit deeper. He replenished it with two sticks this time, and gauged his grip on life by what remained. If Sit-cum-to-ha had only remembered her grandfather, and gathered a larger armful, his hours would have been longer. It would have been easy. But she was ever a careless child, and honored not her ancestors from the time the Beaver, son of the son of Zing-ha, first cast eyes upon her. Well, what mattered it? Had he not done likewise in his own quick youth? For a while he listened to the silence. Perhaps the heart of his son might soften, and he would come back with the dogs to take his old father on with the tribe to where the caribou ran thick and the fat hung heavy upon them.

He strained his ears, his restless brain for the moment stilled. Not a stir, nothing. He alone took breath in the midst of the great silence. It was very lonely. Hark! What was that? A chill passed over his body. The familiar, long-drawn howl broke the void, and it was close at hand. Then on his darkened eyes was projected the vision of the moose—the old bull moose—the torn flanks and bloody sides, the riddled mane, and the great branching horns, down low and tossing to the last. He saw the flashing forms of gray, the gleaming eyes, the lolling tongues, the slavered fangs. And he saw the inexorable circle close in till it became a dark point in the midst of the stamped snow.

    A cold muzzle thrust against his cheek, and at its touch his soul leaped back to the present. His hand shot into the fire and dragged out a burning faggot. Overcome for the nonce by his hereditary fear of man, the brute retreated, raising a prolonged call to his brothers; and greedily they answered, till a ring of crouching, jaw-slobbering gray was stretched round about. The old man listened to the drawing in of this circle. He waved his hand wildly, and sniffs turned to snarls; but the panting brutes refused to scatter. Now one wormed his chest forward, dragging his haunches after, now a second, now a third; but never a one drew back. Why should he cling to life? He asked and dropped the blazing stick into the snow. It sizzled and went out. The circle grunted uneasily but held its own. Again he saw the last stand of the old bull moose, and Koskoosh dropped his head wearily upon his knees. What did it matter after all? Was it not the law of life?

**Questions**

1. Why was Koskoosh left while the tribe was moving away?
2. Were Koskoosh's son and granddaughter inhuman in leaving Koskoosh behind? Why?
3. What was the purpose of the author by inserting Koskoosh's recalling of the moose story?
4. What is the theme of this story?
5. What is the law of life according to Koskoosh?

# 杰克·伦敦
# (1876—1916)

杰克·伦敦是20世纪初美国最著名的现实主义作家和短篇小说家之一。他的作品不仅在美国本土广为流传，而且长久以来一直受到世界各国人民的欢迎。伦敦于1876年1月12日出生于加利福尼亚州的旧金山。他贫困的童年大部分时间在奥克兰度过，没有机会系统地学习。为了养家他十几岁时就做过各种各样的工作，甚至冒险出海、去阿拉斯加淘金。这些丰富的人生经历给他日后的作品留下了深刻的烙印。他热爱阅读，并通过自学成功地从事了写作。他的写作生涯很短暂，但是他用自身的努力赢得了名誉和尊重。1916年他在自己心爱的农场中自杀身亡，年仅40岁。

伦敦的勤奋让他成为同时代的作家中最多产的一位。在他短暂的一生中共写作了约五十本书，一百多部短篇小说和大量论文、随笔。其中最为著名的包括：《野性的呼唤》（1903）讲述了在与自然的接触中人类意志的力量，《深渊中的人们》（1903）描述了英格兰社会底层人民的贫苦与衰落，以及以自己航海经历为蓝本的《海狼》（1904）、自传体小说《马丁·伊登》（1909）和短篇小说集《丢失的脸》（1910）。

## 生命的法则

《生命的法则》讲述了一个印第安部落中年迈的老酋长在部落迁徙后独自留在原地，在孤独的回忆中阐释了生命的法则，最后在狼群的撕咬下走完了人生旅途的故事。小说采用自然主义的手法描写了老酋长的内心世界，同时，含蓄地向读者揭示了社会达尔文主义所认可的人类社会发展规律。

老科斯克库什贪婪地听着周围的声音。虽然他昏花的双眼已无法看清世间万物，但他敏锐的听力却将整个世界囊括在他那隐藏在布满皱纹的前额后的清晰思维中。啊！那是斯卡图哈。她在尖声训斥着狗，连推带打地把它们套进挽具。斯卡图哈是他的外孙女，她太忙了，不能抽出点儿时间来关照一下年迈的外公。他一个人坐在雪地中，孤独、无助。帐篷都要被拆掉，短暂的白天就要过去，可是他们的路途还很遥远。生命与生活的责任在召唤着斯卡图哈远离死亡。但是，老科斯克库什马上就要走到生命的尽头。

想到这儿，老科斯克库什感到一阵心慌。他伸出已麻木的手，哆哆嗦嗦地摸索着身旁的一小堆干柴。确认了木柴的位置后，他又把手缩回到破烂的皮袄里，继续沉浸在万籁俱寂的世界之中。冻得半硬的皮子被撕裂的沉闷声传来，他知道这时酋长的驼鹿皮帐篷已被拆卸开，也许已经在被折叠成包。酋长是他的儿子，身材魁梧，是部落里的首领，强壮的猎人。只因女人们收拾帐篷行李时慢了一点儿，他便大声责骂。老科斯克库什竖着耳朵仔细地听着，也许这是他最后一次听到这种声音了。基霍的帐篷被拆掉了，塔斯肯的也被拆掉了。七顶、八顶、九顶帐篷都被拆掉了，可能只有巫师的还在那儿。可现在轮到它了。他听到巫师嘟囔着把帐篷放上雪橇。一个小孩在哭泣，边上有个女人在轻声地安慰他。准是那个身体赢弱又烦躁的小科蒂，老人想。这些很快都会消失，或许人们会用火将冰冻的苔原烤出个洞当作墓穴，在上面堆上石块，以免狼獾撕食亡者。可这能怎么样呢？他最多只能再活几年，这几年中饥饱参半。死神在等待，无论什么人，那些脑满肠肥的和那些饥肠辘辘的，最终都将走向死亡。

那是什么？是男人在系紧雪橇的皮带。他仔细地听着，也许以后再也听不到了。带着风声的皮鞭向狗抽去，它们在哀号。它们是多么憎恨这样的工作和旅途啊！他们出发了。一个接着一个，雪橇消失在寂静之中。他们走出了他的生命，他将独自一人面对自己余下的悲伤时光。不，传来鹿皮靴踩在雪地上咯吱咯吱的声音，有个男人走到他的身旁，轻轻地把手放在他的头上。儿子就应该这样做。他还记得其他老人的儿子都跟随着大部队离开，但他的儿子没有那样做。他沉浸在回忆中，直到他儿子的话语把他拉到现实。

"还好吧？"他问。

"很好，"老人答道。

"干柴就放在您身旁，"年轻人继续说道，"火着得很旺。今天早上天灰蒙蒙的，升温了。快要下雪了。哦，现在已经开始下了。"

"嗯，下雪了。"

"部落里的人都很着急，行李都很沉，还都饿着肚子。路远着呢，他们要赶紧上路。我也要走了。好吗？"

"好的。我就像经年的枯叶，轻轻地挂在树枝上。一口气吹过来，我就会落下。我的声音变得像个老女人了，眼睛也看不见脚下的路了，我感觉脚很沉，我累了。走吧。"

最后的抱怨伴着雪地上咯吱的声音消逝了，他满意地低下了头。他知道儿子已经远去，他的手又赶紧摸向木柴，这是一根位于他与永恒之间的木棍，死亡已向他张开了大口。他与死神最后抗争的时间长短完全取决于这堆木柴。木柴将会一根根添到火里，死亡也将一步步逼近。最后一根木柴燃尽时，严寒就会全力袭来。他的脚会先失去知觉，接着是手。麻木会慢慢地从四肢一直蔓延至全身。他的头会径直倒在膝盖上，走向永恒。这很容易。所有人终将会死。

他不再抱怨，这就是生命的规律，对谁都公平。他生于这片土地，长于这片土地，与它紧紧相连。这里的法则对他来说并不陌生，这是所有生物的法则。大自然对众生并不仁慈，她并不在乎所谓的个体的具体的生命，她关注的是整体的种族的延续。这是科斯克库什尚不开化的头脑中所能悟出的最深刻的真理，于是他紧紧地把握着这一点。他在所有的生命中都看到了这一点。树液上升，嫩绿的柳树芽绽开，枯黄的树叶飘落。这就是整个生命的历史。然而，自然的任务就是规定个体的生命活动。不遵守这一规律，要死；遵循了，同样也要死。自然对此从不在乎，而许多人都恪守此道，尽管只是顺从这件事本身。然而并不是顺从了的人都会永生。科斯克库什生活在一个古老的部落中，当他还是小孩子的时候，他就认识许多老人，还知道一些更老的人。因此，这个部落的存在是真实的，部落所有成员都顺从自然的规律。谁也不记得死去老人的坟墓。这些老人只是一段插曲，不能算在内，他们就像夏天的乌云那样消散了。他本人也只是一段插曲，也会死去。自然不会关心这一点。对于生命，自然只有一个任务，就是制定法则。延续生命是生命的任务，而生命的法则却是死亡。一个容颜姣美的少女，胸丰体健，脚步轻盈，目光闪闪。但她的任务就在眼前。她眼光流转，步履轻佻，博得小伙子们的爱慕。她春心萌动，弄得他们也心神不安。她会越长越漂亮，越长越耐看。直到有个猎手再也无法控制自己，把她娶到家中，她便开始辛苦操劳家务，变成孩子的母亲。随着孩子的出生，她的美貌也渐渐消逝，她的手脚变得粗大笨重，目光会变得污浊朦胧。最后，只有小孩才会乐意和这个坐在火边的容颜衰老的老妇人玩耍。她的任务已经完成了。因而，一旦赶上饥荒或是长途迁移，她就像他现在一样会被留在雪地里，身边只有一小堆干柴。这就是法则。

他小心地把一根木柴架到火堆上，又陷入沉思。无论在世界何处，所有的东西都是一样。蚊子在霜冻来临之时消失，松鼠会爬到窝外死去，兔子年龄一大就变得臃肿笨拙，再也无法从天敌手中逃命。就连那些强壮无比的白脸熊也会因为衰老而变得又大又笨，又瞎又吵，最后也会被一群吵闹的爱斯基摩犬拽倒撕食。他还记得那位传教士带着《圣经》和药箱到来的前一年冬天，他是怎样把自己的父亲留在科隆戴克河上游岸边的。只要一想起那个药箱中的东西，老科斯克库什就会咂舌称赞，可他现在唾液已干，无法咂舌了。止痛药真是个好东西。不过那个传教士也真是个麻烦的人，他从没有给驻地带回过肉，可胃口倒是不小。这引起猎人的不满。他在去爬梅欧河边的分水岭时，寒气侵肺，死了。后来狗找到了他的坟墓，把坟上的石头扒开，争抢他的骨头。

老科斯克库什又往火堆中添了一根柴，再次深深地陷入回忆中。那是一次可怕的大饥荒。那时,老人们饿着肚子蜷缩在火边,他们嘴里唠叨的总是以前育空河接连三个冬天河水滔滔不绝,又接连三个夏天河流冰封的日子。在那次饥荒中他失去了母亲。夏季里,产卵的鲑鱼群没有回来。所以,整个部落就期待着冬天到来,好捕捉驯鹿。冬天来了,却没有驯鹿。在那些老人的一生中,从来没有人听到或见到过类似的情况。连续七个年头,驯鹿也没有回来,连兔子都不多。狗派不上用场,瘦得只剩一把骨头。在漫长的黑夜里,先是孩子们哭着死去,接着是妇女和老人,整个部落只有不到十分之一的人见到第二年春天的太阳。真是一场可怕的饥荒。

不过,他也见过许多次丰饶的年景。那时候,猎到的肉都放坏了。狗吃得胖胖的,干不了什么活,猎物都跑掉了。女人们也生了许多孩子,帐篷里挤满了男孩和女孩。男人们的胃口也变大了,又开始了传统的争斗。他们先到分水岭的南部消灭了帕利人,然后又去西方灭掉了塔那那人。他记得在他小时候的一个丰年里,看到过一只大驼鹿被一群狼捕杀。那是青哈和他一起在雪地中看到的。青哈后来成为猎人中最聪明的人,最后却跌进育空河的冰窟窿里。他们在一个月后找到他,看出他已经从冰窟窿里爬出了半个身子,可却被紧紧地冻在冰上。

那天,青哈和他想学着父辈的样子出去打猎。他们在小溪的河床上发现了一头驼鹿新留下的足迹,边上还有许多狼的足印。"这是一头老家伙,"青哈马上就看出了足印中的信息,"一头老得跟不上同伴的家伙。狼把它从同伴中拦了下来,死死地缠住了它。"的确如此。狼就是这样,他们不管白天黑夜,一刻不停,紧跟在驼鹿后面撕咬它的腿和鼻子,死死缠住它,一直把它咬死。他和青哈都感到嗜血的欲望!最后的场面一定惊心动魄。

他们沿着足迹紧追,虽然科斯克库什眼神不好,经验不足,可是也能追上它们,因为足迹范围太大了。他们紧紧地跟在后面,浑身是汗,猜想着残酷、鲜活的悲剧一步步上演的情形。他们来到了一处驼鹿曾停留的地方,一片雪地被踩得稀烂,雪地的半径有三个男人那么长,中间是这个猎物四腿朝天留下的深深印痕,周围是那些狼踏出的较浅的足迹。它们有的卧在边上稍作休息,而其他的则继续捕杀。它们的身体在雪地上留下的痕迹就如同刚印上去一样清晰。一只狼已死在这头疯狂猎物的突然猛冲和践踏之下。露出体外的骨头证明了这儿发生过的一切。

他们继续追踪,不久,他们穿着雪鞋的双脚停在了驼鹿第二次停留的地方。从雪地上的痕迹可以看出这个大家伙进行了拼命的反抗,它曾两次被扑倒,又两次挣脱袭击者重新站了起来。它已经完成生活的使命,但仍渴望活下去。青哈说一只驼鹿被扑倒了还能再次站起来可真是一件怪事,可这只驼鹿做到了。如果他们把这件事告诉巫师,他也一定会说这是一个奇迹。

他们没有放弃,来到驼鹿沿着山坡打算逃进树丛的地方。但它的仇敌在后面猛咬,它用后腿站立,向后倒了下去,沉重的后背将两只狼压在深深的雪里。很显然，一场杀戮在即，因为其他的狼没有理会那两只狼，而是匆忙从它们身旁跑过，紧紧地跟在驼鹿的后面。不远处，又出现了两处暂停的痕迹，在这儿，足印里开始出现了血迹，原本清晰可辨的驼鹿的足迹开始变得细碎零乱。接着，他们第一次听到厮杀的声音，但已经不是追逐者们放开嗓子的齐声嚎叫，而是短促的猎猎之声，说明短兵相接之后撕咬啃食的开始。青哈爬到逆风处的山坡上，趴在地上。未来将成为部落首领的科斯克库什也跟着爬了上去。他们拨开一株小云杉树垂下的枝条，向前望去，看到了最后一幕。

这一幕，像所有的童年回忆一样，深深地印在他的脑海里。他混浊的眼里又浮现出多年前那活生生的猎杀场面。科斯克库什感到十分奇怪，因为在以后的日子里，当他成为人们的酋长和长老会里的长老时，他做了许多大事，使他的名字成为帕利人的诅咒。他们传说他在一场公开、一对一的决斗中一刀一刀杀死了一个陌生的白人。可这却是根本没有发生过的事。

快要熄灭的火堆和更加刺骨的寒气中断了他对自己年轻时候的回忆。他向火堆里加了两根木棍，又摸了摸剩下的木柴，想知道自己还能活多久。假如斯卡图哈还惦记着她的外公，多给弄些木柴来的话，他就可以多活一点儿时间。对她来说，这不是难事，可她总是那么粗心。当青哈的孙子白渥第一眼看到她时，她就不再以自己的祖先为荣了。好了，这又有什么关系？在他那短暂的年轻时代里，他不也做过同样的事嘛！他在寂静中听了一会儿，或许他的儿子会心软，然后拉着雪橇回来接上他的老父亲和部落一起去驯鹿又多又肥的地方。

他让思绪停了下来，又竖起耳朵。没有动静，什么都没有。寂静中只有他一个人孤独的喘息声。听！那是什么？一股寒气贯穿了他的全身。那熟悉的、长长的嗥叫打破了寂静，而且就在不远的地方。此时，他漆黑一片的眼前又浮现出那头驼鹿的样子——身体两侧被撕烂，肋部鲜血淋漓，鬃毛残缺不全。一只巨大的分叉的角低低地、不断地向上挑着，直到生命的最后一息。他看见灰色的身体、发着光的眼睛、伸在外面的舌头、淋着口水的犬牙，无情的狼群围成的圈子在不断缩小，直到在凌乱的雪地中间聚成一个黑点。

一个冰冷的嘴碰到了他的面颊，他的思绪一下子又回到现实。他的手伸向火边，猛然拽出一根燃着的木柴。出于对人类与生俱来的恐惧，这个畜生退却了。它长声嗥叫，召唤着同伴。它的同伴贪婪地回应着。最后，这些灰毛畜生垂涎地围着他蹲成一个圈。老人听到圈子在缩小，用力地挥舞着木柴，喘息变成了怒吼。但这些喘着粗气的畜生就是不肯离去。有一只匍匐到他的身后，咬住他的臀部，向后拖，接着是第二只、第三只，没有一只后退。"为什么要留恋生命呢？"他自问着，接着把手中的木柴扔到了雪地里。木柴哳哳作响熄灭了。围着的畜生不安地发出呼噜声，但毫无退却之意。他又一次看到那只老驼鹿弥留时停驻的地方。科斯克库什疲惫地把头垂向了膝盖。"这又有什么呢？难道这不正是生命的法则吗？"

## To Build a Fire

*London's prose style influenced many of his stories about animals and environment, including one of his best works, "To Build a Fire" (1908). London had already established his literary status when this short story was published in the* **Century Magazine.** *The story depicts the struggle between man and nature in which the human being was conquered and finally died in the coldness of the polar region. It is typical of London's naturalistic style.*

Day had broken cold and gray, exceedingly cold and gray, when the man turned aside from the main Yukon trail and climbed the high earth-bank, where a dim and little-traveled trail led eastward through the fat spruce timberland. It was a steep bank, and he paused for breath at the top, excusing the act to himself by looking at his watch. It was nine o'clock. There was no sun nor hint of sun, though there was not a cloud in the sky. It was a clear day, and yet there seemed an intangible pall over the face of things, a subtle gloom that made the day dark, and that was due to the absence of sun. This fact did not worry the man. He was used to the lack of sun. It had been days since he had seen the sun, and he knew that a few more days must pass before that cheerful orb, due south, would just peep above the sky line and dip immediately from view.

The man flung a look back along the way he had come. The Yukon lay a mile wide and hidden under three feet of ice. On top of this ice were as many feet of snow. It was all pure white, rolling in gentle, undulations where the ice jams of the freeze-up had formed. North and south, as far as his eye could see, it was unbroken white, save for a dark hair-line that curved and twisted from around the spruce-covered island to the south, and that curved and twisted away into the north, where it disappeared behind another spruce-covered island. This dark hair-line was the trail—the main trail—that led south five hundred miles to the Chilcoot Pass, Dyea, and salt water; and that led north seventy miles to Dawson, and still on to the north a thousand miles to Nulato, and finally to St. Michael, on Bering Sea, a thousand miles and half a thousand more.

But all this—the mysterious, far-reaching hair-line trail, the absence of sun from the sky, the tremendous cold, and the strangeness and weirdness of it all—made no impression on the man. It was not because he was long used to it. He was a newcomer in the land, a *chechaquo*, and this was his first winter. The trouble with him was that he was without imagination. He was quick and alert in the things of life, but only in the things, and not in the significances. Fifty degrees below zero meant eighty-odd degrees of frost. Such fact impressed him as being cold and uncomfortable, and that was all. It did not lead him to meditate upon his frailty as a creature of temperature, and upon man's frailty in general, able only to live within certain narrow limits of heat and cold; and from there on it did not lead him to the conjectural field of immortality and man's place in the universe. Fifty degrees below zero stood for a bite of frost that hurt and that must be guarded against by the use of mittens, ear-flaps, warm moccasins, and thick socks. Fifty degrees below zero was to him just precisely fifty degrees below zero. That there should be anything more to it than that was a thought that never entered his head.

As he turned to go, he spat speculatively. There was a sharp, explosive crackle that startled him. He spat again. And again, in the air, before it could fall to the snow, the spittle crackled. He knew that at fifty below spittle crackled on the snow, but this spittle had crackled in the air. Undoubtedly it was colder than fifty below—how much colder he did not know. But the temperature did not matter. He was bound for the old claim on the left fork of Henderson Creek, where the boys were already. They had come over across the divide from the Indian Creek country, while he had come the roundabout way to take a look at the possibilities of getting out logs in the spring from the islands in the Yukon. He would be in to camp by six o'clock; a bit after dark, it was true, but the boys would be there, a fire would be going, and a hot supper would be ready. As for lunch, he pressed his hand against the protruding bundle under his jacket. It was also under his shirt, wrapped up in a handkerchief and lying against the naked skin. It was the only way to keep the biscuits from freezing. He smiled agreeably to himself as he thought of those biscuits, each cut open and sopped in bacon grease, and each enclosing a generous slice of fried bacon.

He plunged in among the big spruce trees. The trail was faint. A foot of snow had fallen since the last sled had passed over, and he was glad he was without a sled, traveling light. In fact, he carried nothing but the lunch wrapped in the handkerchief. He was surprised, however, at the cold. It certainly was cold, he concluded, as he rubbed his numb nose and cheek-bones with his mittened hand. He was a warm-whiskered man, but the hair on his face did not protect the high cheek-bones and the eager nose that thrust itself aggressively into the frosty air.

At the man's heels trotted a dog, a big native husky, the proper wolf-dog, gray-coated and without any visible or temperamental difference from its brother, the wild wolf. The animal was depressed by the tremendous cold. It knew that it was no time for traveling. Its instinct told it a truer tale than was told to the man by the man's judgment. In reality, it was not merely colder than fifty below zero; it was colder than sixty below, than seventy below. It was seventy-five below zero. Since the freezing point is thirty-two above zero, it meant that one hundred and seven degrees of frost obtained. The dog did not know anything about thermometers. Possibly in its brain there was no sharp consciousness of a condition of very cold such as was in the man's brain. But the brute had its instinct. It experienced a vague but menacing apprehension that subdued it and made it slink along at the man's heels, and that made it question eagerly every unwonted movement of the man as if expecting him to go into camp or to seek shelter somewhere and build a fire. The dog had learned fire and it wanted fire, or else to burrow under the snow and cuddle its warmth away from the air.

The frozen moisture of its breathing had settled on its fur in a fine powder of frost, and especially were its jowls, muzzle, and eyelashes whitened by its crystalled breath. The man's red beard and mustache were likewise frosted, but more solidly, the deposit taking the form of ice and increasing with every warm, moist breath he exhaled. Also, the man was chewing tobacco, and the muzzle of ice held his lips so rigidly that he was unable to clear his chin when he expelled the juice. The result was that a crystal beard of the color and solidity of amber was increasing its length on his chin. If he fell down it would shatter itself, like glass, into brittle fragments. But he did not mind the appendage. It was the penalty all tobacco-chewers paid in that country, and he had been out before in two cold snaps. They had not been so cold as this, he knew, but by the spirit thermometer at Sixty Mile he knew they had been registered at fifty below and at fifty-five.

He held on through the level stretch of woods for several miles, crossed a wide flat of nigger-heads, and dropped down a bank to the frozen bed of a small stream. This was Henderson Creek, and he knew he was ten miles from the forks. He looked at his watch. It was ten o'clock. He was making four miles an hour, and he calculated that he would arrive at the forks at half-past twelve. He decided to celebrate that event by eating his lunch there.

The dog dropped in again at his heels, with a tail drooping discouragement, as the man swung along the creek-bed. The furrow of the old sled-trail was plainly visible, but a dozen inches of snow covered the marks of the last runners. In a month no man had come up or down that silent creek. The man held steadily on. He was not much given to thinking, and just then particularly he had nothing to think about save that he would eat lunch at the forks and that at six o'clock he would be in camp with the boys. There was nobody to talk to; and, had there been, speech would have been impossible because of the ice-muzzle on his mouth. So he continued monotonously to chew tobacco and to increase the length of his amber beard.

Once in a while the thought reiterated itself that it was very cold and that he had never experienced such cold. As he walked along he rubbed his cheek-bones and nose with the back of his mittened hand. He did this automatically, now and again changing hands. But rub as he would, the instant he stopped his cheek-bones went numb, and the following instant the end of his nose went numb. He was sure to frost his cheeks; he knew that, and experienced a pang of regret that he had not devised a nose-strap of the sort Bud wore in cold snaps. Such a strap passed across the cheeks, as well, and saved them. But it didn't matter much, after all. What were frosted cheeks? A bit painful, that was all; they were never serious.

Empty as the man's mind was of thoughts, he was keenly observant, and he noticed the changes in the creek, the curves and bends and timber jams, and always he sharply noted where he placed his feet. Once, coming around a bend, he shied abruptly, like a startled horse, curved away from the place where he had been walking, and retreated several paces back along the trail. The creek he knew was frozen clear to the bottom,—no creek could contain water in that arctic winter,—but he knew also that there were springs that bubbled out from the hillsides and ran along under the snow and on top the ice of the creek. He knew that the coldest snaps never froze these springs, and he knew likewise their danger. They were traps. They hid pools of water under the snow that might be three inches deep, or three feet. Sometimes a skin of ice half an inch thick covered them, and in turn was covered by the snow. Sometimes there were alternate layers of water and ice-skin, so that when one broke through he kept on breaking through for a while, sometimes wetting himself to the waist.

That was why he had shied in such panic. He had felt the give under his feet and heard the crackle of a snow-hidden ice-skin. And to get his feet wet in such a temperature meant trouble and danger. At the very least it meant delay, for he would be forced to stop and build a fire, and under its protection to bare his feet while he dried his socks and moccasins. He stood and studied the creek-bed and its banks, and decided that the flow of water came from the right. He reflected a while, rubbing his nose and cheeks, then skirted to the left, stepping gingerly and testing the footing for each step.

Once clear of the danger, he took a fresh chew of tobacco and swung along at his four-mile gait.

In the course of the next two hours he came upon several similar traps. Usually the snow above the hidden pools had a sunken, candied appearance that advertised the danger. Once again, however, he had a close call; and once, suspecting danger, he compelled the dog to go on in front. The dog did not want to go. It hung back until the man shoved it forward, and then it went quickly across the white, unbroken surface. Suddenly it broke through, floundered to one side, and got away to firmer footing. It had wet its forefeet and legs, and almost immediately the water that clung to it turned to ice. It made quick efforts to lick the ice off its legs, then dropped down in the snow and began to bite out the ice that had formed between the toes. This was a matter of instinct. To permit the ice to remain would mean sore feet. It did not know this, it merely obeyed the mysterious prompting that arose from the deep crypts of its being. But the man knew, having achieved a judgment on the subject, and he removed the mitten from his right hand and helped tear out the ice-particles. He did not expose his fingers more than a minute, and was astonished at the swift numbness that smote them. It certainly was cold. He pulled on the mitten hastily, and beat the hand savagely across his chest.

At twelve o'clock the day was at its brightest. Yet the sun was too far south on its winter journey to clear the horizon. The bulge of the earth intervened between it and Henderson Creek, where the man walked under a clear sky at noon and cast no shadow. At half-past twelve, to the minute, he arrived at the forks of the creek. He was pleased at the speed he had made. If he kept it up, he would certainly be with the boys by six. He unbuttoned his jacket and shirt and drew forth his lunch. The action consumed no more than a quarter of a minute, yet in that brief moment the numbness laid hold of the exposed fingers. He did not put the mitten on, but, instead struck the fingers a dozen sharp smashes against his leg. Then he sat down on a snow-covered log to eat. The sting that followed upon the striking of his fingers against his leg ceased so quickly that he was startled. He had had no chance to take a bite of biscuit. He struck the fingers repeatedly and returned them to the mitten, baring the other hand for the purpose of eating. He tried to take a mouthful, but the ice-muzzle prevented. He had forgotten to build a fire and thaw out. He chuckled at his foolishness, and as he chuckled he noted that the stinging which had first come to his toes when he sat down was already passing away. He wondered whether the toes were warm or numb. He moved them inside the moccasins and decided that they were numb.

He pulled the mitten on hurriedly and stood up. He was a bit frightened. He stamped up and down until the stinging returned to his feet. It certainly was cold, was his thought. That man from Sulphur Creek had spoken the truth when telling how cold it sometimes got in the country. And he had laughed at him at the time! That showed one must not be too sure of things. There was no mistake about it, it was cold. He strode up and down, stamping his feet and threshing his arms, until reassured by the returning warmth. Then he got out matches and proceeded to make a fire. From the undergrowth, where high water of the previous spring had lodged a supply of seasoned twigs, he got his firewood. Working carefully from a small beginning, he soon had a roaring fire, over which he thawed the ice from his face and in the protection of which he ate his biscuits. For the moment the cold of space was outwitted. The dog took satisfaction in the fire, stretching out close enough for warmth and far enough away to escape being singed.

When the man had finished, he filled his pipe and took his comfortable time over a smoke. Then he pulled on his mittens, settled the earflaps of his cap firmly about his ears, and took the creek trail up the left fork. The dog was disappointed and yearned back toward the fire. The man did not know cold. Possibly all the generations of his ancestry had been ignorant of cold, of real cold, of cold one hundred and seven degrees below freezing point. But the dog knew; all its ancestry knew, and it had inherited the knowledge. And it knew that it was not good to walk abroad in such fearful cold. It was the time to lie snug in a hole in the snow and wait for a curtain of cloud to be drawn across the face of outer space whence this cold came. On the other hand, there was no keen intimacy between the dog and the man. The one was the toil-slave of the other, and the only caresses it had ever received were the caresses of the whip-lash and of harsh and menacing throat-sounds that threatened the whiplash. So the dog made no effort to communicate its apprehension to the man. It was not concerned in the welfare of the man; it was for its own sake that it yearned back toward the fire. But the man whistled, and spoke to it with the sound of whiplashes, and the dog swung in at the man's heels and followed after.

The man took a chew of tobacco and proceeded to start a new amber beard. Also, his moist breath quickly powdered with white his mustache, eyebrows, and lashes. There did not seem to be so many springs on the left fork of the Henderson, and for half an hour the man saw no signs of any. And then it happened. At a place where there were no signs, where the soft, unbroken snow seemed to advertise solidity beneath, the man broke through. It was not deep. He wet himself halfway to the knees before he floundered out to the firm crust.

He was angry, and cursed his luck aloud. He had hoped to get into camp with the boys at six o'clock, and this would delay him an hour, for he would have to build a fire and dry out his foot-gear. This was imperative at that low temperature—he knew that much; and he turned aside to the bank, which he climbed. On top, tangled in the underbrush about the trunks of several small spruce trees, was a high-water deposit of dry firewood—sticks and twigs, principally, but also larger portions of seasoned branches and fine, dry, last-year's grasses. He threw down several large pieces on top of the snow. This served for a foundation and prevented the young flame from drowning itself in the snow it otherwise would melt. The flame he got by touching a match to a small shred of birch bark that he took from his pocket. This burned even more readily than paper. Placing it on the foundation, he fed the young flame with wisps of dry grass and with the tiniest dry twigs.

He worked slowly and carefully, keenly aware of his danger. Gradually, as the flame grew stronger, he increased the size of the twigs with which he fed it. He squatted in the snow, pulling the twigs out from their entanglement in the brush and feeding directly to the flame. He knew there must be no failure. When it is seventy-five below zero, a man must not fail in his first attempt to build a fire—that is, if his feet are wet. If his feet are dry, and he fails, he can run along the trail for half a mile and restore his circulation. But the circulation of wet and freezing feet cannot be restored by running when it is seventy-five below. No matter how fast he runs, the wet feet will freeze the harder.

All this the man knew. The old-timer on Sulphur Creek had told him about it the previous fall, and now he was appreciating the advice. Already all sensation had gone out of his feet. To build the fire he had been forced to remove his mittens, and the fingers had quickly gone numb. His pace of four miles an hour had kept his heart pumping blood to the surface of his body and to all the extremities. But the instant he stopped, the action of the pump eased down. The cold of space smote the unprotected tip of the planet, and he, being on that unprotected tip, received the full force of the blow. The blood of his body recoiled before it. The blood was alive, like the dog, and like the dog it wanted to hide away and cover itself up from the fearful cold. So long as he walked four miles an hour, he pumped that blood, willy-nilly, to the surface; but now it ebbed away and sank down into the recesses of his body. The extremities were the first to feel its absence. His wet feet froze the faster, and his exposed fingers numbed the faster, though they had not yet begun to freeze. Nose and cheeks were already freezing, while the skin of all his body chilled as it lost its blood.

But he was safe. Toes and nose and cheeks would be only touched by the frost, for the fire was beginning to burn with strength. He was feeding it with twigs the size of his finger. In another minute he would be able to feed it with branches the size of his wrist, and then he could remove his wet foot-gear, and, while it dried, he could keep his naked feet warm by the fire, rubbing them at first, of course, with snow. The fire was a success. He was safe. He remembered the advice of the old-timer on Sulphur Creek, and smiled. The old-timer had been very serious in laying down the law that no man must travel alone in the Klondike after fifty below. Well, here he was; he had had the accident; he was alone; and he had saved himself. Those old-timers were rather womanish, some of them, he thought. All a man had to do was to keep his head; and he was all right. Any man who was a man could travel alone. But it was surprising, the rapidity with which his cheeks and nose were freezing. And he had not thought his fingers could go lifeless in so short a time. Lifeless they were, for he could scarcely make them move together to grip a twig, and they seemed remote from his body and from him. When he touched a twig, he had to look and see whether or not he had hold of it. The wires were pretty well down between him and his finger-ends.

All of which counted for little. There was the fire, snapping and crackling and promising life with every dancing flame. He started to untie his moccasins. They were coated with ice; the thick German socks were like sheaths of iron halfway to the knees; and the moccasin strings were like rods of steel all twisted and knotted as by some conflagration. For a moment he tugged with his numb fingers, then, realizing the folly of it, he drew his sheath knife.

But before he could cut the strings, it happened. It was his own fault or, rather, his mistake. He should not have built the fire under the spruce tree. He should have built it in the open. But it had been easier to pull the twigs from the brush and drop them directly on the fire. Now the tree under which he had done this carried a weight of snow on its boughs. No wind had blown for weeks, and each bough was fully freighted. Each time he had pulled a twig he had communicated a slight agitation to the tree—an imperceptible agitation, so far as he was concerned, but an agitation sufficient to bring about the disaster. High up in the tree one bough capsized its load of snow. This fell on the boughs beneath, capsizing them. This process continued, spreading out and involving the whole tree. It grew like an avalanche, and it descended without warning upon the man and the fire, and the fire was blotted out! Where it had burned was a mantle of fresh and disordered snow.

The man was shocked. It was as though he had just heard his own sentence of death. For a moment he sat and stared at the spot where the fire had been. Then he grew very calm. Perhaps the old-timer on Sulphur Creek was right. If he had only had a trail-mate he would have been in no danger now. The trail-mate could have built the fire. Well, it was up to him to build a fire over again, and this second time there must be no failure. Even if he succeeded, he would most likely lose some toes. His feet must be badly frozen by now, and there would be some time before the second fire was ready.

Such were his thoughts, but he did not sit and think them. He was busy all the time they were passing through his mind. He made a new foundation for a fire, this time in the open, where no treacherous tree could blot it out. Next, he gathered dry grasses and tiny twigs from the high-water flotsam. He could not bring his fingers together to pull them out, but he was able to gather them by the handful. In this way he got many rotten twigs and bits of green moss that were undesirable, but it was the best he could do. He worked methodically, even collecting an armful of the larger branches to be used later when the fire gathered strength. And all the while the dog sat and watched him, a certain yearning wistfulness in its eyes, for it looked upon him as the fire provider, and the fire was slow in coming.

When all was ready, the man reached in his pocket for a second piece of birch bark. He knew the bark was there, and, though he could not feel it with his fingers, he could hear its crisp rustling as he fumbled for it. Try as he would, he could not clutch hold of it. And all the time, in his consciousness, was the knowledge that each instant his feet were freezing. This thought tended to put him in a panic, but he fought against it and kept calm. He pulled on his mittens with his teeth, and threshed his arms back and forth, beating his hands with all his might against his sides. He did this sitting down, and he stood up to do it; and all the while the dog sat in the snow, its wolf-brush of a tail curled around warmly over its forefeet, its sharp wolf-ears pricked forward intently as it watched the man. And the man, as he beat and threshed with his arms and hands, felt a great surge of envy as he regarded the creature that was warm and secure in its natural covering.

After a time he was aware of the first far-away signals of sensation in his beaten fingers. The faint tingling grew stronger till it evolved into a stinging ache that was excruciating, but which the man hailed with satisfaction. He stripped the mitten from his right hand and fetched forth the birch bark. The exposed fingers were quickly going numb again. Next he brought out his bunch of sulphur matches. But the tremendous cold had already driven the life out of his fingers. In his effort to separate one match from the others, the whole bunch fell in the snow. He tried to pick it out of the snow, but failed. The dead fingers could neither touch nor clutch. He was very careful. He drove the thought of his freezing feet, and nose, and cheeks, out of his mind, devoting his whole soul to the matches. He watched, using the sense of vision in place of touch, and when he saw his fingers on each side the bunch, he closed them—that is, he willed to close them, for the wires were down, and the fingers did not obey. He pulled the mitten on the right hand, and beat it fiercely against his knee. Then, with both mittened hands, he scooped the bunch of matches, along with much snow, into his lap. Yet he was no better off

After some manipulation he managed to get the bunch between the heels of his mittened hands. In this fashion he carried it to his mouth. The ice crackled and snapped when by a violent effort he opened his mouth. He drew the lower jaw in, curled the upper lip out of the way, and scraped the bunch with his upper teeth in order to separate a match. He succeeded in getting one, which he dropped on his lap. He was no better off. He could not pick it up. Then he devised a way. He picked it up in his teeth and scratched it on his leg. Twenty times he scratched before he succeeded in lighting it. As if flamed he held it with his teeth to the birch bark. But the burning brimstone went up his nostrils and into his lungs, causing him to cough spasmodically. The match fell into the snow and went out.

The old-timer on Sulphur Creek was right, he thought in the moment of controlled despair that ensued: after fifty below, a man should travel with a partner. He beat his hands, but failed in exciting any sensation. Suddenly he bared both hands, removing the mittens with his teeth. He caught the whole bunch between the heels of his hands. His arm-muscles not being frozen enabled him to press the hand-heels tightly against the matches. Then he scratched the bunch along his leg. It flared into flame, seventy sulphur matches at once! There was no wind to blow them out. He kept his head to one side to escape the strangling fumes, and held the blazing bunch to the birch bark. As he so held it, he became aware of sensation in his hand. His flesh was burning. He could smell it. Deep down below the surface he could feel it. The sensation developed into pain that grew acute. And still he endured it, holding the flame of the matches clumsily to the bark that would not light readily because his own burning hands were in the way, absorbing most of the flame.

At last, when he could endure no more, he jerked his hands apart. The blazing matches fell sizzling into the snow, but the birch bark was alight. He began laying dry grasses and the tiniest twigs on the flame. He could not pick and choose, for he had to lift the fuel between the heels of his hands. Small pieces of rotten wood and green moss clung to the twigs, and he bit them off as well as he could with his teeth. He cherished the flame carefully and awkwardly. It meant life, and it must not perish. The withdrawal of blood from the surface of his body now made him begin to shiver, and he grew more awkward. A large piece of green moss fell squarely on the little fire. He tried to poke it out with his fingers, but his shivering frame made him poke too far, and he disrupted the nucleus of the little fire, the burning grasses and tiny twigs separating and scattering. He tried to poke them together again, but in spite of the tenseness of the effort, his shivering got away with him, and the twigs were hopelessly scattered. Each twig gushed a puff of smoke and went out. The fire-provider had failed. As he looked apathetically about him, his eyes chanced on the dog, sitting across the ruins of the fire from him, in the snow, making restless, hunching movements, slightly lifting one forefoot and then the other, shifting its weight back and forth on them with wistful eagerness.

The sight of the dog put a wild idea into his head. He remembered the tale of the man, caught in a blizzard, who killed a steer and crawled inside the carcass, and so was saved. He would kill the dog and bury his hands in the warm body until the numbness went out of them. Then he could build another fire. He spoke to the dog, calling it to him; but in his voice was a strange note of fear that frightened the animal, who had never known the man to speak in such way before. Something was the matter, and its suspicious nature sensed danger—it knew not what danger, but somewhere, somehow, in its brain arose an apprehension of the man. It flattened its ears down at the sound of the man's voice, and its restless, hunching movements and liftings and shiftings of its forefeet became more pronounced; but it would not come to the man. He got on his hands and knees and crawled toward the dog. This unusual posture again excited suspicion, and the animal sidled mincingly away.

The man sat up in the snow for a moment and struggled for calmness. Then he pulled on his mittens, by means of his teeth, and got upon his feet. He glanced down at first in order to assure himself that he was really standing up, for the absence of sensation in his feet left him unrelated to the earth. His erect position in itself started to drive the webs of suspicion from the dog's mind; and when he spoke peremptorily, with the sound of whiplashes in his voice, the dog rendered its customary allegiance and came to him. As it came within reaching distance, the man lost his control. His arms flashed out to the dog, and he experienced genuine surprise when he discovered that his hands could not clutch, that there was neither bend nor feeling in the fingers. He had forgotten for the moment that they were frozen and that they were freezing more and more. All this happened quickly, and before the animal could get away, he encircled its body with his arms. He sat down in the snow, and in this fashion held the dog, while it snarled and whined and struggled.

But it was all he could do, hold its body encircled in his arms and sit there. He realized that he could not kill the dog. There was no way to do it. With his helpless hands he could neither draw nor hold his sheath-knife nor throttle the animal. He released it, and it plunged wildly away, with tail between its legs, and still snarling. It halted forty feet away surveyed him curiously, with ears sharply pricked forward. The man looked down at his hands in order to locate them, and found them hanging on the ends of his arms. It struck him as curious that one should have to use his eyes in order to find out where his hands were. He began threshing his arms back and forth, beating the mittened hands against his sides. He did this for five minutes, violently, and his heart pumped enough blood up to the surface to put a stop to his shivering. But no sensation was aroused in the hands. He had an impression that they hung like weights on the ends of his arms, but when he tried to run the impression down, he could not find it.

A certain fear of death, dull and oppressive, came to him. This fear quickly became poignant as he realized that it was no longer a mere matter of freezing his fingers and toes, or of losing his hands and feet, but that it was a matter of life and death with the chances against him. This threw him into a panic, and he turned and ran up the creek-bed along the old, dim trail. The dog joined in behind and kept up with him. He ran blindly, without intention, in fear such as he had never known in his life. Slowly, as he plowed and floundered through the snow, he began to see things again,—the banks of the creeks, the old timber-jams, the leafless aspens, and the sky. The running made him feel better. He did not shiver. Maybe, if he ran on, his feet would thaw out; and, anyway, if he ran far enough, he would reach camp and the boys. Without doubt he would lose some fingers and toes and some of his face; but the boys would take care of him, and save the rest of him when he got there. And at the same time there was another thought in his mind that said he would never get to the camp and the boys; that it was too many miles away, that the freezing had too great a start on him, and that he would soon be stiff and dead. This thought he kept in the background and refused to consider. Sometimes it pushed itself forward and demanded to be heard, but he thrust it back and strove to think of other things.

It struck him as curious that he could run at all on feet so frozen that he could not feel them when they struck the earth and took the weight of his body. He seemed to himself to skim along above the surface, and to have no connection with the earth. Somewhere he had once seen a winged Mercury, and he wondered if Mercury felt as he felt when skimming over the earth.

His theory of running until he reached camp and the boys had one flaw in it; he lacked the endurance. Several times he stumbled, and finally he tottered, crumpled up, and fell. When he tried to rise, he failed. He must sit and rest, he decided, and next time he would merely walk and keep on going. As he sat and regained his breath, he noted that he was feeling quite warm and comfortable. He was not shivering, and it even seemed that a warm glow had come to his chest and trunk. And yet, when he touched his nose or cheeks, there was no sensation. Running would not thaw them out. Nor would it thaw out his hands and feet. Then the thought came to him that the frozen portions of his body must be extending. He tried to keep this thought down, to forget it, to think of something else; he was aware of the panicky feeling that it caused, and he was afraid of the panic. But the thought asserted itself, and persisted, until it produced a vision of his body totally frozen. This was too much, and he made another wild run along the trail. Once he slowed down to a walk, but the thought of the freezing extending itself made him run again.

And all the time the dog ran with him, at his heels. When he fell down a second time, it curled its tail over its forefeet and sat in front of him, facing him, curiously eager and intent. The warmth and security of the animal angered him, and he cursed it till it flattened down its ears appeasingly. This time the shivering came more quickly upon the man. He was losing his battle with the frost. It was creeping into his body from all sides. The thought of it drove him on, but he ran no more than a hundred feet, when he staggered and pitched headlong. It was his last panic. When he had recovered his breath and control, he sat up and entertained in his mind the conception of meeting death with dignity. However, the conception did not come to him in such terms. His idea of it was that he had been making a fool of himself, running around like a chicken with its head cut off—such was the simile that occurred to him. Well, he was bound to freeze anyway, and he might as well take it decently. With this new-found peace of mind came the first glimmerings of drowsiness. A good idea, he thought, to sleep off to death. It was like taking an anesthetic. Freezing was not so bad as people thought. There were lots worse ways to die.

He pictured the boys finding his body next day. Suddenly he found himself with them, coming along the trail and looking for himself. And, still with them, he came around a turn in the trail and found himself lying in the snow. He did not belong with himself any more, for even then he was out of himself, standing with the boys and looking at himself in the snow. It certainly was cold, was his thought. When he got back to the States he could tell the folks what real cold was. He drifted on from this to a vision of the old-timer on Sulphur Creek. He could see him quite clearly, warm and comfortable, and smoking a pipe.

"You were right, old hoss; you were right," the man mumbled to the old-timer of Sulphur Creek.

Then the man drowsed off into what seemed to him the most comfortable and satisfying sleep he had ever known. The dog sat facing and waiting. The brief day drew to a close in a long, slow twilight. There were no signs of a fire to be made, and, besides, never in the dog's experience had it known a man to sit like that in the snow and make no fire. As the twilight drew on, its eager yearning for the fire mastered it, and with a great lifting and shifting of forefeet, it whined softly, then flattened out its ears down in anticipation of being chidden by the man. But the man remained silent. Later, the dog whined loudly. And still later it crept close to the man and caught the scent of death. This made the animal bristle and back away. A little longer it delayed, howling under the stars that leaped and danced and shone brightly in the cold sky. Then it turned and trotted up the trail in the direction of the camp it knew, where were the other food-providers and fire-providers.

**Questions**

1. How does the man's lack of imagination lead to his death? What other factors lead to the man's final destiny?
2. Why are the dog and the "old-timer" able to survive the cold of the winter while the man cannot?

3. How does London's naturalistic prose style influence and serve the mood of the story?
4. What kind of relationship between man and nature is stated by the author?
5. What is the theme of the story? And why?

## 生火

  伦敦的散文体写作风格出现在他多部关于动物和环境的小说中,其中包括他最优秀的作品之一《生火》(1908)。这篇短篇小说在《世纪》杂志发表时,伦敦已经确立了自己在文坛的地位。小说描写了人与自然的斗争,在斗争中人类最终被征服,死于极地的严寒。这是一部典型的自然主义风格的代表作。

  天已破晓,寒冷而阴暗,极其寒冷而阴暗,这时有个男人从育空河主道上转过来,爬上高高的泥岸地,那里有一条模糊的、罕有人迹的小路穿过肥沃的云杉林地向东延伸。这是个陡峭的河岸,男人在岸顶借看表之机稍作停留,歇了口气。九点了。天空虽然没有一片云彩,却也看不到太阳,一点儿太阳的影子也没有。这无疑是个晴天,但看起来就像有一层无形的阴影笼罩于万物表面,这难以察觉的昏暗让天气阴沉,一切都因为没有太阳。但他并没有为此担忧,他早已习惯了没有太阳的日子。他已经很久没有见过太阳了,他知道势必还要过几天那明亮的太阳才会隐约出现在天际线上,但很快又会从视野中再次消失。

  男人向他来时的路瞥了一眼。育空河有一英里宽,上面覆盖着三英尺厚的冰,冰上面是厚厚的雪。在严寒期冰块形成的地方呈和缓的波浪形,一片白茫茫。无论南面还是北面,只要目光所及之处,尽是一望无际的白色,只有一条阴暗的纹线从布满云杉的岛屿蜿蜒向南,又转向北,从那里消失在另一片云杉覆盖的岛屿背后。这条黑线就是那条小路——那条育空河主道——向南五百英里可到达亚的奇尔库特山关隘、戴依和盐水湖,向北七十英里可到道森,再继续向北一千英里可到努拉托,最后如果再继续走上一千五百英里就会到达白令海边的圣·迈克尔。

  但是所有这一切——神秘的、绵延的细小通道,从天空消失的太阳,可怕的严寒,以及所有古古怪怪的事情——都没有给男人留下什么印象。这并不是因为他早就适应了,实际上他在这里只是个新人,这是他在这里的第一个冬天。他的问题在于缺乏想象力。他对生活中的事物反应敏捷而机警,但只是对事物本身,而不是对其所蕴含的意义。零下五十度意味着冰点下八十多度。这样的事实给他的印象只是寒冷和不适,仅此而已。这并不能使他深思他作为有体温的动物的弱点,也不能使他想到人类的这个弱点,就是只能生活在冷与热之间一个狭小的范围内,也没能让他推测出不朽的境界和人类在宇宙中的地位。零下五十度意味着伤人的刺骨寒冷,而那必须用手套、耳包、温暖的棉鞋和厚厚的袜子来抵御。零下五十度对他来说就是精确的零下五十度。除此之外他再没有想到什么更多的东西。

他转过身继续前行,边盘算着边啐了一口唾沫。一个尖利的、爆炸似的噼啪声吓到了他。他又啐了一口,在唾沫落到雪地上之前,又在空气中爆裂开了。他知道零下五十度时唾液会在雪地上冻裂,但在这里唾液在空气中就裂开了,无疑这里的天气比零下五十度要冷——他并不知道究竟冷多少。但是温度不是问题。他正向亨德申河左岔口的老营地行进,同伴们已经到达那里了。他们从印第安河地区直接跨越了分水岭到了那里,而他自己却绕了个弯路想去看一下开春时能不能从育空岛往外运木材。他应该会在六点时到达营地。那时天肯定有点儿黑了,但是同伴们应该已经到了,篝火在燃烧,热腾腾的晚餐也会准备好。至于午餐,他用手按了按外套上那个凸起的包,实际是在衬衫里,用手帕包裹着紧贴着身体。这是唯一避免烤饼被冻住的方法。一想到那些烤饼,切开的每一片都用油脂浸透,并夹着一大片熏肉,他就满意地微笑了。

他一头扎进一大片云杉林中。小路变得越来越模糊。上一回有雪橇经过的地方又积攒了一英尺厚的雪。他庆幸自己没有带雪橇,可以轻快地前行。事实上,他除了包裹在手帕里的午餐什么也没带。但是他惊讶于这里的寒冷。当他用带着手套的手摩挲冻僵了的鼻子和颧骨的时候,他得出结论:确实很冷。他是个大胡子男人,但是他脸上的胡须并不能保护他高高耸立的颧骨和顽强挺立在寒气中的鼻子。

一只狗一路小跑尾随在男人的脚后,这是一只硕大的本地爱斯基摩犬,纯种的灰色狼狗,与他同宗兄弟——野狼——没有任何明显的性情上的差别。这只狗由于寒冷而消沉。它知道这并不是旅行的时候。它的本能比男人的判断要准确得多。事实上,天气并不是比零下五十度要冷,而是比零下六十度、七十度还要冷,是零下七十五度。既然冰点是零上三十二度,这就意味着现在是冰点下一百零七度。狗并不知道什么温度计。也许它的脑子没有像人脑子那样对寒冷那么敏感,但是野兽是有本能的。它体验到了一种模糊的但却极具威胁的恐惧,这种恐惧征服了它,使它跟在男人脚后偷偷摸摸地移动,使它热切地想知道男人的每个不寻常的举动,比如希望他走进帐篷或是找一个避风地生火。狗已经知道什么是火并且需要火,或者在雪下挖个洞来保暖抵御寒气。

狗呼出的湿气在它的皮毛上形成了一层均匀的霜粉,尤其是在它的颌骨和鼻口部,同时眼睫毛也被呼出的霜弄白了。男人的红色胡须也同样布满了霜,但更为坚固,甚至结了冰晶,并且体积随着每一次温暖潮湿的呼气不断增大。男人还在嚼着烟叶,脸上的冰把他的嘴唇冻得僵硬以至于当他喷出烟汁时无法及时擦净下巴颏儿,结果在下巴上挂了一串彩色的像琥珀一样坚固的冰晶并且在不断增长。如果男人跌倒,这冰晶就会像玻璃一样摔得粉碎。但是男人并不在乎这个。这就是嚼烟叶的人在这种国家必须付出的代价。他以前也在这种寒冷天气中出来过两次。他知道那两次没有这次寒冷，但是按"六十里"的酒精温度计记载，那两次的温度分别是零下五十度和零下五十五度。

他继续行进了几英里，穿过了一片平坦的树林，越过了一块腐草丛生的野地，然后跳下河岸到了一条封冻的小河。这就是亨德申河，他知道离河岔口只有十英里了。他看了看表，十点钟。他每小时行进四英里，他估算了一下照这个速度，他会在十二点半的时候到达岔口。为了庆祝一下他决定在那里吃午餐。

当男人沿着冰冻的河床继续蹒跚前行的时候，狗还是随意地跟在他的脚后，尾巴无精打采地低垂着。老雪橇道的车辙痕迹仍然清晰可见，但是在上一个经过的雪橇留下的痕迹上盖着十几英寸厚的雪。可见近一个月来没有人走过这条寂寞的小河。这个男人继续坚定地走着。他不是个勤于思考的人，尤其是在此时他除了会在岔口吃午餐和晚上六点会到营地与孩子们会合之外，他什么都没想。没有人能与之交谈，就算有，他嘴上厚厚的冰也让他无法说话，于是他继续孤独地咀嚼着烟叶，增加着下巴上胡须的长度。

有个想法反复涌现：天气太冷了，他从未经历过这样的寒冷。他边走边用带着棉手套的手背摩擦着颧骨和鼻子。他机械地这么做着，不时地换换手。可是，尽管他不断地揉搓着，他刚刚暖和了面部，鼻尖马上就冻僵了。他知道自己的脸肯定是布满了冻霜，后悔没有设计那种巴德在寒冷天气用的鼻带。这种带子可以横过脸颊保护脸和鼻子。但是这毕竟不那么重要。脸冻僵又怎么样？只是有点儿疼，仅此而已，没什么大不了的。

他的脑子空荡荡的，他的观察力却敏锐起来。他注意着小河的变化。哪里有拐弯，哪里有迂回，哪里是木材集结的地方，他也总是很仔细地留意应该从哪里落脚。一次他从一个转角绕过来的时候，突然像一匹受惊的马一样连连后退，绕过他刚刚踩着的地方，沿着小路后退了几步。他知道小河肯定是一冻到底了——没有河在这样的极地的冬天还能有水的——但是他也知道会有泉水从山侧涌出，在雪下和小河的冰面上流淌。他知道就算是最冷的天气也不会冻结这些泉水，但是他同时也知道这些泉水的危险。它们是陷阱。它们也许在雪下藏着大约三英寸或许是三英尺深的水涡。有时上面会覆盖着半英寸厚的一层薄冰，冰上面又盖着雪。有时薄冰和水交替着，以至于如果有人陷进去，他就会越陷越深，有时水甚至会浸湿到他的腰。

这就是他惊慌失措连连后退的原因。他已经感觉到了脚下的松动，已经听到了雪下面冰层的断裂声。在这样的温度下弄湿了脚就意味着麻烦和危险，至少也意味着时间上的拖延。因为他得被迫停下来生火，在火堆边赤着脚把袜子和靴子弄干。他站住仔细研究着河床和河岸，断定水是从右边流过来的。他又思索了一会儿，用手揉着脸和鼻子，然后绕向左边，小心翼翼地迈步，每走一步都要试试冰面的可靠性。当危险解除时，他重新嚼起了烟叶，继续以四英里的时速飞快前进。

在接下来的两个小时里，他遇到了几个类似的陷阱。通常这样的水涡上面的雪会呈下陷、结晶的状态，而这就预示了危险。然而他又一次次侥幸地脱险。还有一次，当他察觉到了危险，他就逼着他的狗走在前面。狗不愿意走，在那里犹犹豫豫的，直到男人把它推到前面，然后它快速地穿过绵延的白色河面。突然狗陷了进去，它马上挣扎着跳到一边，到了一处安全的冰面。它的前肢都湿了，几乎同时它身上的水就冻成了冰。狗快速地使劲儿舔掉腿上的冰，然后卧倒在雪里开始咬掉脚趾之间的冰。它这么做只是出于本能。不把冰弄掉脚爪就会疼。狗并不知道为什么，它只是服从内心深处的神秘驱动力。但是男人知道，这次他对这种事物的判断是正确的。他摘下右手手套，帮助狗儿清除冰块。他把手暴露出来还不到一分钟，就惊讶地发现手迅速地冻僵了。天真是冷啊！他迅速把手套戴上，并用手在胸前使劲地拍打着。

12点钟应该是这一天中最亮的时候，但是冬天的太阳仍然在远远的南面徜徉，丝毫没有升上水平线的意思。地面的凸起部分在太阳和亨德申河之间交错，这时男人正在晴朗的天空下走在河上，没有投下影子。在十二点半的时候，男人准时到达了河岔口。他对自己的速度很满意。如果他照这个速度继续前进的话，他一定可以在晚上六点与同伴们团聚。他解开夹克和衬衫取出他的午餐。这个动作只用了不到十五秒的时间，但是在这短暂的一瞬麻木的感觉立即袭上他裸露在外面的手指。他没有戴上手套，而只是不断地用力将手指在大腿上敲打。然后他坐在一段盖满了雪的木头上吃起来。用手指撞击大腿产生的刺痛感随即就消失了，这让他很震惊。他没顾得上咬一口烤饼，马上又将手指反复捶打并马上戴上手套，把另一只手拿出来吃东西。他想吃一大口，但是嘴边的冰让他根本张不开嘴。他忘记了应该先生火将冰雪融化。他暗自嘲笑自己的愚蠢，此时他注意到在他一开始坐下来时脚趾传来的刺痛已经消失了。他想知道脚趾是暖和过来了还是冻僵了。他动了动棉靴里面的脚趾，断定它们已经冻僵了。

他快速把手套戴上站了起来。他有点儿害怕。他来来回回地跺着脚，直到脚上又有了刺痛的感觉。天真是冷啊，他想着。原来那个从萨尔弗河回来的人在描述这个地区天气有多么冷的时候说的是事实。当时他还笑话人家！这表明一个人对事情不能过分自信。没错，真是冷啊。他来回踱着步，跺着脚，反复挥打着胳膊，直到又暖和起来才放心。他取出火柴开始生火。去年春天涨潮时在这片矮丛林中留下了一些从前的枝条，他从这里找到了柴火。他小心地从生小火开始，不久就生起了熊熊的火堆，在火旁他脸上的冰融化了，并吃了烤饼。这时，寒冷是被克服了。狗儿也洋洋自得地伸展着四肢尽量靠近火，既要取暖，还要小心别被火烤焦。

吃完午餐后，男人装满了烟斗悠闲地吸了一会儿烟。然后他戴上手套，将帽子两边的耳罩紧紧地扣在耳朵上，沿着小河左岔口的小路继续前进。狗儿很失望，恋恋不舍地回头看着火堆。男人不知道冷。也许他的先辈就不知道什么是寒冷，真正的寒冷，冰点下一百零七度的寒冷。但是狗儿知道，它所有的祖先都知道，因此它也知道。它知道在这令人恐惧的寒冷中不应该四处走，这时候应该暖暖和和地躲在雪洞里等待着有一片云能够把外面的寒冷遮住。另外，男人与狗之间的关系并不亲密。狗是男人的苦力，狗唯一得到的爱抚来自于皮鞭和威胁要鞭打它的尖利刺耳的声音。因此狗儿并不想努力把自己的忧虑告诉男人。它并不关心男人的安全，它只是自己很向往火。但是男人吹口哨了，又用鞭哨声威胁他了，狗儿只好摇摇摆摆地跟在男人的脚后继续前进。

男人又嚼起了烟叶，又开始长起了琥珀的胡须。他呼出的湿气也迅速地将他的胡须、眼眉和睫毛染上了一层白霜。看起来亨德申河的左岔口并没有太多的泉水，半小时了男人没有看到一点儿水涡的迹象。接下来事情就发生了。在一处毫无预警的地方，柔软完好的雪本应预示着下面坚固的冰面，男人却突然陷了进去。水不太深，只湿到了膝盖，他赶紧挣扎着跳到一处安全的冰面上。

他很恼火，大声诅咒着自己的噩运。他原本希望能够在六点钟到营地与同伴们会合，这一来要耽误一小时的时间了，因为他不得不生火来弄干鞋袜。在这种低温下这是必须要做的——他十分清楚这一点。他转过身来爬上河岸。在河岸的高处几株小云杉旁的矮树丛中混着水冲过来的一些木柴——主要是木棍和枝条，还有很大一部分的树杈和去年留下的干草。他在雪上扔了几大块树枝垫底，可以防止细弱的火苗随着雪的融化而被浇灭。男人从口袋里拿出一块白桦树皮，用火柴在上面划出火花。这东西比纸易燃。他把烧着的干树皮放在垫底的树枝上，然后不断地往火堆里添加干草和干燥的嫩树枝。

他弄得缓慢而仔细，因为他清楚地意识到危险。渐渐地，火苗越来越旺，他开始往火堆里添加大一些的枝条。他蹲在雪地上，从纠缠在一起的灌木丛里拽出树枝直接添到火堆里。他知道他不能失败。当气温是零下七十五度的时候，一个人在最初尝试生火的时候一定不能失败——尤其在脚已经湿透的情况下一定不能失败。如果脚是干的，那么要是没生起来火，他可以沿着小路跑上半英里，脚就能恢复血液循环。但是在零下七十五度的温度下，脚又是潮湿僵硬的时候，就无法用奔跑这个方法来恢复血液循环。无论他跑得多快，脚还是会越冻越硬。

这些男人都知道。到过萨尔弗河的老前辈去年秋天曾经告诉过他，而现在他很感激这个忠告。他的脚已经失去了所有知觉。为了生火他不得不摘下手套，手指马上就麻木了。四英里的时速使他的血液能够从心脏源源不断地涌入身体表面和四肢。但是他停下来的这一刹那,这个过程也随即放慢。冷气弥漫在这个毫无防备的地区,而他正不可避免地直接遭受到寒冷最强大的侵袭。在寒冷面前身体里的血液退缩了。血液像狗一样是有生命的,但是也像狗一样想藏起来躲避可怕的寒冷。只要男人保持四英里的时速,血液就会不由分说地传递到身体各个部位;但是如今血液已经消逝在身体的角落里。四肢是最早感受到这一点的。他湿透了的脚越冻越硬,露在外面的手指即使还没有冻僵也变得越来越麻木。鼻子和脸已经冻僵了,同时皮肤也由于缺少血液而越来越冷。

但是他仍是安全的。脚趾、鼻子和脸只是刚刚开始僵硬,因为火已经开始熊熊燃烧了。他正在往里添加手指那么粗的树枝,下一刻他就可以添加手腕那么粗的树枝,然后他就可以脱下湿了的鞋袜将它们烤干,同时还能够让赤着的脚在火旁暖和过来,当然,先要用雪搓一搓。火成功地点起来了,他也安全了。他记起了那位老前辈的忠告,笑了起来。那位老前辈曾经很严肃地断言没人能在零下五十度的时候独自穿越克朗代克地区。可是,他就在这里。他是出了点儿状况;他是孤身一人,但是他可以自救。那些前辈们太婆婆妈妈了,他想,至少有一些是这样的。一个男人应该做的就是保持冷静,那样他就会安然无恙。只要是真正的男人都可以独自走过这里。但是,他还是惊异于脸和鼻子冻僵的速度。他从没想到手指会在这么短的时间里变得毫无生命。说它们毫无生命,因为男人几乎不能移动手指去抓起一根树枝,好像手指已经远离了他的身体。当他抓树枝的时候他不得不看一下手指有没有抓住树枝。他和手指之间的线路好像断掉了。

这些都不算什么。只要有火,噼啪作响跳跃着的火苗预示着充满希望的生命。他开始要脱下麻皮靴。那上面结满了冰;厚实的德国袜像铁壳一样直箍膝盖;鞋带像大火过后缠绕在一起打着结的钢绳。他用冻僵的手指拉扯了一会儿,意识到自己的愚蠢,他取出了鞘刀。

但是在他割开鞋带之前,事情发生了。这完全是他自己的错,或者说,是他的过失。他不应该在树下生火。他应该在一片开阔地生火。但是在这里生火确实离树丛近,很方便拽出树枝直接扔到火里。现在他所生起的火堆上面的树的枝杈都积满了厚厚的雪。已经好几星期都没有风吹过这里,因此每条树杈上都满载着雪。每次男人拽树枝的时候都会给树带来一丝轻微的颤动——就男人而言,这种颤动是不易察觉的,但是足够的颤动就会导致灾难。高处的一条树杈上的雪翻了下来,砸到下面的枝杈,把它们上面的雪也弄翻了。这个过程在继续,不断地蔓延以至于波及整棵树。雪越来越多,如同雪崩,毫无预警地落了下来,火被浇灭了!刚刚火焰燃烧的地方如今是一堆凌乱的新雪。

男人惊呆了。这如同他听到了自己的死刑判决。他坐了一阵,瞪着刚刚火堆燃烧的地方。随即他冷静下来。也许萨尔弗河上的那位老前辈是对的。如果他有一个同伴，现在就不会身处险境。同伴还会生一堆火。现在得靠他自己再生起一堆火来，这第二次绝对不能失败。即使成功了，他也很可能会失去脚趾。他的脚现在已经冻坏了，而下一堆火生起来还需要些时间。

这些念头在他脑中转动的时候他并没有呆坐在那里。在他想这些事情的时候手里是在忙的。他重新又弄了个火堆的底座，这次是在空地上，上面没有讨厌的树会再把火弄灭。然后他在之前洪水的漂浮物中收集了一些干草和嫩树枝。他已经无法拢起手指去抓这些东西了，但是他可以两只手一起抱。这样，他弄到了很多腐烂了的枝条和一点儿不需要的绿苔，但是这已经是他能做到的权限了。他有条不紊地工作着，甚至收集了一抱的粗树枝以备火烧旺的时候用。狗儿始终蹲在那里看着男人，眼睛里充满了焦急的渴望，因为只有男人能够给它提供火，而火来得太慢了。

当一切就绪，男人把手伸到衣袋里又取出了一块白桦树皮。尽管他的手指感觉不到树皮的存在，他仍然知道树皮就在那里，因为当他摸索的时候能听到清脆的沙沙声。他竭尽全力也无法抓住树皮。他始终清醒地意识到每过一秒他的脚都会冻得越来越厉害。这个想法使他恐慌，但是他尽量克制着，保持镇静。他在牙齿的帮助下戴上手套，反复挥舞着胳膊，手用尽全力击打身体两侧。他一开始坐着拍打，后来又站起来继续挥舞；狗儿始终卧在雪地上，它像狼一样的尾巴弯过来暖暖和和地包裹住前爪，像狼一样尖尖的耳朵向前方耸立着，看着男人。男人在用手臂和手拍打时看到那只狗在自然皮毛的保护下温暖而安全，不由得嫉妒起来。

过了一会儿男人感觉到了拍打的手指末端有了一些知觉。这种微弱的酥麻的感觉越来越强烈直到发展成了一种折磨人的刺痛，但是男人却很愿意接受这种感觉。他右手剥掉手套去拿树皮。露在外面的手指很快又麻木了。他紧接着取出那捆硫黄火柴。但是无比的寒冷又夺去了他手指的知觉。在他竭力地想从一捆火柴中分出一根时，整捆火柴掉在了雪地上。他想把它从雪地上捡起来，没有成功。失去知觉的手指根本碰不到火柴，更别说拿起来了。他小心翼翼，尽量不去想冻僵的脚、鼻子和脸，而把全部精力放在火柴上。他注视着自己的手指，用他的视觉来代替触觉，当他看到手指放在了火柴的两侧时，他就收拢它们——或者说，他希望能并拢手指，因为手指已经不像身体的一部分，不听使唤了。他把右手的棉手套戴上，用力在膝盖上敲打。然后用戴着手套的双手，把那捆火柴连同很多雪一起捧了起来放在大腿上的外套衣襟里。但是状况仍然很糟糕。

经过一番周折，男人终于成功地用戴着手套的手掌夹住了火柴。借这个姿势将火柴送向嘴边。他使劲挣裂了脸上的冰，张开了嘴。他把下颚收紧，把上嘴唇撇到一边，用上牙蹭那捆火柴想分出一根来。他终于成功地拿出了一根，把它放在大腿上。情况还没有好转。他捡不起来火柴。他想出了一个办法。他用牙捡起了火柴放在腿上刮擦。试了二十来次才把火柴点着。然后用牙齿叼着燃着的火柴送向树皮。但是燃烧的硫黄味窜到了他的鼻孔，吸进了肺部，引起了一阵断断续续的咳嗽。火柴掉在雪里熄灭了。

那位萨尔弗河的老前辈是对的，紧接着他在勉强压抑住绝望的那一刻想道：在零下五十度的天气里，应该找一个伙伴同行。他使劲拍打着手，但是唤不起任何知觉。突然他用牙齿脱掉手套，露出双手。用手掌夹住整捆火柴。他还没有冻僵的手臂使他可以合起手掌紧紧压住火柴。然后他将这整捆火柴往腿上擦去。火柴燃起了火焰，70根火柴同时被点着了！没有风吹灭火柴。他把头偏向一边躲开让人窒息的浓烟，用燃烧着的一捆火柴去接近树皮。他这样抓着，感觉到手上有了知觉。他的肉烧着了。他能够闻得到。体内也能够感觉到。这种知觉发展为愈演愈烈的疼痛。他仍然坚持着，笨拙地握住这捆火柴去点树皮。树皮不那么容易点燃，因为他烧着的双手挡在前面，遮住了大部分的火苗。

最后，当他再也无法忍受的时候，他猛地把手拿开。燃烧着的火柴嗞嗞响着掉到了雪中，但是好在树皮已经点着了。他开始往火里放干草和小树枝。他没办法挑挑拣拣的，因为他只能用手捧着这些燃料。小块的朽木和绿苔与枝条绞缠在一起，他尽力用牙齿咬着把它们分开。他笨拙而小心地弄着火苗。这关乎生命，一定不能熄灭。身体表层的血在慢慢消失，男人开始颤抖，于是他的动作就变得更加的笨拙。一大块绿苔垂直落在了小火苗上。男人努力想用手指把它拨开，但是他颤抖的身体使他拨得太远了，还弄散了火苗，燃烧着的草和小树枝四散分开。他竭力想把它们重新聚拢到一起，但是无论他多么努力，颤抖着的身体不听使唤，树枝还是令人绝望地散落了一地。每根树枝都冒着一股青烟熄灭了。他终于没能生起火。男人无动于衷地四处看着，偶然看到了那只一直蹲在灰烬对面的雪地上的狗，不安地弓背耸肩，轻轻抬起一只前腿，然后另一只，来回地把身体的重量在两只脚上转移着。

男人看到了狗，他有了一个很疯狂的想法。他想起了一个陷在暴风雪中的人，杀了一头牛，躲在它的尸体里爬行，最终获救的故事。他可以把狗杀掉，然后把手塞进它温暖的身体里直到恢复知觉。然后他就可以再生一堆火。他冲着狗喊了一声叫它过来。然而他的声音里含着一种古怪的恐惧的声调，吓到了这只畜牲，男人以前从来没用这种方式招呼过它。一定有问题，狗多疑的天性使它嗅到了危险——虽然不知道是什么危险，但是不知何故，狗的脑子里浮现出对男人的恐惧。它听到男人的声音后把耳朵耷拉下来，它不安的弓背、交替脚爪的动作越来越明显；但是它就是不到男人那里去。男人用手和膝盖支撑着爬向狗。这个不寻常的姿势再次引起了狗的怀疑，狗悄然地跑开了。

男人在雪地上坐了片刻，极力保持冷静。然后他用牙把手套戴上，站了起来。他先向下瞄了一眼，确认自己真的站起来了，因为脚已经完全失去了知觉，让他觉得自己的脚没着地。他直立的姿势消除了狗对他的怀疑。因此当男人像往常一样专横地用鞭哨的声音呼唤它时，狗还是习惯性地、顺从地走到男人边来了。当狗走到伸手能够到的地方时，男人再也控制不住自己了。他伸出胳膊猛地扑向狗，当他发现他的手冻得已经无法抓住东西的时候他着实吃了一惊，他的手指既不能弯曲也没有知觉。他刚才竟然一时忘记了自己的手已经冻僵了而且冻得越来越严重。所有这一切发生得太快，狗来不及逃掉，男人就用手臂圈住了狗的身体。他坐在雪地上，用这个姿势紧紧抱着狗，而狗咆哮着、哀鸣着、挣扎着。

但是他只能做到这些，用手臂抱住狗，坐在那里。他意识到他根本不能杀了这只狗。他没办法做到。他麻木的手既不能拔刀也不能握住刀，更别说杀狗了。他于是把狗放开，狗急忙发疯似的夹着尾巴逃开了，仍然在咆哮着。狗退到离他40英尺的地方停下来，好奇地看着男人，耳朵向前方耸立着。男人向下看了看手，想找到它们的位置，发现它们都悬在手臂的末端。男人觉得要靠眼睛来找手在哪里真是挺有意思的。他开始来回挥舞手臂，把戴着手套的手在身侧敲打。他猛烈地做了五分钟，心脏终于涌出了足够的血液到他的身体表面，他停止了颤抖，但是仍然没有唤起手的知觉。他感觉双手像重物一样挂在手臂上。他想驱散这个想法，但是他发现自己竟然忘记要做什么了。

死亡的恐惧隐约而沉重地向他袭来。他意识到这不单单是冻僵手指和脚趾或是失去手足的问题了，而是生死攸关的问题了，此时这种恐惧变得强烈起来。这让他恐慌，他转过身沿着古老模糊的河岸小路奔跑着。狗也加入进来，跟在男人的后面。他在这种生平从未经历过的恐惧中盲目地、无意识地奔跑着。慢慢地，当他在雪地上挣扎狂奔的时候，他又开始能够看清东西了——河岸、老木材堆、光秃秃的白杨树和天空。奔跑使他感觉好了些。他不再颤抖了。也许，如果他一直跑下去的话，他脚上的冰就会融化；并且，如果他跑得够远，他就能到达营地见到他的同伴们。毫无疑问他会失去一些手指和脚趾，还有脸的一部分也会被冻坏，但是只要他到了那里同伴们会照顾他，挽救他身体的其他部分。而同时他的脑海中有另一个声音在响：他永远回不了营地与同伴们相会了。因为离得太远了，他会被冻得越来越严重，不久就会僵硬死去。他把这个想法远远抛在脑后不去想它。有时这个想法会不时地蹦出来，但是他仍然把它塞回去想些别的事情。

他很奇怪自己的脚冻得这样严重，即使他的脚在击打着地面并承载着身体的重量他都毫无知觉，却仍然能够用这双脚奔跑。在他看来他像是在地面上掠过，脚与地面没有接触。他曾在哪里看过长着翅膀的墨丘利神，他想知道墨丘利神飞的时候的感觉是不是和他现在掠过地面的感觉一样。

他想尽快跑到营地和同伴们那里,但却忽略了自己的弱点:缺乏耐力。他几次跌倒又站起来,最后还是蹒跚着,跌跌撞撞倒了下来。他试着站起来,但没有成功。他决定坐下来休息,接下来他要换作走,持续地走。当他坐下来喘匀了气,他发现自己感觉很温暖、很舒适。他不再颤抖,甚至像是有一股暖流冲向他的胸和四肢。但是当他摸鼻子和脸的时候却没有知觉。奔跑不能融化脸上的冰,也无法融化手脚的冰。然后那个想法涌了出来,他身体冻僵的部分会不断蔓延。他尽量控制这个想法,忘记它,想些别的事情;他意识到这种想法带来的惊慌的情绪,他害怕这种惊慌。然而这种想法不断地涌现着、持续着,直到他似乎看到自己的身体完全冻僵的那一幕。他无法忍受,又开始沿着小路疯狂地奔跑。一旦他慢下来行走,这个冰冻将蔓延的想法马上使他重新奔跑起来。

狗一直跟在男人的后面奔跑。当男人再次倒下来时,狗用尾巴缠住前爪面对面坐在男人面前,十分好奇地看着他。狗很温暖和安全,这激怒了男人,他大声诅咒着直到狗妥协地垂下了耳朵。这时颤抖的感觉更快地袭向男人。他正在与严寒的抗争中败下阵来。冰冻从四面八方向体内蔓延。这个想法促使他继续奔跑,但是只跑了不到一百英尺他就再次蹒跚着一头栽倒了。这是他最后一次恐慌。当他恢复了呼吸和控制力的时候,他坐起来开始在心中盘算要有尊严地去迎接死亡。但是他的想法也不完全是这样的。他想到的是他一直在欺骗自己,像一只被砍掉了头的鸡一样四处乱跑——这就是他所能想到的比喻。无论如何他是一定会被冻死的,他也许可以体面地去接受这一切。这反而使他在体内产生了一种平静,随之而来的是第一丝睡意。他想,在睡梦中死去是个好主意,就像打上了麻药一样。冻僵并不是像人们想象的那样可怕。有很多死法比这糟糕得多。

他想象着同伴们第二天发现他的尸体。突然,他发现他正与他们一起沿着小路寻找着自己。他和同伴们一起绕过小路的一个转弯看到了躺在雪地上的自己。他不再属于他自己了,因为那时他已脱离了自己的身体,与孩子们站在一起看着雪中的自己。天气真是冷啊,这就是他所想的。当他回到美国时,他会告诉人们什么是真正的寒冷。他把思绪拉回到那位萨尔弗河老人。他可以清楚地看到老前辈在吸着烟斗,温暖而舒适。

"你是对的,老家伙;你对了,"男人对着那位萨尔弗河的老人喃喃说道。

然后,男人沉沉地陷入了似乎是他所经历的最满足、最舒适的睡眠中。狗儿仍然在对面蹲坐着,等待着。短暂的白天在漫长的黄昏中渐近结束。仍然没有生火的迹象,并且,在狗看来从不知道一个人会这样一直在雪中坐着而不生火。当夜幕降临的时候,狗对火的渴望紧紧摄住了它,随着每一次抬起和挪动前爪,狗都低低地哀鸣着，然后它又垂下耳朵期待着男人的责骂。但是男人仍然一动不动。后来狗开始大声地嚎叫。再后来它悄悄地靠近男人，闻到了死亡的气息。狗惊得皮毛直竖，连连后退。它迟疑了一小会儿。清冷的天空中，繁星闪烁，狗在天空下哀号着。然后它转过身沿着小路向着它印象中的营地的方向跑去，在那里会有别人给它食物，为它生火。

# Sherwood Anderson
# (1876—1941)

Sherwood Anderson was best-known as an American short story writer whose prose style, based on everyday speech and derived from Gertrude Stein's experimental writing, much influenced Ernest Hemingway, William Faulkner, John Steinbeck and other modern American fiction writers. Young Sherwood took various jobs to help his family. He worked as a manual laborer, enlisted in the US Army, and then enrolled at Wittenberg University. Eventually he secured a job as a copywriter in Chicago. After marriage, he had three children and managed his own business and manufacturing firms. Then he left his business, his wife and children to pursue the writer's life of creativity. When he returned, he worked for a publishing and advertising company in Chicago. Anderson died of peritonitis in Panama at 64.

His first mature book is *Winesburg, Ohio* (1919), a collection of interrelated short stories. His major novels include *Many Marriages* (1923), which focuses on sexual fulfillment; *Dark Laughter* (1925), which values the "primitive" over the "civilized" and *Beyond Desire* (1932), which depicts the Southern textile mill labor struggles. However, his best works are generally considered to be his short stories collected in *The Triumph of the Egg* (1921), *Horses and Men* (1923), *Death in the Woods* (1933), and *Winesburg, Ohio* as mentioned previously.

## Hands

*As the opening story of* **Winesburg, Ohio,** *Anderson claimed "Hands" as the first "real" story he ever wrote. The collection explores the devastating consequences on life in a provincial town due to the repressive conventions. Through the young reporter's sympathetic narrative, Biddlebaum's innocence, kindheartedness, passion and eventual isolation are fully depicted in sharp contrast with the townspeople's prejudice, narrow-mindedness, selfishness and stubborn viciousness. It is an outcry for human understanding, compassion and love.*

Upon the half decayed veranda of a small frame house that stood near the edge of a ravine near the town of Winesburg, Ohio, a fat little old man walked nervously up and down. Across a long field that had been seeded for clover but that had produced only a dense crop of yellow mustard weeds, he could see the public highway along which went a wagon filled with berry pickers returning from the fields. The berry pickers, youths and maidens, laughed and shouted boisterously. A boy clad in a blue shirt leaped from the wagon and attempted to drag after him one of the maidens who screamed and protested shrilly. The feet of the boy in the road kicked up a cloud of dust that floated across the face of the departing sun. Over the long field came a thin girlish voice. "Oh, you Wing Biddlebaum, comb your hair, it's falling into your eyes," commanded the voice to the man, who was bald and whose nervous little hands fiddled about the bare white forehead as though arranging a mass of tangled locks.

Wing Biddlebaum, forever frightened and beset by a ghostly band of doubts, did not think of himself as in any way a part of the life of the town where he had lived for twenty years. Among all the people of Winesburg but one had come close to him. With George Willard, son of Tom Willard, the proprietor of the New Willard House, he had formed something like a friendship. George Willard was the reporter on the *Winesburg Eagle* and sometimes in the evenings he walked out along the highway to Wing Biddlebaum's house. Now as the old man walked up and down on the veranda, his hands moving nervously about, he was hoping that George Willard would come and spend the evening with him. After the wagon containing the berry pickers had passed, he went across the field through the tall mustard weeds and climbing a rail fence peered anxiously along the road to the town. For a moment he stood thus, rubbing his hands together and looking up and down the road, and then, fear overcoming him, ran back to walk again upon the porch of his own house.

In the presence of George Willard, Wing Biddlebaum, who for twenty years had been the town mystery, lost something of his timidity, and his shadowy personality, submerged in a sea of doubts, came forth to look at the world. With the young reporter at his side, he ventured in the light of day into Main Street or strode up and down on the rickety front porch of his own house, talking excitedly. The voice that had been low and trembling became shrill and loud. The bent figure straightened. With a kind of wriggle, like a fish returned to the brook by the fisherman, Biddlebaum the silent began to talk, striving to put into words the ideas that had been accumulated by his mind during long years of silence.

Wing Biddlebaum talked much with his hands. The slender expressive fingers, forever active, forever striving to conceal themselves in his pockets or behind his back, came forth and became the piston rods of his machinery of expression.

The story of Wing Biddlebaum is a story of hands. Their restless activity, like unto the beating of the wings of an imprisoned bird, had given him his name. Some obscure poet of the town had thought of it. The hands alarmed their owner. He wanted to keep them hidden away and looked with amazement at the quiet inexpressive hands of other men who worked beside him in the fields, or passed, driving sleepy teams on country roads.

When he talked to George Willard, Wing Biddlebaum closed his fists and beat with them upon a table or on the walls of his house. The action made him more comfortable. If the desire to talk came to him when the two were walking in the fields, he sought out a stump or the top board of a fence and with his hands pounding busily talked with renewed ease.

The story of Wing Biddlebaum's hands is worth a book in itself. Sympathetically set forth it would tap many strange, beautiful qualities in obscure men. It is a job for a poet. In Winesburg the hands had attracted attention merely because of their activity. With them Wing Biddlebaum had picked as high as a hundred and forty quarts of strawberries in a day. They became his distinguishing feature, the source of his fame. Also they made more grotesque an already grotesque and elusive individuality. Winesburg was proud of the hands of Wing Biddlebaum in the same spirit in which it was proud of Banker White's new stone house and Wesley Moyer's bay stallion, Tony Tip, that had won the two-fifteen trot at the fall races in Cleveland.

As for George Willard, he had many times wanted to ask about the hands. At times an almost overwhelming curiosity had taken hold of him. He felt that there must be a reason for their strange activity and their inclination to keep hidden away and only a growing respect for Wing Biddlebaum kept him from blurting out the questions that were often in his mind.

Once he had been on the point of asking. The two were walking in the fields on a summer afternoon and had stopped to sit upon a grassy bank. All afternoon Wing Biddlebaum had talked as one inspired. By a fence he had stopped and beating like a giant woodpecker upon the top board had shouted at George Willard, condemning his tendency to be too much influenced by the people about him, "You are destroying yourself," he cried.

"You have the inclination to be alone and to dream and you are afraid of dreams. You want to be like others in town here. You hear them talk and you try to imitate them."

On the grassy bank Wing Biddlebaum had tried again to drive his point home. His voice became soft and reminiscent, and with a sigh of contentment he launched into a long rambling talk, speaking as one lost in a dream.

Out of the dream Wing Biddlebaum made a picture for George Willard. In the picture men lived again in a kind of pastoral golden age. Across a green open country came clean-limbed young men, some afoot, some mounted upon horses. In crowds the young men came to gather about the feet of an old man who sat beneath a tree in a tiny garden and who talked to them.

Wing Biddlebaum became wholly inspired. For once he forgot the hands. Slowly they stole forth and lay upon George Willard's shoulders. Something new and bold came into the voice that talked. "You must try to forget all you have learned," said the old man. "You must begin to dream. From this time on you must shut your ears to the roaring of the voices."

Pausing in his speech, Wing Biddlebaum looked long and earnestly at George Willard. His eyes glowed. Again he raised the hands to caress the boy and then a look of horror swept over his face.

With a convulsive movement of his body, Wing Biddlebaum sprang to his feet and thrust his hands deep into his trousers pockets. Tears came to his eyes. "I must be getting along home. I can talk no more with you," he said nervously.

Without looking back, the old man had hurried down the hillside and across a meadow, leaving George Willard perplexed and frightened upon the grassy slope. With a shiver of dread the boy arose and went along the road toward town. "I'll not ask him about his hands," he thought, touched by the memory of the terror he had seen in the man's eyes. "There's something wrong, but I don't want to know what it is. His hands have something to do with his fear of me and of everyone."

And George Willard was right. Let us look briefly into the story of the hands. Perhaps our talking of them will arouse the poet who will tell the hidden wonder story of the influence for which the hands were but fluttering pennants of promise.

In his youth Wing Biddlebaum had been a school teacher in a town in Pennsylvania. He was not then known as Wing Biddlebaum, but went by the less euphonic name of Adolph Myers. As Adolph Myers he was much loved by the boys of his school.

Adolph Myers was meant by nature to be a teacher of youth. He was one of those rare, little understood men who rule by a power so gentle that it passes as a lovable weakness. In their feeling for the boys under their charge such men are not unlike the finer sort of women in their love of men.

And yet that is but crudely stated. It needs the poet there. With the boys of his school, Adolph Myers had walked in the evening or had sat talking until dusk upon the schoolhouse steps lost in a kind of dream. Here and there went his hands, caressing the shoulders of the boys, playing about the tousled heads. As he talked his voice became soft and musical. There was a caress in that also. In a way the voice and the hands, the stroking of the shoulders and the touching of the hair was a part of the schoolmaster's effort to carry a dream into the young minds. By the caress that was in his fingers he expressed himself. He was one of those men in whom the force that creates life is diffused, not centralized. Under the caress of his hands doubt and disbelief went out of the minds of the boys and they began also to dream.

And then the tragedy. A half-witted boy of the school became enamored of the young master. In his bed at night he imagined unspeakable things and in the morning went forth to tell his dreams as facts. Strange, hideous accusations fell from his loose-hung lips. Through the Pennsylvania town went a shiver. Hidden, shadowy doubts that had been in men's minds concerning Adolph Myers were galvanized into beliefs.

The tragedy did not linger. Trembling lads were jerked out of bed and questioned. "He put his arms about me," said one. "His fingers were always playing in my hair," said another.

One afternoon a man of the town, Henry Bradford, who kept a saloon, came to the schoolhouse door. Calling Adolph Myers into the school yard he began to beat him with his fists. As his hard knuckles beat down into the frightened face of the schoolmaster, his wrath became more and more terrible. Screaming with dismay, the children ran here and there like disturbed insects. "I'll teach you to put your hands on my boy, you beast," roared the saloon keeper, who, tired of beating the master, had begun to kick him about the yard.

Adolph Myers was driven from the Pennsylvania town in the night. With lanterns in their hands a dozen men came to the door of the house where he lived alone and commanded that he dress and come forth. It was raining and one of the men had a rope in his hands. They had intended to hang the schoolmaster, but something in his figure, so small, white, and pitiful, touched their hearts and they let him escape. As he ran away into the darkness they repented of their weakness and ran after him, swearing and throwing sticks and great balls of soft mud at the figure that screamed and ran faster and faster into the darkness.

For twenty years Adolph Myers had lived alone in Winesburg. He was but forty but looked sixty-five. The name of Biddlebaum he got from a box of goods seen at a freight station as he hurried through an eastern Ohio town. He had an aunt in Winesburg, a black-toothed old woman who raised chickens, and with her he lived until she died. He had been ill for a year after the experience in Pennsylvania, and after his recovery worked as a day laborer in the fields, going timidly about and striving to conceal his hands. Although he did not understand what had happened he felt that the hands must be to blame. Again and again the fathers of the boys had talked of the hands. "Keep your hands to yourself," the saloon keeper had roared, dancing with fury in the schoolhouse yard.

Upon the veranda of his house by the ravine, Wing Biddlebaum continued to walk up and down until the sun had disappeared and the road beyond the field was lost in the grey shadows. Going into his house he cut slices of bread and spread honey upon them. When the rumble of the evening train that took away the express cars loaded with the day's harvest of berries had passed and restored the silence of the summer night, he went again to walk upon the veranda. In the darkness he could not see the hands and they became quiet. Although he still hungered for the presence of the boy, who was the medium through which he expressed his love of man, the hunger became again a part of his loneliness and his waiting. Lighting a lamp, Wing Biddlebaum washed the few dishes soiled by his simple meal and, setting up a folding cot by the screen door that led to the porch, prepared to undress for the night. A few stray white bread crumbs lay on the cleanly washed floor by the table; putting the lamp upon a low stool he began to pick up the crumbs, carrying them to his mouth one by one with unbelievable rapidity. In the dense blotch of light beneath the table, the kneeling figure looked like a priest engaged in some service of his church. The nervous expressive fingers, flashing in and out of the light, might well have been mistaken for the fingers of the devotee going swiftly through decade after decade of his rosary.

**Questions**
1. What was so special about Wing Biddlebaum's hands?
2. Why was Biddlebaum so cruelly treated in the Pennsylvania town when he was a schoolmaster?
3. What did Biddlebaum try to convey to George Willard when they met?
4. What kind of life did Biddlebaum live near the town of Winesburg?
5. What is the author's attitudes to Biddlebaum and the townspeople respectively? And how does he indicate the differences stylistically?

# 舍伍德·安德森
# (1876—1941)

美国作家舍伍德·安德森以短篇小说闻名于世。他的散文风格基于日常口语，同时也得益于格特鲁德·斯坦实验写作之精华。美国现代小说名家欧内斯特·海明威、威廉·福克纳、约翰·斯坦贝克等都曾直接受其写作风格的影响。舍伍德年轻时曾干过各种工作以补家用。他干过体力活，在美国军队服过役，后来上了威登堡大学。最终他在芝加哥获得了一份编写广告的稳定工作。结婚后，他有三个孩子并经营自己的工厂。后来他突然放弃生意，离开妻子和孩子，去追求一种作家的创作人生。他回来后在芝加哥为一家出版和广告公司工作。安德森最终在巴拿马死于腹膜炎，享年64岁。

他的第一部成名作《小城畸人》（1919）是一部短篇小说集。其主要长篇小说包括：《多次婚姻》（1923），主要探讨性满足问题；《黑暗中的笑声》（1925），赞美"原始人"，贬低"文明人"；《超越欲望》（1932），描写南方纺织厂的工人斗争。然而，其杰作通常被认为是他的短篇小说，收录在《蛋的胜利》（1921）、《马与人》（1923）、《林中之死》（1933），以及前面提到的《小城畸人》等短篇小说集中。

## 手

《手》是安德森《小城畸人》中的开篇。他声称该作品是他第一篇"真正的"故事。该短篇小说集探索了偏远小镇中传统如何压抑人性以及人的心灵遭受摧残的后果。故事通过年轻记者充满同情的叙述，比德尔邦的无辜、好心肠、热情以及后来的孤独被完整地描绘出来，与此形成鲜明对照的是城里人的偏见、狭隘、自私以及极大的恶意。故事呼吁人与人的理解、彼此的同情与爱护。

俄亥俄州瓦恩斯堡镇附近的溪谷边有一座木架屋，在木屋半朽的游廊上，一位又胖又矮的老头神情紧张地来回走动着。伸向远方的田地里本来播种的是三叶草，结果却长出密密麻麻的黄芥末色杂草。老头的目光越过田地可以看见远处的公路，公路上行驶着一辆大车，车上挤满了从地里归来的采浆果的年轻人。这些采果的姑娘、小伙又笑又叫，好不热闹。一个身着蓝衬衫的男孩跳下车，想方设法往前拽一位姑娘,姑娘尖叫着表示抗议。男孩的双脚踢起路上的尘土,飞扬的尘土遮掩了日落的晚霞。从深远的田地那边传来女孩般尖细的叫喊声。"嘿,温·比德尔邦,梳好你的头发,都掉到眼里去了,"那声音命令着老头。老头秃顶,紧张的手神经质地胡乱摸挲着光秃、白皙的脑门儿,就好像在梳理一团杂乱无章的头发。

温·比德尔邦总是因为一大堆疑惑而感到惧怕和困扰,他虽然在本镇住了20年,但从未认为自己与镇里的生活有任何关系。瓦恩斯堡全镇只有一个人亲近他。老头与乔治·威拉德结成了某种友谊,乔治是新威拉德住宅主人汤姆·威拉德的儿子。乔治·威拉德是《瓦恩斯堡鹰报》的记者,他有时晚上沿着公路走出来,走到温·比德尔邦家。眼下这老头在游廊上来回走动,双手紧张地活动着,他希望乔治·威拉德能来与他共度此夜。载着采果人的大车过去后,老头穿过长满高高的芥末色杂草的田地,爬过护栏,焦急地观望通往镇子的大路。他就这样站了一会儿,搓着双手,朝大路东张西望,后来他感到一阵恐惧,就又跑回自家的回廊,独自踱来踱去。

温·比德尔邦20年来一直是镇上的谜,只是在乔治·威拉德面前,他才摆脱掉某种胆怯,他那充满疑惑的阴郁之心才得以出来重见天日。有这位年轻记者在身旁,他才斗胆在光天化日之下走上中心大街,或者在自家摇摇摆摆的阳台上来回大步走动,高谈阔论。原来低沉、颤抖的嗓音也变得尖细、高昂起来,佝偻的身躯也挺直起来。就像渔夫放归溪流的鱼,沉默者比德尔邦扭动着身躯开始讲话,他千方百计地组织语言来表达长时间的沉默在脑海中所积累的念头。

温·比德尔邦多用手来说话。他的手指纤细灵活,富有表现力,总是那么活跃,总是试图藏在兜里或背后,活动起来就成了他那套表达机械的活塞杆。

温·比德尔邦的故事就是手的故事。他那双闲不住的双手活动起来就像被关在笼子里的鸟的翅膀在扑闪,"温"即翅膀的意思,他的名字因此意而得。镇里某个无名诗人想出这么个名字。这双手使其主人感到惊恐。他想把手藏起来,同时惊愕地看着其他人安静而冷漠的手,这些人就是地里在他身旁干活的人们,或在乡村路上昏昏欲睡的一队队人马。

温·比德尔邦与乔治·威拉德谈起话来,总是握着拳头,捶着桌子或房子四周的墙壁。这一动作令他舒服。两人在田野中散步的时候,若讲话之欲袭上心头,温·比德尔邦就找一个树桩或护栏顶板,用手不停地敲打,然后重新悠然自得地讲起来。

有关温·比德尔邦之手的故事本身就值得写一本书。以同情心讲述该故事会开启无名之辈许多奇异、美妙的秉性。这是诗人的事。在瓦恩斯堡,这双手吸引人之处只是其活力。温·比德尔邦用这双手曾经一天采集多达一百四十夸脱的草莓。手是他突出的特征,他名声的来源。同时手也使得他本来已经怪诞、莫测的个性越发怪诞。瓦恩斯堡以温·比德尔邦的手为荣,就如同它以班克·怀特的新石宅和韦斯利·莫耶的栗色公马托尼·蒂普为荣一样,这匹公马曾在克利夫兰秋季赛马会上夺得2分15秒标准轻驾车赛冠军。

就乔治·威拉德来说,他好多次都想问问有关那双手的事。有时候这种好奇攫住他的心,几乎不可抗拒。他感到一定有原因促使那双手异常活跃而且老想藏起来,只是对温·比德尔邦日益增多的敬重才使他没有贸然问出脑中常想的问题。

有一次他准备好了就要问这事。那是一个夏日的下午,俩人在田野里漫步,随后停下来坐在绿草如茵的堤坝上。整个下午温·比德尔邦都在滔滔不绝地说着,灵性大发。在一处护栏边他曾停下来,一边像只大啄木鸟那样敲击着顶板,一边向乔治·威拉德大声喊叫,责备他太容易受周围人的影响。"你是在毁了自己,"他大声说。

"你喜欢独处与梦想,但又惧怕梦想。你想像镇子里其他人一样。你听他们说话,竭力模仿他们。"

在绿草如茵的堤坝上,温·比德尔邦又在竭力阐明自己的观点。他的嗓音变得轻柔而怀旧,随着一声自足的叹息,他开始漫无边际地畅谈起来,就如同痴人说梦。

在梦中,温·比德尔邦为乔治·威拉德描绘了一幅图景。图景中,人们又生活在一个田园般的黄金时代。从碧绿、宽阔的田野对面来了一队身姿矫健的小伙子,有的徒步,有的骑马。小伙子们齐聚在一位老人脚下,老人坐在小花园里的树下,对他们说话。

温·比德尔邦完全在灵感的驱使之下。仅此一次他忘却了自己的手。此时他那双手缓缓地、不知不觉地伸了出来,搭在了乔治·威拉德的肩膀上。某种新颖、大胆的东西传进他的嗓音,在述说。"你必须尽力忘掉所学的一切,"老头说,"你一定要开始梦想。从现在起你一定要关闭耳朵、弃绝各种声音的喧嚣。"

温·比德尔邦说话间停了一会儿,长久而真挚地望着乔治·威拉德。他的双眼炯炯发亮。他再一次举起手抚摩这孩子,突然一阵恐惧的表情掠过他的脸庞。

随着身体一阵抽动,温·比德尔邦跳起身来,将手深深地插入裤兜。他的双眼沁满泪水。"我得回家了。我不能再跟你说了,"他紧张地说。

老人头也不回,急匆匆地走下山坡,穿过草地,撇下乔治·威拉德在草坡上困惑不解、心存恐惧。这孩子害怕地颤抖起来,沿着大路朝镇里走去。"我不问他手的事了,"他思忖着,想起老人眼中的恐惧仍感到心动。"一定有事儿,但我也不想知道是什么了。他的手与害怕我和害怕其他人有关。"

乔治·威拉德是对的。让咱们简略地回顾一下有关这双手的故事。也许对手的述说会触动诗人讲述一个秘而不宣、非同寻常的故事，而手只是某种招展的锦旗，似乎在透露这个故事潜移默化的影响。

在他的青年时代，温·比德尔邦曾在宾夕法尼亚的一个小镇里做教员。他当时并不叫温·比德尔邦，而是叫一个不那么响亮的名字，阿道夫·迈尔斯。当时的阿道夫·迈尔斯深受学校里男孩子们的爱戴。

阿道夫·迈尔斯天生就是教孩子的料。他属于那种少见的、鲜为人知的人，这种人靠文质彬彬的力量来统管一切，而这往往被看作一种可爱的弱点。这种人对自己所负责的孩子们的感情无不像感情细腻的女人对男人的爱。

但这只是粗略地阐述一番，需要诗人描绘才会更生动。阿道夫·迈尔斯与学校里的孩子们在一起，傍晚散步，或坐着畅谈，直到校舍台阶上的黄昏渐渐地消失在梦中。他那双手四处忙碌着，抚摸孩子们的肩膀，把玩他们蓬松的头发。他说着话，嗓音柔和而悦耳。他的话音里也有一种爱抚。从某个方面讲，那嗓音、那双手，还有拍打肩膀和抚弄头发都是这位老师努力向孩子们头脑中灌输梦想的一部分。他通过手指间的爱抚表达自己。他这类人的生命力是发散型的，而不是集中型的。在他的双手爱抚下，孩子们头脑中的疑惑与怀疑烟消云散，他们也开始梦想。

而后来，悲剧降临。学校一名笨男孩被这位年轻的老师迷住了。他晚上在床上想象出不可言喻之事，而到了早上就直截了当地把梦说成了事实。也正是从他那把不住门的嘴，怪异、可怕的谴责之词倾泻而来。这个宾夕法尼亚小镇传出一阵震颤。从前潜藏在人们头脑中有关阿道夫·迈尔斯的疑惑被激活成某种信念。

这悲剧未停片刻。胆战心惊的孩子们被拉下床，遭到质问。"他用胳膊搂我，"一个孩子说。"他的手指头老是摆弄我的头发，"另一个说。

一天下午，镇里的头号人物，开酒吧的亨利·布拉德福来到教室门前。他把阿道夫·迈尔斯叫到操场上，随后就开始用拳头揍他。他硬邦邦的手关节狠狠地打在那男教师惊恐万状的脸上，他的愤怒变得越来越可怕。孩子们惊慌地尖叫着，就像被惊动的虫子四处逃窜。"让你用手碰我的孩子，你这畜生，"酒吧老板吼叫着说。他用拳头打够了男教师，开始满院子用脚踢他。

阿道夫·迈尔斯在晚上被赶出了这个宾夕法尼亚小镇。十多个人手提灯笼来到教师独自居住的房前，命令他穿上衣服出来。天下着雨，其中一个人的手里拿着绳子。他们本来想吊死男教师，可是他矮小的身材、白皙的皮肤以及令人怜悯的神情触动了这些人的心，他们也就放他跑了。可一旦他向黑夜逃跑，这些人又后悔自己心太软,于是又追上去,边骂边向那身影扔树枝和硕大的软泥球,直到那身影越跑越快,消失在黑夜之中。

20年来,阿道夫·迈尔斯独自一人生活在瓦恩斯堡镇。他才40岁,但看起来有65岁。比德尔邦这个名字,他取自在货运站所看见的一箱货物,当时他正匆匆路过一个俄亥俄州东部的小镇。他有一个姑妈在瓦恩斯堡镇,姑妈是个牙齿发黑的养鸡老太太,他与姑妈一直生活到她去世。自从宾夕法尼亚那场经历之后,他病了整整一年。身体恢复后,他在地里打散工,出门小心翼翼,竭力掩藏自己的双手。虽然他并不明白发生了什么,但他感到都是手的错。男孩子的父亲们曾屡次三番地说到手的事。"把手放老实点儿,"酒吧老板当时咆哮着说,在学校的操场上暴跳如雷。

在溪谷边木屋的游廊上,温·比德尔邦还在来回走动,直到太阳落下去,田地远处的大路消失在灰茫茫的夜色之中。他走进屋里切了几片面包,然后抹上蜂蜜。晚班快车隆隆作响,拉走满载的一车车白天收获的浆果,轰鸣声过去之后,一切又恢复了夏日夜晚的平静。此时他又走到回廊上,踱着步子。在黑暗中他看不见双手,他的手安静下来。那男孩成为他表达对人类之爱的媒介,虽然他仍渴望男孩的到来,但这种渴望同时也成为他孤独与等待的一部分。温·比德尔邦点上灯,洗了简单的晚饭时用过的几个盘子,在通往阳台的拉门旁架起折叠床,准备脱衣就寝。一些漏掉的白面包渣洒落在桌旁清洗得干干净净的地板上。他把灯放在矮凳子上,开始捡面包渣,飞快地一一送进嘴里。在桌下浓密的灯影里,他跪着的身影就像教堂里正忙着的牧师。那紧张、富于表现力的手指在灯影里闪烁不停,很容易被误认为那是信徒的手指几十年如一日地飞快地捻珠祈祷。

Sherwood Anderson

## Paper Pills

*The short story "Paper Pills" is one of the 25 short stories in* **Winesburg, Ohio**. *It tells us a "strange" marriage, and it expresses a deep sense of frustration in modern people.*

He was an old man with a white beard and huge nose and hands. Long before the time during which we will know him, he was a doctor and drove a jaded white horse from house to house through the streets of Winesburg. Later he married a girl who had money. She had been left a large fertile farm when her father died. The girl was quiet, tall, and dark, and to many people she seemed very beautiful. Everyone in Winesburg wondered why she married the doctor. Within a year after the marriage she died.

The knuckles of the doctor's hands were extraordinarily large. When the hands were closed they looked like clusters of unpainted wooden balls as large as walnuts fastened together by steel rods. He smoked a cob pipe and after his wife's death sat all day in his empty office close by a window that was covered with cobwebs. He never opened the window. Once on a hot day in August he tried but found it stuck fast and after that he forgot all about it.

Winesburg had forgotten the old man, but in Doctor Reefy there were the seeds of something very fine. Alone in his musty office in the Heffner Block above the Paris Dry Goods Company's store, he worked ceaselessly, building up something that he himself destroyed. Little pyramids of truth he erected and after erecting knocked them down again that he might have the truths to erect other pyramids.

Doctor Reefy was a tall man who had worn one suit of clothes for ten years. It was frayed at the sleeves and little holes had appeared at the knees and elbows. In the office he wore also a linen duster with huge pockets into which he continually stuffed scraps of paper. After some weeks the scraps of paper became little hard round balls, and when the pockets were filled he dumped them out upon the floor. For ten years he had but one friend, another old man named John Spaniard who owned a tree nursery. Sometimes, in a playful mood, old Doctor Reefy took from his pockets a handful of the paper balls and threw them at the nursery man. "That is to confound you, you blithering old sentimentalist," he cried, shaking with laughter.

The story of Doctor Reefy and his courtship of the tall dark girl who became his wife and left her money to him was a very curious story. It is delicious, like the twisted little apples that grow in the orchards of Winesburg. In the fall one walks in the orchards and the ground is hard with frost underfoot. The apples have been taken from the trees by the pickers.

They have been put in barrels and shipped to the cities where they will be eaten in apartments that are filled with books, magazines, furniture, and people. On the trees are only a few gnarled apples that the pickers have rejected. They look like the knuckles of Doctor Reefy's hands. One nibbles at them and they are delicious. Into a little round place at the side of the apple has been gathered all of its sweetness. One runs from tree to tree over the frosted ground picking the gnarled, twisted apples and filling his pockets with them. Only the few know the sweetness of the twisted apples. The girl and Doctor Reefy began their courtship on a summer afternoon. He was forty-five then and already he had begun the practice of filling his pockets with the scraps of paper that became hard balls and were thrown away. The habit had been formed as he sat in his buggy behind the jaded white horse and went slowly along country roads. On the papers were written thoughts, ends of thoughts, beginnings of thoughts.

One by one the mind of Doctor Reefy had made the thoughts. Out of many of them he formed a truth that arose gigantic in his mind. The truth clouded the world. It became terrible and then faded away and the little thoughts began again.

The tall dark girl came to see Doctor Reefy because she was in the family way and had become frightened. She was in that condition because of a series of circumstances also curious.

The death of her father and mother and the rich acres of land that had come down to her had set a train of suitors on her heels. For two years she saw suitors almost every evening. Except two they were all alike. They talked to her of passion and there was a strained eager quality in their voices and in their eyes when they looked at her. The two who were different were much unlike each other. One of them, a slender young man with white hands, the son of a jeweler in Winesburg, talked continually of virginity. When he was with her he was never off the subject. The other, a black-haired boy with large ears, said nothing at all but always managed to get her into the darkness, where he began to kiss her.

For a time the tall dark girl thought she would marry the jeweler's son. For hours she sat in silence listening as he talked to her and then she began to be afraid of something. Beneath his talk of virginity she began to think there was a lust greater than in all the others. At times it seemed to her that as he talked he was holding her body in his hands. She imagined him turning it slowly about in the white hands and staring at it. At night she dreamed that he had bitten into her body and that his jaws were dripping. She had the dream three times, then she became in the family way to the one who said nothing at all but who in the moment of his passion actually did bite her shoulder so that for days the marks of his teeth showed.

After the tall dark girl came to know Doctor Reefy it seemed to her that she never wanted to leave him again. She went into his office one morning and without her saying anything he seemed to know what had happened to her.

In the office of the doctor there was a woman, the wife of the man who kept the bookstore in Winesburg. Like all old-fashioned country practitioners, Doctor Reefy pulled teeth, and the woman who waited held a handkerchief to her teeth and groaned. Her husband was with her and when the tooth was taken out they both screamed and blood ran down on the woman's white dress. The tall dark girl did not pay any attention. When the woman and the man had gone the doctor smiled. "I will take you driving into the country with me," he said.

For several weeks the tall dark girl and the doctor were together almost every day. The condition that had brought her to him passed in an illness, but she was like one who has discovered the sweetness of the twisted apples, she could not get her mind fixed again upon the round perfect fruit that is eaten in the city apartments. In the fall after the beginning of her acquaintanceship with him she married Doctor Reefy and in the following spring she died. During the winter he read to her all of the odds and ends of thoughts he had scribbled on the bits of paper. After he had read them he laughed and stuffed them away in his pockets to become round hard balls.

## Questions

1. The girl was quiet, tall, and beautiful, but the doctor was 45 years old, so why did she marry the doctor?
2. Who was the biological father of the girl's baby?
3. What did the doctor write on the paper? And what did he do with it after writing?
4. Did the girl and the doctor have a happy life in the end?
5. What is the general meaning of the story?

## 纸团

短篇小说《纸团》是《小城畸人》25篇短篇小说中的一篇，这篇小说描写了一桩"离奇"的婚姻，表达了现代人深沉的挫折感。

他是一位有着白胡子、大鼻子、大手掌的老人。在认识他之前的很长一段时间，他在瓦恩斯堡行医，赶着一匹白色的老马走街串巷，为人治病。后来他和一位富有的姑娘结了婚。这个姑娘的父亲去世的时候给她留下一个富饶的大农场。这姑娘个子高挑、皮肤黝黑、性格文静，许多人认为她很漂亮，瓦恩斯堡的每个人都说不清为什么她会嫁给那个医生。结婚不到一年她就死了。

这个医生的指关节大得出奇。当他握紧双手时，指关节宛如一串未上漆的木球，形同用钢条串在一起的核桃。他叼着一支用玉米棒子做的烟斗。妻子死后，他整天坐在空荡荡的诊所中的一扇挂满蜘蛛网的窗户旁。他从未打开过这扇窗户。有一次，在8月的一个酷暑难耐的日子里，他试图打开窗户，却发现窗户牢牢地卡住，打那儿之后，开窗的事他便忘在脑后了。

瓦恩斯堡的人已经忘记了这位老人。可在利菲医生的心底却埋藏着一些美好的种子。在海夫纳街区巴黎纺织品商店楼上散发着霉味的诊所里，他独自不停地工作着，把毁掉的东西重新建好。他竖立起一座座真理的小金字塔，立起之后又拆掉，以便有可能获得新的真理，再建新的金字塔。

利菲医生个子高高的，身上穿着的那套衣服已有10年了。衣服的袖口被磨破了，而且膝盖和肘部已露出了小洞。在诊所里他还穿着一套有大口袋的亚麻布工作服，不断地往衣袋里塞小纸片。几周后纸片成了一个小而硬的圆纸团。当衣袋被塞满时，他便把纸团倒在地板上。10年来，他只有一个朋友，也是一位老人，名叫约翰·斯潘尼尔德，他有一个苗圃。有时老利菲医生也会开玩笑地从口袋里掏出一把纸团，扔向苗圃主。"去你的！你这个唠唠叨叨、多愁善感的老东西。"他喊道，笑得前仰后合。

有关利菲医生以及他追求那个个子高挑、皮肤黝黑的姑娘，后来这个姑娘成为他妻子，并留给他一笔钱的故事很是离奇。这个故事就像长在瓦恩斯堡果园里的小苹果，看上去歪歪扭扭，可味道却很甘甜。秋天人们漫步在果园里，脚下的地面上结了霜，变得硬硬的。苹果从树上被人们摘下来。

苹果被放进桶里，运到城里，在满是书籍、杂志、家具和人的公寓里被吃掉。树上仅剩下摘果人不要的疙疙瘩瘩的苹果。它们看上去像利菲医生的指关节，咬一口却感到甘甜无比。它的甜度全都集中在疙疙瘩瘩的地方。人们在结了霜的地面上一棵树一棵树地去摘歪扭结疤的苹果装满衣袋，只有为数不多的人知晓这种疙疙瘩瘩、歪歪扭扭的苹果甘甜可口。姑娘与利菲医生的恋情始于一个夏天的下午。那时利菲医生45岁，已经有了往衣袋里塞碎纸片，等纸片变成硬纸团就把它扔掉的习惯。这种习惯是他乘坐白色老马马车，缓慢行驶在乡间路上时形成的。他在纸片上写下他思考的问题、思考的开端及其心得。

利菲医生的脑海中闪现出一个又一个想法，从许多想法中又形成一个巨大的真理。这种真理遮蔽世界。世界变得恐怖起来，继而消失，接着小小的思绪又涌上心头。

这个高挑、黝黑的姑娘有了身孕，很恐慌，于是来找利菲医生。她之所以到了这种地步，是她所处的奇特的环境所致。

她父母去世后，给她留下大量的良田，众多求婚者接踵而至。两年来，她几乎每天晚上都在会见求婚者。绝大多数求婚者向她袒露情怀，从说话的语气中流露出迫不及待的心情，看她眼神充满了渴望。这些求婚者当中只有两个与众不同。一个是瓦恩斯堡城里珠宝商的儿子，身材瘦高，双手白皙。他喋喋不休地谈论着女人的贞操。和她在一起时，他从不谈论别的话题。另一个是黑头发大耳朵的小伙子，跟她在一起的时候什么也不谈，总是试图把她弄到黑暗处吻她。

个子高挑、皮肤黝黑的姑娘一度打算嫁给珠宝商的儿子。她一连几个小时静静地坐着听他侃侃而谈，过后她又害怕起来。她开始意识到在他谈论女人贞操的背后，有一种比其他人更强烈的情欲。有时她觉得他侃侃而谈的同时，已经把她的身体置于他的手掌之中。她想象她的身体在他白皙的双手间慢慢地翻来覆去，任他凝视玩弄，夜里她梦见他在啃咬她的身体，他的下巴滴着血。她做过三次这样的梦，后来她就怀孕了，使她怀孕的是那个什么也不谈的小伙子，当他性欲高涨时，他真的咬她的肩膀，以致在她肩膀上留下的齿痕过了好几天还依稀可见。

这个高个、黑皮肤的姑娘在逐渐了解利菲医生之后，她觉得再也不想离开他了。一天早上，她来到他的诊所，还没说一句话，利菲医生似乎已经明白她怎么了。

在医生的诊所里有一个女人，她是城里书店老板的妻子。和所有老式乡下医生一样，利菲医生也拔牙。那个等着拔牙的女人，用手帕捂着牙呻吟。她的丈夫陪着她，当牙被拔出来时，夫妇俩都尖叫起来，血流到那个女人的白衣服上。那个高个、黑皮肤的姑娘对此却毫不在意。那对夫妇走后，医生笑着说道："我赶车带你去乡下。"

一连几周这位高个黑皮肤的姑娘和医生几乎天天在一起。她找他要做的事就在一场疾病中过去了。然而,她像发现歪歪扭扭的苹果的甘甜的人那样,不再理会城里公寓中所吃的那些圆圆的精美苹果。在他们相识后的那个秋天,她就嫁给了医生。第二年春天她就死了。那年冬天,他把写在碎纸片上的那些零散的想法读给她听。读过之后他便哈哈大笑,随后把它们塞进口袋,让它们变成又圆又硬的纸团。

# H. L. Mencken
# (1880—1956)

Henry Louis Mencken was an American editor, author, and critic. He was born and died in Baltimore. He studied at the Baltimore Polytechnic. Probably America's most influential journalist, he began his career on the Baltimore *Herald* at the age of 18, became editor of the Baltimore *Herald*, and from 1906 until his death was on the staff of the Baltimore *Sun*. He also played a key role in the production of the two extremely influential national magazines *Smart Set* and *American Mercury*.

Mencken's pungent, iconoclastic criticism and scathing invective, although aimed at all smugly complacent attitudes, was chiefly directed at what he saw as the ignorant, self-righteous, and overly credulous American middle class. His essays were collected in a series of six volumes, *Prejudices* (1919—1927). In the field of philology he compiled a monumental and lively study, *The American Language* (1919). Among his other works are *George Bernard Shaw: His Plays* (1905), *In Defense of Women* (1917), and the autobiographical trilogy *Happy Days, 1880—1892* (1940), *Newspaper Days, 1899—1906* (1941), and *Heathen Days, 1890—1936* (1943), collected in one volume in 1947. In American literature, Mencken was an important literary champion of such writers as Theodore Dreiser, Sherwood Anderson, Sinclair Lewis, and Eugene O'Neill. His keen interest in and intelligent appraisal of 20th-century American letters are evident in the posthumously collected essays of *H. L. Mencken on American Literature* (2002).

## A Girl from Red Lion, P.A.

*The following story, published in* **The New Yorker,** *February 15, 1941, tells the story of a country girl who, misled by the books she and her boy friend read together and believing that she has sinned after spending the night together with her boy friend, leaves her home and wants to find an ill-famed house and spend the rest of her life there. But she falls into a good hand, for the strange but kind-hearted hack-driver takes her to the high-toned studio of Miss Nellie d'Alembert. As the story unfolds, readers are informed that the girl is persuaded and goes back home. The*

***writer is known for his iconoclastic criticism which finds full expression in the story.***

  Somewhere in his lush, magenta prose Oscar Wilde speaks of the tendency of nature to imitate art—a phenomenon often observed by persons who keep their eyes open. I first became aware of it, not through the pages of Wilde, but at the hands of an old-time hack-driver named Peebles, who flourished in Baltimore in the days of this history. Peebles was a Scotsman of a generally unfriendly and retiring character, but nevertheless he was something of a public figure in the town. Perhaps that was partly due to the fact that he had served twelve years in the Maryland Penitentiary for killing his wife, but I think he owed much more of his eminence to his adamantine rectitude in money matters, so rare in his profession. The very cops, indeed, regarded him as an honest man, and said so freely. They knew about his blanket refusal to take more than three or four times the legal fare from drunks, they knew how many lost watches, wallets, stick-pins and walking-sticks he turned in every year, and they admired as Christians, though deploring as cops, his absolute refusal to work for them in the capacity of stool-pigeon.

  Moreover, he was industrious as well as honest, and it was the common belief that he had money in five banks. He appeared on the hack-stand in front of the old Eutaw House every evening at nine o'clock, and put in the next five or six hours shuttling merrymakers and sociologists to and from the red-light district. When this trade began to languish he drove to Union Station, and there kept watch until his two old horses fell asleep. Most of the strangers who got off the early morning trains wanted to go to the nearest hotel, which was only two blocks away, so there was not a great deal of money in their patronage, but unlike the other hackers Peebles never resorted to the device of driving them swiftly in the wrong direction and then working back by a circuitous route.

  A little after dawn one morning in the early Autumn of 1903, just as his off horse began to snore gently, a milk-train got in from lower Pennsylvania, and out of it issued a rosy-cheeked young woman carrying a pasteboard suitcase and a pink parasol. Squired up from the train-level by a car-greaser with an eye for country beauty, she emerged into the sunlight shyly and ran her eye down the line of hacks. The other drivers seemed to scare her, and no wonder, for they were all grasping men whose evil propensities glowed from them like heat from a stove. But when she saw Peebles her feminine intuition must have told her that he could be trusted, for she shook off the car-greaser without further ado, and came up to the Peebles hack with a pretty show of confidence.

"Say, mister," she said, "how much will you charge to take me to a house of ill fame?"

In telling of it afterward Peebles probably exaggerated his astonishment a bit, but certainly he must have suffered something rationally describable as a shock. He laid great stress upon her air of blooming innocence, almost like that of a cavorting lamb. He said her two cheeks glowed like apples, and that she smelled like a load of hay. By his own account he stared at her for a full minute without answering her question, with a wild stream of confused surmises racing through his mind. What imaginable business could a creature so obviously guileless have in the sort of establishment she had mentioned? Could it be that her tongue had slipped—that she actually meant an employment office, the Y.W.C.A., or what not? Peebles, as he later elaborated the story, insisted that he had cross-examined her at length, and that she had not only reiterated her question in precise terms, but explained that she was fully determined to abandon herself to sin and looked forward confidently to dying in the gutter. But in his first version he reported simply that he had stared at her dumbly until his amazement began to wear off, and then motioned to her to climb into his back. After all, he was a common carrier, and obliged by law to haul all comers, regardless of their private projects and intentions. If he yielded anything to his Caledonian moral sense it took the form of choosing her destination with some prudence. He might have dumped her into one of the third-rate bagnios that crowded a street not three blocks from Union Station, and then gone on about his business. Instead, he drove half way across town to the high-toned studio of Miss Nellie d'Alembert, at that time one of the leaders of her profession in Baltimore, and a woman who, though she lacked the polish of Vassar, had sound sense, a pawky humor, and progressive ideas.

I had become, only a little while before, city editor of the *Herald*, and in that capacity received frequently confidential communications from her. She was, in fact, the source of a great many useful news tips. She knew everything about everyone that no one was supposed to know and had accurate advance information, in particular, about Page 1 divorces, for nearly all the big law firms of the town used her facilities for the manufacture of evidence. There were no Walter Winchells in that era, and the city editors of the land had to depend on volunteers for inside stuff. Such volunteers were moved (a) by a sense of public duty gracefully performed, and (b) by an enlightened desire to keep on the good side of newspapers. Not infrequently they cashed in on this last. I well remember the night when two visiting Congressmen from Washington got into a debate in Miss Nellie's music-room, and one of them dented the skull of the other with a spittoon. At my suggestion the other city editors of Baltimore joined me in straining journalistic ethics far enough to remove the accident to Mt. Vernon place, the most respectable neighborhood in town, and to lay the fracture to a fall on the ice.

My chance leadership in this public work made Miss Nellie my partisan, and now and then she gave me a nice tip and forgot to include the other city editors. Thus I was alert when she called up during the early afternoon of Peebles' strange adventure, and told me that something swell was on ice. She explained that it was not really what you could call important news, but simply a sort of human-interest story, so I asked Percy Heath to go to see her, for though he was now my successor as Sunday editor, he still did an occasional news story, and I knew what kind he enjoyed especially. He called up in half an hour, and asked me to join him. "If you don't hear it yourself," he said, "you will say I am pulling a fake."

When I got to Miss Nellie's house I found her sitting with Percy in a basement room that she used as a sort of office, and at once she plunged into the story.

"I'll tell you first," she began, "before you see the poor thing herself. When Peebles yanked the bell this morning I was sound asleep, and so was all the girls, and Sadie the coon had gone home. I stuck my head out of the window, and there was Peebles on the front steps. I said: 'Get the hell away from here! What do you mean by bringing in a drunk at this time of the morning? Don't you know us poor working people gotta get some rest? But he hollered back that he didn't have no drunk in his hack, but something he didn't know what to make of, and needed my help on, so I slipped on my kimono and went down to the door, and by that time he had the girl out of the hack, and before I could say 'scat' he had shoved her in the parlor, and she was unloading what she had to say."

"Well, to make a long story short, she said she came from somewhere near a burg they call Red Lion, P.A., and lived on a farm. She said her father was one of them old rubes with whiskers they call Dunkards, and very strict. She said she had a beau in York, P.A., of the name of Elmer, and whenever he could get away he would come out to the farm and set in the parlor with her, and they would do a little hugging and kissing. She said Elmer was educated and a great reader, and he would bring her books that he got from his brother, who was a train butcher on the Northern Central, and him and her would read them. She said the books were all about love, and that most of them were sad. Her and Elmer would talk about them while they set in the parlor, and the more they talked about them the sadder they would get, and sometimes she would have to cry."

"Well, to make a long story short, this went on once a week or so, and night before last Elmer came down from York with some more books, and they set in the parlor, and talked about love. Her old man usually stuck his nose in the door now and then, to see that there wasn't no foolishness, but night before last he had a bilious attack and went to bed early, so her and Elmer had it all to theirself in the parlor. So they quit talking about the books, and Elmer began to love her up, and in a little while they were hugging and kissing to beat the band. Well, to make a long story short, Elmer went too far, and when she came to herself and kicked him out she realized she had lost her honest name."

"She laid awake all night thinking about it, and the more she thought about it the more scared she got. In every one of the books her and Elmer read there was something on the subject, and all of the books said the same thing. When a girl lost her honest name there was nothing for her to do except to run away from home and lead a life of shame. No girl that she ever read about ever done anything else. They all rushed off to the nearest city, started this life of shame, and then took to booze and dope and died in the gutter. Their family never knew what had became of them. Maybe they landed finally in a medical college, or maybe the Salvation Army buried them, but their people never heard no more of them, and their name was rubbed out of the family Bible. Sometimes their beau tried to find them, but he never could do it, and in the end he usually married the judge's homely daughter, and moved into the big house when the judge died.

"Well, to make a long story short, this poor girl lay awake all night thinking of such sad things, and when she got up at four thirty A.M. and went out to milk the cows her eyes were so full of tears that she could hardly find their spigots. Her father, who was still bilious, gave her hell, and told her she was getting her just punishment for setting up until ten and eleven o'clock at night, when all decent people ought to be in bed. So she began to suspect that he may have snuck down during the evening, and caught her, and was getting ready to turn her out of the house and wash his hands of her, and maybe even curse her. So she decided to have it over and done with as soon as possible, and last night, the minute he hit the hay again, she hoofed in to York, P.A., and caught the milk-train for Baltimore, and that is how Peebles found her at Union Station and brought her here. When I asked her what in hell she wanted all she had to say was

'Ain't this a house of ill fame?' and it took me an hour or two to pump her story out of her. So now I have got her upstairs under lock and key, and as soon as I can get word to Peebles I'll tell him to take her back to Union Station, and start her back for Red Lion, P.A. Can you beat it?"

Percy and I, of course, demanded to see the girl, and presently Miss Nellie fetched her in. She was by no means the bucolic Lillian Russell that Peebles' tall tales afterward made her out, but she was certainly far from unappetizing. Despite her loss of sleep, the dreadful gnawings of her conscience and the menace of an appalling retribution, her cheeks were still rosy, and there remained a considerable sparkle in her troubled blue eyes. I never heard her name, but it was plain that she was of four-square Pennsylvanian Dutch stock, and as sturdy as the cows she serviced. She had on her Sunday clothes, and appeared to be somewhat uncomfortable in them, but Miss Nellie set her at ease, and soon she was retelling her story to two strange and, in her sight, probably highly dubious men. We listened without interrupting her, and when she finished Percy was the first to speak.

"My dear young lady," he said, "you have been grossly misinformed. I don't know what these works of fiction are that you and Elmer read, but they are as far out of date as Joe Miller's Jest-Book. The stuff that seems to be in them would make even a newspaper editorial writer cough and scratch himself. It may be true that, in the remote era when they appeared to have been written, the penalty of a slight and venial slip was as drastic as you say, but I assure you that it is no longer the case. The world is much more humane than it used to be, and much more rational. Just as it no longer burns men for heresy or women for witchcraft, so it has ceased to condemn girls to lives of shame and death in the gutter for the trivial dereliction you acknowledge. If there were time I'd get you some of the more recent books, and point out passages showing how moral principles have changed. The only thing that is frowned on now seems to be getting caught. Otherwise, justice is virtually silent on the subject.

"Inasmuch as your story indicates that no one knows of your crime save your beau, who, if he has learned of your disappearance, is probably scared half to death, I advise you to go home, make some plausible excuse to your pa for lighting out, and resume your care of his cows. At the proper opportunity take your beau to the pastor, and join him in indissoluble love. It is the safe, respectable and hygienic course. Everyone agrees that it is moral, even moralists. Meanwhile, don't forget to thank Miss Nellie. She might have helped you down the primrose way; instead, she has restored you to virtue and happiness, no worse for an interesting experience."

The girl, of course, took in only a small part of this, for Percy's voluptuous style and vocabulary were beyond the grasp of a simple milkmaid. But Miss Nellie, who understood English much better than she spoke it, translated freely, and in a little while the troubled look departed from those blue eyes, and large tears of joy welled from them. Miss Nellie shed a couple herself, and so did all the ladies of the resident faculty, for they had drifted downstairs during the interview, sleepy but curious. The practical Miss Nellie inevitably thought of money, and it turned out that the trip down by milk-train and Peebles' lawful freight of $1 had about exhausted the poor girl's savings, and she had only some odd change left. Percy threw in a dollar and I threw in a dollar, and Miss Nellie not only threw in a third, but ordered one of the ladies to go to the kitchen and prepare a box-lunch for the return to Red Lion.

Sadie the coon had not yet come to work, but Peebles presently bobbed up without being sent for, and toward the end of the afternoon he started off for Union Station with his most amazing passenger, now as full of innocent jubilation as a martyr saved at the stake. As I have said, he embellished the story considerably during the days following, especially in the direction of touching up the girl's pulchritude. The cops, because of their general confidence in him, swallowed his exaggerations, and I heard more than one of them lament that they had missed the chance to handle the case professionally. Percy, in his later years, made two or three attempts to put it into a movie scenario, but the Hays office always vetoed it.

How the girl managed to account to her father for her mysterious flight and quick return I don't know, for she was never heard from afterward. She promised to send Miss Nellie a picture postcard of Red Lion, showing the new hall of the Knights of Pythias, but if it was ever actually mailed it must have been misaddressed, for it never arrived.

## Questions

1. Please identify the narrator/narrators.
2. How is Peebles generally viewed? And what do you personally think of him and the people concerned after reading the story?
3. Why does the girl run away from home? What do you think is the root cause?
4. H. L. Mencken is known for his iconoclastic criticism. Can you justify this statement by citing specific examples from the story?
5. What would you say about the style Mencken employs in this story?

# H. L. 门肯
# （1880—1956）

亨利·路易斯·门肯是美国新闻记者、作家及评论家。他生于并死于巴尔的摩。他就读于巴尔的摩理工专科学校。门肯可以说是美国最具影响力的记者，18岁开始在巴尔的摩《先驱报》工作，后来成为该报编辑。从1906年起直至他去世，他一直都在巴尔的摩《太阳报》工作。他在创办两个相当有影响力的国家杂志《时髦人物》和《美国信使》的过程中起了重要作用。

门肯辛辣、反传统的批评虽然是针对所有沾沾自喜的态度，但它们的主要目标是那些他认为无知、自以为是、过于轻信别人的中产阶级。他的散文被收入共有六册的《偏见集》（1919—1927）中。在哲学领域，他编撰了具有里程碑意义的《美国语言》（1919）。其他作品包括《萧伯纳的戏剧》（1905）、《为妇女辩护》（1917）；自传三部曲，即：《幸福的日子，1880—1892》（1940）、《做编辑的日子，1899—1906》（1941）和《异教徒的日子，1890—1936》（1943）。这三部曲于1947年收成一集。在美国文学领域，门肯对西奥多·德莱塞、舍伍德·安德森、辛克莱·刘易斯以及尤金·奥尼尔等美国作家给予了充分肯定。他的遗作《门肯论美国文学》（2002）充分显示了他对20世纪美国文学的强烈兴趣和明智评价。

## 来自宾州红狮村的姑娘

下面这个故事刊登在1941年2月15日的《纽约人》杂志上。故事讲述的是一个乡村姑娘由于书籍的误导，认为在和男友度过了一个夜晚后犯下了罪过，因此，离开家乡，想找一家妓院了却此生。但是，她遇到了好人。怪异但热心的出租车夫把她拉到了一个名声不错的内利小姐的艺术室。随着故事的展开，读者知道这位姑娘在好心人的劝说下又返回了家乡。作者以反传统的辛辣批评著称，而这一点在小说中得以充分体现。

奥斯卡·王尔德在他华美、绚烂的散文中谈及自然模仿艺术之倾向，善于观察的人都注意到了这一现象。当初我注意到这种现象并不是通过阅读王尔德的文章，而是从一个名叫皮布尔斯的老出租车夫那里得知的。那会儿，皮布尔斯在巴尔的摩可是名声大振啊。皮布尔斯是苏格兰人，不太友好，性格也比较孤僻，但他却是城里的公众人物。这也许是由于他因杀妻而在马里兰州监狱服刑12年的缘故吧。可在我看来他的显赫更多的是因为他在金钱问题上的坚毅与正直,这一点在他的行当中是极为少见的。的确,警察都认为他是一个诚实的人,而且是不由自主地这么说的。他们知道他曾全盘拒绝接受酒鬼高于合理费用三四倍的车费,他们也知道他每年上交的丢失的手表、钱包、装饰别针及手杖不计其数。尽管作为警察,他们表示不满,但是作为基督徒,他们佩服他拒绝做他们眼线的坚决态度。

此外,他既诚实又勤奋,人们知道他在五家银行都有存款。每天晚上9点钟他出现在幽托楼前的停车场,在接下来的五六个小时里他忙于接送在红灯区寻欢作乐者以及社会学家们。当这儿的活儿不景气时,他就去联合车站揽活。在那儿,他会守到他那两匹老马都睡着了。下早班车的外地人大多数要去最近的宾馆,这儿与最近的宾馆只隔两个街区,所以也没有多少赚头。但是不像其他司机,皮布尔斯从来不耍花招把乘客快速拉向错误的方向,然后顺着过回的道路再拉回来。

1903年初秋的一天早上,正当他那匹闲马开始打呼噜时,从宾夕法尼亚州南部开来的拉牛奶的车进站了。一个脸颊红润的年轻女子手提纸板箱,打着粉色阳伞走下车来。她在一个专门盯着乡村美女的车厢润滑工的引领下走下车,很羞涩地走到阳光下,顺着排成行的马车望去。别的车夫让她害怕,这也不足为奇,因为他们都是贪心的人,就如同炉火散热,他们个个都散发出恶气。但是,当看到皮布尔斯时,她的女性直觉告诉她他可以信赖,于是她立即摆脱了那个润滑工,颇自信地朝皮布尔斯的车走过来。

"喂,先生,"她说,"送我去一家妓院要多少钱?"

后来皮布尔斯讲到这件事时,他对自己当时吃惊程度的描绘可能有些夸张,但是他肯定是经历了完全可以称之为震惊之类的感觉。他强调了她那十足的无知劲儿,几乎是那种轻浮的小羊羔的神情。他说她双颊红如苹果,闻上去像一堆干草。据他说,他足足凝视她一分钟没有回答她的问题,满脑子的迷惑。这么一个天真无邪的小东西在她所提到的那个地方能干什么呢?她是不是说走嘴了?实际上她是不是想说就业办公室、女青年基督协会什么的?后来,当皮布尔斯详细描述此事时,他说他详细问过她,并且说她不仅用十分准确的字眼重复了她的问题,而且还解释说她决心沉溺于罪过,期盼着死于贫民窟。但是在故事的第一个版本中,他只是说他傻傻地望着她,直到他的惊异消失殆尽,然后示意她上了车。他毕竟只是一个普通的车夫,按法律规定必须拉任何来者,不管他们的私人计划如何,也不管他们有何企图。如果他还有一点儿苏格兰的道德观念的话,那就是他谨慎地为她选择目的地。他完全可以将她拉到离车站只有三个街区的满街都是的三类妓院，扔下她，然后再揽别的活儿。但他没有这样做，他跑了大半个城，把她拉到了格调高雅的内利·阿兰波小姐的艺术室。这家艺术室在巴尔的摩那个行当中是数一数二的。内利小姐虽然没有瓦萨的优雅，但她却是一位理性、机敏并且思想进步的妇女。

前不久我成了本市《先驱报》的编辑。作为编辑，我经常收到她的机密信息。实际上，她是许多有用的新闻密报的来源。她知道其他人不知道的任何人的任何事情，特别是头版离婚案的消息，她的信息总是准确并且提前，因为城里所有大的律师事务所都利用她的方便条件得到证据。那个地区没有像沃尔特·温切尔那样的花边专栏编辑，所以那里的编辑只好依靠志愿者搞到内幕。使这些志愿者为之动容的，一是通过优雅的方式所表现出来的公众责任感，二是通过启发而表现出来的保持报纸正义性的欲望。他们通常是靠这第二点而获得成功的。我清楚地记得，那天晚上，在内利小姐的音乐室里，两位来访的华盛顿国会议员争吵起来，其中的一个用痰盂把另一个的脑壳打瘪了。在我的建议下，巴尔的摩市的其他记者和我一起充分运用新闻道德准则，将事件的发生地点移至该城附近一个最体面的地方叫弗农山，报道说脑袋的伤是摔倒在冰上所致。

在这次公众事件中的偶然领导地位使内利小姐成了我圈子里的人。她时常给我提供一些较为有价值的内幕消息，而忘了告诉其他的城市编辑。因此，那天下午早些时候她打电话告诉我皮布尔斯有离奇经历，并且告诉我说"冰上"又有精彩之事时，我就来了精神。她说这不是什么重要新闻，只是一种人们感兴趣的故事。所以，我让帕西·希思去见她，因为尽管他现在继我之后任周日编辑，但他仍偶尔做一些新闻报道，而且我知道他喜欢做那类的报道。半小时后他打电话来让我过去。他说："如果你不亲自听听，你会说我在胡编。"

当我赶到内利小姐的公寓时，我发现她和帕西正坐在她当作办公室的一个地下室房间里。我一到，内利小姐就开始讲起事情的来龙去脉。

她说："在你见那个可怜的姑娘之前，我先给你讲一讲。今天早上皮布尔斯拉门铃时，我睡得正香，其他姑娘也是如此，黑人赛迪回家了。我把头探出窗外，看到皮布尔斯站在台阶上。我说，快他妈的走开！大清早的把醉鬼带到这儿来干什么？难道你不知道我们这些可怜的劳动者也得休息吗？但是他大声回答说他车上坐的不是酒鬼，可是也不知道是个什么样的人，需要我帮忙判断一下。所以我就穿上晨衣下楼开了门。这会儿他已经让那姑娘下了车。还没等我说'走开'他就一把将姑娘推进了客厅。接下来，她一股脑儿地讲了事情的前后。"

"嗨，长话短说，她说她是从宾州一个叫红狮的地方来的，住在农场。她说她爸爸是个他们称之为德美浸礼会教派留着八撇胡的乡巴佬，非常严厉。她说她在宾州约克有个男友，叫埃尔默。一有机会他就会来到农场和她在客厅坐着，他们会来点儿拥抱和亲吻什么的。她说埃尔默受过教育，很爱读书。他有个兄弟在中北线火车上做屠夫。他会把他兄弟的书带给她，他们一起读书。她说那些书都是有关爱情的，大多都是悲伤的。她和埃尔默会坐在客厅谈论这些故事。他们越讨论就越觉得难过，有时她竟哭起来。

"嗨，长话短说，这事大约每周一次。前天晚上埃尔默从约克来了，带来了更多的书。他们坐在客厅谈论爱情。她老爸平时都探头看看，确保没发生什么傻事。但是前天晚上他胆病发作早早睡了。客厅里就只有她和埃尔默了。他们不再谈论书籍，埃尔默开始挑逗她，没多久他们就起劲地拥抱亲吻。嗨，长话短说，埃尔默做得有点儿过分，当她缓过神儿将他踢开时，她意识到自己已经失去了好名声。"

"她一宿没睡想着这事，越想越害怕。她和埃尔默读的每一本书都有此类话题，而且所有的书说的都是同样的事。一个女孩失去好名声后，她唯一能做的就是离家出走，羞辱地过一生。她所读到的女孩无一例外。她们都跑到附近的城市，开始这羞辱的生活，然后就开始酗酒吸毒，最后死在贫民窟。她们的家人不会知道她们的境况。也许她们最终落到医学院，也许救世军将她们埋葬。她们的家人不再有她们的消息，她们的家谱上也不再有她们的名字。有时候她们的男友找她们，但是他找不到。最终，他娶了法官大人的相貌平平的女儿，在法官死后搬进了大房子。"

"嗨，长话短说，这个可怜的女孩一宿没睡，思考这些悲伤的事情。早上四点半起床出去挤奶时，她满眼泪水难以找到管子的插口。她爸爸胆病仍没好，把她臭骂了一通，说这就是好人家都该睡觉而你却在晚上十点十一点还坐着所应得的惩罚。她开始怀疑他那天晚上也许偷偷地溜下来，逮了她个正着，准备把她赶出家门不再管她了，甚至诅咒她。所以，她决定尽快了结。昨晚，她老爸刚一上床，她就跑到宾州约克，赶上了开往巴尔的摩送牛奶的火车。后来皮布尔斯就在车站发现了她并把她带到了这儿。当我问她究竟想做什么，她所说的就是'这是不是一家妓院？'我用了一两个小时的工夫才使她说出事情的来龙去脉。我把她锁在楼上了，我已打发人通知皮布尔斯，就让他把姑娘送回车站，让她回宾州红狮。你能抢先报道吗？"

我和帕西当然要见见这个姑娘。不一会儿内利小姐就把她带了进来。她绝不是后来皮布尔斯荒诞不经的故事中所描述的那个田园风味十足的大明星莉莲·拉塞尔，当然她也远非那种见了就让人倒胃口的女子。尽管她睡眠不足，遭受良心谴责的痛苦并且受到可怕的惩罚的威胁，但她仍双颊红润，充满忧虑的蓝色眼睛中仍显出神采。我从来没听说过她的名字，但显而易见，她是个坚毅的宾州荷兰人的后代，就像她所伺候的那些母牛那样。她身着周日服装，显得有点儿不太舒服,但是内利小姐使她放松下来,很快她就向两个在她眼里也许是非常可疑的陌生人讲了她的事情。我们只是听着,没有打断她。当她讲完,帕西先开了口。

"亲爱的年轻女士,"他说,"你所知道的情况完全不正确。我不知道你和埃尔默读的是些什么书,但是它们就像乔·米勒的笑话集一样早就过时了。书中谈到的事可能会使报社的编辑都咳嗽不止、抓耳挠腮。也许在这些书发表的那个遥远时代,对一个很小的失足的惩罚会像你说的那样严厉,但我向你保证这类事情不会再出现了。当今的世界比过去文明多了,也更理性了。人们不再因异端邪说而烧死男人,不再因施巫术而烧死女人。所以,人们也不再因为小的疏忽而让女孩子生于羞辱、死于贫民窟。如果有时间,我想给你一些新近出版的书籍,向你指出一些段落说明道德准则早已改变。现在人们唯一不赞同的好像是被当场捉住。否则,对此类事情,法律实际上是不会做任何判断的。

"鉴于你的事情除了你的男友还没有人知道,而你的男友若是听说你失踪了会吓得半死,我建议你回家,找些可行的借口向你爸爸解释你离开的原因,然后重新照料他的牛吧。找个适当的机会带你的男友去牧师那儿和他海誓山盟,终生相爱。这是一件安全、体面也健康的事。人人都认为这是道德的,就连道德家们也会这样认为。同时,别忘了感谢内利小姐。她完全可以引你进烟花柳巷,但她没这样做,而是还你纯洁和幸福,没什么的,只是一次有趣的经历。"

小女孩当然只领会了其中的一小部分,因为帕西华丽的表述风格和辞藻让这个头脑简单的挤奶女孩难以理解。但是内利小姐听明白了,她的英语听力要比说的好多了,她很自如地将意思转达过去。不一会儿,那双蓝色眼睛中的疑惑不见了,喜悦的泪水如泉涌。内利小姐也流泪了,所有在场的女士们都流泪了。这些人是在采访期间溜下楼的,她们虽然困倦但十分好奇。实际的内利小姐不可避免地想到了钱,结果是来时的火车票和皮布尔斯那合法的一块钱车费耗尽了这可怜孩子所有的积蓄,她只剩一点儿零钱了。帕西拿了一美元,我拿了一美元,内利小姐不仅拿了一美元,她还让一位女士去厨房准备了盒饭好让她在返回红狮的路上吃。

黑人赛迪还没来上班,但皮布尔斯自己来了。傍晚时分他拉着他那十分神奇的乘客朝车站驶去。这位乘客就像被从火刑柱上救下来的无辜殉难者一样满怀惊喜。正如我所说,在以后的几天里他对这事大肆渲染,特别是对她的美丽更是添油加醋。警察们对他十分信任,也都轻信了他的夸张之辞。我还听说他们都为痛失亲自以专业的方式处理此事的良机而感到遗憾。帕西在其有生之年曾两三次想把它写成电影脚本,但都被海斯公司给否决了。

那姑娘是如何向她的父亲解释她神秘的出走和迅速的归来,我不得而知,因为打那以后就再也没有她的消息。她答应给内利小姐寄红狮村印有皮西厄斯骑士新大厅的明信片,但是即便是发出来了,也肯定是写错了地址,因为从来就没收到。

# Ring W. Lardner
# (1885—1933)

Ring W. Lardner, American short story writer, is famous for his concise, conversational style in which he wrote the comic and satirical stories. Born in Niles, Michigan, Lardner began his career as a sports writer on newspapers in South Bend, Chicago, St. Louis and Boston. From 1913 to 1919 he wrote a daily sports column for the *Chicago Tribune* and published a number of stories and sketches in various magazines. During this period he also published some of these writings in book form. During the twenties, he continued to write for newspapers but was concentrating on stories and sketches. Lardner's style had influenced many writers, notable Hemingway and Salinger.

Lardner's early books displayed his talent for the humourous use of the vernacular in portraying typical Americans, including *Bib Ballads* (1915), a collection of verse; *You Know Me, Al* (1916), a collection of humour stories; *Gullible's Travels* (1917), satirical stories; *Treat 'Em Rough* (1918), and *The Big Town* (1921), a humourous novel. Later collections, noted for their irony, by which Lardner exposed and satirized the follies and vices in the life, include *How to Write Short Stories* (1924) and *The Love Nest* (1926). He also wrote for the theater, his only notable success being *June Moon* (1929).

## Old Folk's Christmas

*The following story is about a married couple, earnestly waiting for their own children to go home for Christmas in order to enjoy family happiness together. They carefully made preparations, and especially bought many expensive Christmas presents for their children. As contrasted with the old folk's arrangements, their children did not seem to mind. They only showed solicitude for their own affairs. This story is written in a concise and conversational style. Its theme sets people thinking. It reveals the truth that the parental love and the generation gaps are at all places.*

Tom and Grace Carter sat in their living-room on Christmas Eve, sometimes talking, sometimes pretending to read and all the time thinking things they didn't want to think. Their two children, Junior, aged nineteen, and Grace, two years younger, had come home that day from their schools for the Christmas vacation. Junior was in his first year at the university and Grace attending a boarding-school that would fit her for college.

I won't call them Grace and Junior any more, though that is the way they had been christened. Junior had changed his name to Ted and Grace was now Caroline, and thus they insisted on being addressed, even by their parents. This was one of the things Tom and Grace the elder were thinking of as they sat in their living-room on Christmas Eve.

Other university freshmen who had lived here had returned on the twenty-first, the day when the vacation was supposed to begin. Ted had telegraphed that he would be three days late owing to a special examination which, if he passed it, would lighten the terrific burden of the next term. He had arrived at home looking so pale, heavy-eyed and shaky that his mother doubted the wisdom of the concentrated mental effort, while his father secretly hoped the stuff had been non-poisonous and would not have lasting effects, Caroline, too, had been behind schedule, explaining that her laundry had gone astray and she had not dared trust others to trace it for her.

Grace and Tom had attempted, with fair success, to conceal their disappointment over this delayed home-coming and had continued with their preparations for a Christmas that would thrill their children and consequently themselves. They had bought an imposing lot of presents, costing twice or three times as much as had been Tom's father's annual income when Tom was Ted's age, or Tom's own income a year ago, before General Motors' acceptance of his new weather-proof paint had enabled him to buy this suburban home and luxuries such as his own parents and Grace's had never dreamed of, and to give Ted and Caroline advantages that he and Grace had perforce gone without.

Behind the closed door of the music-room was the elaborately decked tree. The piano and piano bench and the floor around the tree were covered with beribboned packages of all sizes, shapes and weights, one of them addressed to Tom, another to Grace, a few to the servants and the rest to Ted and Caroline. A huge box contained a sealskin coat for Caroline, a coat that had cost as much as the Carters had formerly paid a year for rent. Even more expensive was a "set" of jewelry consisting of an opal brooch, a bracelet of opals and gold filigree, and an opal ring surrounded by diamonds.

Grace always had preferred opals to any other stone, but now that she could afford them, some inhibition prevented her from buying them for herself; she could enjoy them much more adorning her pretty daughter. There were boxes of silk stockings, lingerie, gloves and handkerchiefs. And for Ted, a three-hundred-dollar watch, a deluxe edition of Balzac, an expensive bag of shiny, new steel-shafted golfclubs and the last word in portable phonographs.

But the big surprise for the boy was locked in the garage, a black Gorham sedan, a model more up to date and better-looking than Tom's own year-old car that stood beside it, Ted could use it during the vacation if the mild weather continued and could look forward to driving it around home next spring and summer, there being a rule at the university forbidding undergraduates the possession or use of private automobiles.

Every year for sixteen years, since Ted was three and Caroline one, it had been the Christmas Eve custom of the Carter's to hang up their children's stockings and fill them with inexpensive toys. Tom and Grace had thought it would be fun to continue the custom this year; the contents of the stockings—a mechanical negro dancing doll, music-boxes, a kitten that meowed when you pressed a spot on her back, etcetera—would make the "kids" laugh. And one of Grace's first pronouncements to her returned offspring was that they must go to bed early so Santa Claus would not be frightened away.

But it seemed they couldn't promise to make it so terribly early. They both had long-standing dates in town. Caroline was going to dinner and a play with Beatrice Murdock and Beatrice's nineteen-year-old brother Paul. The latter would call for her in his car at half past six. Ted had accepted an invitation to see the hockey match with two classmates, Herb Castle and Bernard King. He wanted to take his father's Gorham, but Tom told him untruthfully that the foot-brake was not working; Ted must be kept out of the garage till tomorrow morning.

Ted and Caroline had taken naps in the afternoon and gone off together in Paul Murdock's stylish roadster, giving their word that they would be back by midnight or a little later and that tomorrow night they would stay home.

And now their mother and father were sitting up for them, because the stockings could not be filled and hung till they were safely in bed, and also because trying to go to sleep is a painful and hopeless business when you are kind of jumpy.

"What time is it?" asked Grace, looking up from the third page of a book that she had begun to "read" soon after dinner.

"Half past two," said her husband. (He had answered the same question every fifteen or twenty minutes since midnight.)

"You don't suppose anything could have happened?" said Grace.

"We'd have heard if there had," said Tom.

"It isn't likely, of course," said Grace, "but they might have had an accident some place where nobody was there to report it or telephone or anything. We don't know what kind of a driver the Murdock boy is."

"He's Ted's age. Boys that age may be inclined to drive too fast, but they drive pretty well."

"How do you know?"

"Well, I've watched some of them drive."

"Yes, but not all of them."

"I don't doubt whether anybody in the world has seen every nineteen-year-old boy drive."

"Boys these days seem so kind of irresponsible."

"Oh, don't worry! They probably met some of their young friends and stopped for a bit to eat or something." Tom got up and walked to the window with studied carelessness. "It's a pretty night," he said. "You can see every star in the sky."

But he wasn't looking at the stars. He was looking down the road for headlights. There were none in sight and after a few moments he returned to his chair.

"What time is it?" asked Grace.

"Twenty-two of," he said.

"Of what?"

"Of three."

"Your watch must have stopped. Nearly an hour ago you told me it was half past two."

"My watch is all right. You probably dozed off."

"I haven't closed my eyes."

"Well, it's time you did. Why don't you go to bed?"

"Why don't you?"

"I'm not sleepy."

"Neither am I. But honestly, Tom, it's silly for you to stay up. I'm just doing it so I can fix the stockings, and because I feel so wakeful. But there's no use of your losing your sleep."

"I couldn't sleep a wink till they're home."

"That's foolishness! There's nothing to worry about. They're just having a good time. You were young once yourself."

"That's just it! When I was young, I was young." He picked up his paper and tried to get interested in the shipping news.

"What time is it?" asked Grace.

"Five minutes of three."

"Maybe they're staying at the Murdocks' all night."

"They'd have let us know."

"They were afraid to wake us up, telephoning."

At three-twenty a car stopped at the front gate.

"There they are!"

"I told you there was nothing to worry about."

Tom went to the window. He could just discern the outlines of the Murdock boy's roadster, whose lighting system seemed to have broken down.

"He hasn't any lights," said Tom. "Maybe I'd better go out and see if I can fix them."

"No, don't! " said Grace sharply. "He can fix them himself. He's just saving them while he stands still."

"Why don't they come in?"

"They're probably making plans."

"They can make them in here. I'll go out and tell them we're still up."

"No, don't!" said Grace as before, and Tom obediently remained at the window.

It was nearly four when the car lights flashed on and the car drove away. Caroline walked into the house and stared dazedly at her parents.

"Heavens! What are you doing up?"

Tom was about to say something, but Grace forestalled him.

"We were talking over old Christmases, she said. "Is it very late?"

"I haven't any idea, " said Caroline.

"Where is Ted?"

"Isn't he home? I haven't seen him since we dropped him at the hockey place."

"Well, you go right to bed," said her mother. "You must be worn out."

"I am, kind of. We danced after the play. What time is breakfast?"

"Eight o'clock."

"Oh, Mother, can't you make it nine?"

"I guess so. You used to want to get up early on Christmas."

"I know, but…"

"Who brought you home?" asked Tom.

"Why, Paul Murdock—and Beatrice."

"You look rumpled."

"They made me sit in the 'rumple' seat."

She laughed at her joke, said good night and went upstairs. She had not come even within hand-shaking distance of her father and mother.

"The Murdocks ," said Tom, "must have great manners, making their guest ride in that uncomfortable seat."

Grace was silent.

"You go to bed, too," said Tom. "I'll wait for Ted."

"You couldn't fix the stockings."

"I won't try. We'll have time for that in the morning; I mean, later in the morning."

"I'm not going to bed till you do," said Grace.

"All right, we'll both go. Ted ought not to be long now. I suppose his friends will bring him home. We'll hear him when he comes in."

There was no chance not to hear him when, at ten minutes before six, he came in. He had done his Christmas shopping late and brought home a package.

Grace was downstairs again at half past seven, telling the servants breakfast would be postponed till nine. She nailed the stockings beside the fireplace, went into the music-room to see that nothing had been disturbed and removed Ted's hat and overcoat from where he had carefully hung them on the hall floor.

Tom appeared a little before nine and suggested that the children ought to be awakened.

"I'll wake them," said Grace, and went upstairs. She opened Ted's door, looked, and softly closed it again. She entered her daughter's room and found Caroline semiconscious.

"Do I have to get up now? Honestly I can't eat anything. If you could just have Molla bring me some coffee. Ted and I are both invited to the Murdock's for breakfast at half past twelve, and I could sleep for another hour or two."

"But dearie, don't you know we have Christmas dinner at one?"

"It's a shame, Mother, but I thought of course our dinner would be at night.

"Don't you want to see your presents?"

"Certainly I do, but can't they wait?"

Grace was about to go to the kitchen to tell the cook that dinner would be at seven instead of one, but she remembered having promised Signe the afternoon and evening off, as a cold, light supper would be all anyone wanted after the heavy midday meal.

Tom and Grace breakfasted alone and once more sat in the living-room, talking, thinking and pretending to read.

"You ought to speak to Caroline," said Tom.

"I will, but not today. It's Christmas."

"And I intend to say a few words to Ted."

"Yes, dear, you must. But not today."

"I suppose they'll be out again tonight."

"No, they promised to stay home. We'll have a nice cozy evening."

"Don't bet too much on that," said Tom.

At noon the "children" made their entrance and responded to their parents' salutations with almost the proper warmth. Ted declined a cup of coffee and he and Caroline apologized for making a "breakfast" date at the Murdock's.

"Sis and I both thought you'd be having dinner at seven, as usual."

"We've always had it at one o'clock on Christmas," said Tom.

"I'd forgotten it was Christmas," said Tom.

"Well, those stockings ought to remind you."

Ted and Caroline looked at the bulging stockings.

"Isn't there a tree?" asked Caroline.

"Of course," said her mother. "But the stockings come first."

"We've only a little time," said Caroline. "We'll be terribly late as it is. So can't we see the tree now?"

"I guess so," said Grace, and led the way into the music-room.

The servants were summoned and the tree stared at and admired.

"You must open your presents," said Grace to her daughter.

"I can't open them all now," said Caroline. "Tell me which is special."

The cover was removed from the huge box and Grace held up the coat.

"Oh, Mother!" said Caroline. "A sealskin coat!"

"Put it on," said her father.

"Not now. We haven't time."

"Then look at this!" said Grace, and opened the case of jewels.

"Oh, Mother! Opals!" said Caroline.

"They're my favorite stone," said Grace quietly.

"If nobody minds," said Ted, "I'll postponed my personal investigation till we get back. I know I'll like everything you've given me. But if we have no car in working order, I've got to call a taxi and catch a train."

"You can drive in," said his father.

"Did you fix the brake?"

"I think it's all right. Come up to the garage and we'll see."

Ted got his hat and coat and kissed his mother good-bye.

"Mother," he said, "I know you'll forgive me for not having any presents for you and Dad. I was so rushed the last three days at school. And I thought I'd have time to shop a little when we got in yesterday, but I was in too much of a hurry to be home. Last night, everything was closed."

"Don't worry," said Grace. "Christmas is for young people. Dad and I have everything we want."

The servants had found their gifts and disappeared, expressing effusive Scandinavian thanks.

Caroline and her mother were left alone.

"Mother, where did the coat come from?"

"Lloyd and Henry's."

"They keep all kinds of furs, don't they?"

"Yes."

"Would you mind horribly if I exchanged this?"

"Certainly not, dear. You pick out anything you like, and if it's a little more expensive, it won't make any difference. We can go in town tomorrow or next day. But don't you want to wear your opals to the Murdock's?"

"I don't believe so. They might get lost or something. And I'm not—well, I'm not so crazy about—"

"I think they can be exchanged, too," said Grace. "You run along now and get ready to start."

Caroline obeyed with alacrity, and Grace spent a welcome moment by herself.

Tom opened the garage door.

"Why, you've got two cars!" said Ted.

"The new one isn't mine," said Tom.

"Whose is it?"

"Yours. It's the new model."

"Dad, that's wonderful! But it looks just like the old one."

"Well, the old one's pretty good. Just the same, yours is better. You'll find that out when you drive it. Hop in and get started. I had her filled with gas."

"I think I'd rather drive the old one."

"Why?"

"Well, what I really wanted, Dad, was a Barnes sport roadster, something like Paul Murdock's, only a different color scheme. And if I don't drive this Gorham at all, maybe you could get them to take it back or make some kind of a deal with the Barnes people.

Tom didn't speak till he was sure of his voice. Then: "All right, son. Take my car and I'll see what can be done about yours."

Caroline, waiting for Ted, remembered something and called to her mother. "Here's what I got for you and Dad," she said. "It's two tickets to 'Jolly Jane,' the play I saw last night. You'll love it!"

"When are they for?" asked Grace.

"Tonight," said Caroline.

"But dearie," said her mother, "we don't want to go out tonight, when you promised to stay home."

"We'll keep our promise," said Caroline, "but the Murdocks may drop in and bring some friends and we'll dance and there'll be music. And Ted and I both thought you'd rather be away somewhere so our noise wouldn't disturb you."

"It was sweet of you to do this," said her mother, "but your father and I don't mind noise as long as you're enjoying yourselves."

"It's time anyway that you and Dad had a treat."

"The real treat," said Grace, "would be to spend a quiet evening here with just you two."

"The Murdocks practically invited themselves and I couldn't say no after they'd been so nice to me. And honestly, Mother, you'll love this play!"

"Will you be home for supper?"

"I'm pretty sure we will, but if we're a little late, don't you and Dad wait for us. Take the seven-twenty so you won't miss anything. The first act is really the best. We probably won't be hungry, but have Signe leave something out for us in case we are."

Tom and Grace sat down to the elaborate Christmas dinner and didn't make much impression on it. Even if they had had any appetite, the sixteen-pound turkey would have looked almost like new when they had eaten their fill. Conversation was intermittent and related chiefly to Signe's excellence as a cook and the mildness of the weather. Children and Christmas were barely touched on.

Tom merely suggested that on account of its being a holiday and their having theatre tickets, they ought to take the six-ten and eat supper at the Metropole. His wife said no; Ted and Caroline might come home and be disappointed at not finding them. Tom seemed about to make some remark, but changed his mind.

The afternoon was the longest Grace had ever known. The children were still absent at seven and she and Tom taxied to the train. Neither talked much on the way to town. As for the play, which Grace was sure to love, it turned out to be a rehash of "Cradle Snatchers" and "Sex," retaining the worst features of each.

When it was over, Tom said: "Now I'm inviting you to the Cove Club. You didn't eat any breakfast or dinner or supper and I can't have you starving to death on a feastday. Besides, I'm thirsty as well as hungry."

They ordered the special table d'hôte and struggled hard to get away with it. Tom drank six high-balls, but they failed to produce the usual effect of making him jovial. Grace had one highball and some kind of cordial that gave her a warm, contented feeling for a moment. But the warmth and contentment left her before the train was half way home.

The living-room looked as if Von Kluck's army had just passed through. Ted and Caroline had kept their promise up to a certain point. They had spent part of the evening at home, and the Murdocks must have brought all their own friends and everybody else's, judging from the results. The tables and floors were strewn with empty glasses, ashes and cigaret stubs. The stockings had been torn off their nails and wrecked contents were all over the place. Two sizable holes had been burnt in Grace's favorite rug.

Tom took his wife by the arm and led her into the music-room.

"You never took the trouble to open your own present," he said.

"And I think there's one for you, too," said Grace. "They didn't come in here," she added. "so I guess there wasn't much dancing or music."

Tom found his gift from Grace, a set of diamond studs and cuff buttons for festive wear. Grace's present from him was an opal ring.

"Oh, Tom!" she said.

"We'll have to go out somewhere tomorrow night, so I can break these in," said Tom.

"Well, if we do that, we'd better get a good night's rest."

"I'll beat you upstairs," said Tom.

## Questions

1. What preparations have Ted and Caroline done for the Christmas?
2. Why do Ted and Caroline sleep so late during the Christmas Eve?
3. Do the children like the presents their parents prepare for them? Why?
4. Where do the old folks get the tickets to "Jolly Jane"? Do they love the play?
5. What's your feeling after reading this story?

# 林·威·拉德纳
# （1885—1933）

美国短篇小说作家林·威·拉德纳以其简洁、口语化的风格撰写幽默讽刺作品而享有盛誉。拉德纳生于密歇根州的奈尔斯，曾经在南本德、芝加哥、圣路易斯和波士顿等地担任体育新闻记者。1913—1919年他为《芝加哥论坛报》体育专栏撰稿，并在各种杂志上发表了许多短篇小说和随笔，在此期间他也结集出版了一些作品。在20世纪20年代，他依旧为报社撰稿，但主要撰写短篇小说和随笔。拉德纳简洁的写作风格影响了后来的许多作家，如著名的作家海明威和赛林格。

拉德纳的早期作品显露出他善于用口语幽默地描写典型美国人的卓越才能，这些作品包括诗集《比布民谣》（1915），幽默小说集《阿尔，你了解我》（1916），讽刺小说《格利布莱游记》（1917）、《你对他们无礼》（1918）和幽默小说《大城市》（1921）等。拉德纳后期的作品则巧妙地运用反语揭露和讽刺生活中的愚蠢与邪恶，这些作品包括《怎样写短篇小说》（1924）和《爱巢》（1926）等。他也撰写剧本，唯一获得成功的是《六月的月亮》（1929）。

## 一对双亲的圣诞节

下面的作品讲述了一对夫妇热切等待一双儿女回家过圣诞节的故事。这对夫妇精心地为过节做了准备，特别为孩子们买了许多昂贵的圣诞礼物，并盼望他们能够早点儿回家共享天伦之乐。而年轻人却对父母的安排不以为然，只关心自己的事情。这个故事以简洁、口语化的写作风格，展示了"可怜天下父母心"的事实，揭示了"代沟"现象普遍存在的问题，主题令人深思。

圣诞节前夕，卡特夫妇——汤姆和格雷丝坐在客厅里，一会儿唠唠家常，一会儿伴装读书，还一直想着令他们烦心的事情。他们的两个孩子：朱尼尔，19岁，格雷丝，比哥哥小两岁，这天他们就要离校回家过圣诞节了。朱尼尔是大一的学生，格雷丝在一所大学预科学校里寄宿读书。

我以后就不再称他们为格雷丝和朱尼尔了，虽然那是他们在接受洗礼时起的名字。朱尼尔已改名为特德，格雷丝也改叫卡罗琳，并且他们让别人包括他们的父母也这样称呼。这是汤姆和老格雷丝此时坐在客厅里思考的事情之一。

在这座城市里读书的其他大一学生，已经在圣诞节放假的第一天——21日就回家了。那天，特德打电报告诉家里他因为参加一个临时的考试要晚三天回来，如果他考试通过了，会减轻下学期的负担。今天他回到家时，面色苍白、眼神忧郁，一副衰弱不适的样子，以致他的妈妈怀疑他是学傻了，而他爸爸则在默默地祝福他会平安无事的。卡罗琳也姗姗来迟，解释说她要洗的脏衣服不知了去向，又不放心让别人为她寻找而耽搁了时间。

格雷丝和汤姆不动声色地掩饰着对他们迟归的沮丧，继续为过节做着准备，以使孩子们对节日产生浓厚的兴趣，随之也使自己兴奋起来。他们买了许多昂贵的礼物，花销相当于汤姆十几岁时爸爸年收入的两到三倍，也就是汤姆自己一年前的收入。现在汤姆因发明一种新式抗风化油漆，通用汽车公司兑现给他一大笔钱，使他能够买下这幢别墅和这些奢侈品，这是他父母和岳父母做梦也想不到的。同时，也为特德和卡罗琳创造了他和格雷丝从前不曾拥有的优越条件。

在家中关闭着的琴房门后，摆放着一棵精心装饰的圣诞树；在钢琴、琴凳及圣诞树周围的地板上，散放着饰以缎带的大大小小、形状不同、重量不等的礼包。其中，一个是送给汤姆的，另一个是送给格雷丝的，有几个是送给佣人的，其余的就都是送给特德和卡罗琳的。一个大礼盒内装着一件为卡罗琳买的海豹皮大衣，这件大衣的价钱是从前卡特夫妇一年的房租；甚至还有更昂贵的一"套"珠宝——一个猫眼石胸针、一个镶有猫眼石和金丝线的手镯、一个镶嵌着钻石的猫眼石戒指。

格雷丝喜欢猫眼石总是胜过其他任何宝石。她现在能够买得起宝石了，却又不舍得为自己买，只是为女儿买，打扮女儿更令她高兴，她还为卡罗琳买了几盒丝制长筒袜、女式内衣、手套和手帕等。为特德买的礼物是一只价值三百美元的手表、一部精装的巴尔扎克著作、一个精致的袋子里装着多把新式闪亮的钢柄高尔夫球杆，还有一台最新型的便携式留声机。

然而，给特德最大的惊喜是锁在车库里的那辆黑色戈勒姆轿车。这辆车比停在它旁边的汤姆的旧车型号更新，外观更漂亮。如果天气持续晴朗的话，特德在这个假期里就可以驾驶它；到了明年的春夏之季也能够在家的附近兜风。大学里有规定，禁止在校大学生拥有和使用私家车。

16年以来，也就是从特德三岁、卡罗琳一岁起，过圣诞节悬挂起长筒袜，里面装满孩子们廉价的玩具，已经是卡特家节前的惯例。汤姆和格雷丝认为今年仍沿用以往的做法还会是很有趣的：长筒袜里放入新式的玩具——一个机械黑人舞娃、多个音乐盒、一只你用手按她背上的斑点会"喵喵"叫的玩具猫等一些会使"孩子们"发笑的东西。格雷丝对回家过节的孩子首先提出要求——他们必须早早睡觉，这样圣诞老人才不会被吓走。

可是，孩子们却没有傍晚待在家里的打算，他们俩在城里都有各自的约会：卡罗琳要去吃饭，然后和比阿特丽斯·默多克和她19岁的哥哥保罗去看戏，保罗将在六点半开车来接她；特德已接受邀请与两个同学赫布·卡斯尔和伯纳德·金一起去看冰上曲棍球比赛。他想用爸爸的戈勒姆轿车，但汤姆谎称刹车失灵，他必须等到明早才能进入车库。

特德和卡罗琳在下午都睡了一会儿，然后坐上保罗·默多克那漂亮的敞篷车一起去赴约了，并说他们半夜才能回来，或者更晚些；明天晚上他们会待在家里的。

他们走后，汤姆和格雷丝就开始了牵肠挂肚、漫长的等待，因为长筒袜只有在孩子们平安地躺在床上时才能装满、悬挂；再有人们在处于惦念和盼望的兴奋状态下刻意入睡也是很难做到。

"几点了？"格雷丝从她在晚饭后就开始看的那本书的第三页抬起头来问。

"两点半。"她的丈夫说。（从半夜开始，他每隔15分钟或20分钟就回答一次这样的问题。）

"你想他们不会出事吧？"格雷丝说。

"如果有事会有人告诉我们的。"汤姆说。

"当然，不可能出事，"格雷丝说，"可他们如果在某个地方出了车祸，那里无人报告、打电话或者什么的可咋办啊！我们不知道默多克家的男孩车开得怎么样。"

"他和特德同岁，这个年龄的男孩容易开快车。但他们开得非常好。"

"你怎么知道的？"

"哦，我看过一些男孩那样开车。"

"那倒是，但并不是所有男孩都开快车。"

"我不能确定世界上所有的人都见过19岁的男孩开快车。"

"这个年龄的男孩似乎缺少一些责任感。"

"噢，别担心！他们或许遇到一些同龄的朋友，停下来吃点儿东西或者在一起交流什么的。"汤姆站起身来故作镇静地走到窗前。"天太黑了，"他说，"能看见天上的每一颗星星。"

其实，他没有看星星，却在看路上的车，可他没有看见想要看的车。过了一会儿，他坐回到椅子上。

"几点了？"格雷丝问。

"差二十二分，"他说。

"几点差二十二分？"

"三点差二十二分。"

"你的表一定是停了！差不多一个小时前你就告诉我两点半了。"

"我的表没问题！你可能刚才打瞌睡了。"

"我一直都没合眼。"

"啊，该到你睡觉的时候了，你为什么不去睡觉呢？"

"那你为什么不去睡觉？"

"我不困！"

"我也不困！说实在的，你熬夜太傻了！我熬夜是因为我感觉特别精神，还能整理整理长筒袜，你不去睡觉可是白搭。"

"等他们到了家我才去睡觉。"

"那就太愚蠢了！没有什么可担心的。说不定他们现在正玩得开心呢！你也是从那时过来的。"

"那倒是！我年轻时，我年轻时……"他拿起报纸留意起运输业新闻来了。

"几点了？"格雷丝问。

"差五分三点。"

"或许他们在默多克家过夜了。"

"他们应该告诉我们一下啊。"

"他们怕打电话吵醒我们呗！"

在三点二十分时，一辆车停在了门前。

"他们回来了！"

"我早就告诉你没什么可担心的。"

汤姆走到窗前向外看，他只能分辨出默多克男孩那辆敞篷车的轮廓，感觉车的照明系统似乎出了毛病。

"他没开车灯，"汤姆说，"我出去看看，说不定我帮助修理一下会好的。"

"不，不要去！"格雷丝严厉地说，"他自己会修的。他停车时不开灯或许是为了节省而已。"

"他们为什么不进来呢？"

"他们可能在商量着什么。"

"他们可以回屋里来商量啊！我出去告诉他们我们还没有睡呢。"

"不，不要去！"格雷丝像刚才一样严厉地说，汤姆顺从地待在那里。

当车灯闪亮、汽车开走时，时间已接近四点钟了。卡罗琳走进房门迷迷糊糊地看着她的父母。

"天哪！你们没睡觉在做什么？"

汤姆想要说些什么，但格雷丝抢先制止了他。

"我们在谈论以前的圣诞节,"她说,"时间很晚了吧?"

"我不知道,"卡罗琳说。

"特德在哪儿?"

"他没回家吗?自从他在曲棍球场下了车,我就没见到他。"

"哦,你马上上床休息吧!"她妈妈说,"你一定很累了。"

"是的,有点儿。在看完戏后我们又跳舞去了。什么时候吃早饭啊?"

"八点钟。"

"噢,妈妈,你能不能定在九点钟啊?"

"我想,你过去经常在圣诞节那天早早起床,所以,就定在了八点钟。"

"我知道,但——"

"谁送你回家的?"汤姆问。

"哦,保罗·默多克——和比阿特丽斯。"

"你的头发太乱了。"

"他们让我坐在座位的'夹缝'里弄的。"

她听了自己的戏言笑了起来,随即道一声晚安便上楼了,与父母连手都没握一下。

"默多克家人,"汤姆说,"真是与众不同,让客人坐在那么不舒服的座位上。"

格雷丝沉默不语。

"你也去睡觉吧,"汤姆说,"我要等特德。"

"你不会整理长筒袜。"

"我不做那事。上午有时间再整理,我的意思是中午再整理。"

"你睡觉,我才去睡。"格雷丝说。

"那好,咱俩都去睡吧。特德也该回来了,我觉得,他的朋友会送他回家的。他回来时,我们也能听得到。"

在五点五十分时,特德回来了,家人听到了他的动静,没人理会他。他昨天很晚才去办年货,今早只带回家一个小包裹。

格雷丝又在七点半下楼来,告诉佣人早餐推迟到九点钟。她把长筒袜钉在了壁炉旁;走进琴房看了看一切如故的陈设,并把特德轻轻地放在门厅地板上的帽子和大衣取走。

汤姆在九点前就起床了,并建议叫醒孩子们。

"我会叫醒他们的,"格雷丝说,接着就上了楼。她打开特德的房门看了看,又轻轻地关上;她走进女儿的房间,发现卡罗琳正半睡半醒着。

"我用现在起床吗?说实在的,我不想吃什么东西。如果能让莫拉给我送来一杯咖啡就好啦！我和特德都被邀请在十二点半到默多克家吃饭，所以我还能再睡上一两个小时。"

"可是，亲爱的，你不知道我们在一点钟要吃圣诞正餐吗？"

"不好意思，妈妈，我一直认为我们的正餐时间是在晚上。"

"你不想看一看你的礼物吗？"

"我当然想，难道是它们等不及了吗？"

格雷丝打算去厨房告诉厨师正餐时间由一点钟改在七点钟，可她想起曾向西格尼承诺下午和晚上放假之事；又想到孩子们在吃过了丰盛的午餐之后晚餐就应该吃一些简单清淡的食物了。因此，她打消了这个念头。

汤姆和格雷丝单独吃了早饭，又坐在客厅里聊着家常、想着心事、佯装读书。

"你应该劝劝卡罗琳，"汤姆说。

"我会劝的，但不是今天，今天是圣诞节。"

"我打算跟特德说几句话。"

"是的，亲爱的，应该的。但不是今天。"

"他们今晚还会出去。"

"不会的，他们已经答应待在家里。我们将度过一个美好温馨的夜晚。"

"你别想美事儿啦！"汤姆说。

中午时分，"孩子们"回来了，他们很得体地表达了对父母问候的感激之情。特德谢绝了为其送上的一杯咖啡，他和卡罗琳一同为去默多克家"早餐"约会而表示歉意。

"我和妹妹都认为，你们会像往常一样在七点钟吃正餐。"

"我们总是在圣诞节那天一点钟吃正餐。"汤姆说。

"我忘记了今天是圣诞节！"特德说。

"哦，那些长筒袜总该提醒你们吧！"

特德和卡罗琳看了看那鼓鼓囊囊的长筒袜。

"没有圣诞树啊？"卡罗琳问。

"当然有，"她妈妈说，"但长筒袜在先。"

"我们仅有一点儿时间了，"卡罗琳说，"按照往年的时间现在已经晚了，我们看不到圣诞树了吧？"

"你们会看到的，"格雷丝边说边带着他们走进了琴房。

佣人们也被召集来了，大家一同仔细端详着圣诞树并赞不绝口。

"打开你的礼包看看吧！"格雷丝对女儿说。

"我现在不能把所有的礼包都打开看，"卡罗琳说，"告诉我哪个最好。"

格雷丝拿过一个大盒子并拿掉盒盖儿，取出了里面的大衣。

"噢！妈妈，"卡罗琳说，"一件海豹皮大衣！"

"穿上吧！"他爸爸说。

"现在我不能穿，没有时间了。"

"你再看看这个！"格雷丝打开那个珠宝盒儿说。

"噢！妈妈，猫眼石！"卡罗琳说。

"它们是我最喜欢的宝石。"格雷丝平静地说。

"如果没人介意的话，"特德说，"我暂时不看我的礼物，等回来后再看。我肯定喜欢你们送给我的所有礼物。但是，如果我没有可开的车，就只好打的和赶火车去赴约了。"

"你有好车开啊！"他爸爸说。

"修好刹车了吗？"

"没问题。走，我们到车库去看看！"

特德戴上了帽子，穿好了衣服，与妈妈吻别，准备去车库。

"妈妈，"他说，"我知道，您会原谅我没有为您和爸爸头什么圣诞礼物。在学校的最后三天我实在是太忙了，原以为昨天回来时会有时间买些东西，但我匆忙回家，昨天晚上所有的商店又都打烊了。"

"别在意，"格雷丝说，"圣诞节是年轻人的节日，我和你爸爸什么也不缺。"

佣人们分别找到了自己的圣诞礼物，并表达了真诚的谢意，然后离去。琴房里只有卡罗琳和她妈妈了。

"妈妈，这大衣是从哪里买的？"

"劳埃德和亨利百货公司。"

"那里还有其他种类的皮大衣吗？"

"有的。"

"如果我调换一下，您不介意吧！"

"当然不会，亲爱的！你可以挑选你喜欢的任何一件，价钱贵一点儿也没关系。我们明后天就进城！你为什么不戴猫眼石饰物去默多克家呢？"

"我不想戴，万一丢了呢！我身体不——好，我对——不感兴趣。"

"我觉得，宝石也能调换。"格雷丝说，"你现在要去赴宴，准备走吧！"

卡罗琳爽快地答应了，格雷丝的内心感到非常的惬意。

特德与爸爸来到车库，汤姆打开了车库门。

"哎呀——，您有两辆车！"特德说。

"那辆新车不是我的，"汤姆说。

"是谁的呀？"

"送给你的，新款车。"

"爸爸，太好了！可它看上去像那辆旧车似的。"

"的确，那辆旧车不错。但你的新车更好。当你驾驶它时，就会知道了。你上车，发动吧！我已经加满了油。"

"我想我还是开那辆旧车吧！"

"为什么？"

"哦，爸爸，我真正想要的是一辆巴恩斯运动敞篷汽车，像保罗·默多克那样的，只是配色不同就可以了。如果这辆新车我不开的话，能否让车行取回去？或者与巴恩斯车行协商调换一下。"

汤姆清了清嗓子，然后说："好的，儿子。你先开我的车吧！接下来我再考虑给你换车的事。"

卡罗琳在等特德时，忽然想起一件事，对她妈妈高声说："这是我给您和爸爸的两张《乔利·简》戏票。我昨晚看过了，你们一定会喜欢的。"

"什么时候的？"格雷丝问。

"今天晚上的。"卡罗琳说。

"可是，亲爱的，"她妈妈说，"你们答应过今晚待在家里，我们晚上就不想出去了。"

"我们一定在家，"卡罗琳说，"但默多克兄妹以及他们的朋友可能来访，我们要一起随着音乐跳舞娱乐。我和特德认为你们最好外出回避一下，以免噪声打扰你们。"

"你们这样考虑，真是善解人意啊！"她妈妈说，"但我和你爸爸不在乎噪声，只要你们开心就行。"

"不管怎么样，应该是您和爸爸出去享受一下的时候了。"

"真正的享受是待在家里与你们俩一起度过一个安静的夜晚。"格雷丝说。

"可实际上是默多克兄妹主动要来我家串门儿的，他们以前对我很好我又无法回绝。妈妈，去吧！您会喜欢这出戏的。"

"你们晚上回家吃饭吗？"

"我们一定在家里吃。如果回来晚些的话，您和爸爸不用等我们。你们看七点二十分那场戏剧情更完整些。第一幕是最精彩的。晚上我们可能不会饿，但还是让西格尼给我们留点儿吃的，我们可能会吃。"

汤姆和格雷丝坐在精心准备好的圣诞正餐桌前，没有动桌上的饭菜。尽管他们此时很有食欲，但仍没有吃那16磅的火鸡和其他菜肴。他俩的谈话是断断续续的，主要谈到的是西格尼高超的厨艺和温暖的天气，对孩子们和圣诞节的事几乎没有提及。

汤姆针对此次看戏提出了自己的建议：我们应该看六点十分那场，并在城里吃晚饭。他的妻子则不同意，说特德和卡罗琳如果回到家里，会因为看不到父母而失望。汤姆对此似乎想要说些什么，可他没再说下去。

这天下午对于格雷丝来说真是过得漫长而难耐。孩子们在七点钟时仍没有回来，她和汤姆打的去火车站。在路上，他俩沉默不语。对于这场戏格雷丝的确很喜欢，它是一出以"老少配"与"性爱"为题材编排的喜剧，喜剧色彩很浓厚，引人发笑。

看完戏后，汤姆说："我请你去海湾俱乐部餐馆吃饭。你还没吃早饭、正餐或者晚饭呢，我不能让你在节日里饿肚子；我也是又饿又渴啊！"

他们在餐馆点了一桌特色美食，并吃了个精光。汤姆喝了六杯饮料，但没能产生往常那种舒服的感觉；格雷丝喝了一杯普通饮料和一杯提神饮料，为她带来了片刻温馨、惬意的感觉，但这种感觉在他们乘车回家的途中很快就消失了。

回到家里，他们看到客厅的景象犹如冯·克卢克将军的部队刚刚撤离一般。从现场可以断定：特德和卡罗琳真是信守了诺言，他们的确是在家里与默多克兄妹带来的朋友们度过了一个疯狂的夜晚。你看，桌子和地板上散落着空瓶子、灰烬和烟蒂，长筒袜也被扯了下来，被毁的礼物满地都是；格雷丝心爱的地毯也被烧了两个大窟窿。

汤姆挽着他的妻子走进了琴房。

"你不用费力就可以找到你的礼物了，"他说。

"你的礼物也一样好找。"格雷丝说，"他们没来过这里，"她接着说，"那么，他们没有什么轻歌曼舞啊！"

汤姆找到了格雷丝送给他的礼物——一套用于节日穿着的钻石钮扣和袖扣；汤姆送给格雷丝的是一个猫眼石戒指。

"哦，汤姆！"她说。

"明晚我们得出去走走，这样我好穿戴试用一下这些东西。"汤姆说。

"哦，如果那样的话，我们今晚就要好好休息啦！"

"我就先上楼啦！"汤姆说。

# John McNulty
# (1895—1956)

John McNulty, US journalist and author, was born in Lawrence, Massachusetts. During his service in *The New Yorker*, he launched a new career writing stories and articles, which enlivened that magazine in the 1940s. He was best-known for his humorous dispatches from an Irish saloon of quotable regulars on Third Avenue (the real-life Costello's on East 44th Street). To readers, McNulty's characters became a sort of ensemble group, as indeed they were in life. His 26 New York profiles and saloon sketches from the Forties and Fifties show McNulty's perfect pitch for the uncommon speech of ordinary people. McNulty came from the world of newspapers, where one awed reporter observed that "just as dogs will make up with some people and not with others, the English language will do things for Mr. McNulty which it will not do for the rest of us."

From 1937 until his death in 1956, John McNulty walked many beats for *The New Yorker*, but his favorite — and the one that he made famous—was Tim & Joe Costello's, an old-fashioned Irish saloon at Third Avenue and Forty-fourth Street. Some of his stories include, "This Place on Third Avenue," "Atheist Hit by a Truck," "Man Here Keeps Getting Arrested All the Time," "Argument outside a Gin Mill Here," "This Lady Was a Bostonian They Call Them," "The Fight in the Hallway," etc.

## Cluney McFarrar's Hardtack

*Fifth Avenue bus drivers and conductors often congregate in a coffee pot around 168 St. Most of them are old 69th men and they talk about the last war. Cluney McFarrar tells about an experience he had in a wood in France in 1918, when he had to run past a can of hardtack a dead soldier had dropped. McFarrar was hungry and wanted that hardtack badly but couldn't stop to pick it up. He made up his mind to come back for it later in the evening when the firing ceased. He did come back, but found he just couldn't go into the wood, thinking of all the boys lying dead there.*

The only trouble with this coffee pot around a Hundred and Sixty-eighth Street is it's practically one whole war behind the times. Dozens of guys who go in there off the Fifth Avenue buses are old Sixty-ninth men and they keep some track of the war in the *News* every morning. But no sooner do they talk ten minutes about this war than back they hop into the other war because it is still more familiar to them. The result was they got this war into France before it really got there. They're always talking about Looneyville — that was a spot in France in the other war—and about LaFurty Millon, they call it, that was also in the other war.

They're bus drivers and conductors on the buses, and this coffee pot is a hangout for them. Sometimes they get talking the other war and they get carried away by their own talk so that once in a while it makes quite a story they tell, in its own way. The other day it was Cluney McFarrar talking. He just finished up work on the Burma Road line, they call it, because it's the Number Two that goes through Harlem.

Cluney McFarrar was a sergeant in the Sixty-ninth and it is practically a miracle how he weaves around in traffic with that big bus, considering the right arm he got. It was hit by a machine gun in a wheat field and later on he developed a thing in it called osteomyelitis. He knows the medical name for it because he heard the doctors in the hospitals talking about it a million times. But osteomyelitis or no osteomyelitis, he can jockey that bus around O.K., and not only that but with his bum arm he can maneuver the door open and shut in traffic in the twinkle of an eye, so that he can spit tobacco into the street as he goes along. One conductor that works with him says McFarrar is a marvel of timing, opening and shutting the door for this purpose.

This day, a couple days ago, McFarrar finished on the Burma Road, had a slug or two in a place next door to this coffee pot, then came in for coffee and to sit around talking. One thing led to another and McFarrar told about one time in a woods in France—still back a whole war, into 1918.

"There was no more trenches than a rabbit," McFarrar said, "because it was July, around that sometime, and we were chasing them but still plenty of our fellers getting killed. You don't know really what's happening in a war like that until a couple years later when you come home and read in a slow-written book just what the hell was going on that time, like for instance the day I'm talking about."

"We couldn't go up the road, so we were going ahead the best we could through a woods, the woods on both sides the road. They were shelling the road so you couldn't go up it."

"Guys would see Germans here and there ahead of them in the woods, so the way you'd have to do is stand behind a tree and fire a few, then run up and get behind another tree like the goddam Indians they used to have here in this country, except the only Indians most of us knew was those cop-shooters and wild men used to be around the West Side, Tenth Avenue and around there."

"That was the best way to do it, behind trees, everybody separated, but it's hell to keep soldiers separated. Or deployed, if you want to call it that. The toughest thing a sergeant has to do is keep the troops spread out, because as soon as there's shooting, they bunch up, usually around the sergeant, which'd make a fine target out of him."

"We kept separated pretty good through that woods, though, going ahead a little at a time. I come across McElroy, from Eight Avenue, behind one tree, smoking his pipe and shooting one shot after the other. He says to me when I bunched behind the same tree, 'Have you got a match, McFarrar? This pipe keeps going out, and I ought to hold up a minute for a smoke anyway. The bolt of this rifle is getting hot, so help me God.'"

"All that has no bearing on what I was going to say, I mean about the hardtack. Well, after I left McElroy and ran for another tree ahead a little bit and McElroy found himself another tree, I saw something out of the corner of my eye while I was running up to this other tree."

"What I saw was a nice new can of hardtack lying there, and jeez, was I hungry. I forgot to say the chow wagons didn't get up, and everybody was hungry. And there was this can of hardtack some poor guy dropped. He was dead near it. I had to run past it, but I never saw anything so clear as that hardtack."

"So when I got behind the tree I says to myself, 'I'll come back and get that hardtack if I ever live through this day.' And to make sure where I was, I mean where the hardtack was, I took a good look around. I looked up at how the trees set with regards to the road, and how if a man was walking on the road he could look in and tell this part of the woods exactly. Like distinguishing marks, I mean, that you'd see from the road, how the trees grew and the like of that. 'If it's the last thing I ever do, I'll get that hardtack tonight,' I says to myself."

"Well, the day come to an end, and us maybe two miles ahead of where McElroy and me was behind the tree and the hardtack was."

Then McFarrar said they had a funny thing about that other war, compared to this war they got now. He said in some ways that other war was a union war, like. In some places, anyway, it seemed to have regular hours.

"Near this woods was one of those places where the war kept regular hours," McFarrar went on. "It seemed to stop almost altogether at night, even before night. What you might call twilight, it stopped, only the way I remember it, this twilight come at pretty near ten o'clock. Not dark yet, only getting gray and birds going to bed in the trees."

"The birds were funny. I remember them because when everything come to a halt and I was still alive for the end of that day, I says to myself, 'Now I'll go back and get the hardtack.' And I started all alone back down the road. They wasn't shelling it any more, because whether it seems logical or not, the war come to a stop, I tell you, right about that hour. Not a stop for good I don't mean, but a stop for that day. And I walked back down the road toward the place where the hardtack was. Jeez, I was hungry — no chow wagons yet."

"About the birds. While I was walking back the road, I could hear them loud and busy, getting ready for the night. Banging and shooting sounds all the day, and there were the birds singing or at least talking, at this kind of twilight, as if nothing happened. It seemed funny, and it was that quiet I could hear my feet scrunching the gravel down the road."

"Of course I kept glancing into the woods, so I wouldn't pass where the hardtack was. It got silenter and silenter except for the birds, and gradually they started to shut up and it got a little darker, only not what you'd call dark. For some reason there was nobody on the road but me. The stuff like camions and chow wagons wouldn't come up until real black dark."

"There was beginning to be a little smell from the woods. They were the quietest woods I ever seen then, even though they were certainly noisy all that day we just pulled through."

"I came to the place I marked in my mind's eye, and my stomach gave a jump because I knew the hardtack was right in there. Honest to God, I was near starved. I stood a minute in the road and checked up. I wanted to make sure by the shape of the trees I was right and that was the place. And I started to go into the woods after the hardtack."

"Then the silence came over me. Every bird quit all to once. My feet stopped going into the woods. It came over me how there was all the guys, some of them I knew, would never come out of those woods again. Some of them from New York. Most of them, you might say, because don't forget this was the Sixty-ninth. I thought how they'd never walk around on the New York streets any more, Ninety-sixth or anywhere, and not ever get drunk in New York on Saturday night the way you do. And on top of all that, this silence I got to explain to you but I can't."

"And that was the last step I took toward that hardtack when I thought all that. I turned around and went up the road again."

"I couldn't have gone in those woods if there was Fig Newtons in there."

## Questions

1. How do you understand the title of the story?
2. What personal details do we know about McFarrar?
3. Did McFarrar get the hardtack? Why?
4. Why did the narrator talk about the birds?
5. What kind of social significance does the story have?

# 约翰·麦克纳尔蒂
# （1895—1956）

约翰·麦克纳尔蒂，美国新闻记者、作家，出生于马萨诸塞州的劳伦斯市。他在《纽约客》杂志供职期间，撰写了一系列别具一格的故事，使得该杂志在20世纪40年代充满生机。他最著名的作品是对纽约市第三大道的一个爱尔兰沙龙（现实生活中的东44街上的科斯特洛之家）的一些常客的幽默报道。麦克纳尔蒂塑造的人物犹如一个特别的团体，其中包括了各色人等，他们形象鲜明、栩栩如生，就像现实生活中的人物一样。麦克纳尔蒂在四五十年代所著的26个纽约剪影和沙龙素描中，展示了他对普通人不寻常谈话的完美刻画，麦克纳尔蒂来自新闻界，他对语言的驾驭出神入化，惟妙惟肖，其中一位对他充满敬畏的报界同行曾经这样评述："正像狗会与一些人合得来，与另一些人却合不来一样，英语语言会为麦克纳尔蒂先生效力，却不会听其他人的差遣。"

从1937年到1956年他去世之前，约翰·麦克纳尔蒂为《纽约客》奔走了很多地方，但是他最钟爱的——并使其声名远扬的——是蒂姆和乔·科斯特洛之家，一家位于纽约第三大道和44街的老式爱尔兰沙龙。他最有名的故事便来自此处，其中包括：《第三大道的这个地方》《无神论者被卡车撞了》《这里的人总是不断地被捕》《这边酒厂外的争论》《他们说这位女士是一个波士顿人》《走廊里的打斗》等。

## 柯拉内·麦克法若的硬饼干

第五大道的公交车司机和售票员经常在168大街附近的一个咖啡屋里聚集起来。他们绝大多数是六十九军团的老兵，常常谈论过去的那场战争。柯拉内·麦克法若讲述了自己1918年在法国一个树林里的一次经历，当时他不得不从一罐硬饼干旁跑过去，那是从一个阵亡士兵身上掉落的。麦克法若当时很饿，特别想拿到那罐饼干，但因为枪炮阻击，他不能停下来去拿。他暗下决心，那天傍晚炮火停下的时候他就回来取那罐饼干。他的确回来了，但是当他想到那些躺在树林里死去的战友们，便无法走近去拿那罐饼干。

这个位于168街区的咖啡屋的唯一问题是，它实际上是一个谈论战争的场所。很多从第五大道上下公交车到这个咖啡屋去的都是六十九军团的老兵，他们每天上午从《新闻》报上了解战事。但是关于眼下的战争，他们谈论了还不到十分钟就跳到了另一场战争上，因为他们更熟悉那场战争。结果，这场战争还没有打到法国，他们已经开始大谈那边的战场了。他们总是谈论卢内维尔——那场战争中的一个法国战场——还谈论他们称为拉法蒂·米伦的地方，也是那场战争中的一个战场。

他们是公交车司机和售票员，这个咖啡屋是他们经常光顾的地方。有时他们谈论那场战争的时候，情绪会变得异常激动，有时会以独有的方式讲得绘声绘色。有一天，柯拉内·麦克法若在高谈阔论。他刚结束了博尔马路线的工作，称其为博尔马是因为那是穿越哈雷姆区的二号线。

柯拉内·麦克法若曾经是六十九军团的中士。就他的右臂而言，他能开着那辆大巴在繁忙的车辆中间穿梭实在是个奇迹。有一次在麦地里交战时，他的右臂被机枪击中，后来得了骨髓炎。因为听医生说过上百万次了，所以他知道这个医学名称。但不管有没有骨髓炎，他都能游刃有余地驾驶他的巴士。不仅如此，他还能在眨眼之间用他的残臂灵巧地开门、关门，把烟头吐到街上，同时还不耽误他开车前行。因此，一位跟他共事的售票员说麦克法若在这方面是一个奇才。

几天前，麦克法若干完了博尔马路的工作，先到咖啡屋隔壁的酒馆儿喝了一两杯酒，然后走进来要了一杯咖啡，便坐下闲聊起来。他谈了一件事又联系到另一桩，后来他开始谈起1918年发生在法国的一个丛林里的一场战争。

"根本就没有像样的战壕，"麦克法若说，"因为是七月份左右，我们在追击敌人，但我们还是有很多弟兄被击毙。直到多年以后你回到家读了有关战争的书，你才了解到那时候究竟是怎么回事，但身处战争现场你根本不知道发生了什么，比方说我要讲的这一天发生的事。"

"我们不能沿着大路前进，所以我们费尽全力穿越道路两边的树林前进。他们一直在用炮轰炸这条路，所以我们不能沿大路前进。"

"弟兄们看到前面树林里到处都是德国人，所以我们只能先躲在一棵树后放上几枪，然后往前跑几步，再躲到另一棵树后，就像这个国家以前该死的印第安人那样，只是我们大多数人了解的印第安人都是警察杀手和疯子，他们原来常在城西和第十大道周围的地方出现。"

"那就是当时最好的前进方式，藏在树后，大家单独行动，或者分散部署，如果你想这样说的话，但使士兵们保持分散太难了。中士要做的最棘手的事就是使军队保持分散状态，因为一有枪响，士兵们就会往一块儿跑，通常是围到中士身边，这就使中士成了极易被打中的靶子。"

"虽然每次我们只能前进一点儿，但我们在穿过那片林地时保持着相当好的分散状态。后来我碰到了来自第八大道的麦克艾罗伊，他正躲在一棵树后面，一边抽烟斗一边打了一枪又一枪。我跳到他藏身的那棵树后面，他对我说："麦克法若，你有火柴吗？这烟斗老是灭，不管怎样，我得在这里撑一会儿，吸两口烟。这步枪的枪栓越来越热，老天帮帮我吧。"

"上面讲的这些跟我要说的事儿没有多大关系，我是说跟那罐硬饼干没关系。就这样，我离开了麦克艾罗伊，跑到往前一点儿的另一棵树后，麦克艾罗伊自己也躲到了另外一棵树后面，就在我往前面的那棵树跑的当儿，眼角的余光看到了一样东西。"

"我看到的是一罐包装精美的、还未开封的硬饼干，天哪，当时我饿坏了。刚才我忘了说，军用食品车还没赶到，所以人人都很饿。就在这时，我看到了不知哪个可怜的家伙掉的硬饼干。那家伙就死在饼干旁边。我没法去拿，不得不越过它，但我从没有见过比那罐硬饼干更清晰的东西。"

"所以当我躲到那棵树后时，对自己说：'如果我能活过今天，我就回来拿那罐饼干。'为了确定我的位置，我是说那罐硬饼干的位置，我仔细地打量了一下周围。我抬头看看这棵树离大路多远、在大路的哪个方向，如果从大路上走过来，怎样才能准确地找到这个地方。我是说可以从路上看到的很明显的记号，比如树的长势等。'如果我这辈子要做最后一件事，那就是今晚拿到那罐硬饼干，'我自言自语道。"

"就这样，这一天结束了，我们离我和麦克艾罗伊藏身的那棵树，还有那罐硬饼干大约两英里。"

然后麦克法若说跟眼下正在进行的这场战争相比，他们那场战争有一点挺搞笑。他说从某种程度上讲，那场战争有点儿像联盟作战。至少在有些地方是这样，因为作战好像有固定的时间。

"这片树林附近就是一个有固定战斗时间的战场，"麦克法若继续讲道。"看起来这仗一到夜晚，甚至在夜晚之前就完全停下来了。或者在你们称作黄昏的时候就停了，我记得那天的黄昏接近十点才到来。天还没黑，只是有点儿灰暗，鸟儿都回到树上打算睡觉了。"

"那些鸟儿很有意思。我记得它们，是因为那天傍晚当一切都停息了的时候，我还活着，我自言自语道：'现在我要回去拿那罐饼干。'随后我独自一人顺着大路往回走。他们已经不再轰炸大路，因为不管讲得通还是讲不通，战斗结束了。我是说就在那个时候。我不是说完全结束了，只是那天的战斗结束了。我朝着饼干所在的地方往回走。哎呀，我好饿——食品车还是没有到。"

"再说说那些鸟儿。当我往回走时，我能听见它们嘈杂忙碌的声音，准备好过夜。一整天都是砰砰啪啪的枪击声，这时候终于有了鸟儿的鸣唱，或者至少是叽叽喳喳的交谈声，在这样的一个黄昏，好像什么都没有发生过。这看起来很滑稽。夜晚很安静,我都能听见脚踩在石子路上发出的嘎吱声。"

"我不停地往树林里看,这样我就不会错过硬饼干所在的地方。除了鸟声,周围越来越静了,后来鸟儿也逐渐闭上了嘴,天变得暗些,但还不是很黑。出于某种原因,路上只有我一个人。像军用卡车和食品车这类东西只有在深夜才会出现。"

"我开始闻到森林里散发出的一股异味儿。那是我到过的最安静的树林,虽然就在我们刚刚熬过的那个白天,这林子曾经噪声不断。"

"我走到了在心里记下的那个地方,胃抽动了一下,因为我知道饼干就在那儿。说实话,我快要饿死了。我在路边站了一会儿,查看了一下周围的情况。我想根据树的长势确定这就是我要找的地方,然后走进树林去找那罐饼干。"

"这时我感到异常安静。所有的鸟儿突然间不再出声,我停下了前进的脚步。我突然想到树林里躺着那么多战死的伙计,其中一些人我还认识,他们再也走不出这片林子了。其中一些人来自纽约,也许你会说绝大多数是从纽约来的,因为别忘了这是六十九军团。我想到他们再也不能走在纽约街头,96号大街或其他地方了,而且也没法在星期六的晚上像你们一样喝醉了。我很想给你们说说那种死一般的沉寂,可我讲不出来。"

"一想到这些,我就再也没往前去找那罐饼干了。我转过身,又走回到大路上。"

"就算那林子里有美味的菲格牛顿甜饼,我也不会进去。"

# William Faulkner
# (1897—1962)

William Cuthbert Faulkner was an American writer and Nobel Prize laureate from Oxford, Mississippi. Faulkner wrote novels, short stories, plays, poems, essays, and screenplays. He is primarily known for his novels and short stories set in the fictional Yoknapatawpha County, based on Lafayette County, Mississippi, where he spent most of his life.

Faulkner was one of the most celebrated writers in American literature generally and Southern literature specifically. Though his work was published as early as 1919, and largely during the 1920s and 1930s, Faulkner was not widely known until we received the 1949 Noble Prize in Literature, for which he became the only Mississippi-born Nobel winner. Two of his works, *A Fable* (1954) and his last novel *The Reivers* (1962), won the Pulizer Prize for Fiction. In 1998, the Modern Library ranked his 1929 novel *The Sound and the Fury* sixth on its list of the 100 best English-language novels of the 20th Century; also on the list were *As I Lay Dying* (1930) and *Light in August* (1932). *Absalom, Absalom!* (1936) appeared on similar lists. His first published story, "A Rose for Emily" is one of the most famous an American has written.

## Dry September

*"Dry September" is a short story published in 1931. It describes a lynch mob forming despite of ambiguous evidence on a hot September evening to avenge an alleged (and unspecified) insult or attack upon a white woman by a black watchman, Will Mayes. Told in five parts, the story includes the perspective of the rumored female victim, Miss Minnie Cooper, and of the mob's leader, John McLendon.*

## I

Through the bloody September twilight, aftermath of sixty-two rainless days, it had gone like a fire in dry grass: the rumor, the story, whatever it was. Something about Miss Minnie Cooper and a Negro. Attacked, insulted, frightened: none of them, gathered in the barber shop on that Saturday evening where the ceiling fan stirred, without freshening it, the vitiated air, sending back upon them, in recurrent surges of stale pomade and lotion, their own stale breath and odors, knew exactly what had happened.

"Except it wasn't Will Mayes," a barber said. He was a man of middle age; a thin, sand-colored man with a mild face, who was shaving a client. "I know Will Mayes. He's a good nigger. And I know Miss Minnie Cooper, too."

"What do you know about her?" a second barber said.

"Who is she?" the client said. "A young girl?"

"No," the barber said. "She's about forty, I reckon. She ain't married. That's why I don't believe—"

"Believe, hell!" a hulking youth in a sweat-stained silk shirt said. "Won't you take a white woman's word before a nigger's?"

"I don't believe Will Mayes did it," the barber said. "I know Will Mayes."

"Maybe you know who did it, then. Maybe you already got him out of town, you damn niggerlover."

"I don't believe anybody did anything. I don't believe anything happened. I leave it to you fellows if the ladies that get old without getting married don't have notions that a man can't—"

"Then you are a hell of a white man," the client said. He moved under the cloth. The youth had sprung to his feet.

"You don't?" he said. "Do you accuse a white woman of lying?"

The barber held the razor poised above the half-risen client. He did not look around.

"It's this darn weather," another said. "It's enough to make a man do anything. Even to her."

Nobody laughed. The barber said in his mild, stubborn tone: "I ain't accusing nobody of nothing. I just know and you fellows know how a woman that never—"

"You damn niggerlover!" the youth said.

"Shut up, Butch," another said. "We'll get the facts in plenty of time to act."

"Who is? Who's getting them?" the youth said. "Facts, hell! I—"

"You're a fine white man," the client said. "Ain't you?" In his frothy beard he looked like a desert rat in the moving pictures. "You tell them, Jack," he said to the youth. "If there ain't any white men in this town, you can count on me, even if I ain't only a drummer and a stranger."

"That's right, boys," the barber said. "Find out the truth first. I know Will Mayes."

"Well, by God!" the youth shouted. "To think that a white man in this town—"

"Shut up, Butch," the second speaker said. "We got plenty of time."

The client sat up. He looked at the speaker. "Do you claim that anything excuses a nigger attacking a white woman? Do you mean to tell me you are a white man and you'll stand for it? You better go back North where you came from. The South don't want your kind here."

"North what?" the second said. "I was born and raised in this town."

"Well, by God!" the youth said. He looked about with a strained, baffled gaze, as if he was trying to remember what it was he wanted to say or to do. He drew his sleeve across his sweating face. "Damn if I'm going to let a white woman—"

"You tell them, Jack," the drummer said. "By God, if they—"

The screen door crashed open. A man stood in the floor, his feet apart and his heavy-set body poised easily. His white shirt was open at the throat; he wore a felt hat. His hot, bold glance swept the group. His name was McLendon. He had commanded troops at the front in France and had been decorated for valor.

"Well," he said, "are you going to sit there and let a black son rape a white woman on the streets of Jefferson?"

Butch sprang up again. The silk of his shirt clung flat to his heavy shoulders. At each armpit was a dark halfmoon, "That's what I been telling them! That's what I—"

"Did it really happen?" a third said. "This ain't the first man scare she ever had, like Hawkshaw says. Wasn't there something about a man on the kitchen roof, watching her undress, about a year ago?"

"What?" the client said. "What's that?" The barber had been slowly forcing him back into the chair; he arrested himself reclining, his head lifted, the barber still pressing him down.

McLendon whirled on the third speaker. "Happen? What the hell difference does it make? Are you going to let the black sons get away with it until one really does it?"

"That's what I'm telling them!" Butch shouted. He cursed, long and steady, pointless.

"Here, here," a fourth said. "Not so loud. don't talk so loud."

"Sure," McLendon said; "no talking necessary at all. I've done my talking. Who's with me?" He poised on the balls of his feet, roving his gaze.

The barber held the drummer's face down, the razor poised. "Find out the facts first, boys. I know Willy Mayes. It wasn't him. Let's get the sheriff and do this thing right."

McLendon whirled upon him his furious, rigid face. The barber did not look away. They looked like men of different races. The other barbers had ceased also above their prone clients. "You mean to tell me," McLendon said, "that you'd take a nigger's word before a white woman's? Why, you damn niggerloving—"

The third speaker rose and grasped McLendon's arm; he too had been a soldier. "Now, now. Let's figure this thing out. Who knows anything about what really happened?"

"Figure out hell!" McLendon jerked his arm free. "All that're with me get up from there. The ones that ain't—" He roved his gaze, dragging his sleeve across his face.

Three men rose. The drummer in the chair sat up. "Here," he said, jerking at the cloth about his neck; "get this rag off me. I'm with him. I don't live here, but by God, if our mothers and wives and sisters—" He smeared the cloth over his face and flung it to the floor. McLendon stood in the door and cursed the others. Another rose and moved toward him. The remainder sat uncomfortable, not looking at one another, then one by one they rose and joined him.

The barber picked the cloth from the floor. He began to fold it neatly. "Boys, don't do that. Will Mayes never done it. I know."

"Come on," McLendon said. He whirled. From his hip pocket protruded the butt of a heavy automatic pistol. They went out. The screen door crashed behind them, reverberant in the dead air.

The barber wiped the razor carefully and swiftly, and put it away, and ran to the rear, and took his hat from the wall. "I'll be back as soon as I can," he said to the other barbers. "I can't let—" He went out, running. The two other barbers followed him to the door and caught it on the rebound, leaning out and looking up the street after him. The air was flat and dead. It had a metallic taste at the base of the tongue.

"What can he do?" the first said. The second one was saying "Jees Christ, Jees Christ" under his breath. "I'd just as lief be Will Mayes as Hawk, if he gets McLendon riled."

"Jees Christ, Jees Christ," the second whispered.

"You reckon he really done it to her?" the first said.

## II

She was thirty-eight or thirty-nine. She lived in a small frame house with her invalid mother and a thin, sallow, unflagging aunt, where each morning between ten and eleven she would appear on the porch in a lace-trimmed boudoir cap, to sit swinging in the porch swing until noon. After dinner she lay down for a while, until the afternoon began to cool. Then, in one of the three or four new voile dresses which she had each summer, she would go downtown to spend the afternoon in the stores with the other ladies, where they would handle the goods and haggle over the prices in cold, immediate voices, without any intention of buying.

She was of comfortable people— not the best in Jefferson, but good people enough— and she was still on the slender side of ordinary looking, with a bright, faintly haggard manner and dress. When she was young she had had a slender, nervous body and a sort of hard vivacity which had enabled her for a time to ride upon the crest of the town's social life as exemplified by the high school party and church social period of her contemporaries while still children enough to be unclassconscious.

She was the last to realize that she was losing ground; that those among whom she had been a little brighter and louder flame than any other were beginning to learn the pleasure of snobbery— male— and retaliation— female. That was when her face began to wear that bright, haggard look. She still carried it to parties on shadowy porticoes and summer lawns, like a mask or a flag, with that bafflement of furious repudiation of truth in her eyes. One evening at a party she heard a boy and two girls, all schoolmates, talking. She never accepted another invitation.

She watched the girls with whom she had grown up as they married and got homes and children, but no man ever called on her steadily until the children of the other girls had been calling her "aunty" for several years, the while their mothers told them in bright voices about how popular Aunt Minnie had been as a girl. Then the town began to see her driving on Sunday afternoons with the cashier in the bank. He was a widower of about forty—a high-colored man, smelling always faintly of the barber shop or of whisky. He owned the first automobile in town, a red runabout; Minnie had the first motoring bonnet and veil the town ever saw. Then the town began to say: "Poor Minnie." "But she is old enough to take care of herself," others said. That was when she began to ask her old schoolmates that their children call her "cousin" instead of "aunty."

It was twelve years now since she had been relegated into adultery by public opinion, and eight years since the cashier had gone to a Memphis bank, returning for one day each Christmas, which he spent at an annual bachelors' party at a hunting club on the river. From behind their curtains the neighbors would see the party pass, and during the over-the-way Christmas day visiting they would tell her about him, about how well he looked, and how they heard that he was prospering in the city, watching with bright, secret eyes her haggard, bright face. Usually by that hour there would be the scent of whisky on her breath. It was supplied her by a youth, a clerk at the soda fountain: "Sure; I buy it for the old gal. I reckon she's entitled to a little fun."

Her mother kept to her room altogether now; the gaunt aunt ran the house. Against that background Minnie's bright dresses, her idle and empty days, had a quality of furious unreality. She went out in the evenings only with women now, neighbors, to the moving pictures. Each afternoon she dressed in one of the new dresses and went downtown alone, where her young "cousins" were already strolling in the late afternoons with their delicate, silken heads and thin, awkward arms and conscious hips, clinging to one another or shrieking and giggling with paired boys in the soda fountain when she passed and went on along the serried store fronts, in the doors of which the sitting and lounging men did not even follow her with their eyes any more.

### III

The barber went swiftly up the street where the sparse lights, insect-swirled, glared in rigid and violent suspension in the lifeless air. The day had died in a pall of dust; above the darkened square, shrouded by the spent dust, the sky was as clear as the inside of a brass bell. Below the east was a rumor of the twice-waxed moon.

When he overtook them McLendon and three others were getting into a car parked in an alley. McLendon stooped his thick head, peering out beneath the top, "Changed your mind, did you?" he said. "Damn good thing; by God, tomorrow when this town hears about how you talked tonight—"

"Now, now," the other ex-soldier said. "Hawkshaw's all right. Come on, Hawk; jump in."

"Will Mayes never done it, boys," the barber said. "If anybody done it. Why, you all know well as I do there ain't any town where they got better niggers than us. And you know how a lady will kind of think things about men when there ain't any reason to, and Miss Minnie anyway—"

"Sure, sure," the soldier said. "We're just going to talk to him a little; that's all."

"Talk hell!" Butch said. "When we're through with the—"

"Shut up, for God's sake!" the soldier said. "Do you want everybody in town—"

"Tell them, by God!" McLendon said. "Tell every one of the sons that'll let a white woman—"

"Let's go; let's go: here's the other car." The second car slid squealing out of a cloud of dust at the alley mouth. McLendon started his car and took the lead. Dust lay like fog in the street. The street lights hung nimbused as in water. They drove on out of town.

A rutted lane turned at right angles. Dust hung above it too, and above all the land. The dark bulk of the ice plant, where the Negro Mayes was night watchman, rose against the sky. "Better stop here, hadn't we?" the soldier said. McLendon did not reply. He hurled the car up and slammed to a stop, the headlights glaring on the blank wall.

"Listen here, boys," the barber said; "if he's here, don't that prove he never done it? Don't it? If it was him, he would run. Don't you see he would?" The second car came up and stopped. McLendon got down; Butch sprang down beside him. "Listen, boys," the barber said.

"Cut the lights off!" McLendon said. The breathless dark rushed down. There was no sound in it save their lungs as they sought air in the parched dust in which for two months they had lived; then the diminishing crunch of McLendon's and Dutch's feet, and a moment later McLendon's voice: "Will!... Will!"

Below the east the wan hemorrhage of the moon increased. It heaved above the ridge, silvering the air, the dust, so that they seemed to breathe, live, in a bowl of molten lead. There was no sound of nightbird nor insect, no sound save their breathing and a faint ticking of contracting metal about the cars. Where their bodies touched one another they seemed to sweat dryly, for no more moisture came. "Christ!" a voice said; "let's get out of here."

But they didn't move until vague noises began to grow out of the darkness ahead; then they got out and waited tensely in the breathless dark. There was another sound: a blow, a hissing expulsion of breath and McLendon cursing in undertone. They stood a moment longer, then they ran forward. They ran in a stumbling clump, as though they were fleeing something. "Kill him, kill the son," a voice whispered. McLendon flung them back.

"Not here," he said. "Get him into the car." "Kill him, kill the black son!" the voice murmured. They dragged the Negro to the car. The barber had waited beside the car. He could feel himself sweating and he knew he was going to be sick at the stomach.

"What is it, captains?" the Negro said. "I ain't done nothing. For God, Mr. John." Someone produced handcuffs. They worked busily about the Negro as though he were a post, quiet, intent, getting in one another's way. He submitted to the handcuffs, looking swiftly and constantly from dim face to dim face. "Who is here, captains?" he said, leaning to peer into the faces until they could feel his breath and smell his sweaty reek. He spoke a name or two. "What you all say I done, Mr. John?"

McLendon jerked the car door open.

"Get in!" he said. The Negro did not move. "What you all going to do with me, Mr John? I ain't done nothing. White folks, captains, I ain't done nothing: I swear before God." He called another name.

"Get in!" McLendon said. He struck the Negro. The others expelled their breath in a dry hissing and struck him with random blows and he whirled and cursed them, and swept his manacled hands across their faces and slashed the barber upon the mouth, and the barber struck him also. "Get him in there," McLendon said. They pushed at him. He ceased struggling and got in and sat quietly as the others took their places. He sat between the barber and the soldier, drawing his limbs in so as not to touch them, his eyes going swiftly and constantly from face to face. Butch clung to the running board. The car moved on. The barber nursed his mouth with his handkerchief.

"What's the matter, Hawk?" the soldier said.

"Nothing," the barber said. They regained the highroad and turned away from town. The second car dropped back out of the dust. They went on, gaining speed; the final fringe of houses dropped behind.

"Goddamn, he stinks!" the soldier said.

"We'll fix that," the drummer in front beside McLendon said. On the running board Butch cursed into the hot rush of air. The barber leaned suddenly forward and touched McLendon's arm.

"Let me out, John," he said.

"Jump out, niggerlover," McLendon said without turning his head. He drove swiftly. Behind them the sourceless lights of the second car glared in the dust. Presently

McLendon turned into a narrow road. It was rutted with disuse. It led back to an abandoned brick kiln—a series of reddish mounds and weed- and vine-choked vats without bottom. It had been used for pasture once, until one day the owner missed one of his mules. Although he prodded carefully in the vats with a long pole, he could not even find the bottom of them.

"John," the barber said.

"Jump out, then," McLendon said, hurling the car along the ruts. Beside the barber the Negro spoke:

"Mr. Henry."

The barber sat forward. The narrow tunnel of the road rushed up and past. Their motion was like an extinct furnace blast: cooler, but utterly dead. The car bounded from rut to rut.

"Mr. Henry," the Negro said.

The barber began to tug furiously at the door. "Look out, there!" the soldier said, but the barber had already kicked the door open and swung onto the running board. The soldier leaned across the Negro and grasped at him, but he had already jumped. The car went on without checking speed.

The impetus hurled him crashing through dust-sheathed weeds, into the ditch. Dust puffed about him, and in a thin, vicious crackling of sapless stems he lay choking and retching until the second car passed and died away. Then he rose and limped on until he reached the highroad and turned toward town, brushing at his clothes with his hands. The moon was higher, riding high and clear of the dust at last, and after a while the town began to glare beneath the dust.

He went on, limping. Presently he heard cars and the glow of them grew in the dust behind him and he left the road and crouched again in the weeds until they passed. McLendon's car came last now. There were four people in it and Butch was not on the running board.

They went on; the dust swallowed them; the glare and the sound died away. The dust of them hung for a while, but soon the eternal dust absorbed it again. The barber climbed back onto the road and limped on toward town.

## IV

As she dressed for supper on that Saturday evening, her own flesh felt like fever.

Her hands trembled among the hooks and eyes, and her eyes had a feverish look, and her hair swirled crisp and crackling under the comb. While she was still dressing the friends called for her and sat while she donned her sheerest underthings and stockings and a new voile dress. "Do you feel strong enough to go out?" they said, their eyes bright too, with a dark glitter. "When you have had time to get over the shock, you must tell us what happened. What he said and did; everything."

In the leafed darkness, as they walked toward the square, she began to breathe deeply, something like a swimmer preparing to dive, until she ceased trembling, the four of them walking slowly because of the terrible heat and out of solicitude for her. But as they neared the square she began to tremble again, walking with her head up, her hands clenched at her sides, their voices about her murmuring, also with that feverish, glittering quality of their eyes.

They entered the square, she in the center of the group, fragile in her fresh dress. She was trembling worse. She walked slower and slower, as children eat ice cream, her head up and her eyes bright in the haggard banner of her face, passing the hotel and the coatless drummers in chairs along the curb looking around at her: "That's the one see? The one in pink in the middle." "Is that her? What did they do with the nigger? Did they—?" "Sure. He's all right." "All right, is he?" "Sure. He went on a little trip." Then the drug store, where even the young men lounging in the doorway tipped their hats and followed with their eyes the motion of her hips and legs when she passed.

They went on, passing the lifted hats of the gentlemen, the suddenly ceased voices, deferent, protective. "Do you see?" the friends said. Their voices sounded like long, hovering sighs of hissing exultation. "There's not a Negro on the square. Not one."

They reached the picture show. It was like a miniature fairyland with its lighted lobby and colored lithographs of life caught in its terrible and beautiful mutations. Her lips began to tingle. In the dark, when the picture began, it would be all right; she could hold back the laughing so it would not waste away so fast and so soon. So she hurried on before the turning faces, the undertones of low astonishment, and they took their accustomed places where she could see the aisle against the silver glare and the young men and girls coming in two and two against it.

The lights flicked away; the screen glowed silver, and soon life began to unfold, beautiful and passionate and sad, while still the young men and girls entered, scented and sibilant in the half dark, their paired backs in silhouette delicate and sleek, their slim, quick bodies awkward, divinely young, while beyond them the silver dream accumulated, inevitably on and on. She began to laugh. In trying to suppress it, it made more noise than ever; heads began to turn. Still laughing, her friends raised her and led her out, and she stood at the curb, laughing on a high, sustained note, until the taxi came up and they helped her in.

They removed the pink voile and the sheer underthings and the stockings, and put her to bed, and cracked ice for her temples, and sent for the doctor. He was hard to locate, so they ministered to her with hushed ejaculations, renewing the ice and fanning her. While the ice was fresh and cold she stopped laughing and lay still for a time, moaning only a little. But soon the laughing welled again and her voice rose screaming.

"Shhhhhhhhhhh! Shhhhhhhhhhhhhh!" they said, freshening the icepack, smoothing her hair, examining it for gray; "poor girl!" Then to one another: "Do you suppose anything really happened?" their eyes darkly aglitter, secret and passionate. "Shhhhhhhhhh! Poor girl! Poor Minnie!"

## V

It was midnight when McLendon drove up to his neat new house. It was trim and fresh as a birdcage and almost as small, with its clean, green-and-white paint. He locked the car and mounted the porch and entered. His wife rose from a chair beside the reading lamp. McLendon stopped in the floor and stared at her until she looked down.

"Look at that clock," he said, lifting his arm, pointing.

She stood before him, her face lowered, a magazine in her hands. Her face was pale, strained, and weary-looking. "Haven't I told you about sitting up like this, waiting to see when I come in?"

"John," she said. She laid the magazine down. Poised on the balls of his feet, he glared at her with his hot eyes, his sweating face.

"Didn't I tell you?" He went toward her. She looked up then. He caught her shoulder. She stood passive, looking at him.

"Don't, John. I couldn't sleep... The heat; something. Please, John. You're hurting me."

"Didn't I tell you?" He released her and half struck, half flung her across the chair, and she lay there and watched him quietly as he left the room. He went on through the house, ripping off his shirt, and on the dark, screened porch at the rear he stood and mopped his head and shoulders with the shirt and flung it away. He took the pistol from his hip and laid it on the table beside the bed, and sat on the bed and removed his shoes, and rose and slipped his trousers off. He was sweating again already, and he stooped and hunted furiously for the shirt. At last he found it and wiped his body again, and, with his body pressed against the dusty screen, he stood panting. There was no movement, no sound, not even an insect. The dark world seemed to lie stricken beneath the cold moon and the lidless stars.

**Questions**
1. Why does the author repeatedly mention "hot" and "dust"?
2. What role does the character Barber Hawk Shawn play in the whole story?
3. Does McLendon really care about or respect the dignity of women? Why? Or why not?
4. In Part IV, Faulkner provides many detailed descriptions about Miss Minnie Cooper. What is the use of Part IV? And what does the author try to imply here?
5. Explain the meaning of the story's title.

# 威廉·福克纳
# （1897—1962）

威廉·卡斯伯特·福克纳是美国作家，来自密西西比州牛津郡的诺贝尔奖得主。福克纳写长篇小说、短篇小说、戏剧、诗歌、散文和电影剧本。他最出名的就是他的长篇小说和短篇小说，都以虚构的约克纳帕塔法县为背景，以密西西比州的拉法耶特县为原型，他在那里度过了人生的大部分时间。

福克纳是美国文学史上最有名的作家之一，特别是在美国南方文学方面。尽管他早在1919年就有作品出版，大部分作品是在20世纪20年代和30年代出版，但直到1949年获得诺贝尔文学奖，他才声名远播，也因此成为唯一在密西西比出生的诺贝尔奖得主。他的两部作品，《寓言》（1954）和他最后一部长篇小说《掠夺者》（1962）获得普利策文学奖。1988年，现代图书公司将其1929年的长篇小说《喧哗与骚动》评为20世纪100本最佳英文长篇小说的第六名，入选名单的还有《我弥留之际》（1930）和《八月之光》（1932）。《押沙龙，押沙龙！》则出现在类似的名单中。他首次出版的短篇小说《献给艾米丽的玫瑰》是最有名的美国短篇小说之一。

## 干旱的九月

《干旱的九月》是发表于1931年的一部短篇小说。故事描述了在9月的一个炎热的晚上，尽管证据模糊不清，一群暴徒集结要为声称（然而并不具体）是被黑人看守威尔·梅耶斯凌辱或袭击的白人女子报仇。故事分五个部分讲述，包括从传言中的女性受害者米妮·库珀小姐的角度，以及从暴徒的领头人约翰·麦克莱顿的角度。

一

9月的黄昏，残阳如血。62天没下雨的结果就是——那谣言，那故事，不管它是什么，都像干草里的火苗一样蔓延开来。反正是有关米妮·库珀小姐和一个黑人的事儿。那个星期六傍晚，人们聚集在理发店里。吊扇转动着，不但没把污浊的空气变清新，反而混合着变质的护发油和洗发水的阵阵气味，把人们身上和嘴里散发出来的种种臭味一股脑儿又吹了回来。没人知道到底发生了什么事情，却都感觉似乎遭受了袭击、侮辱和惊吓。

"反正不是威尔·梅耶斯。"一个理发师说。他是个中年男子,瘦瘦的,沙土色的皮肤,面色温和可亲。他正在给一位顾客刮脸。"我了解威尔·梅耶斯。他是个规规矩矩的黑人。我也了解米妮·库珀小姐。"

"你了解她什么?"另一个理发师问道。

"她是谁?"顾客问道,"是个年轻的姑娘?"

"不是,"理发师说,"我估计她快四十了,还没结过婚。所以我才不相信——"

"相信?见鬼去吧!"一个穿着汗渍斑斑的丝绸衬衫的大个子年轻人说,"难不成你不相信白人女子说的话,却相信黑鬼说的?"

"我不相信威尔·梅耶斯做那样的事儿。"理发师说,"我了解威尔·梅耶斯。"

"或许,你知道是谁干的?或许你已经把他送到城外去了,你他妈还真是爱黑鬼啊!"

"我不信有谁干了什么事儿。我就不信出过事儿。你们大伙儿想想:那些年纪不小没有结婚的老小姐是不是会胡思乱想,觉得男人不能——"

"那你就是个混账白人。"顾客说,他在围布下动了动。那年轻人就已经从座位上跳了起来。

"你不相信?"他说,"你是指责一个白人妇女撒谎吗?"

理发师拿着剃刀,举在半起身的顾客头上,他没有回头。

"都怪这该死的天气。"另一个人说,"这天热得足以让男人什么事都干得出来。即便是对她。"

没有人发笑。理发师慢条斯理地,语气又颇为固执地说:"我不是要指责什么人什么事。我只知道,你们大伙儿也知道,一个女人,从不——"

"你这个爱黑鬼的该死东西!"年轻人说。

"闭嘴!布奇,"另一个人说,"我们有的是时间采取行动去了解真相。"

"谁?谁要调查真相?"年轻人说,"真相!见鬼!我——"

"你是个好样的白人,"顾客说,"不是吗?"他胡须上涂满了泡沫,看上去像电影里见过的沙漠鼠。"杰克,你告诉他们,"他对年轻人说,"就算这镇上的白人死绝了,你还能指望我。尽管我只是个旅行推销员,而且还不是本地人。"

"说得对,伙计们,"理发师说,"先搞清楚事实。我了解威尔·梅耶斯。"

"啊呀,上帝啊!"年轻人喊道,"想不到,这镇上居然会有个白人——"

"闭嘴，布奇，"第二个开口的人说，"我们有的是时间。"

顾客坐了起来。他看着说话的人。"你是说，啥事都可以是宽恕黑鬼侵犯白人妇女的理由？你是想告诉我，你是个白人可又支持这种事？你还是回去吧，回你的北方去吧。南方不要你这样的人。"

"什么北方啊？"第二个人反驳道，"我可是在这镇上土生土长的。"

"唉，上帝啊。"年轻人说。他不知所措地环顾四周，仿佛在努力回忆自己要说或要做什么。他用袖子擦了擦淌汗的脸。"妈的，要是我让一个白人妇女——"

"杰克，你告诉他们，"旅行推销员说，"上帝啊，要是他们——"

纱门被撞开了。一个人站在门口，双腿叉开，身材魁梧，从容自如，白衬衫领口敞着，戴顶毡帽。他目光犀利，无所顾忌地扫视了一圈屋内的人。他叫麦克莱顿，曾在法国前线指挥过部队作战，因为英勇过人而获嘉奖。

"怎么，"他说，"你们打算就坐在这儿，任凭黑崽子在杰弗逊的大街上强奸白人妇女？"

布奇又跳了起来。他的丝绸衬衣紧紧粘在宽厚的肩膀上，两个腋窝下都是半月形的汗渍。"我就一直跟他们这么说的！我就是这么——"

"真出事了？"第三个人说，"就像霍克肖说的，这可不是她第一次说有男人对她不怀好意了。大约一年前，不是说有个男的在厨房屋顶上看她脱衣服吗？"

"什么？"顾客问，"那是怎么回事？"理发师慢慢地把他往下按回椅子上。他不肯往后躺，使劲抬起头来，理发师还在用力让他坐下。

麦克莱顿猛地转向第三个说话的人。"出事？出没出事有什么关系？你打算让这黑崽子就这么溜掉，真跑去干这事？"

"我就这么跟他们说的。"布奇喊道。他骂骂咧咧的，没完没了又没有重点。

"喂，喂，"第四个说，"别那么大声。别那么大声说话。"

"真是！"麦克莱顿说，"根本没必要说。我要说的都说完了。谁跟我来？"他稳稳地站在那儿，环顾四周。

理发师把旅行推销员的脸按下去，举着剃刀。"先把事实弄弄清楚，伙计们。我了解威尔·梅耶斯。不是他干的。咱们把治安官找来，公正地处理这事。"

麦克莱顿把那愤怒僵硬的脸转向理发师，理发师也没躲闪。他们俩看着就像不同种族的人。其他的理发师都停下手中的活，让顾客躺着。"你是对我说，"麦克莱顿说，"你相信一个黑鬼的话，不相信一个白人妇女的话？为什么，你这

个喜欢黑鬼的混账东西——"

第三个开口的人站起身来,抓住麦克莱顿的胳膊,他也曾当过兵。"好了,好了。咱们一起来琢磨一下这事。谁知道到底出了什么事儿吗?"

"琢磨个鬼!"麦克莱顿使劲挣脱胳膊。"要跟我干的人都站起来。那些不——"他瞪起眼睛四下看着,用袖子擦了把脸。

三个人站了起来。椅子里的旅行推销员坐起身子。"喂!"他说,使劲拽脖子上的围布,"把这破布给我扯掉。我跟他干。我不住在这儿,但上帝,要是我们的母亲、妻子和姐妹——"他抓着围布擦了把脸,把布朝地上一扔。麦克莱顿站在屋里,大声咒骂剩下的人。又一个人站起来朝他们走去。剩下的人坐在那儿都很不自在,互相也不看。随后他们一个接一个站起来,走到麦克莱顿身边。

理发师从地上捡起围布,叠得整整齐齐的。"伙计们,别这么干。威尔·梅耶斯绝没干过。这我知道。"

"快点儿。"麦克莱顿说。他转过身子,屁股兜露出一把重型自动手枪的枪把。他们走了出去。纱门在他们身后猛地撞上又弹开,撞击声回荡在死寂的空气中。

理发师仔细又快速地擦了剃刀,收拾起来,然后向屋后方跑去,从墙上取下他的帽子。"我尽快回来,"他对别的理发师说,"我不能让——"他出了门,跑了起来。其他两个理发师跟着他走到门口,抓住弹回来的门。他们向门外探身,看着他在街上渐渐远去。空气凝固而死寂。舌头根有股含了块铁似的味道。

"他能做什么?"第一个人说。第二个人压着声念叨:"耶稣基督,耶稣基督。""要是霍克惹怒了麦克莱顿,我倒宁愿威尔·梅耶斯干过这种事。"

"耶稣基督,耶稣基督。"第二个人喃喃自语。

"你认为他真对她干出了那种事?"第一个人问道。

## 二

她三十八九岁,跟久病不起的母亲和面黄肌瘦却精力充沛的姨妈住在一座小木屋里。每天上午十点到十一点之间,她戴着有花边的睡帽来到门廊,荡秋千荡到中午时分。饭后,她躺下休息一会儿,直到炎热的下午开始凉爽一些,她便穿上一件新的巴里纱裙——她每年夏天总做三四件新的薄纱裙服——去镇里,和其他小姐太太们一起逛商店,消磨时光。她们在那儿摸摸看看,虽无意购买,却总是用想买不买又急切的语气讨价还价。

她家境不错,虽在杰弗逊算不上最好的,但也是富有的人家。她长相平常,但身材至今还很苗条。她爱穿颜色鲜亮的衣服,神情喜悦又略显憔悴。年轻时,她身材修长苗条，亭亭玉立，活泼热情，这使她曾在杰弗逊镇社交生活里独占鳌头。那时候，孩子们还没有等级观念，因而，她在高中舞会和教会组织的活动中可是同龄人的佼佼者。

她一直没有意识到她在失去优势。她一向比其他的同伴聪明活跃，像一团更明亮耀眼的火焰。但她没有认识到，她的那些同伴，男的变得自大、势力；而女的学会心机暗藏，打击报复，并以此为乐。她从那时起就表面看着欢愉，内心憔悴失意。她依旧带着这副样子参加在暗影斑驳的回廊或夏天草坪上的舞会，既像是个面具，又好像是面旗子，眼光流露出矢口否认现实却困惑不已的神情。在一次舞会上，她听见一个男同学和两个女同学的谈话。从此，她再也不接受任何邀请了。

她眼看着和她一起长大的女孩们结婚生子，建立家庭。然而，没有男人一如既往地倾心于她，直到朋友的孩子大了，叫了她好多年"阿姨"。孩子的母亲们常常绘声绘色地给孩子们讲米妮阿姨少女时如何惹人喜爱。后来，镇上的人开始看她和银行出纳员星期天下午一起开车兜风。他是个四十来岁的鳏夫——面色红润，常常散发着淡淡的发油或威士忌的气味。他拥有镇上第一辆汽车，一辆红色轻便小汽车。米妮有着全镇第一个坐车兜风时戴的软帽和面纱。随后镇上的人开始说："可怜的米妮。"也有人说："她年纪够大了，可以照料自己。"她也是那个时候开始要求老同学让她们的孩子叫她"表姐"，不要叫"阿姨"。

公众舆论指责她私通是十二年前的事情了，出纳员去孟菲斯一家银行工作也有八年了。他每年圣诞节回到镇上待一天，参加在河边的狩猎俱乐部举行的一年一度的单身汉聚会。邻居们在窗帘背后偷着看聚会的整个过程。然后，在圣诞节过街拜访时，就跟她不停地讲他，说他气色如何如何好，他们听说他在城里的日子如何如何富裕，还时不时地用明亮又神秘的眼神看她欢愉又憔悴的面容。往往在这个时刻，她嘴里会有威士忌酒味。酒是一位年轻人给她的，是个冷饮店的店员："没错，是我给老姑娘买的酒。我认为她有权稍稍快活一下。"

她的母亲足不出户，干瘦的姨妈操持家务。相比之下，米妮颜色亮丽的裙子，悠闲而空虚的日子有种强烈的不真实特质。她现在只和邻居女人们晚上出去看电影。每天下午，她便穿上其中一身新裙子，独自去市区。她的"表妹"们下午晚些时候就在那儿游逛。她们秀发如丝，胳膊纤细而笨拙，臀部故意扭动。她们和男友成双成对，相互偎依，站在冷饮柜前尖叫或咯咯嬉笑。她从他们身边走过，顺着一排排密集的商店铺面向前走。倚坐在门框或懒躺在门口的男人们，甚至都不再多看她一眼了。

## 三

　　理发师快步走到街上，稀疏的路灯在死气沉沉的空中投下强烈的光，虫子绕着飞来扑去的。白天已经在一片尘土中消失殆尽；昏暗的广场上空，笼罩着一层精疲力竭的尘土，天空像铜钟的内里一样澄亮。东方天际低垂着一轮比平时大两倍的月亮。

　　追上他们的时候，麦克莱顿和另外三个人正要钻进一辆停在小巷里的汽车。麦克莱顿低下头发蓬松的脑袋，从车顶篷下向外看去。"改主意了，是吗？"他说，"太他妈好了；上帝啊，明天要是全镇人听到你今晚说的——"

　　"好了，好了，"另一个退伍兵说，"霍克肖也没错。进来吧，霍克，快坐进来。"

　　"威尔·梅耶斯从没干过那事，伙计们。"理发师说，"就算真有人干过。唉，你们跟我一样清楚，都知道我们镇上的黑鬼比哪儿的都要好。而且你们也知道，女人有时会无缘无故地想着男人的事儿。反正米妮小姐——"

　　"对的，对的，"退伍士兵说，"我们只是去跟他谈谈，仅此而已。"

　　"谈个屁！"布奇说，"当我们完事的时候——"

　　"看在上帝的份上，闭嘴！"退伍兵说，"你想让全镇每个人都——"

　　"上帝啊，告诉他们！"麦克莱顿说，"告诉那些崽子，那会让白人妇女——"

　　"走，我们走吧。这儿还有辆车。"第二辆车从飞扬的尘土中滑行出巷口，发出刺耳的声响。麦克莱顿发动汽车，在前面带路。尘土像雾一样弥漫整个街道。悬挂在半空的街灯像在水中一样带着光轮。他们驶出了镇子。

　　一条布满车辙的小路向右拐去。路面尘土飞扬，整个大地都尘土飞扬。夜空下耸立着黑黢黢的制冰厂厂房，黑人梅耶斯在那当守夜人。"最好停在这儿，对吗？"退伍士兵说。麦克莱顿并不作答。他猛地把车开上前，猛地刹车，前灯直射在白墙上。

　　"听我说，伙计们，"理发师说，"他要是人在这儿，不就能证明他没干过那事？对吗？如果是他干的，他就逃跑了。难道你们不觉得他会逃跑吗？"第二辆车开过来，停下。麦克莱顿下车；布奇跳下车站在他身边。"听我说，伙计们。"理发师又说。

　　"把车灯关了！"麦克莱顿说。无声无息的黑暗倾泻而来。四周一片寂静，他们只听见自己在持续两个多月的焦热的尘土中寻找空气的喘息声。接着是麦克莱顿和布奇渐渐走远的脚步声。过了一会儿响起麦克莱顿的声音：

　　"威尔……威尔！"

东方天际，一轮淡血色的月亮冉冉升起。月亮升上山脊，给空气、给尘土镀上一层银色，仿佛它们是在一碗炽烈的铅水中呼吸生存。四周一片寂静，没有鸟啼也没有虫鸣；只有人的喘息和汽车熄火后金属冷却时的轻微声响。他们的身体挨着彼此，似乎只出干汗，因为已经没有湿气出来。"上帝啊，"有个人开口说，"咱们下车吧。"

但是，直到前面黑暗中隐约传来嘈杂的声音，他们才开始动身。他们下了车，在无声的黑暗里紧张地等待着。又传来另一个声音：殴打声，嘶嘶的出气声和麦克莱顿低声的咒骂。他们又站了一会儿，然后跑过去。他们跑得跌跌撞撞的，像是躲避什么。"杀了他，杀了这鬼崽子。"一个声音低声说。麦克莱顿猛地把他们推了回去。

"别在这儿，"他说，"把他弄进车去。""杀了他，杀了这个黑畜生。"那个声音还在嘟囔。他们把黑人拖到车跟前，理发师一直在车边等，他能感觉到自己在流汗，也知道自己很快要吐了。

"怎么回事，长官们？"黑人说，"我什么也没干，上帝作证，约翰先生。"有人拿出手铐，他们围着黑人忙乎，一声不吭，全神贯注又彼此碍事，仿佛黑人只是一根柱子。黑人顺从地戴上手铐，眼睛不停地迅速打量着黑暗中看不清楚的面孔。"都谁在这儿，长官们？"他说着，身子向前倾盯着每张脸，他们都能感觉到他的呼吸，闻到他身上的汗臭味。他说出一两个名字。"你们都说我干了什么事，约翰先生？"

麦克莱顿一把拽开车门。

"进去！"他说。黑人没有动。"你们要对我干什么，约翰先生？我什么也没干。白人先生们，长官们，我什么也没干。我向上帝发誓。"他又说出一个名字。

"进去！"麦克莱顿说。他打了黑人一下。其他人嘘出一口长气，跟着朝黑人身上打去。他转过身大声咒骂，戴着手铐的双手朝着他们的脸抡去。划伤了理发师的嘴，理发师也出手打了他。"把他弄上车。"麦克莱顿说。他们推搡着他。他不再挣扎，他上了车，安静地坐着。其余人纷纷上车坐下。他坐在理发师和退伍士兵的中间，两腿并拢，胳膊紧紧地抱着身子，以免碰到他们，他的目光不断飞快地从一张一张脸上扫过去。布奇紧贴着车窗站在踏脚板上。汽车开动了。理发师用手帕捂住了嘴。

"怎么了，霍克？"退伍兵问。

"没事。"理发师说。汽车又上了公路，离开镇子。第二辆车在后面飞扬的尘土里跟着。他们加速继续开，最后一排房屋向车后掠去，消失了。

"该死的，他真臭！"士兵说。

"我们会治好他的。"坐在前面麦克莱顿旁边的推销员说。布奇站在踏脚板上迎着扑面而来的热风大声咒骂着。理发师突然倾身向前,碰碰麦克莱顿的胳膊。

"让我下车,约翰。"他说。

"跳下去,你这个喜欢黑鬼的人。"麦克莱顿头也不回地说。他开得飞快。他们后面第二辆车跟了上来,看不清来处的灯光在尘土里十分晃眼。一会儿,麦克莱顿拐入一条狭窄的小路。这条路坑坑洼洼的,长久未用,通向一座废弃的砖窑——一连串红色的土堆和一个个杂草藤蔓丛生、深不见底的洞穴。这里曾被用作牧场,直到有一天主人丢了一头骡子。尽管他用一根长长的竹竿小心地在洞里打捞,却始终够不到洞底。

"约翰。"理发师说。

"那你跳出去。"麦克莱顿说着,沿着路上错乱交叠的车辙把车开得飞快。理发师边上的黑人说:

"亨利先生。"

理发师向前倾身坐起。路上狭窄的坑道疾驰而来,飞驰而去。他们的移动像是火炉熄灭后的气流,虽是比较凉爽,却了无生气。汽车在满是车辙的路上颠来颠去的。

"亨利先生。"黑人说。

理发师开始使劲拽门。"当心!别……"退伍兵说。但理发师已经踢开车门,转身踩在踏脚板上。退伍兵隔着黑人去抓理发师,可他已经跳下汽车。车没有减速,依然向前疾驰。

车行驶的惯性把他猛甩出去,滚过落满尘土的草丛,摔进沟里。灰尘在他四周飘散开来,干枯的草茎发出细微却似乎带有恶意的断裂声。他躺在枯草上,喘不上气又干呕,直到第二辆车开近又走远,才好了一些。他站起来,一瘸一拐地往前走,一直走上公路,然后向镇里走去,边走边用双手拍掉身上的土。月亮升得更高了,终于升上高空脱离尘土,过了一会儿,杰弗逊镇在一片尘土下闪烁可见。

他继续一瘸一拐地走着。没一会儿,他听见汽车声,身后车灯在飘浮的尘土中越来越亮。他离开大路,蜷伏在杂草丛里等汽车过去。这时,麦克莱顿的车最后过来,车里坐着四个人,布奇也没站在踏脚板上。

汽车继续向前,尘土吞没了他们的踪影,强烈的车灯和轰轰的车声也消失了。汽车扬起的尘土在空中飘了一会儿,很快就跟永恒的尘土合为一体。理发师爬回大路,跛着脚朝镇子走去。

## 四

那个星期六晚上,她换好衣服准备吃晚饭时,感觉浑身发烫。她两手颤抖着扣上扣儿,眼睛有发烧的神情。梳头时,头发在梳子下打卷,发出噼啪的静电声。她的衣服还没穿好,朋友们就来了。她们坐在那儿看她穿上最轻薄的内衣、长袜和一件新的巴里纱裙。"你觉得有力气出门吗?"她们问道,她们的眼睛亮晶晶的,黑眼珠泛着光。"等你回过神了,你一定要告诉我们发生了什么事,他说了什么,干了什么,都详详细细给我们讲讲。"

她们沿着树荫走向广场。她开始深呼吸,像游泳的人入水前那样,直到她不再颤抖。她们四个人走得很慢,一来是因为天气热,二来也是出于关心她。但当她们快到广场时,她又开始颤抖,她抬着头走路,两手握拳垂在身体两边;她们在她耳边絮絮叨叨的,她们的眼神带着狂热和闪闪发光的特性。

她们走进广场,她走在中间,穿着新裙子,看着弱不禁风。她颤抖得更厉害了,走得越来越慢,像小孩们在吃冰激凌,她抬着头,明亮的眼睛在憔悴的脸上扑闪,她走过旅馆,坐在路边椅子上没穿外套的旅行推销员们转过头看她:"就那个,看见没?中间穿粉红衣服的那个。""那就是她?他们怎么处理黑鬼的?他们是不是——""当然。他没事。""没事,是吗?""当然了。他出去旅行了。"她们走近药店,连懒懒地靠在门口的年轻人都向她脱帽致意。她走过药店,他们的目光追着她,看她的屁股和大腿扭动。

她们继续走,走过脱帽致敬的绅士,人们的说话声戛然而止,都恭恭敬敬、小心翼翼的。"看见没?"朋友们问。她们的声音听上去好似拖长又犹豫的叹气,又满含着洋洋得意。"广场上一个黑人都没有。一个都没有。"

她们走进电影院。电影院像小型的仙境一样,休息室灯火辉煌,墙上满是彩印的画,画里都是生活中又美丽又可怕的画面。她的嘴唇开始有些刺痛。黑暗中,等电影开始,一切就都好了;她就不至于笑容消耗得又快又早。于是,她对着看向她的一张张面孔和压低了声音的惊讶语气快步向前。她们在老座位上坐下来,借着银幕上的白光,她能看到过道,看见年轻的男男女女成双成对地走进场内。

灯熄灭了,幕布泛出银光。于是,生活画面开始展现:美丽的、热情的和忧伤的男女青年还在继续进场,半明半暗的光线下,他们身上的香水味四散开来,在场里嘶嘶细语,成双成对的背影优美柔滑,他们苗条的身材有的敏捷,有的笨拙,散发着神圣的青春魅力。他们身后,银色的美梦还在继续,无可阻挡地继续。她开始大笑起来,她努力想忍住,反而笑得更厉害。人们转过头看她。朋友们把她搀起来,领出影院,她都一直在笑。她站在马路边上尖声大笑,笑个没完，直到来了一辆出租车，她们把她扶上车。

她们帮她脱掉粉色的巴里纱裙、薄内衣和长筒袜，把她放到床上，砸碎冰块给她敷太阳穴，又派人去请大夫。大夫没找到，她们就照顾她，压低声音说话，为她换冰块，扇扇子。冰块刚换上还没有融化时，她会停止狂笑，安静地躺一会儿，偶尔发出低低的呻吟声。过不了一会儿，笑声又涌上来，她便尖声狂笑。

"嘘！嘘！"她们哄着她，一边换冰袋，一边抚摸她的头发，找白头发。"可怜的姑娘！"她们互相问，"你觉得真出事了吗？"她们的眼睛闪烁着黑黝黝的亮光，诡秘而又兴奋。"嘘！可怜的姑娘！可怜的米妮！"

## 五

麦克莱顿驱车回到整洁的新家时已是午夜。新家整齐清新，白绿相间的油漆明亮悦目，只是跟鸟笼一样小。他锁了车，走上门廊，进了屋。他的妻子从台灯旁边的椅子里站起来。麦克莱顿站在门跟前，瞪着她，直到瞪得她垂下了头。

"你看看几点了。"他说，抬起胳膊指着钟。

她站在他面前，低着头，拿着一本杂志。她脸色苍白，神色紧张又疲倦。"我没跟你说过，不要这样坐着等我，看我什么时候回家吗？"

"约翰。"她说，她放下杂志。他稳稳地站在那儿，满脸大汗，愤怒的眼睛使劲地瞪着她。

"我没跟你说过吗？"他朝她走过去，她抬起了头。他抓住她的肩膀；她呆呆地站在那儿，看着他。

"别这样，约翰。我睡不着……天太热了，不知怎么回事。求你了，约翰。你弄疼我了。"

"我没跟你说过吗？"他松开她，半推半搡地把她摔倒在椅子里。她躺在那儿，静静地望着他离开房间。他穿过房子，扯下衬衣。黑暗中，他站在装着纱窗的屋后阳台上，用衬衣擦了擦头和肩膀，然后把衬衣扔到一边。他从裤子后兜掏出手枪，放在床边的桌子上，坐在床上，脱了鞋子，又站起来脱下裤子。他又出了一身汗，他弯下腰四处乱找那件衬衣。总算找到了，又用它把身子擦了一遍。他身子贴着落满尘土的纱窗，站在那儿直喘粗气。四下里没有任何动静，没有一丝声音，连虫声也没有。黑暗的世界像患了重病一样，躺在冷月昏星下沉沉睡去。

# Stephen Vincent Benét
# (1898—1943)

Stephen Vincent Benét was an American poet and novelist, best-known for *John Brown's Body*, a long epic poem on the Civil War, which he wrote in France. Benét received two Pulitzer prizes for his poetry. He was one of those rare poets who were both popular and critically acclaimed.

Stephen Vincent Benét was born in Bethlehem, Pennsylvania, into an army family. His father was Colonel J. Walker Benét. Frances Neill (Rose) Benét, Stephen's mother, was a descendant of an old Kentucky military family. Because his father was an avid reader, who especially loved poetry, Benét grew up at home, where literature was valued and enjoyed. Benét spent most of his boyhood in Benicia, California. At the age about ten, Benét was sent to the Hitchcock Military Academy. However, he preferred reading to athletics and did not like the insensitivity of his schoolmates. Benét's first book, *Five Men and Pompey* (1915), a collection of verse, was published when he was 17. It showed the romantic influence of William Morris as well as the influence of modern realism.

Benét's first novel, the autobiographical *The Beginning of Wisdom* (1921), showed the influence of F. Scott Fitzgerald. He continued his studies at Sorbonne, France, where he lived somewhat bohemian life and met his wife, the writer and journalist Rosemary Carr. In 1923 he returned to the United States. During the 1920s he wrote three other novels, *Young People's Pride* (1922), serialized in *Harper's Bazaar, Jean Huguenot* (1923), and *Spanish Bayonet* (1926), a historical novel about the 18th-century Florida. It focused on Benét's ancestors. *James Shore's Daughter* (1934), a story about wealth and responsibility, is usually considered among Benét's best achievements. His work is filled with mysteries, ghosts and scares, which touch his readers' deep heart.

## By the Waters of Babylon

*The story follows John on his initiation quest, a journey he undertakes in order to be recognized by his tribe as a man and a priest. Exposed to his father's teaching of reading, writing, healing, and "magic", John has been fascinated by the stories about the gods and sets out on his pursuit of his manhood. John's desire for new knowledge leads him to break many of the laws of his tribe. He travels to the Place of the Gods, even though he is afraid that he will die there. His journey ends up in a new discovery contrary to what his father has taught him. The discovery is that the island is not filled with magical mists, the ground is not burning with eternal flames, nor is it populated by spirits and demons. Instead, John finds a vast Dead Place, a city of ruined towers. As he explores the city and learns more and more, John's sense of fear diminishes. He becomes a real man. It is an initiative story for anyone who happens to read it.*

The north and the west and the south are good hunting ground, but it is forbidden to go east. It is forbidden to go to any of the Dead Places except to search for metal and then he who touches the metal must be a priest or the son of a priest. Afterwards, both the man and the metal must be purified. These are the rules and the laws; they are well made. It is forbidden to cross the great river and look upon the place that was the Place the Gods—this is most strictly forbidden. We do not even say its name though we know its name. It is there that spirits live, and demons—it is there that there are the ashes of the Great Burning. These things are forbidden—they have been forbidden since the beginning of time.

My father is a priest; I am the son of a priest. I have been in the Dead Places near us, with my father—at first, I was afraid. When my father went into the house to search for the metal, I stood by the door and my heart felt small and weak. It was a dead man's house, a spirit house. It did not have the smell of man, though there were old bones in a corner. But it is not fitting that a priest's son should show fear. I looked at the bones in the shadow and kept my voice still.

Then my father came out with the metal—a good, strong piece. He looked at me with both eyes but I had not run away. He gave me the metal to hold—I took it and did not die. So he knew that I was truly his son and would be a priest in my time. That was when I was very young— nevertheless, my brothers would not have done it, though they are good hunters. After that, they gave me the good piece of meat and the warm corner of the fire. My father watched over me—he was glad that I should be a priest. But when I boasted or wept without a reason, he punished me more strictly than my brothers. That was right.

After a time, I myself was allowed to go into the dead houses and search for metal. So I learned the ways of those houses—and if I saw bones, I was no longer afraid. The bones are light and old—sometimes they will fall into dust if you touch them. But that is a great sin.

I was taught the chants and the spells—I was taught how to stop the running of blood from a wound and many secrets. A priest must know many secrets—that was what my father said.

If the hunters think we do all things by chants and spells, they may believe so—it does not hurt them. I was taught how to read in the old books and how to make the old writings—that was hard and took a long time. My knowledge made me happy—it was like a fire in my heart. Most of all, I liked to hear of the Old Days and the stories of the gods. I asked myself many questions that I could not answer, but it was good to ask them. At night, I would lie awake and listen to the wind—it seemed to me that it was the voice of the gods as they flew through the air.

We are not ignorant like the Forest People—our women spin wool on the wheel, our priests wear a white robe. We do not eat grubs from the trees; we have not forgotten the old writings, although they are hard to understand. Nevertheless, my knowledge and my lack of knowledge burned in me —I wished to know more.

When I was a man at last, I came to my father and said, "It is time for me to go on my journey. Give me your leave."

He looked at me for a long time, stroking his beard, then he said at last, "Yes. It is time. " That night, in the house of the priesthood, I asked for and received purification. My body hurt but my spirit was a cool stone. It was my father himself who questioned me about my dreams.

He bade me look into the smoke of the fire and see—I saw and told what I saw. It was what I have always seen—a river, and, beyond it, a great Dead Place and in it the gods walking. I have always thought about that. His eyes were stern when I told him—he was no longer my father but a priest. He said, "This is a strong dream. "

"It is mine," I said, while the smoke waved and my head felt light. They were singing the Star song in the outer chamber and it was like the buzzing of bees in my head.

He asked me how the gods were dressed and I told him how they were dressed. We know how they were dressed from the book, but I saw them as if they were before me. When I had finished, he threw the sticks three times and studied them as they fell.

"This is a very strong dream, " he said. "It may eat you up."

"I am not afraid," I said and looked at him with both eyes. My voice sounded thin in my ears but that was because of the smoke.

He touched me on the breast and the forehead. He gave me the bow and the three arrows.

"Take them," he said. "It is forbidden to travel east. It is forbidden to cross the river. It is forbidden to go to the Place of the Gods. All these things are forbidden."

"All these things are forbidden," I said, but it was my voice that spoke and not my spirit. He looked at me again.

"My son," he said. "Once I had young dreams. If your dreams do not eat you up, you may be a great priest. If they eat you, you are still my son. Now go on your journey."

I went fasting, as is the law. My body hurt but not my heart. When the dawn came, I was out of sight of the village. I prayed and purified myself, waiting for a sign. The sign was an eagle. It flew east.

Sometimes signs are sent by bad spirits. I waited again on the flat rock, fasting, taking no food. I was very still—I could feel the sky above me and the earth beneath. I waited till the sun was beginning to sink. Then three deer passed in the valley going east—they did not mind me or see me. There was a white fawn with them—a very great sign.

I followed them, at a distance, waiting for what would happen. My heart was troubled about going east, yet I knew that I must go. My head hummed with my fasting—I did not even see the panther spring upon the white fawn. But, before I knew it, the bow was in my hand. I shouted and the panther lifted his head from the fawn. It is not easy to kill a panther with one arrow but the arrow went through his eye and into his brain. He died as he tried to spring—he rolled over, tearing at the ground. Then I knew I was meant to go east—I knew that was my journey. When the night came, I made my fire and roasted meat.

It is eight suns' journey to the east and a man passes by many Dead Places. The Forest People are afraid of them but I am not. Once I made my fire on the edge of a Dead Place at night and, next morning, in the dead house, I found a good knife, little rusted. That was small to what came afterward but it made my heart feel big. Always when I looked for game, it was in front of my arrow, and twice I passed hunting parties of the Forest People without their knowing. So I knew my magic was strong and my journey clean, in spite of the law.

Toward the setting of the eighth sun, I came to the banks of the great river. It was half-a-day's journey after I had left the god-road—we do not use the god-roads now for they are falling apart into great blocks of stone, and the forest is safer going. A long way off, I had seen the water through trees but the trees were thick. At last, I came out upon an open place at the top of a cliff. There was the great river below, like a giant in the sun. It is very long, very wide. It could eat all the streams we know and still be thirsty. Its name is Qu-dis-sun, the Sacred, the Long. No man of my tribe had seen it, not even my father, the priest. It was magic and I prayed.

Then I raised my eyes and looked south. It was there, the Place of the Gods.

How can I tell what it was like—you do not know. It was there, in the red light, and they were too big to be houses. It was there with the red light upon it, mighty and ruined. I knew that in another moment the gods would see me. I covered my eyes with my hands and crept back into the forest.

Surely, that was enough to do, and live. Surely it was enough to spend the night upon the cliff. The Forest People themselves do not come near. Yet, all through the night, I knew that I should have to cross the river and walk in the places of the gods, although the gods ate me up. My magic did not help me at all and yet there was a fire in my bowels, a fire in my mind. When the sun rose, I thought, "My journey has been clean. Now I will go home from my journey." But, even as I thought so, I knew I could not. If I went to the Place of the Gods, I would surely die, but, if I did not go, I could never be at peace with my spirit again. It is better to lose one's life than one's spirit, if one is a priest and the son of a priest.

Nevertheless, as I made the raft, the tears ran out of my eyes. The Forest People could have killed me without fight, if they had come upon me then, but they did not come. When the raft was made, I said the sayings for the dead and painted myself for death. My heart was cold as a frog and my knees like water, but the burning in my mind would not let me have peace. As I pushed the raft from the shore, I began my death song—I had the right. It was a fine song.

"I am John, son of John," I sang.

"My people are the Hill People. They are the men.

I go into the Dead Places but I am not slain.

I take the metal from the Dead Places but I am not blasted.

I travel upon the gods-roads and am not afraid.

E-yah! I have killed the panther, I have killed the fawn!

E-yah! I have come to the great river. No man has come there before.

It is forbidden to go east, but I have gone, forbidden to go on the great river, but I am there.

Open your hearts, you spirits, and hear my song.

Now I go to the Place of the Gods, I shall not return.

My body is painted for death and my limbs weak, but my heart is big as I go to the Place of the Gods!"

All the same, when I came to the Place of the Gods, I was afraid, afraid. The current of the great river is very strong—it gripped my raft with its hands. That was magic, for the river is wide and calm. I could feel evil spirits about me, in the bright morning; I could feel their breath on my neck as I was swept down the stream. Never have I been so much alone—I tried to think of my knowledge, but it was a squirrel's heap of winter nuts. There was no strength in my knowledge any more and I felt small and naked as a new—hatched bird—alone upon the great river, the servant of the gods.

Yet, after a while, my eyes were opened and I saw. I saw both banks of the river—I saw that once there had been gods-road across it, though now they were broken and fallen like broken vines. Very great they were, and wonderful and broken—broken in the time of the Great Burning when the fire fell out of sky. And always the current took me nearer to the Place of the Gods, and the hug ruins rose before my eyes.

I do not know the customs of rivers—we are the People of the Hill. I tried to guide my raft with the pole but it spun around. I thought the river meant to take me past the Place of the Gods and out into the Bitter Water of the legends. I grew angry then—my heart felt strong. I said aloud, "I am a priest and the son of a priest!" The gods heard me—they showed me how to paddle with the pole on one side of the raft. The current changed itself—I drew near to the Place of the Gods.

When I was very near, my raft struck and turned over. I can swim in our lakes—I swam to the shore. There was a great spike of rusted metal sticking out into the river—I hauled myself up upon it and sat there, panting. I had saved my bow and tow arrows and the knife I found in the Dead Place but that was all. My raft went whirling downstream toward the Bitter Water. I looked after it, and thought if it had trod me under, at least I would be safely dead. Nevertheless, when I had dried my bowstring and re-strung it, I walked forward to the Place of the Gods.

It felt like ground underfoot; it did not burn me. It is not true what some of the tales say, that the ground there burns forever, for I have been there. Here and there were the marks and stains of the Great Burning, on the ruins, that is true. But they were old marks and old stains. It is not true either, what some of our priests say, that it is an island covered with fogs and enchantments. It is not. It is a great Dead Place—greater than any Dead Place we know. Everywhere in it there are god-roads, though most are cracked and broken. Everywhere there are the ruins of the high towers of the gods.

How shall I tell what I saw? I went carefully, my strung bow in my hand, my shin ready for danger. There should have been the wailings of spirits and the shrieks of demons, but there were not. It was very silent and sunny where I had landed—the wind and the rain and the birds that drop seeds had done their work—the grass grew in the cracks of the broken stone. It is a fair island—no wonder the gods built there. If I had come there, I also would have built.

How shall I tell what I saw? The towers are not all broken—here and there one still stands, like a great tree in a forest, and the birds nest high. But the towers themselves look blind, for the gods are gone. I saw a fish-hawk, catching fish in the river. I saw a little dance of white butterflies over a great heap of broken stones and columns. I went there and looked about me—there was a carved stone with cult—letters, broken in half. I can read letters but I could not understand these. They said UBTREAS. There was also the shattered image of a man or a god. It had been made of white stone and he wore his hair tied back like a woman's. His name was ASHING, as I read on the cracked half of a stone. I thought it wise to pray to ASHING, though I do not know that god.

How shall I tell what I saw? There was no smell of man left, on stone or metal. Nor were there many trees in that wilderness of stone. There are many pigeons, nesting and dropping in the towers—the gods must have loved them, or, perhaps, they used them for sacrifices. There are wild cats that roam the god—roads, green-eyed, unafraid of man. At night they wail like demons but they are not demons. The wild dogs are more dangerous, for they hunt in a pack, but them I did not meet till later. Everywhere there are the carved stones, carved with magical numbers or words.

I went north—I did not try to hide myself. When a god or a demon saw me, then I would die, but meanwhile I was no longer afraid. My hunger for knowledge burned in me—there was so much that I could not understand. After a while, I know that my belly was hungry. I could have hunted for my meat, but I did not hunt. It is known that the gods did not hunt as we do—they got their food from enchanted boxes and jars.

Sometimes these are still found in the Dead Places—once, when I was a child and foolish, I opened such a jar and tasted it and found the food sweet. But my father found out and punished me for it strictly, for, often, that food is death. Now, though, I had long gone past what was forbidden, and I entered the likeliest towers, looking for the food of the gods.

I found it at last in the ruins of a great temple in the mid-city. A mighty temple it must have been, for the roof was painted like the shy at night with its stars—that much I could see, though the colors were faint and dim. It went down into great caves and tunnels—perhaps they kept their slaves there. But when I started to climb down, I heard the squeaking of rats, so I did not go—rats are unclean, and there must have been many tribes of them, from the squeaking. But near there, I found food, in the heart of a ruin, behind a door that still opened. I ate only the fruits from the jars—they had a very sweet taste. There was drink, too, in bottles of glass—the drink of the gods was strong and made my head swim. After I had eaten and drunk, I slept on the top of a stone, my bow at my side.

When I woke, the sun was low. Looking down from where I lay, I saw a dog sitting on his haunches. His tongue was hanging out of his mouth; he looked as if he were laughing. He was a big dog, with a gray-brown coat, as big as a wolf. I sprang up and shouted at him but he did not move—he just sat there as if he were laughing. I did not like that. When I reached for a stone to throw, he moved swiftly out of the way of the stone. He was not afraid of me; he looked at me as if I were meat. No doubt I could have killed him with an arrow, but I did not know if there were others.

Moreover, night was falling. I looked about me—not far away there was a great, broken god-road, leading north. The towers were high enough, but not so high, and many of the white dead-houses were wrecked, there were some that stood. I went toward this god-road, keeping to the heights of the ruins, while the dog followed. When I had reached the god-road, I saw that there were others behind him. If I had slept later, they would have come upon me asleep and torn out my throat. As it was, they were sure enough of me; they did not hurry. When I went into the dead-house, they kept watching at the entrance—doubtless they thought they would have a fine hunt. But a dog cannot open a door and I knew, from the books, that the gods did not like to live on the ground but on high.

I had just found a door I could open when the dogs decided to rush. Ha! They were surprised when I shut the door in their faces—it was a good door, of strong metal.

I could hear their foolish baying behind it but I did not stop to answer them. I was in darkness—I found stairs and climbed. There were many stairs, turning around till my head was dizzy. At the top was another door—I found the knob and opened it. I was in a long small chamber—on one side of it was a bronze door that could not be opened, for it had no handle. Perhaps there was a magic word to open it but I did not have the word. I turned to the door in the opposite side of the wall. The lock of it was broken and I opened it and went in.

Within, there was a place of great riches. The god who lived there must have been a powerful god. The first room was a small ante-room—I waited there for some time, telling the spirits of the place that I came in peace and not as a robber. When it seemed to me that they had had time to hear me, I went on. Ah, what riches! Few, even, of the windows had been broken—it was all as it had been. The great windows that looked over the city had not been broken at all though they were dusty and streaked with many years. There were covering on the floors, the colors not greatly faded, and the chairs were soft and deep. There were pictures upon the walls, very strange, very wonderful—I remember one of a bunch of flowers in a jar—if you came close to it, you could see nothing but bits of color, but if you stood away from it, the flowers might have been picked yesterday. It made my heart feel strange to look at this picture—and to look at the figure of a bird, in some hard clay, on a table and see it so like our birds. Everywhere there were books and writings, many in tongues that I could not read. The god who lived there must have been a wise god and full of knowledge. I felt I had right there, as I sought knowledge also.

Nevertheless, it was strange. There was a washing-place but no water—perhaps the gods washed in air. There was a cooking place but no wood, and though there was a machine to cook food, there was no place to put fire in it. Nor were there candles or lamps—there were things that looked like lamps but they had neither oil nor wick. All these things were magic, but I touched them and lived—the magic had gone out of them. Let me tell one thing to show. In the washing-place, a thing said "Hot" but it was not hot to the touch—another thing said "Cold" but it was not cold. This must have been a strong magic but the magic was gone. I do not understand—they had ways—I wish that I knew.

It was close and dry and dusty in their house of the gods. I have said the magic was gone but that it not true—it had gone from the magic things but it had not gone from the place. I felt the spirits about me, weighing upon me. Nor had I ever slept in a Dead Place before—and yet, tonight, I must sleep there. When I thought of it, my tongue felt dry in my throat, in spite of my wish for knowledge. Almost I would have gone down again and faced the dogs, but I did not.

I had not gone through all the rooms when the darkness fell. When it fell, I went back to the big room looking over the city and made fire. There was a place to make fire and a box with wood in it, though I do not think they cooked there. I wrapped myself in a floor-covering and slept in front of the fire—I was very tired.

Now I tell what is very strong magic. I woke in the midst of the night. When I woke, the fire had gone out and I was cold. It seemed to me that all around me there were whisperings and voices. I closed my eyes to shut them out. Some will say that I slept again, but I do not think that I slept. I could feel the spirits drawing my spirit out of my body as a fish is drawn on a line.

Why should I lie about it? I am a priest and the son of a priest. If there are spirits, as they say, in the small Dead Places near us, what spirits must there not be in that great Place of the Gods? And would not they wish to speak? After such long years? I know that I felt myself drawn as a fish is drawn on a line. I had stepped out of my body—I could see my body asleep in front of the cold fire, but it was not I. I was drawn to look out upon the city of the gods.

It should have been dark, for it was night, but it was not dark. Everywhere there were lights—lines of light—circles and blurs of light—ten thousand torches would not have been the same. The sky itself was alight—you could barely see the stars for the glow in the sky. I thought to myself "This is strong magic" and trembled. There was a roaring in my ears like the rushing of rivers. Then my ears grew used to the light and my ears to the sound. I knew that I was seeing the city as it had been when the gods were alive.

That was a light indeed—yes, that was a light: I could not have seen it in the body—my body would have died. Everywhere went the gods, on foot and in chariots—there were gods beyond number and counting and their chariots blocked the streets. They had turned night to day for their pleasure—they did not sleep with the sun. The noise of their coming and going was the noise of the many waters. It was magic what they could do—it was magic what they did.

I looked out of another window—the great vines of their bridges were mended and the god-roads went east and west. Restless, restless, were the gods and always in motion! They burrowed tunnels under rivers—they flew in the air. With unbelievable tools they did giant works—no part of the earth was safe from them, for, if they wished for a thing, they summoned it from the other side of the world. And always, as they labored and rested, as they feasted and made love, there was a drum in their ears—the pulse of the giant city, beating and beating like a man's heart.

Were they happy? What is happiness to the gods? They were great, they were mighty, they were wonderful and terrible. As I looked upon them and their magic, I felt like a child—but a little more, it seemed to me, and they would pull down the moon from the sky. I saw them with wisdom beyond wisdom and knowledge beyond. And yet not all they did was well done—even I could see that—and yet their wisdom could not but grow until all was peace.

Then I saw their fate come upon them and that was terrible past speech. It came upon them as they walked the streets of their city. I have been in the fights with the Forest People—I have seen men die. But this was not like that. When gods war with gods, they use weapons we do not know. It was fire falling out of the sky and a mist that poisoned. It was the time of the Great Burning and the Destruction. They ran about like ants in the streets of their city—poor gods, poor gods! Then the towers began to fall. A few escaped—yes, a few. The legends tell it. But, even after the city had become a Dead Place, for many years the poison was still in the ground. I saw it happen, I saw the last of them die. It was darkness over the broken city and I wept.

All this, I saw. I saw it as I have told it, though not in the body. When I woke in the morning, I was hungry, but I did not think first of my hunger for my heart was perplexed and confused. I knew the reason for the Dead Places but I did not see why it had happened. It seemed to me it should not have happened, with all the magic they had. I went through the house looking for an answer. There was so much in the house I could not understand—and yet I am a priest and the son of a priest. It was like being on one side of the great river, at night, with no light to show the way.

Then I saw the dead god. He was sitting in his chair, by the window, in a room I had not entered before and, for the first moment, I thought that he was alive. Then I saw the skin on the back of his hand—it was like dry leather. The room was shut, hot and dry—no doubt that had kept him as he was. At first I was afraid to approach him—then the fear left me. He was sitting looking out over the city—he was dressed in the clothes of the gods. His age was neither young nor old—I could not tell his age. But there was wisdom in his face and great sadness. You could see that he would have not run away. He had sat at his window, watching his city die—then he himself had died. But it is better to lose one's life than one's spirit—and you could see from the face that his spirit had not been lost. I knew, that, if I touched him, he would fall into dust—and yet, there was something unconquered in the face.

That is all of my story, for then I knew he was a man—I knew then that they had been men, neither gods nor demons. It is a great knowledge, hard to tell and believe. They were men—they went a dark road, but they were men. I had no fear after that— I had no fear going home, though twice I fought off the dogs and once I was hunted for two days by the Forest People. When I saw my father again, I prayed and was purified. He touched my lips and my breast, he said, "You went away a boy. You come back a man and a priest." I said, "Father, they were men! I have been in the Place of the Gods and seen it! Now slay me, if it is the law—but still I know they were men."

He looked at me out of both eyes. He said, "The law is not always the same shape—you have done what you have done. I could not have done it my time, but you come after me. Tell!"

I told and he listened. After that, I wish to tell all the people but he showed me otherwise. He said, "Truth is a hard deer to hunt. If you eat too much truth at once, you may die of the truth. It was not idly that our fathers forbade the Dead Places." He was right—it is better the truth should come little by little. I have learned that, being a priest. Perhaps, in the old days, they ate knowledge too fast.

Nevertheless, we make a beginning. It is not for the metal alone we go to the Dead Places now—there are the books and the writings. They are hard to learn. And the magic tools are broken—but we can look at them and wonder. At least, we make a beginning. And, when I am chief priest we shall go beyond the great river. We shall go to the Place of the Gods—not one man but a company. We shall look for the images of the Gods and find the god ASHING and the others—the gods Lincoln and Biltmore and Moses. But they were men who built the city, not gods or demons. They were men. I remember the dead man's face. They were men who were here before us. We must build again.

## Questions

1. What does the stone stand for? Is there any significance of finding the stone?
2. What does the narrator's father do?
3. What drives the narrator to take the risk?
4. If we say it is a story of development, do you agree and why?
5. What can you as a reader sense from the end of the story?

# 斯蒂芬·文森特·波奈特
# (1898—1943)

斯蒂芬·文森特·波奈特是美国诗人、小说家。他最有名的内战长篇史诗《约翰·布朗的身体》完成于法国。波奈特以诗歌见长,曾两次获得普利策奖。他是为数不多深受大众和评论界好评的作家。

斯蒂芬·文森特·波奈特出生在宾夕法尼亚州伯利恒市的一个军旅世家。父亲是上校沃克·波奈特。斯蒂芬的母亲弗朗西斯·尼尔·波奈特出身当地名门望族,肯塔基军人家庭。波奈特的父亲痴迷于书籍,尤爱诗歌,具有浓郁文学氛围的家庭环境造就了波奈特。波奈特在加州的伯尼西亚度过大部分童年时光。在大约10岁时,波奈特被送往希区柯克军事学院学习。但是他厌恶体育,钟情于读书,更不屑与那些呆头呆脑的同学们同流合污。17岁时,波奈特发表了他的第一本诗集,《五名男子和庞培》(1915)。这部诗集深受威廉·莫里斯的浪漫主义及当代现实主义的影响。

波奈特的第一部自传体小说是《智慧的开端》(1921),从中不难看出斯科特·菲茨杰拉德对其的影响。他继续求学于法国索邦大学,该校的放荡不羁的生活方式冲击着波奈特。正是在这种生活氛围中,他遇到了他的生活伴侣,作家和新闻记者罗斯玛丽·卡尔。1923年波奈特回到美国。在19世纪20年代波奈特写了其他三部小说,即连载于《哈珀街》的《年轻人的傲慢》(1922),还有《让胡格诺派》(1923)和《西班牙刺刀》(1926)。最后一部历史小说以18世纪的美国佛罗里达州为原型,侧重于对波奈特的祖先的追忆。关于财富和责任故事的《詹姆斯·索尔的女儿》(1934)通常被认为是波奈特的佳作。他的小说充满了神秘、诡异和恐怖,动人心魄。

## 巴比伦河畔

故事讲述了小约翰的成长历程,一次为了赢得部落认可,进而正式成人和被膏为法师的冒险历程。自小耳濡目染父亲的口述故事、阅读书籍、祛病及法术等经历,小约翰着迷于魔幻传说,踏上成人的历程。约翰渴望知识,不惜打破部落的陈规,历经艰险发现了众神之所,尽管担心死神牵绕,他的旅程还是给他带来了惊喜的发现。与父亲的说教不同,众神之所并没有迷雾弥漫,没有永生之火燃手,亦没有精灵魔鬼聚集,而是一座座废弃已久的塔楼,漫无尽头的死亡之地。随着约翰探险的深入，揭开了死亡之城的秘密，约翰开始克服了自身的恐惧心理。最终他成为了一个男子汉。凡读此故事者皆会有所启迪。

  南部、西部和北部是绝好的猎奇之地，但是东部是禁地。死亡之地的任何一个部位都是禁地，不过去找金属例外，不过任何碰到金属之人必须是牧师或牧师的儿子。之后，人和金属都必须净化。这些都是清规戒律，而且制定得很完备。渡过大河去看神之地是被禁止的——这是绝对被禁止的。虽然我们知道其名，但都闭口不谈。那里就是神灵、鬼怪的居所——那里有着大火燃烧的烟尘。这些都是禁忌——自从开天辟地之时就都是禁忌了。

  我父亲是牧师，我是牧师之子。我曾同父亲去过附近的死亡之地——开始我害怕。父亲进到房子里找寻金属时，我站在门边，心变得紧缩、虚弱。那房主死后，房子成了鬼魂之地。房子里没有人气，屋角只有白骨。可是牧师之子不应该显露胆怯。我看着暗处的尸骨，默不作声。

  不久，父亲从房子里走了出来，手里拿着一块铁——坚硬无比。他两只眼睛紧紧地盯着我，我没有跑开。他示意让我接过那块铁块——我接过来，但没死。现在他认识到我的确配做他的儿子，此生也当牧师。那时我还小——不过，我的哥哥们也会这么做，虽然他们都是好猎手。之后，他们给我好肉吃，让我坐在暖和处。父亲望着我——很高兴我当牧师。不过每当我大放厥词或无端哭泣，父亲惩罚我比哥哥们更严厉。这没错儿。

  一段时间以后，父亲就允许我一人走进死亡之屋，寻找金属。渐渐地我对这些屋子的布局了如指掌，再看到那些白骨，也不再恐惧了。那些白骨很轻，年日悠久，一碰就会变成灰尘。这可是个大罪过呀。

  父亲教会我很多东西，魔咒、魔法我都细心学习——我还知道怎样止血及许多秘密。牧师必须要洞穿好多秘密——父亲就是这么说的。

  如果猎手们以为我们很多事情仅凭魔咒或魔法，那就由他们去吧——对他们无碍。我还掌握了诠释古书奥秘的能力，还有用古语写作——这很难，需要很长时间。知识的积累令我欢愉，好像心中燃着一团火焰。此外，我还醉心于古老的传说，诸神的故事令我神往。我常自言自语地问自己一些无法回答的问题，无论怎么说好奇总归是好事。夜深人静的时候，我会躺下，聆听风声，就好像是诸神交谈的声音，他们正飞过天空。

  同居住在森林里的人相比，我们要比他们睿智，更有知识。我们的女人用轮子纺线，我们的牧师身穿白色的魔法袍，我们没有吃树上幼虫的习惯。尽管古老的文献晦涩难懂，但我们也会代代相传。还有，我的见识，对知识的渴求像烈焰在心中燃烧，愈来愈强。

当我真正成为男子汉的时候，我找到父亲，对他说："父亲，时候到了。我已经成为男子汉了，该去远行了。让我出行吧。"

父亲看了我好长一段时间，默不作声，用手捋着胡须，半天儿他才说："是呀，是到时候了。"那天晚上，在牧师的房子里，我要求并接受了洁净礼。我的身体疼痛难忍，但灵魂静如岩石。父亲亲自质询我的梦想！

父亲让我盯着冒着蓝烟的火焰，仔细观察——我看见了并述说所见。那是我一贯所见———一条河，对岸是一个巨大的死亡之地，诸神在那里穿行。我一直在思考这些。我把看到的一切告诉父亲，他双眼深邃且严厉。此时的他不再是父亲而是牧师。他说："这是个强大的梦想。"

"这是我的梦想，"我说。烟火在我身旁起舞，我感到头轻飘飘的。外屋响起星星之歌，在我脑中嗡嗡作响。

父亲问我神的装束，我回答了神是如何装束的。我们从书中了解到神的装束，但我感觉神就在我眼前。当我把所见到的一切讲完，父亲做了三次占卜并仔细琢磨木棍倒下的样子。

"这是个很强大的梦想，"父亲说，"它有可能把你吞噬。"

"我不怕，"我注视着父亲说道。我的声音自己听起来缥缈，但那是因为烟火的缘故。

父亲拍拍我的胸脯，摸了摸我的脑门儿。他给了我弓和三支箭。

"拿着，"他说，"禁止去东边，禁止过河，禁止去神之地。这些都是禁忌。"

"这些都是禁忌，"我说。但这只是我的嗓音在说话，而不是我的灵魂在说话。父亲又看了看我。

"儿子，"父亲说，"我年轻时也有梦想。假如梦想不吞噬你，你可能成为伟大的牧师。假如梦想吞噬了你，你还是我的儿子。现在走自己的路吧。"

按照教规，我开始禁食，苦修身体，净化灵魂。当黎明降临时，我已远离村子。我祈祷、净化自我，等待神迹。神迹是一只鹰，飞向东方。

有些时候神迹是邪灵发出的。我坐在一块平滑的岩石上等待，不吃不喝，心如止水，感知高高在上的苍穹，感知脚下厚厚的大地。我静静地等待，直到夕阳西沉。突然峡谷中出现三只鹿，向东奔驰，它们没有在意我，或根本没看到我。后边紧紧尾随着一头幼鹿，这可是个大兆头。

我尾随其后，保持一定的距离，不知接下来会发生什么。我拿不准是不是该往东边走，但我必须往东去。由于禁食，头嗡嗡作响，我甚至都没发现一头黑豹扑向了那只白色幼鹿。出乎我的意料，不知不觉中我早已弓在手。我狂吼，那只黑豹仰起头松开了到口的幼鹿。手里的弓箭不足以杀死一头黑豹，但我射出去的利箭穿透了黑豹的眼睛，射进了它的头颅。黑豹向前跃了两下，应声倒地，爪子深深地抓入地里,一命呜呼。这时我才开始意识到我应该往东去,东部才是我行程的目的地。夜色渐浓,我生了一堆火,美美地吃了一顿烤豹肉。

往东得走整整八天,还要穿越许多死亡之地。林子里的居民害怕这些死亡之地,而我却不怕。一天夜里,我在一处死亡之地的边缘生起了篝火,第二天一早,我竟然在死人之屋找到一把不错的匕首,略有点儿锈。这与后来发生的一切相比微不足道,但却使我信心倍增。以后每当我找猎物,猎物都会出现在我的箭头之前,有两次我竟然悄无声息地躲过林中猎人,没被发觉。这下我更加自信了,我的魔法无边,征途顺畅,再也不去理会圣书上那些陈规陋习。

第八天,黄昏时分,我来到一条大河的边上。这距离我离开诸神之地又有小半天的路程。我们一般不走诸神之路,一是道路已被乱石堵塞,再就是穿林子更安全。走了很久,我透过树木缝隙隐约看到有水。终于,我来到了悬崖峭壁上的一处开阔地。脚下就是大河,阳光下宛如一个巨人呈现在眼前。河道宽广,河水悠长,有一种气吞千条大河之势,气势磅礴。它的名字叫丘——迪——逊,圣河,长河之意。我们部落没有一人见过此河,我做牧师的父亲也没见过。这太神奇了,我祷告起来。

然后,我举目朝南远眺。那里是诸神之地。

我相信你一定没有见过如此神奇的景象。正是在那里,在诸神禁忌之地,红灯下,一排排,大过房子,如梦如幻。红光绕顶,体积硕大,残垣断壁。我意识到,要换个时间,诸神一定会发现我。于是我手遮双眼,猫腰潜回林子。

当然,这一切足矣,一生足矣。当然,能在悬崖峭壁上过一夜,此生足矣。林子里的居民压根就不敢越雷池半步。整个晚上我都在盘算我是否真的应该趟过那条大河,走进诸神之地,哪怕冒被诸神吃掉的风险,也在所不惜。我的法力毫无效果,但欲望之火在心中燃烧,难以平息。太阳高高升起,我想,"我的行程一帆风顺。现在我该返程回家吧。"但即使有这样的念头,我也心知肚明我不会这样做。如果我真的踏入诸神之地,我将必死无疑,但是如果不去,我又如何安抚我的灵魂。听从心灵的呼唤总比丧命要好吧,谁让你是牧师呢,况且还是牧师的儿子。

想到此,我开始制造木筏,泪水夺眶而出。要是被林子里的人们撞上,他们会轻易把我杀死,好在他们没出现。筏子做好了,我祷告亡者的庇护,身上涂上迷彩,迎接死亡。我漠视一切,且腿脚乏力。心中欲望搅得我魂不守舍。不过我一直努力克制,使自己神智清醒。我将筏子推向河边,唱响了一首死亡之歌——我有这样的权利。这真是一首好歌。

"我是约翰,约翰的儿子,"我唱道。

"我的人民是大山之子。他们个个豪气英武。

我走进死亡之地,却安然无恙。

我拿到死谷之铁,却性命犹存。

我踏上诸神之路,毫不畏惧。

咿呀呀!黑豹倒在我的箭下,幼鹿闻风丧胆!

咿呀呀!我趟过先人没有趟过的大河。

禁忌的东部我到过,禁忌的河我趟过,而今,身在此处。

敞开你的心胸,你的灵魂,聆听我歌唱吧。

而今我要踏入诸神之地,我将一去不返。

我身涂迷彩,面对死亡,我四肢无力,但勇气十足,敢于走向诸神之地。"

当来到诸神之地,恐惧在我心底还是油然而生,我胆怯,我害怕。湍流不息的大河有如一双大手紧紧攥住我的木筏。这就是魔法,河道宽敞,河水静谧,悄无声息。明媚的早上,我可以感觉到众多邪灵围绕着我。激流将我冲向下流,我可以感觉到他们在冲我的脖子吹气。一种从未体验到的孤寂,我试图寻求知识的帮助,但却像松鼠冬天储藏坚果。知识不再起作用,独自一人矗立在大河沿,它唯听命于众神,在这里我是那样的渺小、无助,犹如新孵化的雏鸟一切尽暴露无遗。

过了一会儿,我睁开双眼,环顾四周,看到了。我看到了大河的两岸,我看到了曾几何时这里有一条众神穿越的路径横跨大河,尽管现在已是残垣断壁,像断了的常青藤,如此浩大、壮观、残破,令人叹为观止。河流就这样把我一路冲到诸神之地,眼前豁然出现一派巨大的破败景象。

我一点儿都不了解河上的习俗,我是大山之子。我试图借助木杆划动筏子,但筏子只是一味地原地打旋。我以为大河要将我带出诸神之地,进入到传说中的苦涩水域。我有些恼怒,倔强不服。我大声叫道:"我是一个牧师,还是牧师的儿子!"诸神听到我的喊叫,他们教我如何在筏子的一边用木杆划动筏子。水流改变了方向,我接近了诸神之地。

咫尺之遥,筏子陷住不动,翻了船。我能在家乡的水里游泳,很快就到了岸边。一根巨大的锈迹斑斑的铁棍伸向河流。我紧紧抓住这根铁棍,坐在那儿,喘口气。好在我的弓、箭、那把在死亡之地捡到的刀还在,仅此而已。筏子顺流而下,奔向苦涩水域。我回头看,这才感到一旦被冲到水底,想必这时已是孤魂野鬼了。我拧干弓弦,重新系牢,甩开膀子大步流星地朝诸神之地走去。

我的脚感觉落地了,但并没有感到灼热。并不像传说的那样,那里的大地燃烧不止,这是我亲眼所见。各处的确会有大燃烧留下的痕迹和残留,但都是遗迹。也不像一些牧师所言,这座岛屿遍布迷雾。不对。这是一个巨大的死亡之地，超过我们所知。四处都是断裂、颓败的神路。四处都是高耸神塔的残迹。

我所见到的一切，从何说起呢？我谨慎地前行，紧紧地握着弓箭，做好了应对一切危险的准备。这里本该有精灵的呼号，邪灵的咆哮，但却悄无声息。我踏足之地万籁寂静，阳光普照，时而刮起阵风，时而飘起阵雨，时而小鸟飞过播下种子，仿佛一切都恪尽其职。断裂的岩石缝隙簇簇，青草摇曳。这真是绝妙之处，怪不得诸神居住在这个岛上。我要是早来此地，也会在此定居。

我听见的一切，从何说起呢？塔楼并没有全部坍塌，时不时还可以看到依然耸立的塔楼，犹如森林中突兀而起的一棵参天大树，鸟儿高高地栖息在上。塔楼面目狰狞，毫无生气，因为不再有神灵居住，我看到鱼鹰在河里捕鱼。我看到一大堆碎石块上方盘旋飞舞着一群白色的蝴蝶，翩翩起舞。我走近一看，那是一根拦腰断裂的石柱，上面刻满了文字。我认识上面的字母，但一个字都不认识。上面写着UBTREAS的字样。还有一尊破败不堪的人像或神像，是用白色石头雕刻的，他的头发像女人那样盘在脑后，他的名字叫ASHING，我是在石头的缝隙中看到这几个字的。我意识到我该祈求ASHING的帮助，尽管我不认识这尊神。

我所见到的一切，从何说起呢？无论是石头还是金属上都没有遗留下任何人的气息。满是碎石的荒野也没有多少树。塔楼上下栖息着无数只鸽子，筑巢、排粪，诸神一定很眷顾这些鸽子，也许诸神用这些鸽子祭祀。还有些野猫游荡在诸神之地，这些绿眼睛野猫对人一点儿都不害怕。夜色中时不时传来幽灵般的猫叫，但他们并不是幽灵。而那些野狗最令我胆战，它们成群结队猎食，但后来我才同野狗相遇。这里随处都是刻着文字的石碑，有的是晦涩难懂的文字，有的是数字。

我一路向北走去，没有躲藏。要是被神或魔鬼瞧见，我必死无疑，但是此时我却一点儿都不害怕。我的心中涌动着对知识的渴望，好奇的欲火在心中燃烧，这里有许许多多我无法解释的东西。过了一会儿，我感到有点儿饿，我本可以打猎获取食物，但却没这样做。人们都知道，神不像我们那样猎食，他们从魔匣或魔罐中取食。有时在死亡之地还能找到这些魔匣、魔罐。记得儿时有一次我愚蠢地打开了一个魔罐，品尝了里面的东西，发现里面的食物很香甜。后来被父亲发现，狠狠地揍了我一顿，因为吃这些食物会死人的。而今，今非昔比了，我早已过了受约束的年龄，我大胆地走进这些塔楼里，寻找诸神的食物。

最终我在城中央的一座寺庙的废墟中找到了食物。那座寺庙一定很大，尽管色彩暗淡，光线幽暗，我还是能看清寺庙顶部的装饰犹如繁星闪耀的夜空。这个岩洞一直延伸进去，里面是宽敞的岩洞和层层的洞穴，想必早年是用于囚禁奴隶的场所。但当我往下爬行的时候，隐约听见阵阵老鼠的尖叫声，我最讨厌不干净的老鼠，听声音数量还很多，我停住脚步，没有往前爬。但就在此处，在一堆废墟中我发现了可食用的东西，废墟后是一扇敞开的门。我从罐中拿了几个水果尝尝，味道还不错，很甜。此外，还有饮料，一瓶瓶的，诸神的饮料度数很高，立马我觉得头重脚轻，晕乎乎的。吃完喝完，我把弓箭放置一边，躺在一块大石头上美美睡了一觉。

醒来时，夕阳西下，已是黄昏时分。环顾了一下我躺着的四周，发现一条狗蜷缩在一旁。舌头耷拉在外，望着我，似乎在嘲笑我。那是一条很大的野狗，身上披着灰褐色的皮毛，像一条狼一样硕大无比。我噌的从地上跃起，一边吼着一边驱赶着它。这条狗待在那儿，纹丝不动，一脸的嘲讽。这我可不喜欢，我拿起块石头朝它打了过去，它毫不含糊，根本不害怕。它一定把我当成它的美餐，就这样一动不动地盯着我。没错，我一箭就会要了它的命，但我不敢含糊，害怕不止这一条狗。

夜幕降临。我环顾四周，不远处是一条宽广且凹凸不平的神路，一直通向北边。座座高塔林立，但还没有高得不能攀越，一排排白色的死亡之屋早已是残垣断壁，星星点点的几个屋子还矗立在那儿。我朝着神路走去，尽量走废墟的高处，那条狗一直尾随着我。来到神路时，我冷不丁地发现不止这一条狗，还有好多狗尾随到此。如果我醒来稍晚一点，想必这些狗早已扑过来，撕裂我的喉咙了。看样子它们也明白我的想法，他们不急不忙。当我走进死亡之屋时，他们蜷缩在门口盯着，毫无疑问，这些狗把我当成了一顿美餐。有一点我敢肯定，狗是不会开门的，这些书上早就说过，而诸神也不会住在地上，而是居高临下居住在"天堂"。

我刚找到一扇可以开启的门，突然这群野狗猛地向我扑来。哈哈！我迅速地关上门，门很结实，是铁门，这些狗也一定很吃惊，我竟然当着它们的面把门关上了。远处传来一阵阵带有不甘的犬吠之声，我没敢停下应付它们，四周漆黑一团，我摸索着找到楼梯，向上攀爬。楼梯蹬很多，七拐八拐搞得我晕头转向。来到楼梯顶又是一扇门，我摸到门把手，推开门。发现自己身处一间狭小的屋子里，屋子的一端有一扇铜门，没有把手，打不开。也许开这扇门需要魔咒，但我没有魔咒。我转向对面的门，门上的锁早已破旧，推开门我走了进去。

进到里面，我发现里面到处是宝藏。住在里面的神一定威力无比。第一间屋子有一个小储藏室，我停下脚步犹豫了一会儿，告诉这里的神，我来此处寻求平安，而非要掠夺什么。当我意识到诸神在听我的祈祷的时候，我走了进去。啊，这么多的宝藏！尽管有几扇窗户被打碎，一切还都保持原样。硕大的窗户完好无损，俯瞰着整个城市，时间久了，窗户上布满了灰尘和雨渍。地上铺设的颜色依旧，没有因年代久远而褪色。椅子松软，座背很高。墙上挂着各种画，看起来怪怪的，又令人赏心悦目。我记得看见一幅中有一束鲜花插在瓶里，走到近前看，除了颜色什么都看不见，但远看，犹如昨天刚刚摘的艳丽的花。看到这幅画，我觉得怪怪的，桌子上摆放着一只硬泥土捏成的鸟的塑像，同我们家的鸟一模一样。到处是书籍和写成的文字，各种语言，全是一些我看不懂的文字。住在这里的神一定聪明绝顶，知识渊博。我觉得自己来对了地方，我不是在寻找知识嘛。

不管怎么说，这里太奇怪了。一个巨大的澡盆，里面没有一滴水，也许神们在空气中沐浴。做饭的地方没有劈柴，虽然这里有一个做饭的家什，却没有点火的地方。屋子里也没有蜡烛，没有灯。有些东西看似像灯，但既没有灯油也没有灯捻。这里的一切都太神了，我摸了摸这些东西，命还在。这些东西已没了魔法。让我讲一件事儿吧。厨房的一处标有"热"，但摸起来一点儿都不热；另一处标有"冷"，但一点儿都不冷。这一定是魔法，只不过是法力已经尽失。我不明白，但也知道它们有它们的存在方式，这是我希望知道的。

这些诸神之屋，密不透风，干燥无比，布满灰尘。我已经说过法力消失了，但这不是真的。法力从这些东西上消失，但这个地方还有法力。我感觉到身边到处是神，就在我身旁，压迫着我。我以前从没在诸神之屋睡过觉，但今夜，我一定要睡在这里。一想到这儿，我的舌头发干，尽管我渴求知识，但还是有点儿心虚。我几乎放弃，宁愿下去面对那些狗，但我没那样做。

夜色降临时，我各个屋子看了一遍。天彻底黑下来时，我回到那间大屋子，俯瞰远处的城池，升起一堆火。有生火的地方，尽管我不相信它们会在这里做饭，但这里有一个装满劈柴的箱子。我用地毯将自己包裹起来，睡在火前，我实在太疲劳了。

现在来说说什么叫法力无边。子夜时我从睡梦中醒来，睁开双眼，我发现火已经熄灭了，寒气逼人。好像周边到处是低语的声音，有人在窃窃私语。我合上眼，想把这些声音从眼前赶走。我假装睡熟，其实不然，我压根就没睡着。我觉得就好像鱼儿咬钩不停地拽鱼线，那些精灵不断地将我的灵魂拽出我的身体。

我为何要说谎呢？我是一个牧师，牧师的儿子。假如正如人们说的那样，我四周的死亡之屋真有幽灵存在的话，那么在这些诸神之屋里有什么幽灵呢？难道他们就不希望同我交谈吗？过去了这么多年，又会怎样呢？我想我就像鱼儿咬钩，被一根渔线拽住了。我已经离开了我的肉身，看到我的身体睡在一堆火旁，但那又不是我。我被拽着、拉着去看诸神之城。我如梦如幻在梦境与现实间徘徊！

因为是晚上，天应该很黑，但却不黑，而是灯火通明。随处都是灯火，一排排的灯火，一圈圈耀眼的灯火，远比成百上千的火炬耀眼夺目。天空明亮，你都无法看清天上的繁星。我自言自语："难道这就是魔法？"身子不由自主地战栗起来。耳边传来阵阵轰鸣声，犹如大河奔腾咆哮而过。渐渐地眼睛适应了这些光芒,耳朵辨清了声音。我知道我看到的是这座城市,同诸神曾经住过时一模一样。

那确实是光,就是光线:我无法用身体体会的光,我的身体已死。诸神所到之处,无论是步行,还是驾车,数量之多数不胜数,车骑阻塞马路。为了取乐,他们将黑夜变成白昼,他们不同太阳一道入睡。他们来去匆匆,声音嘈杂,犹如洪水。这就是他们施的法术。

我往另一扇窗外看,楼上的常青藤被人修剪过,诸神之路通向东西。魂不守舍,坐卧不宁,这些神也是如此,他们一刻也不休息。他们在水下挖涵洞,他们在空中飞行。他们的工具神奇,他们的成果巨大,地上每一寸都逃不过他们,因为他们想要的东西没有得不到的,东、西、南、北,他们一声呼唤,招之即来。总是这样,他们劳作,休憩,欢宴,做爱,他们耳中就像乐鼓一样,回响着大城市的躁动,像一个人的心脏跳个不停。

他们快乐吗?对这些神来说,快乐意味着什么?他们英明无比,他们力大无穷,他们帅气十足,他们狰狞恐怖。当我举头眺望他们和他们的魔法,感觉自己十分渺小,犹如孩童那样无助,而他们可以不费吹灰之力做他们想做的事情,叫从九天揽月。他们在我眼里,智慧超群,无所不知。但并不是他们所做的一切都是那么尽善尽美,这我一眼就能看穿,只有一切相安无事,他们的智慧才会不断地增长。

接着,我看到他们的命运攫住了他们,现在想起来还令人不寒而栗。他们在大街上穿梭时,命运扑住了他们。我同森林人战斗过,见证了这些人的死亡。但事情并非如此。当诸神展开激战时,他们使用的武器人类没有见过。火从天降,毒雾缭绕。那就是大火燃烧的时刻,毁灭的时刻。他们像蚂蚁那样在大街上四处逃窜,可怜的神,可怜的神啊。接着,塔楼坍塌,幸免于难的人寥寥无几,活下来讲述这段经历。这座城市成为废墟,残垣断壁,多年后,地上仍然弥漫着毒气。我见证了这一切,目睹了最后一个人死亡。破败的城市上空黑色密布,我哭了起来。

我目睹了所有这一切,尽管没亲身经历,看到的一切也足以让我一五一十地告诉你。第二天早上当我醒来时,大脑空空,思绪凌乱如麻,肚子也开始咕咕直叫,饿了也没想到该找点吃的了。我知道了死亡之地产生的原因,却百思不得其解,这一切到底为什么发生。他们有这样那样的魔法,我看来这一切原本该避免。我一间屋子又一间屋子地看,想要找出答案。屋子里令人费解的东西数不胜数,牧师儿子,又是牧师的我,却一窍不通。就好像夜幕下,站在河对岸,没有一丝光线,前路漫漫。

突然,我看到了死神。他就坐在椅子上,靠近窗户,这间屋子我以前没进去过,乍一看,我还以为他活着。我看到他手背上的皮肤,干瘪得像皮革。门紧闭,闷热,干燥,毫无疑问他就这样一直被关在里面。起初我不敢走近他,转眼恐惧消失。他就坐在那注视着远处的城池,身上穿着神的装束。他到底多大年纪,我搞不准,不年轻,也不年老,一脸的智慧和沧桑。一眼就能看出他不会逃跑,他就这样坐在窗前,眼看着城市死亡,然后自己死亡。生命不足惜,只要人的灵魂还在那就比什么都强。从他的脸上不难看出,他的灵魂还在,我知道一碰,他的身体就会化为灰烬,但他的脸上却有种不屈的东西。

这就是我的故事,那时我才知道他是活生生的人,他们既不是神也不是鬼。这种事情难以讲述,也不会让人相信。他们是人,走上了一条黝黑的旅程,但他们就是人。那以后,我再也不害怕,勇敢地踏上回家之旅,一路上驱散狗群,躲过森林人两天的追逐。但当我再次见到我父亲时,我祈祷、净化自己。父亲拂着我的嘴唇,拍着我的胸脯,说:"你离家时还是个孩子,归来时已是大人、牧师了。"我说:"父亲,他们是人!我到过诸神之地,看到了一切。现在杀了我吧,如果教规如是。但我依然认为他们就是人。"

父亲看着我,双目紧紧地注视着我。他说:"教规并非一成不变,你做了你该做的,我年轻时却做不来,但你完成了我未完成的事。难道不是这样吗?"

我说,他听。这以后,我希望告诉所有的人,但父亲却不这样认为。他说:"真理不是像猎鹿那样容易。如果你一次就消化过多的真理,你可能会为真理丧命。我们的祖先禁止人们进入死亡之地是有道理的,绝不是空穴来风。"父亲说的没错,最好是把真理慢慢地渗透给大家伙儿。我理解了,学会了牧师该尽的本分。也许,那时先人们了解的只是太多了。

不管怎么说,我们有了开端。我们走进死亡之地不仅仅是为了金属,那里还有书籍和文字。它们不是很好懂。魔法工具已断,但我们可以观察、思索这些东西。至少,我们有了个开端。我一旦成为大祭司,将带领大家穿越那条大河。我们将走进诸神之地,我不是一个人,而是与人同去。我们将寻找诸神的画像,找到艾星神以及超人林肯、比尔摩神殿和先知摩西。他们是建造这座城池的人,而非神,非鬼。他们是人。我记得那个死人的脸。他们是先于我们到此地的人。我们必须重建。

# Ernest Hemingway
# (1899—1961)

Ernest Hemingway, the American novelist, short story writer and 1954 Nobel Prize winner, enjoys international reputation for his succinct and natural writing style and portrayal of the "tough guy" image. His adventurous life and 4 marriages attract equal attention. Born in Oak Park, Illinois, the son of a well-to-do physician, Hemingway began his earliest writing career as a reporter for the *Kansas City Star* after graduation from high school in 1917. As an ambulance driver in WWI, he was wounded in the Italian front. After the war, he worked as a correspondent for the *Toronto Star* in Paris, where he became one of the expatriated Americans in the literary circle around Gertrude Stein and Ezra Pound. He reported the Spanish Civil War on the loyalist side. After experiencing WW II, he settled in Cuba in 1945. In his last years in Idaho, he suffered from both physical and mental illness, which eventually led to his suicide.

Hemingway's early novel *The Sun Also Rises* (1926) made him spokesman of the "lost generation." His next important novel *A Farewell to Arms* (1929) tells of a tragic wartime love affair, which reflects his bitter resentment against war. *For Whom the Bell Tolls* (1940), depicting the Spanish Civil War, argues for human brotherhood. His novelette *The Old Man and the Sea* (1952) celebrates the indomitable courage of an aged Cuban fisherman. In addition, Hemingway also wrote numerous short stories such as the masterful "Hills like White Elephants," "The Short Happy Life of Francis Macomber," and "The Snows of Kilimanjaro."

## A Clean, Well-Lighted Place

*The following story from* **Winner Take Nothing** *(1933) tells about two waiters in a café, waiting for their last customer, an old man who has attempted suicide, to leave. In contrast to the younger waiter who is eager to get home, the older waiter is sympathetic to the old man's basic needs for both physical and spiritual comfort. Despite its compactness and simplicity, the story has tremendous impact. It explores the philosophical question of human existence and loneliness.*

It was late and every one had left the café except an old man who sat in the shadow the leaves of the tree made against the electric light. In the day time the street was dusty, but at night the dew settled the dust and the old man liked to sit late because he was deaf and now at night it was quiet and he felt the difference. The two waiters inside the café knew that the old man was a little drunk, and while he was a good client they knew that if he became too drunk he would leave without paying, so they kept watch on him.

"Last week he tried to commit suicide," one waiter said.

"Why?"

"He was in despair."

"What about?"

"Nothing."

"How do you know it was nothing?"

"He has plenty of money."

They sat together at a table that was close against the wall near the door of the café and looked at the terrace where the tables were all empty except where the old man sat in the shadow of the leaves of the tree that moved slightly in the wind. A girl and a soldier went by in the street. The street light shone on the brass number on his collar. The girl wore no head covering and hurried beside him.

"The guard will pick him up," one waiter said.

"What does it matter if he gets what he's after?"

"He had better get off the street now. The guard will get him. They went by five minutes ago."

The old man sitting in the shadow rapped on his saucer with his glass. The younger waiter went over to him.

"What do you want?"

The old man looked at him. "Another brandy," he said.

"You'll be drunk," the waiter said. The old man looked at him. The waiter went away.

"He'll stay all night," he said to his colleague. "I'm sleepy now. I never get into bed before three o'clock. He should have killed himself last week."

The waiter took the brandy bottle and another saucer from the counter inside the café and marched out to the old man's table. He put down the saucer and poured the glass full of brandy.

"You should have killed yourself last week," he said to the deaf man. The old man motioned with his finger. "A little more," he said. The waiter poured on into the glass so that the brandy slopped over and ran down the stem into the top saucer of the pile. "Thank you," the old man said. The waiter took the bottle back inside the café. He sat down at the table with his colleague again.

"He's drunk now," he said.

"He's drunk every night."

"What did he want to kill himself for?"

"How should I know."

"How did he do it?"

"He hung himself with a rope."

"Who cut him down?"

"His niece."

"Why did they do it?"

"Fear for his soul."

"How much money has he got?"

"He's got plenty."

"He must be eighty years old."

"Anyway I should say he was eighty."

"I wish he would go home. I never get to bed before three o'clock. What kind of hour is that to go to bed?"

"He stays up because he likes it."

"He's lonely. I'm not lonely. I have a wife waiting in bed for me."

"He had a wife once too."

"A wife would be no good to him now."

"You can't tell. He might be better with a wife."

"His niece looks after him."

"I know. You said she cut him down."

"I wouldn't want to be that old. An old man is a nasty thing."

"Not always. This old man is clean. He drinks without spilling. Even now, drunk. Look at him."

"I don't want to look at him. I wish he would go home. He has no regard for those who must work."

The old man looked from his glass across the square, then over at the waiters.

"Another brandy," he said, pointing to his glass. The waiter who was in a hurry came over.

"Finished," he said, speaking with that omission of syntax stupid people employ when talking to drunken people or foreigners. "No more tonight. Close now."

"Another," said the old man.

"No. Finished." The waiter wiped the edge of the table with a towel and shook his head.

The old man stood up, slowly counted the saucers, took a leather coin purse from his pocket and paid for the drinks, leaving half a peseta tip.

The waiter watched him go down the street, a very old man walking unsteadily but with dignity.

"Why didn't you let him stay and drink?" the unhurried waiter asked. They were putting up the shutters. "It is not half-past two."

"I want to go home to bed."

"What is an hour?"

"More to me than to him."

"An hour is the same."

"You talk like an old man yourself. He can buy a bottle and drink at home."

"It's not the same."

"No, it is not," agreed the waiter with a wife. He did not wish to be unjust. He was only in a hurry.

"And you? You have no fear of going home before your usual hour?"

"Are you trying to insult me?"

"No, hombre, only to make a joke."

"No," the waiter who was in a hurry said, rising from pulling down the metal shutters. "I have confidence. I am all confidence."

"You have youth, confidence, and a job," the older waiter said. "You have everything."

"And what do you lack?"

"Everything but work."

"You have everything I have."

"No. I have never had confidence and I am not young."

"Come on. Stop talking nonsense and lock up."

"I am of those who like to stay late at the café," The older waiter said. "With all those who do not want to go to bed. With all those who need a light for the night."

"I want to go home and into bed."

"We are of two different kinds," the older waiter said. He was now dressed to go home. "It is not only a question of youth and confidence although those things are very beautiful. Each night I am reluctant to close up because there may be some one who needs the café."

"Hombre, there are bodegas open all night long."

"You do not understand. This is a clean and pleasant café. It is well-lighted. The light is very good and also, now, there are shadows of the leaves."

"Good night," said the younger waiter.

"Good night," the other said. Turning off the electric light he continued the conversation with himself. It is the light of course but it is necessary that the place be clean and pleasant. You do not want music. Certainly you do not want music. Nor can you stand before a bar with dignity although that is all that is provided for these hours. What did he fear? It was not fear or dread. It was a nothing that he knew too well. It was all a nothing and a man was nothing too. It was only that and light was all it needed and a certain cleanness and order. Some lived in it and never felt it but he knew it all was nada y pues nada y nada y pues nada. Our nada who art in nada, nada by thy name thy kingdom nada thy will be nada in nada as it is in nada. Give us this nada our daily nada and nada us our nada as we nada our nadas and nada us not into nada but deliver us from nada; pues nada. Hail nothing full of nothing, nothing is with thee. He smiled and stood before a bar with a shining steam pressure coffee machine.

"What's yours?" asked the barman.

"Nada."

"Otro loco más," said the barman and turned away.

"A little cup," said the waiter.

The barman poured it for him.

"The light is very bright and pleasant but the bar is unpolished," the waiter said.

The barman looked at him but did not answer. It was too late at night for conversation.

"You want another copita?" the barman asked.

"No, thank you," said the waiter and went out. He disliked bars and bodegas. A clean, well-lighted café was a very different thing. Now, without thinking further, he would go home to his room. He would lie in the bed and finally, with daylight, he would go to sleep. After all, he said to himself, it is probably only insomnia. Many must have it.

## Questions

1. How does the first dialogue between the two waiters establish the differences between them?
2. Compare the younger waiter and the older waiter in their attitudes toward the old man. Whose attitude do you take to be closer to that of the author? Even though Hemingway does not editorially state his own feelings, how does he make them clear to us?
3. Point to sentences that establish the style of the story. What is distinctive in them? What repetitions of words or phrases seem particularly effective? Does Hemingway seem to favor a simple or an erudite vocabulary?
4. What is the story's point of view? Discuss its appropriateness.
5. Explain the meaning of the story's title.

# 欧内斯特·海明威
# (1899—1961)

美国作家欧内斯特·海明威，长、短篇小说俱佳，1954年获诺贝尔文学奖，他以简洁、自然的写作风格以及对"硬汉"形象的刻画，享有国际盛誉。他的冒险生涯与四次婚姻同样引人关注。海明威生于伊利诺伊州的橡树园，父亲是内科医生，家境殷实。他1917年高中毕业后当了《堪城星报》记者，从此开始写作生涯。第一次世界大战期间，他当救护车司机，在意大利前线受伤。战后，他侨居巴黎，任《多伦多星报》记者，成为以格特鲁德·斯泰因和埃兹拉·庞德为首的文学圈中的一员。西班牙内战期间，海明威报道战况，支持民主政府。在亲身经历了第二次世界大战之后，他于1945年定居古巴。在爱达荷州的最后岁月里，海明威不堪身心痛苦而自杀。

海明威的早期小说《太阳照常升起》（1926）使他成为"迷惘的一代"的代言人。他的另一部重要小说《永别了，武器》（1929）讲述了战时的悲剧爱情故事，反映了作者对战争的痛恨。《丧钟为谁而鸣》（1940）讲述的是西班牙内战，歌颂了兄弟般的情谊。他的中篇小说《老人与海》（1952）歌颂了一个古巴老渔夫与强大的自然界进行斗争、永不言败的精神。海明威还创作了大量的短篇小说，如《白象般的群山》《弗朗西斯·麦康勃短促的快乐生活》《乞力马扎罗山的雪》等名篇。

## 一个干净、明亮的地方

下面的故事选自《胜者无所得》（1933），讲述了小餐馆里两个服务员等待最后一位顾客离去的故事。这位顾客年迈体衰，曾试图自杀。年轻服务员急着回家，而年长者则对老人的身心基本需求抱以同情。尽管情节紧凑、简洁，但故事的感染力巨大，它探寻到人类生存与孤独的深处。

时间很晚了，大家都离开了餐馆，只有一位老人还坐在阴影里，这阴影是灯光照射到树叶上形成的。白天大街上尘土飞扬，但到了夜里，露水使得尘埃落地。这位老人喜欢在餐馆里待到很晚，因为他耳聋，此时的夜晚万籁俱寂，他觉得与白天不同。在餐馆里两个服务员知道这位老人有点儿醉了，虽然他是个诚实守信的顾客，但是他们知道如果他喝得酩酊大醉，他就会忘记付账而离开，因此他们紧盯着他。

"上周他试图自杀，"一个服务员说。

"为什么？"

"他绝望了。"

"怎么啦？"

"没事。"

"你怎么知道没事。"

"因为他有很多钱。"

他们一起坐在紧靠餐馆门墙边的一张桌子旁，望着平台，那儿的桌旁空无一人，只有这位老人还坐在微风摇曳的树影里。一个姑娘和一个士兵在大街上走过，大街上的灯光照在士兵领章的铜号码上。那个姑娘没戴帽子，从士兵身旁匆匆走过。

"巡逻队会把他抓起来，"一个服务员说。

"即使他得到他要的东西，又有什么关系？"

"他最好现在离开大街，否则巡逻队会抓他，5分钟前他们刚刚路过这儿。"

坐在阴影里的老人用酒杯敲着茶托。那个年纪小一点儿的服务员走到他旁边。

"你要什么？"

老人看了他一眼，说："再来一杯白兰地。"

"你会喝醉的，"那个服务员说。老人望着他，服务员走开了。

"他会通宵待在这儿，"他对他的同事说。"我这会儿有些困，我从来没有在3点钟之前睡过觉。他本应该在上周自杀死去。"

那个服务员从餐馆的柜台上拿了一瓶白兰地和茶托走到那个老人桌前。他放下茶托，把酒杯倒满白兰地。

"你上周自杀死了就好了，"他对这位耳聋的老人说道。老人用手指打了个手势。"再倒点儿，"他说，服务员又往杯子倒酒，酒溢了出来，顺着杯缘流进了一摞茶托的最上面一个。"谢谢！"老人说。服务员把酒瓶拿回到餐馆里。他又和同事坐在桌旁。

"他这会儿已经醉了，"他说。

"他每天晚上都喝得醉醺醺的。"

"他干嘛要自杀呀？"

"我怎么知道？"

"他是怎么自杀的？"

"他用绳子上吊。"

"谁救的他？"

"他侄女。"

"为什么救他？"

"为他的灵魂担忧。"

"他有多少钱？"

"他有很多钱。"

"他准有80岁喽。"

"我想，怎么说也有80岁。"

"我希望他能回家。3点钟之前我从没睡过觉。那他什么时间睡觉？"

"他因为不喜欢睡觉才熬夜。"

"他孤身一人。可我不是单身汉。我的老婆在床上等我呢。"

"他也有过老婆。"

"这会儿要是有老婆对他可没好处。"

"不能这么说。要是有老婆他会好些。"

"他侄女在照顾他。"

"我知道。你刚才说是他侄女救的他。"

"我可不想那么老。人老了会变得很脏。"

"也不一定。这个老人就很干净。他喝酒不往外洒，即使是现在喝醉了也是这样。瞧。"

"我不想看他。我希望他回家。他不尊重别人的劳动。"

"那个老人透过瓶子看广场对面，然后又看服务员。"

"再来一杯白兰地。"他指着瓶子说。那个想快点儿下班的服务员走了过来。

"没了，"他说。说话方式形同傻瓜对醉汉或外国人那样忽略句法。"今晚不能再喝了。现在要关门了。"

"再来一杯，"老人说。

"不，没了。"那个服务员一边用毛巾擦着桌边，一边摇着头说。

老人站了起来，慢慢地数着茶托，从衣袋里掏出一个皮钱包，付了酒钱，留下半个比塞塔做小费。

服务员看着他走到大街上，一个老态龙钟的老人走起路来摇摇晃晃，但却不失风度。

"你为什么不把他留下来喝酒？"那个不急于下班的服务员问道。他们拉上百叶窗。"现在还不到两点半。"

"我想回家睡觉。"

"一个小时算啥？"

"他无所谓，我可很在意。"

"不就是一个小时吗？"

"你说话就像一个老头儿。他可以买瓶酒在家喝嘛。"

"那可不一样。"

"是啊，不一样，"有妻子的那个服务员附和道。他不希望做事不公道。他只是急于回家。

"那么你呢？比平时早回家你不害怕吗？"

"你在侮辱我？"

"不，老兄，我只是开个玩笑。"

"不，"那个急于回家的服务员说着，放下金属百叶窗后，站了起来。"我很自信。我非常自信。"

"你年轻、自信，还有工作。"那个年纪稍大的服务员说。"你拥有一切。"

"那么你缺什么？"

"我除了有工作，什么都缺。"

"我有的你都有。"

"不，我没有自信，也不再年轻。"

"过来。别废话了，上锁。"

"我是那种喜欢待在餐馆到很晚的人，"那个年纪稍大的服务员说。"我同情那些不想睡觉的人，同情那些夜晚需要亮光的人。"

"我要回家睡觉。"

"我们是两种不同的人，"那个年纪稍大的服务员说。他现在换好衣服准备回家。"这不仅仅是年轻和自信的问题，尽管年轻和自信很美妙。每天夜里我都不愿意关店，因为可能有人要来餐馆。"

"老兄，开通宵的酒店有的是。"

"这你就不懂了。这是一个干净、舒适的餐馆。它很明亮。这里的光线很好，还有树荫。"

"再见，"年纪稍小的服务员说。

"再见，"另一个说道。他一边关灯，一边继续自言自语。灯固然很亮，但这个地方必须干净、舒适。你不需要音乐。你当然不需要音乐。你也不会神气地站在酒吧前面，尽管这会儿只供应酒。他怕什么？他不怕也不畏惧。他非常了解虚无缥缈。一切都是虚无缥缈，人也是虚无缥缈。人们所需要的只是亮光、干净及井井有条。有些人生活在虚无缥缈之中，却从没感觉到，但他知道一切除了虚无缥缈，还是虚无缥缈，虚无缥缈。我们的虚无缥缈就在虚无缥缈中，虚无缥缈的是你的名字，是你的王国，你将是虚无缥缈中的虚无缥缈，原本就在虚无缥缈中。给我们这个虚无缥缈吧,我们每天的虚无缥缈,虚无缥缈是我们的,我们的虚无缥缈,因为我们是虚无缥缈的,我们无不在虚无缥缈中,可是把我们从虚无缥缈拯救出来吧,为了虚无缥缈。向虚无缥缈中的虚无缥缈欢呼,虚无缥缈与你同在。他笑着站在一个酒吧前,吧台上有一台闪光的气压咖啡机。

"你要什么?"酒吧男招待问道。

"虚无缥缈。"

"又一个疯子。"那个酒吧男招待说着转过脸去。

"来一小杯,"那个服务员说。

酒吧男招待为他倒了一小杯。

"灯光很亮,也使人很惬意,但酒吧间却擦得不亮,"那个服务员说。

酒吧男招待看着他,没有回答。夜深了,不便谈话。

"你还要一小杯吗?"酒吧男招待问道。

"不,谢谢,"那个服务员说着走了出去。他不喜欢酒吧和酒店。一个干净、明亮的餐馆是另一码事。现在他不再想其他的事,只想回家,回到自己的房间。他想躺在床上,直到天亮,他将入睡。最后,他自言自语,或许只是失眠。许多人一定都会失眠。

# Thomas Wolfe
## (1900—1938)

Thomas Wolfe, the American novelist and short story writer, established his literary reputation chiefly for his masterly command of language, impressive portrayal of characters, vivid description of the American experience, and lyrical style. Born in Asheville, North Carolina, the son of a tombstone carver, Wolfe studied first at the University of North Carolina and then at Harvard University. In 1924 Wolfe took up a teaching job in New York University and worked there intermittently until 1930. After his attempts to write plays ended in failure, he devoted himself to fiction writing. Meanwhile, Wolfe traveled extensively in Europe and America. He died in Baltimore in 1938.

*Look Homeward, Angel* (1929), Wolfe's first and autobiographical novel, recounts the growth of the protagonist Eugene Gant. *Of Time and the River* (1935), the sequel to his first novel, presents the maturing of the protagonist and explores various relationships. His major works that were published posthumously include *The Web and the Rock* (1939), *Your Can't Go Home Again* (1940) and *The Hills Beyond* (1941).

## Circus at Dawn

*The following story from* **From Death to Morning** *(1935) tells about what a circus means to two children. The two brothers regard the coming of the circus to the town as the most important event in their life, deeply impressed by whatever is related to it. It presents a vivid and detailed description of an unforgettable experience in boyhood, concentrating on the things that are seen, heard, smelt and felt.*

There were times in early autumn—in September—when the greater circuses would come to town—the Ringling Brothers, Robinson's, and Barnum and Bailey shows, and when I was a route-boy on the morning paper, on those mornings when the circus would be coming in I would rush madly through my route in the cool and thrilling darkness that comes just before break of day, and then I would go back home and get my brother out of bed.

Talking in low excited voices we would walk rapidly back toward town under the rustle of September leaves, in cool streets just grayed now with that still, that unearthly and magical first light of day which seems suddenly to re-discover the great earth out of darkness, so that the earth emerges with an awful, a glorious sculptural stillness, and one looks out with a feeling of joy and disbelief, as the first men on this earth must have done, for to see this happen is one of the things that men will remember out of life forever and think of as they die.

At the sculptural still square where at one corner, just emerging into light, my father's shabby little marble shop stood with a ghostly strangeness and familiarity, my brother and I would "catch" the first streetcar of the day bound for the "depot" where the circus was—or sometimes we would meet someone we knew, who would give us a lift in his automobile.

Then, having reached the dingy, grimy, and rickety depot section, we would get out, and walk rapidly across the tracks of the station yard, where we could see great flares and steamings from the engines, and hear the crash and bump of shifting freight cars, the swift sporadic thunders of a shifting engine, the tolling of bells, the sounds of great trains on the rails.

And to all these familiar sounds, filled with their exultant prophecies of flight, the voyage, morning, and the shining cities—to all the sharp and thrilling odors of the trains—the smell of cinders, acrid smoke, of musty, rusty freight cars, the clean pine-board of crated produce, and the smells of fresh stored food—oranges, coffee, tangerines and bacon, ham and flour and beef—there would be added now, with an unforgettable magic and familiarity, all the strange sounds and smells of the coming circus.

The gay yellow sumptuous-looking cars in which the star performers lived and slept, still dark and silent, heavily and powerfully still, would be drawn up in long strings upon the tracks. And all around them the sounds of the unloading circus would go on furiously in the darkness. The receding gulf of lilac and departing night would be filled with the savage roar of the lions, the murderously sudden snarling of great jungle cats, the trumpeting of the elephants, the stamp of the horses, and with the musty, pungent, unfamiliar odor of the jungle animals: the tawny camel smells, and the smells of panthers, zebras, tigers, elephants, and bears.

Then, along the tracks, beside the circus trains, there would be the sharp cries and oaths of the circus men, the magical swinging dance of lanterns in the darkness, the sudden heavy rumble of the loaded vans and wagons as they were pulled along the flats and gondolas, and down the runways to the ground. And everywhere, in the thrilling mystery of darkness and awakening light, there would be the tremendous conflict of a confused, hurried, and yet orderly movement.

The great iron-gray horses, four and six to a team, would be plodding along the road of thick white dust to a rattling of chains and traces and the harsh cries of their drivers. The men would drive the animals to the river which flowed by beyond the tracks, and water them; and as first light came one could see the elephants wallowing in the familiar river and the big horses going slowly and carefully down to drink.

Then, on the circus grounds, the tents were going up already with the magic speed of dreams. All over the place (which was near the tracks and the only space of flat land in the town that was big enough to hold a circus) there would be this fierce, savagely hurried, and yet orderly confusion. Great flares of gaseous circus lights would blaze down on the seared and battered faces of the circus toughs as, with the rhythmic precision of a single animal—a human riveting machine—they swung their sledges at the stakes, driving a stake into the earth with the incredible instancy of accelerated figures in a motion picture. And everywhere, as light came, and the sun appeared, there would be a scene of magic, order, and of violence. The drivers would curse and talk their special language to their teams; there would be the loud, gasping and uneven labor of a gasoline engine, the shouts and curses of the bosses, the wooden riveting of driven stakes, and the rattle of heavy chains.

Already in an immense cleared space of dusty beaten earth, the stakes were being driven for the main exhibition tent. And an elephant would lurch ponderously to the field, slowly lower his great swinging head at the command of a man who sat perched upon his skull, flourish his gray wrinkled snout a time or two, and then solemnly wrap it around a tent pole big as the mast of a racing schooner. Then the elephant would back slowly away, dragging the great pole with him as if it were a stick of match-wood.

And when this happened, my brother would break into his great "whah-whah" of exuberant laughter, and prod me in the ribs with his clumsy fingers. And further on, two town darkeys who had watched the elephant's performance with bulging eyes, would turn to each other with ape-like grins, bend double as they slapped their knees and howled with swart rich nigger-laughter, saying to each other in a kind of rhythmical chorus of question and reply:

"He don't play with it, do he?"

"No, suh! He don't send no boy!"

"He don't say 'Wait a minute,' do he?"

"No, suh! He say 'Come with me!' That's what he say!"

"He go boogety—boogety!" said one, suiting the words with a prowling movement of his black face toward the earth.

"He go rootin' faw it!" said the other, making a rooting movement with his head.

"He say 'Ar-rumpf'!" said one.

"He say 'Big boy, we is on ouah way'!" the other answered.

"Har! Har! Har! Har! Har!"—and they choked and screamed with their rich laughter, slapping their thighs with a solid smack as they described to each other the elephant's prowess.

Meanwhile, the circus food-tent—a huge canvas top without concealing sides—had already been put up, and now we could see the performers seated at long trestled tables underneath the tent, as they ate breakfast. And the savor of the food they ate—mixed as it was with our strong excitement, with the powerful but wholesome smells of the animals, and with all the joy, sweetness, mystery, jubilant magic and glory of the morning and the coming of the circus—seemed to us to be of the most maddening and appetizing succulence of any food that we had ever known or eaten.

We could see the circus performers eating tremendous breakfasts, with all the savage relish of their power and strength: they ate big fried steaks, pork chops, rashers of bacon, a half dozen eggs, great slabs of fried ham and great stacks of wheat-cakes which a cook kept flipping in the air with the skill of a juggler, and which a husky-looking waitress kept rushing to their tables on loaded trays held high and balanced marvelously on the fingers of a brawny hand. And above all the maddening odors of the wholesome and succulent food, there brooded forever the sultry and delicious fragrance—that somehow seemed to add a zest and sharpness to all the powerful and thrilling life of morning—of strong boiling coffee, which we could see sending off clouds of steam from an enormous polished urn, and which the circus performers gulped down, cup after cup.

And the circus men and women themselves—these star performers—were such fine-looking people, strong and handsome, yet speaking and moving with an almost stern dignity and decorum, that their lives seemed to us to be as splendid and wonderful as any lives on earth could be. There was never anything loose, rowdy, or tough in their comportment, nor did the circus women look like painted whores, or behave indecently with the men.

Rather, these people in an astonishing way seemed to have created an established community which lived an ordered existence on wheels, and to observe with a stern fidelity unknown in towns and cities the decencies of family life. There would be a powerful young man, a handsome and magnificent young woman with blonde hair and the figure of an Amazon, and a powerfully-built, thick-set man of middle age, who had a stern, lined, responsible-looking face and a bald head. They were probably the members of a trapeze team—the young man and woman would leap through space like projectiles, meeting the grip of the older man and hurling back again upon their narrow perches, catching the swing of their trapeze in mid-air, and whirling thrice before they caught it, in a perilous and beautiful exhibition of human balance and precision.

But when they came into the breakfast tent, they would speak gravely yet courteously to other performers, and seat themselves in a family group at one of the long tables, eating their tremendous breakfasts with an earnest concentration, seldom speaking to one another, and then gravely, seriously and briefly.

And my brother and I would look at them with fascinated eyes: my brother would watch the man with the bald head for a while and then turn toward me, whispering:

"D-d-do you see that f-f-fellow there with the bald head? W-w-well he's the heavy man," he whispered knowingly. "He's the one that c-c-catches them! That f-f-fellow's got to know his business! You know what happens if he m-m-misses, don't you?" said my brother.

"What?" I would say in a fascinated tone.

My brother snapped his fingers in the air.

"Over!" he said. "D-d-done for! W-w-why, they'd be d-d-d-dead before they knew what happened. Sure!" he said, nodding vigorously. "It's a f-f-f-fact! If he ever m-m-m-misses it's all over! That boy has g-g-g-got to know his s-s-s-stuff!" my brother said. "W-w-w-why," he went on in a low tone of solemn conviction, "it w-w-w-wouldn't surprise me at all if they p-p-p-pay him s-s-seventy-five or a hundred dollars a week! It's a fact!" my brother cried vigorously.

And we would turn our fascinated stares again upon these splendid and romantic creatures, whose lives were so different from our own, and whom we seemed to know with such familiar and affectionate intimacy. And at length, reluctantly, with full light come and the sun up, we would leave the circus grounds and start for home.

And somehow the memory of all we had seen and heard that glorious morning, and the memory of the food-tent with its wonderful smells, would waken in us the pangs of such a ravenous hunger that we could not wait until we got home to eat. We would stop off in town at lunch-rooms and, seated on tall stools before the counter, we would devour ham-and-egg sandwiches, hot hamburgers red and pungent at their cores with coarse spicy sanguinary beef, coffee, glasses of foaming milk and doughnuts, and then go home to eat up everything in sight upon the breakfast table.

**Questions**

1. Where is the exposition put in the story?
2. What does the circus mean to the narrator and his brother?
3. What is the theme of the story?
4. How is the style of the story established?
5. How do you comment on the author's attitude towards the black reflected in this story?

# 托马斯·沃尔夫
（1900—1938）

美国小说家托马斯·沃尔夫在语言运用和人物形象塑造方面均取得了突出的艺术成就，他以诗意的笔触形象地表现了美国人所特有的经历。沃尔夫出生于北卡罗来纳州的阿什维尔，父亲是一名墓碑雕刻匠。沃尔夫先后就读于北卡罗来纳大学和哈佛大学。从1924年到1930年，沃尔夫断断续续地在纽约大学任教。当戏剧创作以失败告终之后，沃尔夫开始专门从事小说写作。在此期间，沃尔夫在美国和欧洲各地广泛游历。1938年，沃尔夫在马里兰州的巴尔的摩病逝。

沃尔夫的第一部自传体小说《天使，望故乡》（1929）叙述了男主人公尤金·甘特的成长经历。《时间与河流》（1935）是沃尔夫第一部小说的续集，呈现了甘特成熟的过程，同时探讨了各种不同的关系。沃尔夫去世之后，出版的主要作品有《网与石》（1939）、《你不能再回家》（1940）和《远山》（1941）。

## 黎明时的马戏团

下面的故事选自短篇故事集《从死亡到早晨》(1935)，讲述了马戏团在小镇的出现对两个男孩所具有的特殊意义。在孩子的眼中，马戏团的到来是生活中最重要的一件事，与之相关的一切都给他们留下了深刻的印象。这篇故事通过兄弟俩的所见、所闻和所感，生动而又详细地描写了童年时期的一段难忘经历。

初秋的九月，瑞格林兄弟、罗宾逊、巴纳姆和贝利这样一些大马戏团有时会来到小镇表演。那时，我是一个送报员，每天早晨按照固定的路线送报纸。马戏团要来时，不管天多凉多黑，我都一定会赶在黎明前把报纸送完，然后回家叫弟弟起床。

我们一边急急忙忙地向小镇走去，一边激动地低声谈论着。脚下的落叶沙沙作响，空中出现了第一道阳光，静止不动，既神秘又奇妙，清冷的街道一片灰白。黑暗中的大地似乎突然被重新发现，它就像一尊令人敬畏的、辉煌的、静止的雕塑。正如我们的祖先一样，看到它，我们感到既欣喜又疑惑。我们会终生铭记这样的景象，即使离开人世，也依然会想起它。

雕塑般的广场一片寂静。在它的一角，我父亲经营的那家破旧的大理石小店正像幽灵一样慢慢地浮现出来，显得既陌生又熟悉。我和弟弟总是"乘坐"当天第一班开往马戏团所在车站的电车，遇到熟人时，我们就搭他的便车去。

到达又黑又脏、摇摇欲坠的车站以后，我们下车迅速穿过站场的轨道。在这里，可以看到大信号灯和火车头喷出的蒸汽，可以听到移动的货车发出的碰撞和颠簸声，机车调速时突然传来的零星的轰鸣声、钟鸣声，以及大型火车在铁轨上行驶时产生的隆隆声。

这些声音预示着让人欢欣鼓舞的飞行、航海、早晨和闪闪发光的城市，而且火车上还散发着刺鼻的气味——煤渣味，辛烟味，货车的锈霉味，装农产品箱子的清新的松木板味，储藏的新鲜食物——橙子、咖啡、橘子、熏肉、火腿、面粉和牛肉的气味。除了这些熟悉的声音和气味以外，现在又增添了即将到来的马戏团的奇怪的声音和气味，既奇妙又熟悉，真是让人难以忘记。

那些鲜黄色的华丽车厢是马戏团著名演员生活和睡觉的地方，现在还是一片黑暗，寂静无声。它们巨大无比，气势非凡，一动不动地停在那里，在铁轨上长长地排成队。车周围，马戏团卸东西的声音在黑暗中热闹地迸发着。正在消逝的淡紫色的夜晚充斥着狮子凶暴的咆哮声、大型丛林猫突然发出的凶残的怒吼声、大象吹喇叭似的吼声和马蹄的踏踏声，以及这些丛林动物散发的发霉的刺鼻怪味——黄褐色骆驼、美洲狮、斑马、老虎、大象和熊的气味。

在铁轨边上，马戏团车厢旁边，马戏团演员尖叫着、诅咒着，一盏盏灯在黑暗中神奇地摇摆着，装货的篷车和无盖货车在平板车和拖车上被拉着下坡时，突然发出沉重的隆隆声。在黑暗与黎明交汇的神秘时刻，处处都是一个矛盾体：匆匆忙忙，又井然有序，让人困惑不已。

那些铁灰色的大马，四五匹组成一个马队，踏着地上厚厚的白色尘土向前走着，锁链和缰绳发出咔嗒咔嗒的声音，赶马人尖声喊叫着。他们要把马赶到铁轨那边的河边去饮水。当第一缕阳光出现时，人们会看到大象在熟悉的河中打滚，而那些马则慢慢地、小心地下河去饮水。

在马戏场，帐篷已经以梦幻般的速度搭起来了。这个地方在铁轨附近，是小镇上唯一一块大得能够进行马戏表演的平地。在这里，到处都让人感觉到热烈、迅速而有序所带来的混乱。马戏团的汽灯照在那些硬汉饱经风霜的脸上，他们这种独一无二的动物，就像一台人类铆钉机，用大锤有节奏地、准确地打着木桩。正如电影中人物的快镜头一样，他们以快得让人难以置信的速度将木桩钉入土中。天亮了，太阳出来了，到处都是井井有条和热火朝天的神奇景象。赶马人咒骂着，对他们的马队讲着一种特殊的语言，汽油发动机发出很大的、不均匀的突突声，老板们高喊着、咒骂着，工人们毫无表情地铆接着木桩，沉重的铁链在咯咯作响。

满是尘土的地上已经清理出一块很大的空间，人们正在钉演出主帐篷的木桩。一头大象笨重地、步履蹒跚地向场地内走去，一个人骑在它的头上。在这个驯象师的指挥下，大象慢慢地低下它那摇摆着的大头，舞动了一两下布满皱纹的灰白鼻子，接下来庄严地把像赛船桅杆一样大的帐篷杆子卷起来。然后，大象拖着如同火柴棒一样的杆子，慢慢地向后退去。

当这一幕发生时，弟弟"哈，哈"地大笑起来，还用他笨拙的手指捅一捅我的肋骨。离我们远一点的地方，小镇上两个一直鼓着眼睛观看大象表演的黑人，像猩猩一样咧开嘴冲着对方笑。他们拍打着膝盖，以黑人特有的方式大笑着、大叫着，腰都直不起来了。他们有节奏地一问一答，就像在合唱一样。

"他没有和它玩，是吗？"

"没有，先生！他没有和他玩！"

"他没有说'等一会儿'，是吗？"

"没说，先生！他说'跟我来！'他说的是这个！"

"他一扭一扭地往前走！"一个边说边把他的黑脸朝地模仿大象徘徊的动作。

"他用鼻子拱地找东西！"另一个说，同时他做了一个用鼻子拱地的动作。

"他说'啊，跑！'"一个人说。

"他说'小子，咱们跑！'"另一个说。

"哈！哈！哈！哈！哈！"——他们一边向对方描述大象的高超本领，一边用力拍打着大腿，笑得话都说不出来了。

同时，马戏团的餐厅帐篷已经搭起来了。这个帐篷很大，顶是帆布的，四周都露着。我们看到演员们已经坐在帐篷下长长的搁板桌旁吃早餐了。当食物散发出的味道与我们极度的兴奋，与那些动物浓烈的气味以及那天早晨随马戏团而来的喜悦、甜蜜、神秘、神奇和壮丽混合在一起时，我们感觉这是我们所知道的和吃过的食物中最诱人、最开胃、最鲜美的。

我们看到马戏团演员都有一种原始的旺盛食欲，因为他们的工作是力气活，所以早餐时的饭量很大。他们吃大块的炸牛排、连骨头的猪排、咸肉片、半打鸡蛋、煎火腿片和一摞摞的面粉烙饼。厨师像变戏法一样将这些饼在空中翻转着，然后健壮的女招待用结实的手指把盛饼的盘子举得高高的，稳稳地端到他们的桌上。除了这些食物的诱人气味，那里总是弥漫着一股煮咖啡的浓郁香味。光滑的大咖啡壶里，冒出云雾般的蒸汽，这些演员一杯杯地一饮而尽。这一切都给那天早晨本已令人兴奋的生活增添了新的趣味和生机。

这些马戏团的男女演员个个都长得很好看，既强壮又英俊，而言行之中又几乎总是透着坚定、威严和得体。在我们看来，他们所过的生活是世界上最精彩的生活。他们的举止永远不会给人以散漫、吵闹和粗暴的感觉。女演员们看起来也绝不像浓妆艳抹的妓女，与男人在一起时，她们从没有轻浮的表现。

更确切地说，这些人好像已经建立了一个新的社会。他们在汽车上过着一种井井有条的生活，严格遵守着城里人不知道的家庭生活礼仪，这真让人感到惊讶。小伙子强壮有力，年轻女子长着一头金发，很漂亮，身材像女战士。中年人是个秃顶，体格健壮，脸上布满了皱纹，神情严肃，看起来很有责任心。他们可能是高空秋千队的成员，两个年轻人像抛射物一样在空中跳，被年长的那个人接住以后，又被抛回到窄窄的杆上去，抓住半空中的秋千，旋转三次之后，再抓住秋千。这种表演既充满危险又给人以美感，展示了人类在动作完成的准确性和控制身体平衡方面具有的高超能力。

但是当他们走进早餐帐篷时，会与其他演员交谈几句，严肃但又不失礼貌。然后，他们一家人坐在一条长桌旁，专注地吃着面前的大份早餐。他们之间很少说话，即使说话，也很庄重、严肃、简短。

我和弟弟入迷地看着他们。弟弟注视了一会儿那个秃顶的人，然后转过身，对我耳语道：

"你，你，你看到那个秃顶的人了吗？我，我，我说，他力气很大，"他好像什么都懂似的低声说。"他要接，接，接住他们！他，他，他得干好自己的工作！你知道，如果他失，失，失手，将会发生什么，不是吗？"弟弟说。

"什么？"我会着迷地问。

弟弟就会在空中打个响指。

"完蛋！"他说。"完，完，完蛋！唉，唉，唉，他们还不知道怎么回事，就先死……死……死……死了。"他用力地点头说。"这是事……事……事……事实！如果他失……失……失……失手，一切就都完了！他必……必……必……必须要干好他的活，活，活儿！"弟弟说。"这……这……这……这个，"他继续小声说，口气很坚定、很严肃，"如果他们付……付……付……付给他一周七……七……七十五美元或一百美元，我都不……不……不……不会感到惊讶！这是事实！"弟弟使劲喊道。

着迷的我们再次把目光投向了这些了不起的传奇人物。虽然他们的生活与我们的生活大不相同，但是他们对我们来说既熟悉又亲切。最后，天全亮了，太阳升起来了，我们才很不情愿地离开马戏场回家。

不知怎么的，一想起那个美好早晨所看到的和听到的以及散发着美味的餐厅帐篷，我们的体内就会莫名其妙地产生强烈的饥饿感。我们等不及回家吃饭，就在小镇上的便餐馆前停下来。坐在柜台前的高凳子上，对着夹火腿和鸡蛋的三明治、用粗劣、带血的牛肉做成的辛辣热汉堡、咖啡、冒着泡沫的牛奶和炸面饼圈就开始狼吞虎咽地吃起来。回家后，我们又把早餐桌上的所有食物吃了个一干二净。